1

SWAMP RITES

SWAMP RITES

A NOVEL

JUDITH D. HOWELL

THE SWAMP SERIES – BOOK I

1945 Publishing

Virginia

©2015 Judith D. Howell All Rights Reserved
©2019 Revised 2nd Edition

ISBN: 978-1796324068

Yancy Arceneaux stood on the top step of the gallery. She had awakened when the rooster crowed first light and started a fire to chase the chill way from inside the house. The sun made a rosy-gold strip on the horizon, while a gray mist crawled across the ground. An egret swooped low over the yard, slid between cypress trees, and brought its wings in tight to land in the bayou, alert eyes on the brassy-dark water.

A grayish undershirt showed through her thin blouse; a plain scarf held back her hair. She picked up a dented, rust-speckled bucket and, holding on to the baluster, struggled down the steps with a stiff, awkward gait. When she unlatched the door of the wire coop, the chickens burst out and scurried around. She shushed them away from her bare feet by flapping her shirt. There were thirteen, twelve *poules* and a *gaime*, and they clucked and scratched as she tossed feed. They supplied basic needs, but they were also pets of a sort. As the sun became a pleasant glow over the eastern horizon, reflective orange streaks fanning across the surface of the water, she tilted back her head, closing her eyes and taking in deep breaths, a touch of warmth spreading over her face.

She was an unattractive woman and she was no longer young. Her round eyes, like huge brown marbles, were prominent above bony cheekbones. Her eyelids glowed with a peculiar translucence, one side of her mouth twisted out of shape.

It had been a difficult twenty years.

Most days had been lonely and empty. At times she felt as if a living something had crawled up inside her, ruthlessly gnawing away her guts, leaving only empty space behind.

Not much longer now; the twenty years were almost over.

She wasn't sure what to expect when she saw them—life in French Gap had taught her never to place hope or need in someone else's hands—but she had thought about them often and knew life hadn't been the same for them. What they looked like, what kind of women they had become, she had no idea, but she knew they would be different from her. Her hands, fingers wrapped tightly around the wooden handle of the bucket, had twisted scarred knuckles bright against the leathery copper of the rest of her skin. Their hands would be different, soft, with manicured nails. She looked at her dirty feet. Their feet wouldn't be like hers either. No bunions and hard broken toenails.

They wouldn't understand the way she'd lived

all these years. Sometimes she didn't understand herself. Especially late at night, when the pain and loneliness twisted itself around her heart and dug into her mind like a strand of barbed wire. But it was her life, the only way she knew, not subject to change.

A breeze lifted from the surface of the bayou and skipped through curling leaves, scuffed across the yard, leaving behind white chalk of crushed oyster shell from the road beyond the trees. She raised her face into it, focusing her eyes on a live oak draped in Spanish moss. There was sudden heat in her stomach. Troubled thought wrinkled up her face. She knew they wouldn't want to come. Guilty consciences and memories of long ago promises couldn't be relied upon, but maybe she shouldn't have meddled.

Everything had been important when it all started, but now, was it really so important? Sometimes she thought so, but sometimes she didn't know . . . *she just didn't know.*

She walked back to the house, put aside the bucket and lowered herself to the gallery stoop, running her hands slowly over her face. She was worried, thinking too much. Thinking too much always gave her a headache. She squeezed her eyes tight against the tingle in her fingers and toes, a shiver along her spine like dripping ice water—and was instantly lost in smoky fingers of memory drawing her into . . . .

. . . another muggy Louisiana midnight.

A sudden erratic storm had brought rain most of the day. Heavy drops pelted the windows, danced off the sides of the house, while rainwater sluicing off the metal roof made a muddy trench around the entire structure. Wind spun the rain into shifting gray shadow that seemed to echo wetly inside. As thunder broke, brilliant lightning split the distance. The water had thumped and pounded everything for hours. Eventually, it stopped, midnight plastering its black fire across the sky. Condensation blanketed window-panes and drops of water clung to gallery rails, brilliant facets of shine in the wispy moonlight. Insects came out of hiding, their sounds an annoying palpitation of air beyond windows.

Her nose wrinkled up in the air that was spoiled from disuse. She'd opened a window earlier, but the air still remained musty. Chest squeezed tight, her lungs struggled against humidity's sticky restraint. It was difficult to catch a deep breath, the air as thick and oppressive inside as it was outside. A knot of un-defined emotion painfully tightened in her stomach.

This had been *Grandmere's* room until she passed. The drawers were still filled with her meager posess-ions. Her mother had thrown nothing away before locking the door.

It had remained closed, an extra room waiting for

its purpose.

Waiting for tonight—for her to be eighteen and a day.

There was a braided rug, a narrow bed covered with a crocheted spread that had sun-faded and tattered with time, an irregular lump of pillow, a single cracked lamp that leaned crookedly beneath its warped and torn shade.

On the triangular handmade shelf nailed high up in one corner, a statue squatted squarely in the center.

The statue was of a creature that walked upright like a man, with pointed ears, an elongated face and a pendulous abdomen made prominent by long forward-bent legs. Between those legs sprouted a massive knobby male organ.

She studied the statue from beneath half-lowered lids. It seemed to return her stare with a knowing one of its own.

Her pulse tipped up a notch or two.

She could feel the taut draw of flesh around her lips, her mouth filled with a sudden, absolute dryness. *Grandmere* had called the silvery rock moonstone. She'd never touched it before. She ran her hesitant fingertips over the shiny surface. With her touch came a crawling flash of light, a quick, soft warmth running along the stone.

She jerked her hand away. Her heart tapped wildly inside her chest.

Breathless, fear clutching firm at her heart, she

reached out before she lost her courage, and carefully lifted the statue. She was afraid, but no matter how scared she might be, tonight was a familial obligation. She must fulfill it.

The weight of the statue awed her. She held it tight against her breasts. It was heavier than she'd imagined, seemed to tug at her arms, almost as if it wanted to get away from her. She tightened her grip, frightened it would slip away and break, that she would fail and not complete her task. If she dropped it, it could shatter, and the purpose of this night would be destroyed, lost, gone forever.

Her heart thumped with almost blind panic.

She hesitated, filled with sudden burning resentment toward her mother, the one person who should be with her. *Grandmere* had told her that everyone before her had never been alone. A relative had always been present. She was so young and she had no one. It was unfair. Since this duty had been passed to her, was required of her, she should have the same support. She felt pretty sure she understood what she must do and what would happen to her, but even if not, she knew she couldn't turn back. Everything depended on her.

Grandmere had made the fat dark candles years ago and she placed the statue between them, in the middle of the slatted wood, the spot she had carefully prepared, where the statue's big, splayed toes almost covered the faded orange insignia on the crate's side. Never taking her eyes from the statue, she knelt before the upended crate, lit the candles, and began to remove her clothes . . . .

. . . as a loud and familiar sound broke through her trance, jolting Yancy back to the present. She stiffened, and turned her head, her chocolate-marble eyes glassy as she studied a tangle of trees that separated the house from the road. It was an old car struggling along with a coughing rattle. The noise drifted closer, oyster shell skittering under tires, sharp against the underside of the car. Just as quickly as it came, the sound drifted away, finally fading into silence.

Her forehead furrowed, anguish twisted at her face, and a crooked smile appeared on her lips. He was making his rounds, faithful to a fault, guarding a place where there was nothing to guard, and the only things to be afraid of were him . . . and *her*.

2

It was early, just past dawn. Kitty Chauvin didn't so much wake up as much as she became aware. She slid into wakefulness, almost able to touch the quiet that had settled. Something seemed to have purposefully penetrated the warmth of her sleep, causing nerve endings to tingle, making her conscious of something not quite right.

She stiffened as she touched the empty pillow. Her fingertips skimmed over the hollow where his head had been. Sometime during the early morning hours, he had slipped away without waking her. He had never done that before.

Surprised and confused, she listened to the thud of her heart, allowing herself a few moments for her mind to reconnect with her body. Why had he left? If leaving had been necessary, he could have wakened her. Apparently sneaking away had been a planned and perfectly implemented escape.

She opened her eyes, slowly turned her head.

A slip of blue-bordered paper, torn from the memo pad by the kitchen telephone, was attached to the pillowcase with a hairclip.

Kitty pushed herself up on one elbow and stared at the bold scrawl. She read each word carefully, three times. For a second, her heart seemed to have stopped beating.

> K
>
> It's time to move on. I know you
> will think—dirty fucking trick, I
> could have handled it differently.
> Sorry. Think of me sometimes, and
> remember the good times we had.
>
> B

Last night she'd felt but didn't understand that nuance of uncertainty when he unexpectedly appeared at her door. They had no plans, but she'd been glad to see him. Now she understood the reason for the visit, for that fine-wire tension around his mouth. His hard muscled body on top of her, his flavor had filled her; so male, so strong and warm and exciting, and he'd performed excellently, too perfectly. Trying to give her something special to remember him by, or the guilty exuberance of a goodbye fuck? There had never been a hint of anything wrong. Or had there? Had she just been content and blind? How could she have been so blind? She hadn't even guessed what he was about to do.

A shuddering sigh escaped before she could press her lips firmly together. If this had been coming she deserved better. Why had he done it like this, like a thief . . . a one-night stand, waking to discover the partner he remembered from his drunken stupor the previous night wasn't all he had thought her to be. It was *mean* and *cheap*.

It made her feel *cheap*.

Damn him for acting so indifferent, like she didn't matter, or the part of her life he'd been didn't matter.

Kitty took a deep breath. The searing tightness in her chest eased. She curled into a tight ball, caught the soft inner flesh of her trembling lower lip between her teeth, biting down hard. Brief pain and the blood taste in her mouth was warm, not so unpleasant. His sharp musk clung to the sheets and the heat of her body. For a moment she thought she felt the thrust of him deep inside. Her muscles tightened as if to expel the memory.

It echoed inside her head, like the savage beat of a drum—*it's time to move on—it's time to move on.*

What the hell was that supposed to mean?

Move on to *what*—another woman, another experiment, another adventure . . . a different s*ucker*? He was so dry and matter-of-fact, moving so easily from one woman to the next, without a second thought.

Think of me sometimes. . . .

Did he think himself that special? If he did, he was wrong. He was smart enough to know she would be furious. Did he actually believe she would intentionally spend a lot of time thinking about him, after the initial hurt sting wore off?

. . . remember the good times we had

If they had been so good, why was he leaving?

He'd been a part of her life for almost a year. He hadn't been some stranger, miserable and unsatisfying sex viewed afterward with a measure of distaste and regret. Even the times when they had been nothing more than two hungry bodies straining together toward fulfillment, she'd enjoyed his company, had thought he enjoyed hers, had laughed with him, had thought there was some kind of relationship and friendship beyond the sex. She'd never dwelled upon it, but maybe, once or twice, riding the aftermath of orgasmic euphoria, she might have considered it would eventually become something more. Obviously that was her error. She should have given everything more thought, paid more attention. He'd used her. Knowing their affair for exactly what it was, his plan from the beginning? His habit, use and discard women, for whatever reason, when they seemed no longer of value?

Her throat tightened, her eyes stung, but she didn't cry. She wouldn't let herself cry. It would be more painful. Avoid the pain at all costs.

After all, life's not simple, she thought. *No need to muck it up with unnecessary hurt.*

Lust, she told herself, *just sexual lust.* That's all it had been. Obviously he'd never intended for it to be more, had gone into their affair taking away what he wanted; the sex, gifts, money. She should've recognized it, but his fantastic looks, charming smile and big cock had seduced her, allowed him to inch his way into her life. No need to be angry. It wouldn't do any good. She owned this, it was her fault. She'd let it happen.It was a simple as that.

Kitty ripped up the note, watched the pieces float into the wastebasket like white confetti.

She needed to stop the self pity right here, right now. It was unhealthy to wallow in it. She wasn't going to let his rude departure get to her.

Taken by surprise, her pride was wounded, she felt embarrassed, but all it had really cost was time and money and a little heartache. She wasn't a kid, wasn't new to the game, she was capable of handling whatever life threw her way. A relationship started; a relationship ended. She might miss him for a short time, but she could live without him. No imprint, no irreversible damage. A con man, inconsiderate and a complete ass! She could handle it. No need for a pity party.

3

Arcie Becnel frowned at her image in the full-length mirror and pulled at the dress making ungainly pouches around her stomach and hips. She felt abrupt flaming anger, so disgusted with herself, she grabbed a shoe and threw it. It landed against the wall heel-first and left a small dent before dropping to the carpet.

She'd never been pretty, a plain child who turned into an awkward adult too big and tall to be feminine, with a wide, high forehead, a long jaw never fully disguised by fat chipmunk cheeks, and a double chin. Clumsy and insecure, always feeling people were critical of her, she'd tried to convince herself it didn't matter, she didn't care what people thought. Sometimes it worked; mostly it didn't. During rational moments, when her thoughts weren't angry or hadn't lapsed into darkness, she could admit that never once had she overheard anyone say an unpleasant thing about her. If they thought it, they said it behind her back, not to her face, and she'd never overheard it. Women probably accepted she was just fat and ugly, but men, men were wired differently.

She'd had brief glimpses of being noticed by a man, probably because some men were into chubbies. Occasionally she'd dated over the years, but that was all they were single dates. There was never a second one. except maybe with that one guy—the skinny bald one with acne and bad breath who delivered UPS packages. They had dated twice. He didn't count, of course.

She'd went out with him because she'd been at a deep low point, had thought anything better than nothing. Maybe he'd had his own problems and he'd felt the same. She didn't know for sure, she guessed at those things. She couldn't read people very well. When he swooped in for a kiss, she'd pulled away. Her reaction had knocked those terrible green glasses from his horsy face. Making it worse, she'd stepped on the damn things. She'd offered to pay for a replacement, but he'd said nothing, only picked up the pieces and left. A different UPS guy came to the office after that.

She felt foolish assigning an emotional agenda to her life. She already knew it wasn't going to happen. Her life was quiet, but it wasn't so terrible. There wasn't a man in her life, but so what? That didn't mean disaster, it didn't make her worthless.

People would call her introverted, a loner, she guessed. Making friends had always been difficult. She tolerated her executive assistant job—but most people tolerated their jobs, didn't they? It paid well and her boss was unobtrusive, a kind and gentle man she genuinely liked. She didn't socialize, never went to company functions or formed friendships with co-workers. They were simply acquaintances, and she probably knew more about them personally from eavesdropping than they knew about her. She wasn't even sure how many she liked or who might like her.

After all, she had Kitty—didn't she?

Kitty was the high point of her existence.

Dinner in some Garden District or French Quarter restaurant, maybe a movie, or drinks in some club where Kitty knew everyone. Arcie was always uncomfortable in those clubs. She felt a little dirty without really knowing why.

And she was absolutely certain of one thing, had never been wrong about it—men, never a single one, ever looked at her with hungry hopefulness, that naked longing in their eyes, the way they always looked at Kitty. She understood sexual want. There was no question they wanted Kitty.

Arcie had lived with that knowledge forever. She was disgusted with it, hated it.

She had followed Kitty Chauvin to New Orleans because it seemed the logical thing to do. There was nothing to keep her from leaving home. As soon as people found her mother gone, they would contact child services and put her in a state home filled with other unfortunate children. Or some dirty foster home. The thought of being in foster care with other kids who got treated like garbage terrified her far more than living with Kitty in a strange city. So when Kitty decided she wanted to go to New Orleans for Mardi Gras, Arcie had tagged along. That fat, old pervert shrimper from Bayou Lafourche had been after Kitty for a long time, always passing through town every couple of weeks, flashing his money around. Kitty had used him as her ticket out, making Arcie part of the deal. She was still tagging along.

In the middle of carnival mayhem the morning of their arrival in New Orleans, Kitty lifted the guy's wallet. Excusing themselves for the restroom, they had slipped out the back door of the sidewalk café, mingling with the thick costumed foot traffic on a side street. He hadn't wanted Arcie along, had reluctantly accepted the package deal, she was petrified, overcome with crazy ideas of what he'd do if he caught them.

Arcie stepped out her front door and turned back to lock it.

It was only a few minutes after seven. The morning was pale, already filled with damp humidity. It hung like a heavy veil around her face. The sky rolled and slithered with the grayness of imposing storm clouds threatening rain. If the sun came out without rain, the humidity might burn away and it could turn into a comfortable autumn day. It had been a hot summer. Drooping foliage seemed to tremble in anticipation of cooler weather. After dark the air occasionally stirred with a slight wintry nip.

Arcie took a moment to inhale the sweet thick scent of honeysuckle that filled the air from her neighbor's yard, to look at the fern and ivy riffling in their baskets hanging from the eaves of her own front porch.

A colony of gulls had drifted in during the night, taking up quiet residence in the vacant lot across the street, grouped together like a thin gray blanket over snow. She disliked them, their arrival annoyed her. They would stay for days, sometimes weeks, a few remained forever, filling the area with slogs of shit.

Arcie beeped off the alarm to her white Lincoln. It was a luxurious car, far more than she needed, but it had been what she wanted the moment she saw it. When she drove it, she felt comfortable with herself. She was unsure she'd be able to concentrate for the entire day. She should have taken a personal day, a day to herself. She was more than a little antsy as if small bugs were playing a hopscotch game under her skin. She had slipped into one of her incomplete, gray-edged moments. She hated feeling that way. It was as if she, herself, her life, everything about her existence, was inconsequential. She was insignificant, just there.

She'd learned when she felt that way, when one of those unpredictable black *down* moods took hold, she could pop a pill or two and wait for the meds to kick in, help the images recede. Not always, but most times. Such a special world those pharmaceuticals gave her. She knew she shouldn't take more than prescribed, but somehow *more* seemed *better* as she waited for the meds to drive away the bad feelings, bury the black funk somewhere deep in her mind so the creepy fingers of self-doubt and loathing, disgust and wanting it to end, couldn't claw their way to the surface.

The doctors never elucidated on her beyond a wide range of psychological disorders. Diagnoses changed from doctor to doctor, so she didn't have a lot of confidence in them. She'd never fit perfectly into any category in their little black boxes. Sometimes she had lots of symptoms, fewer at others, but always some. None of them seemed to realize—or maybe just didn't care—that she'd learned to work situations to her advantage, to keep the magic pills coming. She'd learned to function well, able to work and talk and smile and laugh—but couldn't always remember with whom or attach a name to a face. No one, including the doctors, seemed to notice, so they didn't need to know, did they?

She was determined not to let herself fall deeper into the dark void that sucked at her. When one of those deep black clouds descended, sometimes she'd remain that way for days, as the distant voice of self-loathing or a need to forfeit her existence would overtake her. That was when she had to be careful. She could get so anxious and worried, she cried for hours, making herself physically sick. Anxiety would add in headaches, turn into a night of insomnia. Other times she would sit motionless, staring into space, listening to all those wicked conversations inside her head, hopelessly lost in the ashen disembodied world her mind had created.

It was urgent she settle things with Kitty, but talking with Kitty had never been easy. Most times it was downright difficult. Their minds never seemed to work on the same wavelength. Whether she meant to or not, Kitty had the ability to make someone feel like nothing. *Nothing.* Never visiting her, never coming to see what she had done with her lovely old house. *Nothing.*

Kitty would fight her. She had to be careful, don't get angry, don't let darkness overtake her.

I shouldn't have waited so long, she thought, furious with herself.

4

Irregular shapes washed across the bedroom walls in early morning ginger shadow. Lacy Kennedy shoved her long hair behind her ear with an unconscious hand movement, exposing a heavy, circular gold earring. Dressed in an olive-colored suit that made her appear thinner than she actually was, she sat on the bed and offered the man under the striped sheet a chilled glass of juice.

Gregor Gilles was a large, powerfully built man with only a few extra inches around the middle. Divorced five years from a loveless, childless marriage, he was charming, intelligent, and passionate with a refreshing spontaneity she found disarming. He was the best thing that had happened in her life in a very long time.

He yawned, stretched, and smiled. Lacy could feel the heat from his hip through the sheet. Their fingers brushed lightly as he took the juice glass. Her senses became instantly and fully awakened. She felt her lower belly turn liquid; the flesh between her legs began a slow pulse of its own.

They had known each other over six years, since he came to work for her, but had been intimate only six months. An evening business meeting turned romantic. The meeting had run long. When it finished up, she'd offered to buy everyone dinner. All begged off to previous commitments, except him. An hour later, at a table in one of her favorite restaurants, when they simultaneously reached for breadsticks, their fingers touched. A warm tingly wave had skipped along the surface of her skin. There was no mistaking he'd felt it also. He hadn't removed his hand or looked away.

She had found herself drowning in the blue of his eyes—a blue so deep and bright she could only wonder why she had never noticed those eyes before—and tried to remind herself: *Don't mix business with pleasure.* She owned the company, he was a valuable employee, it was a disastrous combination—but his touch was almost electric, his stare hypnotic, and not a single particle of her being wanted to listen. She'd been unable to remove her hand when his fingers curled over hers. Forgetting for a moment that she cared if her private life went public, later that night she'd thrown herself headlong into that sudden intense sexual tension between them.

At her condo's door, he'd drawn her into his arms, his tongue caressing the inside of her mouth with excruciating slowness. She knew instantly she as in trouble.

Minutes later, he flipped her around, her ass pressed hard against his erection, the heel of his hand rubbing, pushing down into the swollen wetness at the junction of her thighs.

They fell asleep pressed together, something she hadn't done with anyone in a long time, and in the morning, over coffee and croissants he served her in bed, she'd discovered she liked him, *really* liked him, way beyond the professional level, and the sex had been as satisfying as it was electrifying. Now, if they touched, there were only familiarity and raw desire between them. She'd come to think of their relationship as scary perfect. Occasionally she found herself a little wary she'd grown too comfortable with him. Being too comfortable could mean a slip and their affair would no longer be secret.

Gregg wrapped his big fingers around her hand, bringing her palm down and sliding it under the sheet where it contracted his already heavy sex.

contacted

"Don't make this harder," she whispered, the skin between her thighs quivering.

"Couldn't get much harder," he answered, desire a lightning flash in the cobalt ocean of his eyes.

"What a horny little bastard you are," she teased.

"B-I-G," he corrected, enunciating each letter carefully.

Lacy laughed. "Yes, big," she agreed.

"You know you love it."

"Yes, I do."

It made her nervous to think about falling in love again. Love meant specific things to her and people

who loved with the strength she'd felt in the past was were
fortunate. Sometimes they felt that way only once in
their life. She kept telling herself love had nothing to
do with it, it was lust, pure animalistic simplicity. They
sort of fit snugly together, had a rapport when they
made subtle eye contact or sensed a mutual coveted
response across a crowded room. She had yet to
discover words for the pleasure he gave her, whether
a brush-of-lip kiss or buried deep inside her. He was
a thoughtful companion, a wonderful lover, but that
didn't equal love. Best to leave the love part alone.

"Don't," she murmured, as he attempted to pull
her down against him. "It's going to be a long, busy
day." Lacy pressed her palms against his chest and
pushed away. "Sometimes we behave like—"

"Rabbits," he said, finishing her thought.

"Yes."

He tilted her chin up and studied her, eyes
slightly narrowed, but whatever thought had occurred
to him didn't linger, dismissed or filed away for
another time. Perhaps he sensed she didn't want or
wasn't ready to hear it. He reached for her again.

"Do you think we'll ever get enough of each
other?" she asked, bracing herself away from him
with outstretched arms.

"Damn, I hope not!"

She attempted to stand and his hand whipped
out and grasped her wrist. "I have to go."

Gregg arched a questioning eyebrow, pushed up against the pillows to drink his orange juice, bright points of color high on his cheeks. His hand slid under the sheet, moved in a mischievous suggestive motion as if he thought that would enough to tempt her to change her mind. "But tonight—"

She felt a taut jerk in her lower belly. The tip of her tongue crept out, moistening her lower lip. For several seconds her eyes followed the coaxing movement of his hand, riveted to the leap of his arousal. She reached out and grasped his hand through the sheet, holding it still. "Tonight, as many times as you want. But this morning, if you want sex, you'll have to finish yourself. I don't have time."

He chuckled, but abruptly his expression went serious. Leaning out to place the unfinished juice on the night table, he spoke softly: "After that, how long will it be?"

"Please don't do this, Gregg."

"I'm unhappy."

"I know you're unhappy."

"Let me go with you. We can make it a vacation in the guise of business. It can work."

"No, it can't."

"Tell me why not." He had disappointment in his eyes, maybe a little pain.

"It's only for the girls."

"I can stay in a hotel. You can sneak away."

What hotel? How did one tell someone there wasn't a hotel within spitting distance? There never had been. Only a couple of upstairs rooms rented out by the week in old lady Breaux's house. Lacy shook her head, her eyes sliding away from the tightening of his lips that pulled them down in the corners. "That's impossible."

"You want to make it impossible." A frown etched between his brows. "I need a better answer."

What better answer? *I'd be embarrassed. You'd be horrified.* There was no better answer. She'd have to lie. She didn't want to lie. She hadn't lied to him so far, she'd simply avoided the truth. What she was doing was difficult enough. "You wouldn't like it there." *Close as I can get to the truth.*

"Okay, I wouldn't like it there. I've been other places I didn't like . . . and I don't like what you're doing either." He eyed her skeptically; reached out and traced a fingertip across her breast. "I can work on changing your mind."

Her nipples hardening, she pulled back. "Don't." She knew what his male mind had already concluded: *another man.* A secret rendezvous. She didn't want another man, had no need for one. She thought he knew that. Obviously, he didn't. Jealousy reared its ugly head, weaving like a cobra before the strike. "This has nothing to do with you—certainly not with *us*, Gregg. You don't understand."

"Help me understand."

"It's difficult to explain."

"Try me. I'm easy. Who knows, your friends might like me." He was baiting her.

Lacy leaned toward him, traced the line of his jaw with her finger. A tremor raced across his cheek, muscle clenched beneath her touch. He angled his head away, his eyes narrowed, his lips scrunched tight. As if he was looking at something distasteful.

"Please—don't do this," she begged.

Their glances locked and held. She knew he saw the flaring heat of impatience in her eyes as she felt the beginning of anger crawl up her throat. She saw his reluctance to let it go like she felt the heat spike in her neck and face. He gently cupped her face, attempting to draw her into a kiss, not willing to part angry. She pulled back. She wouldn't let him sway her with a sexual diversion.

"Stop," she said, standing.

Gregg dropped his hands, didn't speak.

"Seven o'clock reservations at Jrat's," she said.

He nodded, not looking at her.

Lacy felt a thickness clog her throat, the muscles tightening against her heart as she turned away. To him, there was only one explanation. He was as much hurt as angry. Was this new, or had she never noticed that he seemed to consider their togetherness a firm commitment?

She went for the door but stopped with her hand on the brass lever when he called her name. She turned, questioning him with her eyes.

"You think you'll always want to win?"

"Do you think you'll let me?" A smile tugged at the corners of her mouth as she blew him a kiss.

Gregg reached into the air for the catch, clenched his fist, pressed his closed hand and against his lips, then threw open his fingers, as if releasing what he'd caught and allowing it to flutter back to her. It was an endearment that caused her throat to tighten. He had never mentioned love, never even implied it during their most intimate moments. Like her, if he felt it, it was probably too soon for him to give up the words. She felt the kiss-thingy was his way of saying it. Even if it wasn't, the endearment pleased her. She stepped from the bed-room, closing the door quietly behind herself.

5

Long after the sound of the car died away, Yancy sat on the stoop, lost, unable to unwrap herself from the cobwebs of her past. She had drifted with the memories so fast she was no longer sure she wasn't back there, that it wasn't happening all over again. One moment she sat on the step thinking about it, the next she was in that musty old bedroom. She could feel everything happening all over again. As she struggled to focus her hazy thoughts, her mind rolled back to when . . . .

. . . she sat naked in front of the crate, scoring her wrists with the carved-bone knife. She bowed her head under the rope curtain of dried herbs, tattered feathers, and rotted bones, dripping blood into the earthenware bowl between the statue's feet, and began to hum softly, then louder, her body undulating to the sound. She could feel her flesh and muscle moving in unison, tendons drawn taut, lips curled back, the tip of her tongue caught between the edges of her teeth.

Lifting the bowl, she drank. Seconds later she felt the piercing power of the herb-drug. A burning flash inside her, it spread through her body, rippling beneath her skin, searing the edges of her brain, singing its eerie music hotly in her veins. Her vision hazed over and the room danced crazily, alive with light and shadow, as she tied the ribbon of tiny bells around her ankle. Candlelight flickered across her skin, turning it coppery cocoa.

Blood ran down her arms, a rich, thick burgundy, almost black, in the shadow box of the small room. Drops of blood slid across her breasts, joined in her cleavage as a single line that trailed down the flat slope of her belly. She waved her arms over each dark candle, and blood dripped into each melting center, as the flames hissed and sputtered. Fumbling to her feet, she turned in tight little circles. Panting, breasts heaving, she stopped the wanton movement as quickly as she had started it, hanging limply over the crate.

Eyes rolling from side to side beneath closed eyelids, she whimpered and grunted, swayed to an intrinsic vibration, fingers trailing bloody sweat in irregular swirls and circles over her body. The energy inside her rose to a static height. *"Ouvri barrier pour moins! Venir plus pres feroce d'un bon age un! Tenir a sa promesse ce union!"* she said, the words falling effortlessly from her tongue, sealing her pact. Open wide the Gate! Come closer Fierce Ancient One! Make good this union! *"Ouvri barrier pour moins! Venir plus pres feroce d'un bon age un! Tenir a sa promesse ce union!"*

Grandmere had made her say the words over and over and over again until she knew them perfectly. She would do exactly as she'd been told. She must not fail. *Grandmere* said the demon creature would be alerted by the bells, would hear her call, know she was ready and waiting. He would come, and when he came, the union would be made.

So she said the words and waited for him.

There was a shimmer in the heart of the moonstone. Filaments of color gleamed where darkness crossed with moonlight, and the temperature in the room rose to the heat of a winter fire as she sensed she was no longer alone. There was a new odor in the room, far more intense than the scent of blood or melted wax or unwashed flesh.

She squeezed her eyes tight, not daring to look.

He had arrived.

A whisper of warmth touched her and she shivered as if it had been cold. She could feel the night air running between her fingers, but she could hardly breathe it, it was so heavy with the foreign odor and drifting heady scent of crushed magnolia blossoms. Fear ran deep inside her.

The blood in her veins accelerated. She thought it might erupt from her skin as she lifted the bowl again, and drank until she'd numbed herself, partially stifling her fear. The drug spread a second time, profound blue-white electricity cascading through her.

She dropped down on hands and knees, head down, arching her body as she presented her buttocks to the ceiling.

Candlelight danced across her body, as perspiration polished her skin. The warmth in the air grew denser; he was nearer, his pungent stench stronger.

She waited, her thoughts sliding between fear, curiosity, and anticipation.

Her eyelids snapped open. It happened so quickly, not enough of the horror was stolen away by the swirling drug vapors.

Pain ripped through her. Her heartbeat raised in a wild tattooing spasm. Her body went rigid as she tried to swallow, clear the dry obstruction from her throat, but her throat muscles were paralyzed. Unable to utter a sound, she shrank away from the insolent touch of proliferating hair. Her skin slackened, trying to melt off her bones as massive arms held her, thick nails raked her breasts, sharp teeth fastened into her shoulder. Her stomach contents rose up the back of her throat, clotted there, like cottage cheese. She finally uttered a choking sound, her entire body trembling beneath the rasp of a wet searching tongue.

She found herself losing awareness, her nostrils flaring with quick and heavy breathing, as each stab of pain edged her toward darkness. Before she went deep into the black, she thought: *I'm going to die . . .and there will be no one to find me.*

In the blackness were moments of oblivion. Two. Three. Four . . . .

The darkness slid across the edges of her vision. It began to fade, bringing back pin-pricks of light, and the pain mercifully passed as quickly as it had come. She was suspended in grayness, most in some nether area of her mind where nothing could harm her.

Consciousness returned; relief washed through her.

She tried to turn her head to catch a glimpse of this massive creature that had mounted her, held her tight with the pointed stab of teeth and nails as the hairy heat of its body pressed into her. She couldn't see it, but its hot wet breath washed against the side of her face, its weight pushing her down. As if in punishment for her attempt, its next thrust was so hard she screamed. Bayonet-sharp teeth made shreds of her shoulder as he withdrew and was abruptly gone.

She collapsed and panted: *"Ainsi soit-il!"* So be it! *"Mais oui, il est apres fait! Ainsi soit-il!"* But yes, it is done! So be it! *"Il est apres fait!"* It is done!

6

Creely Crane walked slowly out of the courthouse. He'd managed to sidestep an interview with eager reporters by backpedaling from the front entrance when he spotted the wave of TV cameras and microphones, but he had watched his client, with his parents, preen for the audience. Creely knew the media would court him for a couple of days, but when the public's crazed thirst for scandal and violence died away, the press would move on. At the moment, he wanted none of it.

It had been a tiring day. The morning had been the last day of a trial: old-New-Orleans-money kid accused of a brutal assault with a tire iron on a mentally-challenged girl who fought off his advances. She hadn't survived. Murder added to the deal. He was held in custody at city lockup, sweated, squeezed, prodded, and released; never enough proof, alibied to the hilt by his best buds, even if the alibis were squishy. A short deliberation brought in a not guilty verdict. Creely was still ambivalent about the kid, but leaned toward guilty.

Some cases were particularly taxing, especially ones where there was little evidence. Sometimes he was quick to develop a taste for his client, and know for certain their guilt or innocence. Not this time. The kid was either innocent or he had given a great performance and should make Hollywood his career choice. Criminal law could be tricky, filled with the unpredictable, yet Creely loved it. All the complex curves and angles that could turn into something slippery moved his blood. He knew his father would never have been pleased with his profession, but the man hadn't lived long enough to protest.

In this instance, his fiancée was close friends with the client's parents. He hadn't wanted the case, had a moment when his faith in doing what he considered the right thing appeared eroded, but she'd stubbornly chided him into accepting it. The boy's possible guilt never seemed to cross her mind. She insisted Creely might one day need a favor and the client's father could be a potential future campaign donor and powerful political ally.

The verdict had come in at quarter past noon. By the time all the hoopla was over, he ate a late lunch and spent too much afternoon time in a hot, over-crowded courtroom waiting for a no-show client a good ways down the docket. Leaving the courtroom, he'd notified the bail bondsman about the skip, and found himself stopped and dragged into an extensive conversation with another lawyer. His lunch had been a meager, questionable tuna salad on wilted lettuce, and now his stomach felt empty. He needed a slab of rare meat between his teeth, a couple of stiff drinks under his belt, and looked forward to a pleasant evening at his brother's French Quarter apartment.

He had found himself thinking of Kitty Chauvin on and off during the day, a pleasant but not productive endeavor. Whatever had been the trigger, there seemed to be something a little off-kilter about his thoughts. Was it an indication of something wrong? He certainly hoped not. It had been some time since he'd seen her. He found himself missing her, wanting to hear her voice. He punched in her number, got a voice mail, and hung up without a message.

There had never been a scarcity of women in his life. There always seemed to be plenty of sex lying around. Since in his teens, all he had to do was pick it up. Yet, he couldn't recall another woman who stirred him to the extent Kitty always had. His feelings for her were never anything planned or anticipated. Like his heartbeat, they just were. Theirs was an occasional, intense, intimate relationship.

Kitty fascinated him, he liked each of her multiple layers, so he never resisted the tug, that feeling of possession that filled up his chest when he held her—hell, when he was even in the same room with her. From the moment they met eighteen years ago a corner of his heart was reserved for her, but he'd never been sure if that strong unspoken something between them could be more than friendship. What-

ever it was, it was special, hard to define, and sometimes taken for granted. It lay tucked away for
months at a time, always easily retrieved and revived.

Nodding to familiar passersby, Creely stood on
the courthouse steps, loosened his tie, and soaked in
the late afternoon sunshine. The air was humid, with
an occasional wisp of breeze. The streets were a little
shiny, with a random dribble in a crack or buckle, no
major water. The weather people at 6:00 A.M. had
called for rain. He had expected a downpour. The
drizzle and localized misting that occurred wasn't
rain.

The cell phone in his pocket vibrated against his
thigh. "Hi," he said.

"Hi," repeated Barbara Mackey's husky voice.
"You sound tired."

"Some."

"You should be flying high. You won."

"You doubted me?" The verdict had been too
late for the noonday news, but he had watched a
semi-high profile bulletin at 1:00 P.M. over lunch.
It would no doubt be on again at 5:00 and 6:00 P.M.

"They won't forget it."

He didn't reply. He didn't particularly care if they
forgot. For several seconds a hollow silence hung
between them. His work schedule sometimes kept
them apart two or three days. They had previously
arranged dinner plans that night, so she might just be

touching base, but he sensed she had more to say. He waited, rolling his shoulders, stretching, impatiently wanting her to get to the point.

"Still on for dinner?"

"We are."

"Going to your brother's?"

"I am." A sudden stiffness entered his voice. He recognized it, knew she would too. He wished they could get past it, knew they probably never would.

"Meet you at The Steakhouse at seven?"

He glanced at his watch. "I can do that." That gave him enough time to go home for a quick shower and change of clothes, with a preparatory double Scotch.

She was silent for a moment. He closed his eyes, ran his fingers through his hair, and wondered why she hesitated over what she wanted to say. Maybe it had something to do with him not going to Carson's the previous two Fridays. He'd spent them with her at black-tie, big-money charity banquets attended by politicians and rich pompous asses that loved to mingle and impress. People that she seemed to think he needed to impress. His celebrity often felt like a curse, putting him on display, but sometimes it was easier to let her win a small victory and save himself for a bigger battle. He couldn't give her too much leeway; he didn't want to completely disillusion her.

"See you then," she said and disconnected.

Creely felt a flicker of irritation. This was the woman he was going to marry. Her disapproval of his brother let her enjoy getting under his skin. Their close relationship had always seemed to unnerve her. She thought Carson's flamboyant homosexuality could be harmful in the political arena. That made the pair of them a challenge, but it reeled her in; she liked a challenge. The bigger the challenge, the more pleasure she got. In most things they were evenly matched, but she thought she could win this. He was uncertain why she thought that.

Barbara wasn't a ravishing beauty, but she was by no means ordinary. Oddly pretty best described her, clever, sophisticated and elegant; beauty wasn't absolutely necessary. Her family had exorbitant wealth and enormous political power. She cared deeply about her social status. She didn't need his money, so he believed the challenge and the win was the strongest part of her attraction to him. He made an excellent opponent and he believed that's what attracted and drew them together in the first place. He'd never been too critical, rarely questioning her motives, because he realized her steel and position have actually been the strongest part of his attraction to her. He would never delude himself by thinking she madly loved him or their sexual relationship was so dynamic she couldn't live without him.

Creely sighed, shook his head. She'd try at dinner

to prevent him from going to Carson's. She'd fail; she wouldn't like it. A couple of strong Scotches would prepare him. He would have liked it to be different but felt it was unlikely to change.

At some point, they seemed to have formed a silent compromise. He'd grown used to it, so he forced himself not to think or care too deeply as he wondered, not for the first time, if she did the same, and exactly what that said about them and the outcome of their relationship and future together.

7

"Oh, damn, Dusty! Really?" Kitty averted her face and caught the second water spray on the side of her head.

Dusty sat looking at her with shiny-white cataract eyes, making small waves in the water with her tail. A generic dog, short ears, short legs, a barrel for a body, a medium-long coat the color of wet sand, she'd been an injured puppy rescued from the side of the interstate. The dog topped the list of the few unconditional things in her life. After Dusty shook off more water, Kitty drained the bathtub, wrapped her in a towel and removed her.

"Hey, you two!" Arcie appeared like an apparition in the bathroom doorway.

Dusty wiggled a greeting, making a soft snuffling noise, Kitty frowned. She didn't want to see Arcie, yet Arcie was there, wanted or not.

"Hey yourself." Kitty continued to rub Dusty dry. She placed a kiss on the top of her head. The dog gave a contented sigh.

"Picked up your mail *again*," Arcie said, her tone slightly peeved.

"Okay."

"It's been a week, the box was stuffed, the electric bill, junk mail, magazines. Why bother ordering?

You never read them. I throw them away or they go to my office."

"I'm a sucker." Kitty shrugged, felt a hitch in her chest. It wasn't a lie. She had thought that of herself earlier.

No, you take advantage, Arcie thought, but said aloud: "Do a pit stop." She knew Kitty never would.

"I have you."

Of course, you do. Arcie closed the toilet seat and sat. "I thought we could grab a bite. Guess I should have called first."

"You should have." Kitty could hear in her tone that Arcie felt neglected.

"You're going out."

"I am."

"Guess I should leave," she said, thinking: *Noooo . . . can't let this happen.*

"Probably."

"What time is Bill coming?"

Kitty stiffened, pushing herself up from the floor so violently the dog tumbled backward into the wall with a soft thud. Dusty struggled upright, staring at Kitty reproachfully from under the towel.

"Sorry, sweet girl." She stepped over the dog and stalked from the bathroom.

Arcie picked up the dog and followed Kitty into the bedroom, toweling Dusty, then deposited her on the carpet. Dusty rolled, threw herself forward and

and rubbed her nose in the carpet with pleasure whines. Kitty stopped in front of the dresser, dragging her fingers through damp hair that tumbled haphazardly electric across her shoulders.

Arcie made admonitory clicks with her tongue. "What took a bite of your ass?"

Kitty picked up her hairbrush and threw it across the room. It bounced off the bed's heavy wooden headboard. This was a spur-of-the-moment visit. She didn't want to talk to Arcie about its purpose. She wasn't prepared for the fight she knew would ensue. She didn't want to fight, hated fighting. She also hated how she felt, all angry and without control, but hating how she felt wouldn't make the feelings go away until Arcie did.

Arcie's eyes followed the trajectory of the brush and settled where it had fallen between the pillows of the unmade bed. A flush darkened her cheeks, her lips twisted. She knew that tone. Her unannounced appearance made her the target, but she knew she wasn't the initial cause. Kitty's behavior meant man trouble.

They simply stared at each other, a standoff, until Arcie said: "It's not me you're mad at. We both know it. Wanna talk about it?" She didn't want to make the offer, but she knew she couldn't leave.

Kitty felt that odd but familiar flash of anger related to Arcie, different from regular anger. She couldn't remember when it first appeared or why, but it came and went over the years, usually triggered by something Arcie said or did. Tonight was no different. It disappeared quickly enough, but at this particular moment, it was burning a hole in her chest.

They had grown up together, Kitty the eldest by a month, but they were nothing alike. If asked, neither would have been able to remember at what point they'd stumbled into friendship. Like a lot of things, it just happened.

Time had been unkind to Arcie. An unexceptional face, the chubbiness of childhood passing through stages that turned into morbid obesity. Sometimes Arcie's mind didn't seem to work quite right, as if she'd been slapped with more than a little bit of crazy, but Kitty had always tried to overlook her faults.

What she had always liked best about her was her smell. It was a fresh smell that seemed to linger without assistance from deodorant or fragrance. And since Arcie was always around when needed, stodgy but dependable, she'd long ago decided to do her best to accept Arcie as she was—because Arcie was *there,* always just *there* somehow.

Her eyes stung, her vision blurred. She thought: *I'm not going to cry . . . I am not going to cry!* The tears came anyway, making her ashamed of her outburst and loss of control. She didn't want Arcie's charity, but she accepted it because she'd never been good at pretense.

She needed an outlet for the anger that had been building all day. Arcie had accidentally walked into it. It wasn't Arcie's fault, she shouldn't blame her. She didn't think Arcie meant to make bad situations worse than they were; sometimes she just did, for no particular reason.

Kitty wiped tears from her face. "He left . . ." she said, almost inaudibly.

Arcie leaned toward her, head cocked sideways, a small frown pulling her eyebrows together, and said, "What?"

"He left me."

"I don't understand." Arcie's shoulders tilted in a confused shrug.

"What don't you understand? *He left me*," Kitty snapped, angrier with herself than Arcie now that she'd allowed herself to cry.

"What happened?"

Kitty shrugged.

"I thought the two of you got along great together."

Kitty had thought so herself, but it wouldn't erase the fact that he'd used her.

"I thought you might be in love this time."

Kitty felt heat flare through her The roots of her hair tingled. *This time?*

Arcie blushed under her frosty scrutiny. "It was almost a year. You never complained, so I just assumed—"

"Never assume." Kitty gave Arcie her back. Arcie made it sound like a year was the goal to strive for. It made Kitty's life sound like a shabby fraud, an endless procession of friendly encounter and sweaty couplings. She resented it.

Silence stretched icily behind her. She turned back around. Arcie had walked to the balcony's sliding doors and stood to look out. Kitty's condo had a beautiful view of the hazy distance, the muddy undulating slowness of the Mississippi River. Kitty could hear the faint metallic rumbles made by a streetcar when it stopped for passengers, trundling its way between St. Charles and Carrollton.

It was a beautiful evening edging toward night, sepia tinged with lavender and pink, the ground filled with a whirligig of oak and magnolia leaves. It hadn't rained, only occasional bursts and drizzles, and the sun had finally appeared later in the day.

"He left a note," Kitty admitted, disliking the childlike pain in her voice. It made her chest hitch tight with each breath; it echoed inside her head. She was furious with herself for allowing the rejection to hurt, even a little.

"He didn't even say goodbye?" Arcie turned around, hair a tumbled halo against the lavender light.

"No."

"I'm sorry," Arcie said, but what in her voice sounded like sympathy didn't quite match the swirl of darkness in her eyes. Her words sounded more like pity.

Kitty had never known Arcie to have a boyfriend. If she'd ever had a male friend, much less a lover, she'd never mentioned him, so Arcie couldn't possibly understand rejection. Sometimes it was hard to believe she'd brought Arcie with her to New Orleans and they had remained together all these years. She couldn't explain their unusual relationship. Like everything else between, it just was.

They weren't intimate confidants. There had always been a peculiar rift that kept their conversations below that level. What they had was more of a workable understanding. It wasn't important that she ever put a name to what was between them. Whatever it was, most of the time it worked.

It was said that opposites attract; in their case, it was true. Arcie was tense and guarded, like a secret room without light, solid like a rock, her life orderly and structured. Kitty, on the other hand, was open, had a blatant disregard for rules and routine. Her life had always been, and still was, spontaneous, undisciplined and even stormy, like now. She could be self-absorbed, never disturbed for long by someone else's problems. It wasn't in her nature to spend much time thinking about things she could do nothing about, she never felt guilty not being involved in Arcie's private life.

She had taken care of Arcie, kept her safe, for the longest time after they came to New Orleans. Even now she supplemented her income by paying her a personal assistant salary. Because she had always known and accepted that Arcie was a little out of tilt with everything around her, she had grown tolerant. She made excuses for her, but knew she couldn't make excuses forever; at some point, it had to stop.

So, Kitty wondered, *why in hell am I beating myself up over Arcie's shortcomings now?*

Kitty knew the reason for Arcie's unexpected visit. It had to do with that stupid promise they made twenty years ago. She was sure of it. She didn't want to go there tonight and indicate she even remembered. Over the last couple of weeks, she'd found herself plagued with thoughts of an unwanted reunion. Arcie knew how she felt, but Arcie would be up her ass anyway, trying to change her mind. To avoid the subject, she had chosen to avoid Arcie. The situation with Bill had come at an inopportune time. Why make a lousy day worse? She wasn't going to do that to herself. She needed to drop it, right now, avoid letting Arcie even bring up the subject.

"He might be back," Arcie suggested.

"Who said I wanted him back?" she snapped.

"I know, I know . . . you don't need him."

"No—I don't need him." But his leaving had left her feeling vulnerable. Her lips twisted into a bitter smile. She had made a mistake. She'd cared for Bill more than she originally meant to. Like him, enjoy him, but don't care. She'd always seemed drawn to things that were bad for her, especially men. Unable to select the right one for her needs, with the exception of sex. When the next one came along, she'd do it right, she promised herself. She would find out everything she needed to know about him before getting too involved with someone that might sense she didn't have the ability to foresee his use of her. She'd use her head instead of her libido.

A mistake was a mistake. She always tried to learn from her mistakes. Tomorrow would be better. If she worked at it a little, maybe tomorrow she wouldn't be so angry over the fool she'd made of herself.

~ 8 ~

The Past

It had been a quiet, uneventful day, a bright, cloud-less day that filled her with a hunger for fresh fish, and urged her toward her favorite fishing spot. Luck was with her. The water was smooth and dark with algae. Where the trees had shed and the leaves had turned to slimy mulch, she'd unearthed enough fat worms to fill a mason jar. The fish were hungry. Several *goujons*, the big, whiskered mud cats, hung in the bayou from a stringer pole leaning against a cypress knee.

As dusk quenched the remainder of daylight, emerging dark shred the last rays of sun into indigo ribbons. Yancy leaned sleepily against a moss-covered live oak stump, admiring the flash of tinsel-silver from the few stars that had appeared.

The moon was full, streaked faintly orange, bathing everything in a pale glow as it slid through smoky tumbling clouds and touched on dark water like spawning metallic fire. Branches of despoiled trees resembled skeletal arms reaching out from the murky water. A chilly wind, heavy with sour and salt and fish spawn odor, whistled through the fern and the reeds, an adagietto that deformed Spanish moss high in the cypress.

A raw itchy discomfort started in her hands. A pin-pricking sensation of pain traveled up her arms. Her vision blurred, tissue vibrated at the corners of her mouth and eyes. Her temples began to throb. She clutched her head, disoriented, confused over what was happening to her.

The jolting pain that followed was agonizing. The force of it threw her to the ground. Face pressed hard against odious soil, she sucked in a hissing breath, the urgent need to vomit overcame her. On fire from the inside out, she rolled herself onto her hands and knees, quivering as the impact of what was happening resonated through flesh and bone. Mucus and blood and pale smoke oozed from her splitting skin. Shock and terror rose as screams that froze inside her chest, her eyes wide reflective pools of fear. She thought she was dying.

A transparent, glistening lump of flesh formed, outlined jutting angular bones, and she was neither what she had been nor what she would be.

The first spiky tufts of fur appeared, flickered into a dark mask and an extraordinary sable pelt that covered her entire body. Her face elongated into a wide black snout, ivory fangs erupted and gleamed in the moonlight. Long muscular legs filled out and hocks and haunches grew thick, extending into massive paws and thick nails cushioned by large soft pads. A broad plume of tail erupted.

The stretching and twisting and popping finally ended. All pain vanished.

She forced herself to her feet and stood, shaky and confused. Her vision cleared, bringing everything sharply into focus. Her skin tingled. Her nostrils quivered and leaked as her olfactory senses exploded. Her hearing amplified. She was fascinated to hear minute sounds: the repetitious *tick-tick* of evening dew sliding off plant leaves, the unfurling of curled fern, a far-off splash of a gator in distant water, fish sluicing their way between tight tree roots. There was a snicker of prey sliding under cover from a predator, a sleepy bird cooing into its breast in a remote tree, a stealthy rabbit sneaking through weeds, and an owl ruffling its feathers.

Her ears twitched with the motion and noise of small things: insects on the wing, small motors whirring through thin steamers of ghost light, stirring the tactile hair on her muzzle. Her tongue glided out and slipped across the sharp, white shine of enamel.

A strange excitement warmed her blood. She yawned, stretched out her front legs, and dug her toenails into the soft earth. Shaking vigorously, head to tail, she delighted in the weight of the heavy pelt. Her skin quickened pleasurably in each wisp of air movement through the riffling motion of fine guard hairs. She snuffled the air, her mind filled with whirling foreign thought.

An anticipatory tremble overtook her . . . she wanted to run, needed to run, completely stretched out, full force, run until she dropped from exhaustion, until all her muscles ached, her heart seized trying to break free of her chest, and her lungs felt as if they would burst.

Hunger came as a surprise, an unexpected deep rumble in her belly.

She lowered her massive head, scented the ground. Her ears flicked, as she heard the hushed movement not so far away. She sniffed the air again, picking up on the rich gamy scent. She could almost taste the hot blood she craved pumping down her throat, the soft melt of tender bruised flesh against her tongue.

Flesh—*alive*—hot and flush with blood.

A yearning quiver began in her nose until her whole body shook with the exhilarating current. Her heart leaped against her ribcage as she coughed up a whisper of sound, a soft *wuff* that turned from a grudging sliver of noise way down in her chest and crawled quickly, like choked-off laugher, up her throat as she threw back her head and gave voice to an experimental howl.

Arcie impulsively brushed a palm down Kitty's arm. She sensed more than felt Kitty flinch away. Dropping her hand, she said, "So you're going out alone?"

"It won't be the first time."

"Where are you going?" Kitty had always been comfortable with or without a male companion. She had always wished she could be that way.

"Carson Crane's."

"Why there?"

"It's been a long time since I was here." She hadn't gone since she began seeing Bill. She had a bad habit of diving headfirst into relationships, so quick—always so quick—to discard old habits and lovers, push aside old friends when settling into a new romance.

"Wouldn't a pizza and a movie work as good?"

"No."

"Why not give it more time—another week, at least—before you do that?"

"No." Kitty glanced at the clock and wandered into the bathroom.

Arcie followed. "Carson—he's the gay one?" She had a hard time remembering Kitty's people, their faces and names. Most were strangers, so it was difficult for her to approve of most of them, invading and filling up, drifting in and out of the gray blur of their relationship over the years. She never accepted Kitty's unstructured lifestyle.

"His brother isn't."

"His brother is engaged to be married shortly." That one Arcie couldn't forget. She knew it was useless to pay much attention to hot guys, but one look at Creely Crane could suck the thought of another male right out of a woman's mind.

"That certainly doesn't make him dead."

"It makes him taken."

"He's a friend."

"Is he gonna be the same kind of friend after he gets married?"

"I certainly hope so."

"It's in his nature to cheat."

"I'm not responsible for him cheating."

"You don't avoid it."

"Knock it off, Arcie." Kitty felt her temper slipping, fought against a blossoming curl of anger.

"I didn't come here to fight," Arcie whispered. "I don't want to fight."

"I don't want to fight either." After a moment: "Why don't you come with me? Play bodyguard." She tried for generosity, already knowing Arcie wouldn't come.

"No, thanks."

"Why not?"

"Men don't have urges for me as they do for you," Arcie whispered.

"You're antisocial."

"I'm not their type." Arcie hated herself for being defensive, but she couldn't help it.

"No one is your type," Kitty responded. All these years, and she still had no idea what was Arcie's type.

"What's that supposed to mean?"

"It's all bullshit. A couple drinks, friendly conversation, a few laughs—maybe snag a date . . . just a damn *date*. No sex involved." It had occurred to Kitty more than a few times that maybe men and sex scared Arcie for some oddball reason. Or maybe it went deeper. She should have asked, maybe she would ask, but she wouldn't do it tonight.

"I realize that, Kitty." Heat crept into Arcie's cheeks. She hated it when Kitty embarrassed her and hated herself when she allowed it to show. Her eyes slid sideways to the glass-encased Oriental painting on the wall. She reached out, straightened it a fraction. A thousand dollar wasteful expenditure, brought early on when Kitty's career was just taking off. It was beautiful and it wasn't Arcie's money, but she'd been miffed over the purchase. Like when she balanced Kitty's checkbook and discovered the checks to Bill amounting to $15,000—now the bastard was gone.

"Just because that's what *you* would do." It just popped out. She hadn't planned to *say* that sort of thing; *think it*, yes, but never say it. Her tongue was so loose. It had slipped out so easily, surprising her as much as Kitty. Too much stress pulling at her.

Kitty jerked around and snarled, "What the hell are you talking about?"

"A-a quickie."

"It's just *sex*, Arcie, not a criminal offense." She would never apologize for wanting or enjoying sex. Sex wasn't the answer to everything, but sometimes it sure helped. What she occasionally thought to apologize for was who she'd had sex with, but she'd never found anything objectionable about the act itself.

"He just left."

"So?"

"You haven't allowed yourself time to—" Arcie found herself floundering, searching for a word— "mourn."

"*Mourn?* He didn't die, Arcie. He sneaked out and left a note. A final fuck, that's all he wanted." Kitty felt itchy with the burn of her anger.

"Don't say it like that."

"Why not?" Kitty's heart was beating rapidly, thunder in her ears.

"Guess it wasn't a very good one either." Arcie's voice dripped sarcasm.

"And that means what?"

"That you're pissed, but you don't have to mess

with other people's lives."

"Now what are you talking about?"

"Creely Crane. Leave him alone. You need to get laid again so badly, just go to a bar and pick up the first available penis." Arcie startled herself, had just jammed her foot down her throat, her mouth moving faster than her mind. She could feel it way back there, thick black funk, closing in like sewage seepage, cold and nasty. Lousy timing. She needed to talk to Kitty. She shouldn't have waited so long. That's why she'd come over, not this; not to argue, not to criticize, never to make Kitty angry.

Anger crawled across Kitty's skin. What the hell! Had that childish promise set all this in motion? This was an Arcie she didn't know. She'd never denied her liberal sexual habits, but Arcie had never before thrown them in her face. Sometimes in the past, when necessary, she'd used sex to her advantage, but it had never been as bad as Arcie made it sound.

"Stop being so sanctimonious," she retorted, smearing cream over her face.

That stupid promise—the provocation for all this nastiness? Screw this! She reached inside the shower, turning the faucets to hot. Steam began to form large teardrops that slid lazily across the Italian tiles. Let Arcie think and say what she wanted. If Creely was at Carson's, he would be a bonus. She genuinely liked and cared about Creely, another of those dependable, unconditional things in her life. Always being able to communicate with each other had led them to continual sexual involvement over the years. Sometimes she thought she felt something more deeply for him, that maybe he felt the same toward her, but she'd never pursued that nudge. Someone new always seemed to pop into her life or his. But he was extra special, always tugging at her heartstrings, and she trusted him. It didn't matter that they always seemed to troll slightly different waters. There was never any pressure, allowing each other freedom to come and go, always welcoming each other back without judgment.

Their last encounter had been thirteen months previous. They had spoken a few times since their last night together, but continual contact on her part had been through television and newspapers. She'd seen him a couple of times from a distance, at parties or an exhibit, overheard his name in conversations, but there had been nothing head-on, face-to-face. Bill had come into her life, and Creely, moving right along with his, became engaged. She'd thought a few times to call, wish him well on his engagement, but something held her back—jealousy, a sense of impending loss, she supposed. Something she didn't want to think too much about or admit out loud. Without reasonable cause, she didn't like this rich bitch she'd heard of but didn't know, had never met but had seen once or twice, the one who could be taking away another unconditional part of her life. And, yeah, maybe—just maybe—because she'd never been able to acknowledge there could've been something more between herself and Creely and she had probably let it slip away.

Arcie seemed to have lost the motivation of her outburst, but her tone remained a little sharp when she stated: "You should be painting."

"I probably should." Kitty felt resentment like a giant balloon inside her chest. "But it isn't gonna happen tonight."

"Or last night or the night before, or last week either, if I recall correctly."

"Not tonight," Kitty repeated.

Arcie sighed heavily. "Suit yourself."

"I usually do." Kitty tamped down her anger. Arcie could survive without her now, but she'd placed herself in a position where she might find it difficult without Arcie. Arcie handled her personal business as well as everything involved with the promotion and sale of her paintings; she did it well, had a knack for it. If things got really bad between them and their friendship completely disintegrated, she would have to replace her. She wasn't sure she was ready to adjust herself to the habits of someone new.

Arcie had come to the city with her as a safety net. The old shrimper had disgusted her, but she'd done what had to be done to get away. With careful rationing, his money had lasted almost two months and gave her a chance to discover that fast food service wasn't for her. Decent money was unlawful and sometimes dangerous, but in the beginning survival for both of them had depended upon her. So she did a stint at a strip joint on Bourbon Street.

Arcie never approved, but it became a lucrative stepping stone. It was tolerable, it paid the bills. She'd always had bigger plans; always felt she just needed the right opportunity to better herself. She'd never doubted she should have more than she did, was meant to be something more than she was.

She had always had to push Arcie, and Arcie had never taken care of her share, so their first real fight was over money. Arcie finally took a wait job in a small French Quarter café, sharing tables with the redhead who pocketed Arcie's tips every chance she got, but she was usually able to salvage enough to pay half the rent, not much else, on the ratty second-floor furnished apartment off Elysian Fields they shared.

They struggled, until the Saturday morning that odd little man sat too close to her on the bench in Jackson Square. She had tried to ignore him, but oblivious to her discomfort, he managed to press himself up against her, squinting over the top of his round steel-framed glasses. She could smell his denture breath, the faint scent of woodsy cologne.

It was her special bench, she wasn't about to move. "Please stop, I'm not interested in dirty old men," she'd said, thinking about how many she fended off each night at the strip joint.

"Moi?" he said, his voice softly musical, staring at her thought those smudged thick lenses, filling the air with his amused laughter. "You think that? *Mon Dieu, chere!* What a beautiful, naive child you are! Females don't interest me that way."

"Then what do you want?" she had demanded.

One bony finger pointed at her drawing tablet, so she showed him her surrealistic and quirky imaginary creatures. Felix Broussard turned out to be an art gallery owner, and he'd fallen in love with each and every one. He became her friend, opened doors in the artistic community she would have never walked through without him, promoting her talent to every art patron that cross the threshold of his galleries as *pas commun cadeau*—a rare gift. Everyone believed him, even her. She'd fallen into her livelihood as she'd fallen into everything of importance in her life.

Her wonderful Felix became one of those un-conditional things she treasured, however briefly. He'd given in to the ravages of cancer nine years ago, but she would never forget him. Her art now commanded high prices. She lived well. She liked what she did. She was good at it. Her time was her own, no structured hours or an insufferable boss.

What more could a person ask?

"I don't know why I bother," Arcie said, pulling Kitty from her reverie.

"Oh, damnit, stop!" Kitty dropped her robe and stepped into the cloud of steam. She had a headache starting, ~~up high,~~ behind her eyes, and tight wires of tension throbbed in her shoulders and neck. Arcie could wear a person's nerves, but Arcie had yet to mention the promise. She needed to stop over-thinking the twenty-year shit, wouldn't be badgered into going back. Until Arcie brought up the subject, she wouldn't touch it

Arcie watched Kitty through the shower stall's hand-etched glass panels. She felt tired and empty. Her stomach was tight with repressed anger and resentment, her mind clogged with disappointment and foggy, dark funk. Her heart beat a little too fast. The urgent need to talk to Kitty, and the ill feelings that had fueled her system, and had given her the courage to accomplish the purpose of her visit, seemed to have evaporated. All she'd succeeded in doing was making Kitty angry.

"It will pass," she said.

"What did you say?" Kitty asked, through the roar of the water.

"It will pass," she repeated, louder.

Kitty felt her body tense up. Her lungs felt spongy, struggling against the stifling hot shower moisture. When she responded, she sounded breathy, "I never imagined it wouldn't."

"Just like the last time," Arcie added.

Kitty pressed her palms against the slick tiles. The water pounded her and she raised her face into the slam of it, sucking steam into her lungs. She felt a little raw inside. It had already been an emotionally draining day. She didn't need Arcie hassling her. She turned her head, ready to argue, eyed Arcie's slumped figure, and found herself deflated. Her shoulders pushed up around her ears, head hung low, Kitty closed her eyes and said nothing.

She knew Arcie was alluding to two years before Bill. His name was David and his memory still elicited a twinge. David had been a twenty-one-year-old student at LSU in Baton Rouge. She had never imagined more than a fling. She never expected to care deeply for him, wished she hadn't cared as much as she did. Sometimes caring led to love. Love could be sweet in the beginning, but the end could be painful, even if there was only a little of it.

On a sparkly winter morning, they had met on the streetcar when it made an Audubon Park stop. She had been searching for inspiration for a new painting. David had bounded on, all smiles: tall, breath-taking, handsome energy. With a dozen empty seats to choose from, he plopped his leggy body down next to her. She found herself immediately lecherous.

Seven months into a delightful relationship, while she was away at an exhibit in Houston, David abruptly disappeared from her life as quickly as he had entered it. She had left dozens of unanswered messages on his cell phone, sent an equal number of emails. Days passed, then a week, two, three without contact, not a single word. She considered all sorts of reasons that would make it impossible for contact, knowing none of them were valid. Never, *never*, wanting to believe David so thoughtless and cruel.

Nine weeks later, she received the phone call.

His voice was tight, ashamed and embarrassed when he apologized. Even before he explained, she already knew he wasn't coming back, she would never see him again. He said he knew he should have called sooner. He was sorry if he'd hurt her, sorry for the irresponsible way he'd handled things. He hadn't meant for it to happen, but it had happened so fast. He got drunk with college buddies the night she left and got seduced. Blind-sided with craziness and lust, he went back the next night for more. He thought after the third time what he felt was love for the willing, barely legal hottie. A month later he realized his mistake. They had nothing in common beyond the physical attraction that was already turning luke-warm. She'd dumped the pregnancy news on him. He had stupidly thought all women used protection and never thought to ask. Unlike Bill, he hadn't asked that Kitty remember their times together, but occasionally she did.

A year later someone they both knew told her more. David had married the girl. They had twin boys. He had moved to Metairie, traded the life he might have had to work double shifts at the shipyard in Avondale.

Kitty felt, beyond survival, life would probably find it easy to get in his way for a long time. They had discussed his want of a family a couple of times. She understood that probably kept him with the girl, might keep them together for years, or maybe not. She had no way of knowing if it hadn't been for his mistake if they would have stayed together.

She also knew she probably wouldn't have given him a child. She'd never given much consideration to a baby, thought maybe she wasn't genetically engineered for motherhood. After the kind of childhood she'd had, she was never comfortable thinking about the complications kids could bring into her life, so it was never at the top of her priority list. She'd never told him that, but maybe he'd sensed it and just knew.

She was glad for him if he was happy. She wondered in the midst of diapers, bottles, and bills, if David had regrets and thought of her. If he might miss her, just a little. If late at night, when sleep escaped him, he remembered their times together and might touch himself.

Kitty tried to reason with herself; David had been far too young and immature. Yet she'd still felt a little broken. The pain of his loss had stayed fresh for months. So, yeah, maybe she had loved him, more than a little.

They hadn't mentioned David in a long time. Perhaps Arcie hadn't meant to now. Or maybe she was just being spiteful, poking at old wounds that no longer bled, only seeped a little. Picking at the scab, not giving the wounds the time they needed to heal up so they wouldn't become infected. This wasn't the Arcie she thought she knew. Her behavior was different. Now, after her unusual outburst, she was self-consciously studying her toes.

"What's going on here?" Kitty asked, turning off the water and drying herself.

"What do you mean?"

"What's *really* on your mind?"

She needed a drink. When Arcie didn't answer, she wrapped the towel around her, brushed past Arcie and sauntered into the kitchen to retrieved a half-full bottle of Moet & Chandon champagne from the fridge. She swallowed down an entire flute, took a refill, and poured one for Arcie. Returning to the bedroom, she prompted, *"Well?"*

Arcie accepted the flute but didn't drink. "You forgot, didn't you?" Color flooded her cheeks.

Kitty turned away. "Forgot what?" *So there it is, finally coming out.*

"Our promise. You know, about going back."

Kitty kept her back to Arcie. "I didn't forget," she said into the uncomfortable silence. "Not. Going. Back." She carefully enunciated each word.

"You always wanted to forget about home."

"What makes you think I feel differently now?"

"It's been a long time."

"What made you think time would make a difference?" Kitty snapped.

"It's important."

"Not to me."

"We promised Yancy. She never left . . . she's waiting for us."

"So? She can wait for the rest of her life, for all I care," Kitty said. "I didn't belong there. I was unfortunate enough to be born there, but I never belonged there. I did something about that." *And not just for me, but for you, you twit, or you'd probably still be rotting away there like Yancy,* she thought, but said aloud, "It was her choice to stay. She fit in there. She was different. I thought you understood that."

"How was she different?"

"She was *weird*, the whole damn family was. Plain crazy, to tell the truth. I used to wonder how we ever got involved with her."

"We just sort of drifted together."

"Yeah, we did, but I always wondered how that happened."

"We all needed friends."

"That doesn't make me responsible for her choices," Kitty said.

"I don't think she had a lot of choices."

"I got out and I took you with me."

"I know . . . I don't think I'd have left if it hadn't been for you."

Kitty didn't reply, glad Arcie had finally admitted what they both knew.

"Why *did* you take me with you, Kitty?" It was a question she had dreamed of asking, but had always been afraid to hear the answer.

"I thought two would be safer than one." *There had been no one else.*

"I kept in touch with her for a while."

"What? *Why?*" Kitty was startled. Why hadn't Arcie ever mentioned keeping in touch with Yancy? Arcie didn't act normal all the time, not quite all there with her brooding mood swings, but Yancy was plain fucking crazy. Kitty had always figured Arcie was wired a little wrong, maybe some kind of mental or personality disorder, that she should see a doctor, maybe spend some time in a psychiatric facility, but she never mentioned it. Arcie wanted to be secretive, so she let her. Now she was thinking she should have taken time to find out more about what was going on with her.

After leaving their joint housing accommodations, Kitty hadn't bothered to delve into Arcie's personal life and the other woman never talked with her about it. While together, Arcie had never had one. When Arcie could afford it, she'd bought that terrible old duplex shotgun house.

Everything wrong with the house would be fixed with time and money, but she knew she'd never live in it, and after her initial visit, Kitty never went back. So Arcie's personal life was mostly a blank. There seemed to be no one special, she spoke infrequently of her job, raised African violets, and kept tropical fish because she found dogs and cats too much trouble. Arcie loved cheeseburgers and fries, Popeye's Fried Chicken, Godiva chocolates, beignets and coffee from Café du Monde. *Shouldn't I know more about her? Shouldn't I have asked or she have told* me?

"I was curious." Arcie shrugged. "I always thought Yancy's family was mysterious and exciting."

"Frightening is more like it."

"What does that mean?"

"They were scary, Arcie. No one likes being afraid. They scared the shit out of me. I was never sure what might happen if we stopped being friendly with her."

"No matter how much you'd like to forget the past, Kitty, the truth is, our families were all strange in their own way."

Kitty felt her throat tighten. She couldn't dispute that. She had overcome the hardship of a bad childhood, had built a good life for herself, but the trauma her family caused in her youth continued to live on inside her. Once you discovered the good things, you tended to ignore the bad, thinking the good would be around forever. It seldom worked out that way. Some memories never went away, they came back to give you an unexpected sharp nip on the ass.

"You always said that."

Arcie spoke so softly Kitty almost didn't hear her. "Said what?"

"She wasn't right upstairs. You really believed those ugly things people said."

"Yeah, I did."

"It wasn't Yancy's fault. I never held it against her. I guess you did."

"I guess I did." Kitty finished her champagne in one gulp. Arcie hadn't touched hers. "Being friends with her caused me trouble at home. I had enough trouble at home."

"We all had our share."

"'Crazy black voodoo people.' Those were my mother's exact words."

"People didn't like them."

"I don't think 'like' was even on the table.

Rituals, potions, and powders—any spell a person wanted, for the right price. They didn't have to like them for those things." Kitty grimaced. Both the Arceneaux women seemed to have powers no one understood, but almost everyone wanted to make use of. Was it possible Yancy had them also?

"I remember." Arcie chewed at her lower lip.

Kitty rolled her eyes. "Anyway, what has any of it got to do with us now?"

"It was always easier for you."

"What did you say?"

"It was always easier for you."

"What was easier for me?" Kitty asked testily.

"Everything."

"Why would you think that?"

"You were beautiful and smart. You wanted to get away from French Gap."

"So that made everything easier for me." Kitty felt as if their brief moments of camaraderie had melted around the edges and were dissolving as if their friendship had become wary and was on the verge of faltering.

"I think so. If you wanted something, you went after it . . . you always seemed to know how to get it." Arcie knew she'd stepped into quicksand. This wasn't the direction she'd wanted their conversation to go. She finally took a deep swallow of champagne.

"If you want more, you do what you have to do

to get it. She couldn't have wanted much if she stayed there. Maybe she wasn't smart enough to make it anywhere else and she knew it."

Arcie sucked in a deep breath. "You're wrong. She did want something else. It just happened to be different from what you wanted."

"Why are you so hot to defend her?" Kitty felt knee-deep in shit from the past and she didn't like it.

"I'm just telling you the way I think it was—*is*—for her."

Kitty's found her curiosity piqued, but she didn't much like the information that kept spewing out of Arcie. Arcie finally stopped talking, finished off her champagne, and set the flute on the dresser. Eyes cloudy, she seemed to have drifted off into some bleak world of thought to which only she had an admission.

"Okay, so what *did* she want?"

Something mercurial flickered in Arcie's eyes. "She wanted a daughter."

"Not any healthy kid, specifically a daughter?"

"Yes." Arcie had turned to face Kitty, her body half-shadowed by light from the bedside lamps.

"I guess she got her."

Arcie's eyes had taken on a peculiar focus. A hint of sadness in her tone sounded like an accusation. Ridiculous to think such a thing, but it was as if Arcie was insinuating it was all her fault that Yancy hadn't gotten the things she'd wanted out of life.

"I don't think so," Arcie said.

"She never married?"

"No."

"Never even had a hot affair that gave her the kid she wanted?"

"Not that I heard."

"There must've been at least one person that found her appealing," Kitty said.

Arcie's head tilted, her face twisting into a knot. "That was an ugly thing to say."

"It's the truth." Kitty frowned. "How long has it been since you've had contact?"

"A long time."

"Why did you stop communicating with her?"

Arcie shrugged. She didn't know. She hadn't stopped writing. Yancy had. Her last two letters had been returned undeliverable.

"A lot could have changed. You can't be sure she's still there, much less expects us to come."

"I am."

"That's ridiculous—just because it's been twenty years? You don't even know if she's still alive."

"She is, I know, I feel it. She's waiting."

"What the hell is she waiting for?" Dusty moved to sit nervously on the edge of Kitty's foot. Kitty picked her up, accepting a swipe of wet tongue on her cheek. Arcie had edged a little closer to her. They stood motionless, faces inches apart, staring at each other over the dog's nose. Arcie didn't answer. "Stop the drama crap, Arcie, tell me what's she waiting for?"

Arcie stared at her without speaking.

A lengthy silence hung between them. Kitty felt an icy tingle of unease. It was as if a blip had broken down their communication link, then a zip shifted like a whoosh of air to bring everything sharply into focus so neither would be aware their conversation had been interrupted.

Arcie's eyes cleared, a smile twitched up the right side of her mouth. "Maybe us—maybe she's just waiting for *us*," she said quietly.

10

The Past

Yancy came to and left the hideous blackness behind. She lay naked in the tall weeds, the grass against her face damp with late-night dew, her mind bogged down. She couldn't remember where she'd been or what had happened. It took several minutes of slow, controlled breathing to gather her thoughts together.

Reality arrived with a painful surge of blood in her temples.

The pain . . . the bestial feelings . . . the hot pump of blood in her veins . . . the solid thrust of muscle in leg and haunch . . . the snap of twigs and the feel of hard ground rushing by beneath her running paws . . . the cut and slap of tall grass and weeds around her muzzle . . . the chilling thrill of crisp night wind whipping through her pelt.

The hunger!

Her heart lunged, nearly stopped, as she recalled snatches of events, her change a motley fluctuation. The exhilarating shock of opening her new body up to the night, seeing everything with sharp awareness, feeling so strong, the strength almost a solid surging through her veins, sepia lightning flashes of the kill.

Her first kill.

She had slipped out of the rising moon's shadow, fastened her canines into the kicking hindquarter of her prey. The struggle, the frightened squeals of death, burned through her. The warm pulse of blood pouring into her mouth electrified her. She sank her fangs into the animal's throat, bearing the thrashing, wild-eyed young doe to the ground. The thrill that came with the weight of the hot hard body under her own, gorging herself on soft innards and tender meat, flashed through her like fire.

Yancy attempted to push herself upright, shivering, but not with cold. She felt dizzy, fell back against the ground, and rested her forehead on her knees as she brought them up tight against her breasts. She gagged, horror and despair rising like bile into the back of her throat. Balling her hands into fists, she stared into the dark. Threads of moonlight filtered through the treetop canopy, but she could see as clearly as if it were daylight. The scattered pieces of torn clothes, the fishing hole several feet away, the catch of fish in the grass, giving off the unpleasant odor of death, stiff and dull, a steely color, their long whiskers like curled wire, their fins hard, flattened, their scales dry and sharp.

She had no concept of time. No idea how long

she'd been away or when she had returned. Her confused mind flipped and rolled, burned with the memory snatches of what she'd done.

Eventually, she curled into a ball and cried.

11

Arcie stepped inside the door, pushing herself into the near-silence of her house. The only sounds were the hiss-murmur of the aquarium's filtration system and brief creaks of the old house adjusting itself. The room's only illumination came from the aquarium light. In the shadowy dark, she watched the angelfish swim in lazy circles. A flame-red male betta passed into view, fins fanned, casting brilliant color on the glass.

She walked through the shadows to the kitchen, not turning on a light, grabbed a Coke from the refrigerator and popped the tab on the drink can. The release sounded explosive. She flinched, scolding herself: *Stupid! Stupid! Stupid!*—and fought back tears. She was infuriated with Kitty. Hell, she was infuriated with herself! The entire situation had been exhausting. It should have been easy and simple, but they had managed to cross an invisible line when something dangerous reared its ugly head and tied itself into a choke-hold knot around her neck.

She snatched a candy from the Godiva box on the counter.

She had thought everything was improving, that they had established a breakthrough, even when things had started off rocky. It turned out they hadn't.

She was nothing more than the ever-faithful pup, obligated to offer a proper response, empathize and most certainly do or say nothing inappropriate while Kitty experienced her emotional distress. She hated herself for accepting it, for allowing it. She should've walked out sooner, knew she couldn't. Tonight had been her compromise. If ever a time for compromise, it certainly was tonight.

She felt a spurt of anger, a flurry of nippy little things wiggled across her skin. Kitty's behavior pissed her off but sometimes made her sad. She had tried to justify it with: *Kitty's always been that way, Kitty's just being Kitty.* But it was demeaning. She disliked it almost as much as he hated herself for being unable to hold onto her tongue tonight. Ugly and judgmental with her comments, she had offended Kitty, but the words had just slipped out. She'd thought the words a thousand times, wanted to shout them at Kitty each of those times, but she hadn't meant to say them, certainly not now, in that way.

Her fingers wrapped the soda can, crushed it until the drink spewed across the counter. She mopped at the mess with paper towels. Her anger had grown stronger, as much with herself as with Kitty, and her blood pressure was elevated, her skin flushed and tingly. She threw the wet paper towels in the trash and grabbed for her purse. She yanked out the plastic bottle, but in her haste, the lid popped off the prescription bottle, the bottle tumbled from her fingers, and the contents scattered along the floor. She crawled around, scooping pills back inside.

She had expected resistance and thought she could handle it, but she'd lost control. Her anger had been boiling hot, a bumblebee buzzing inside her head. The deep dark funk slid forward, starting to clog up her mind. Being antagonistic put her at a disadvantage, and got her nowhere. It only alienated Kitty. She knew she had to leave. And she did, without saying another word.

Attention drifting, running a red light, almost an accident, pissed her off more. She had no tolerance for damage to her precious car. That could have really brought all the black shit forward.

She had been too confident she could change Kitty's mind. It was stupid of her to dump it all out on the table the night before they needed to leave. Now the damage was done. Her own damn fault!

That damn game was supposed to show the faces of their husbands! She hadn't enjoyed it, had been afraid to open her eyes, and never saw the face of her future husband. But she wasn't likely to ever have a husband, was she? A worthless experience for her—only a dumb game Yancy created. Except for Kitty—it was different with Kitty. Kitty *had* seen something. Why had she lied, saying she didn't remember? That wasn't possible. Maybe she didn't remember *everything* about that night, but she remembered *something!* She had no idea what Kitty saw, if it was the face of her future husband—after all, Kitty still didn't have one either and didn't seem particularly motivated about getting one. If it was a face she saw, husband or not, she'd kept it to herself. But whatever she'd seen had frightened her.

They had all shied away from talking about that night afterward. It seemed to have created a barrier between them. Why had they been so quick to allow that, to accept it? They should have talked about it. And they should've talked after Lacy disappeared. They had avoided talking about that, too.

Occasionally, when her meds calmed the wild jangle of her nerves, chased the gooey funk deep inside some hole, put her in that falsely euphoric place they sometimes did, she'd find a trace of courage to ask about it—but she never had. Now this unexpected crap with Bill had come up. It couldn't have happened at a worse time.

Kitty wasn't making this easy. She would have a miserable night. She definitely wouldn't sleep much. What if Kitty wasn't home in the morning? No searching for her, Arcie had no idea where to look. No time left for subtle, to soothe a damaged ego, no time left to play nice.

Arcie stood in front the aquarium and watched the fish forming a multi-colored wave of motion as they flash-danced toward the glass. She pinched flakes of food, allowing them to rain across the water's surface. The fish fed, their darting movements soothing. Or maybe it was the extra meds kicking in. She wasn't sure, but either way, she was glad, she felt nice. She was already drifting, knots of nerves untying themselves to lay flat and smooth. By the time the fish made satisfied circles, she was relaxed, almost calm.

The bedroom curtains were parted enough for a smudge of light. The lamps made a soft glow that shadowed the corners of the room. Moonlight tangled with slashes of hazy pewter in the indigo night. Beyond the overhang of expensive replacement windows lay a tiny yard with a hibachi on bricks, a young magnolia tree, and an empty concrete bird bath. Red-striped lawn chairs were folded against white fence boards; creeping vines, and a few summer flowers with splotchy dull color. *Mine, my place, no one else's, all mine,* she thought.

An overpowering tangle of confusion worked its way to the front of her mind. Sometimes her mind could be a bouncing ball, her thoughts ricocheting in different directions, and she would feel a boiling rage at the injustices life had heaped upon her. She wished whatever was wrong with her would go away; that all the messy goop inside her head would disappear. A genetic disorder, something lacking in her mother's womb to make her the way she was? Or had it come from the other side, the father she'd never known? Which of them had passed along their horrible nasty stuff inside her mind?

There could be lots of reasons Yancy had stopped writing, she supposed—but Yancy wasn't dead. Deep down inside she knew Kitty was wrong. Maybe Yancy had gotten upset with her, considered it none of her business when she asked about Domeno. It hadn't done much good to ask, she hadn't learned much, only that he was still there, had married—her heart had slammed into the soles of her feet—and his wife had died not long after. Almost a tease, like a movie trailer, it only made her want to know more. She hadn't dared ask more. No matter what Kitty thought, she felt it in her bones—Yancy was waiting for them . . . Domeno was waiting for *her*. She knew —she *knew* he was waiting for *her!*

She could make up all kinds of excuses, but he was the real reason for going back. Sometimes she managed to push away thoughts of him. She'd listen to that far away voice that said nothing about him was real, everything was in her mind—*only in my mind*—but she didn't always understand, because for her he never really went away, always seemed to be there. He never left her alone for long. He came to New Orleans to be with her, would suddenly just be *there*. She would see him watching her from a street corner, staring at her from behind a gas pump, looking at her over the canned goods in the grocery aisle. At night he would be in her bedroom, clinging to shadow in a corner, unsure he was wanted, until she motioned him forward.

She could feel his touch, sweet soft fire, gentle caresses moving over her body when he came to her. He would climb on top of her, teasing her, wanting her to beg. And she would, she always did. She would wrap her arms around him, let him push between her legs, and help him shove himself inside her to take her again and again and *again,* until she screamed each time the heat of orgasm overtook her.

The next morning, she'd wake to a cold sheet. No one there, there never had been. Hurt and disappointment settled deep in her belly like a mule's solid kick.

Arcie sat on the edge of the bed, slipped off her jeans. She folded them until it was impossible to fold them again, and staring at the denim, she stroked the material like a small animal. Thoughts of the reunion now made her queasy, torn between uncertainty and expectation. Her calm was evaporating.

The last couple of weeks had taken her back almost where she'd been before any kind of meds. She'd become skittish, anxious, double-dipping into low self-esteem again.

Sometimes she wanted to die. She knew she couldn't kill herself and guessed that made her a coward. She could never swallow a bottle of pills, couldn't get drunk and smash her car into the side of a building or step in front of a bus. She lacked the ability and energy to climb to a rooftop and open wide her arms, like a broken bird still trying to fly, as she simply leaned forward into a fall. She just wanted it to happen. Sort of like when an old or sick person went to sleep and never woke up.

She fully understood climbing back into that bad place. She didn't like being there, didn't want to return, and didn't want anyone to know she'd ever visited. She wondered if one day she'd find herself completely tipped off the edge, totally lost in that ferocious black funk chasm. She'd just go there and not return.

She hadn't felt this bad in a long time. Nothing was going smoothly. The bad things were starting up again. If she wasn't careful it would get worse. She had to regain control or the time would come when she'd end up in that state lunatic asylum in Mandeville. She had to always make sure she took her meds—*keep taking my meds!*—as she wrapped the bedcovers around her and pulled a pillow over her head.

Yancy opened her eyes to the intense pain and the stabbing growl of her stomach. A warm and sleepy purple dusk had gathered, night eating away the day. She squinted into the disappearing sun and sliding shades of twilight. The day was almost gone. It had slipped away while she drowned in her memories.

Her first change had been terrible; the blackout, the hunger, the blood, the confusion afterward. But over the years each shift made it easier to think. The animal instincts no longer fully overpowered the part of her brain that remained human. Shifting was usually easier around the full moons when the amorphous light gave off a strong magnetic pull and brought the shift more quickly, but not always. No, strong emotions made her beast rise as well. She was forever struggling to adjust mind and body to the transformations the first year, eventually sensing them: The tension, the restless tingling of the skin, and the twitching of body. And she was no less enraged each time it happened.

Grandmere never told me! Of everything she said, she should have told her that. She had to give up her virginity to the beast . . . but *Grandmere* never told her—*never even hinted!*—she would become one.

Yancy struggled to her feet; gingerly touched her

face. Her bottom lip was split, there was the taste of blood and dirt on her tongue. A throbbing, goose egg-sized lump had formed on her cheek, half closing her left eye. Her right knee was skinned. At some point, she'd lost her balance and had fallen down the steps. She had been in a trance, mesmerized by her thoughts, thinking about all the bad things too much.

When she thought about the bad things, she felt something hard and painful form in her chest, deep under her breastbone. *Grandmere* had stressed that she fulfill her birthright, understand the importance of her duty, which was the only way to break the family curse. Why hadn't she explained what a monster she would become? Why had she neglected such an important detail? She'd stayed angry for years until she finally understood that anger with the dead only injured her soul and never solved anything.

So each time the shift electrified her body, she begin to tingle, convulse, and rip apart, and the bestial needs overtook her—each time the fogginess departed, leaving her with tattered bits of memory, the taste of bloody flesh in her mouth and a full belly—each time she left a little more of her humanity behind, she thought it might be better if she shifted and never came back, stayed a beast, never human again, no longer having to spend the rest of her life divided, and slipping between two worlds.

~13~

Lacy finished placing underwear in the dark travel bag. She could read the pout in his expression as she turned toward him, in need of something to smooth the rough edges.

They'd had a quiet dinner, with little conversation, as if there were very little to say to each other, but they both knew differently. Afterward, they didn't make love, they had hard, fast sex. He'd gone at her with a fierceness he'd never shown her before. He spread her legs and pushed himself inside her, pounding at her until she came, then followed so closely it seemed the orgasms were simultaneous. Later, she lay a long time beside him without speaking, not sure what to say. She finally left the bed to pack. Now he watched her, reclining naked against the pillows balled up behind his head.

"A nightcap?" she asked.

"Yes." His voice was gruff.

She left the room, returned with snifters and a bottle of Cointreau, sat on the edge of the mattress and poured. He downed the liqueur with an overflow of emotion in his eyes and a sharp downward curve to his mouth, and let her refill his snifter. She knew what was coming before the words passed his lips.

"Cancel this trip. Say you can't make it."

Lacy looked away, slowly shook her head. "I can't do that."

With a defeated sigh, he said, "Why are you being so stubborn?"

"Why are you?" she countered.

"Because something about this doesn't feel right to me."

Lacy didn't reply. She didn't want to go, but couldn't tell him that. If he chastised her too strongly, she knew she would get angry. She didn't want to fight with him. She wished he would just leave the subject alone. She didn't need the added stress of another argument.

"What isn't right about four old friends getting together after twenty years?"

"Don't know. Wish I could tell you." He caught her hand, uncurled her fingers, and held her palm against his lips. "Nothing I suppose . . . but for some reason—look, I know you're annoyed because I keep after you. It's not my intention to make you angry. I can't help feeling you have reservations yourself, even if you won't admit it."

Lacy tried to concentrate on his soft lips and moist warm breath against her palm instead of the cold spot inside that wouldn't go away. He was right, of course. She did have reservations. She felt backed into a corner, faced with a situation that had to be taken care of, like dirty dishes or laundry going to the dry cleaners.

"Since we've been together, you've never mentioned them."

"There was no reason to until now. A few months of intimacy isn't forever, Gregg."

He looked away, hurt. "I just figured if you were that close—"

"In some ways we were."

"I don't understand."

"I can't explain what I never understood myself." In her peripheral vision, she caught the movement of his hand sliding down his body. She pulled the sheet over him, smoothing the edge across his chest. She wouldn't let him distract her. Would he understand how crazy it would sound if she said sometimes she felt the four of them never really liked each other? Would they discover they still didn't?

"Why go?"

Lacy sighed, offering her hands, palm up, in an almost helpless gesture of defeat. "Twenty years ago we made a promise to get together again. I don't know any other way to explain it." If they stayed together, she would tell him everything—one day, but not now.

"What kind of reunion is it?"

"High school?" she suggested.

Gregg gave a short laugh. "So you're being nice . . . you're curious."

It wasn't an act of nicety or curiosity. "I was thinking along the lines of an obligation," she said, standing and walking away, stopping to look out a window. "It's sort of like a kid being forced by their parents to attend the funeral of a distant relative they never met." She had told him nothing more than necessary about her past. She had a fiercely protective need to keep all the dirty little secrets to herself.

"I'm sorry." During their short intimacy Lacy had become far more important than a sexual partner or the person who signed his paycheck, but despite any justifications he made, he knew all of it amounted to jealousy. In his haste to protect her—damnit, only a *feeling*, he didn't even know what he might be protecting her from!—he was pushing her away.

His apology brushed against her like a gentle touch. She understood he meant no harm—his ex-wife had nearly eviscerated him and he'd been single far too long for a man with so much to offer—but their relationship wasn't cemented. She knew what he thought, and she could tell him what he thought wasn't true, but that wouldn't make him believe her. She hated to think something this simple could make things go wrong between them. She hoped the conflict was only temporary. She and Gregg were good together, they seemed so right for each other.

"I'm sorry, too." She was unable to pinpoint why she felt the way she did, and what troubled her most was feeling it mandatory to participate in this reunion. She's thought at the time it was a game none of them really cared about. Now she was honoring a promise she vaguely remembered, a game she thought worthless to recall. As if there was no option, no chance of refusal. It felt as if a command had been issued and she had to obey because something dark had overrun her mind, sucking up her willpower. *And I'm doing exactly that. Why is that?*

Gregg came up behind her, pressed himself against her, and wrapped himself around her. She turned into him with an urgency of her own. He knelt, licking upward from the junction of her thighs. A hot liquid puddle swirled in her stomach. A gasp caught in her throat as he bowed her back. His hands were hard as he pressed her head into the carpet.

Her desire was as strong as his. She arched back her head, the tug of his fingers in her hair pleasureble pain. Every nerve in her body pulsed as he plunged into her. She pushed her hips up to meet him, holding him fast with her thighs and his response was hard invasive thrusts.

When they finished, neither spoke. He rolled to his side with his eyes closed. She lay beside him and tried to doze like him, but she couldn't quite make it. Tension had returned, twisting deep inside of her.

The Quarter was humming, alive with its usual diverse surge of humanity. Kitty pulled her Mercedes CLK350 into a vacant parking spot, shut off the headlights, killed the engine, but made no attempt to climb out the car. She sat amidst flashes of neon, and music trickling out of doorways, holding tightly to the steering wheel. She couldn't quite leave behind her confrontation with Arcie.

Impatience a shrunken vein in her head, tightening, narrow as a thread, the blood no longer seemed to pass through. It had been near the edge of a full-blown argument, and Arcie thought she could sway her. She'd been in no mood for it. The years hadn't changed her mind about the town or Yancy.

It had been a sad little place, full of suspicion and prejudice, narrow-minded people, who accepted superstition as fact. The locals always talked in whispers about the Arceneaux family, rarely acknowledged them until they wanted to court them for spells or sexual favors. Yancy's father's identity remained a mystery. No one new who he was, probably not even him. Or if they did, it was easier never to put a name to a face. Whoever he was, he was white.

If Arcie decided she wanted to defend Yancy, let

her. If Arcie wanted her to know something more, let Arcie tell her. It was so long ago. She had so many scars from her early years, it was hard to recall everything. Memories from those years were filled with more bad than good. She knew she had some good memories, but it wasn't always easy to remember where the bad ones ended and the good ones began, and most just got buried, never fully faded away.

Kitty's mama did laundry and piece work for the people of the parish. By day, baskets of people's filthy linen calloused her hands and stooped her back. By night, Jennet Chauvin spent time recovering from or avoiding the next beating to be administered by Freddie, Kitty's worthless father, a man who lived in his own black hell of an alcoholic creation. He had no reason to beat his wife; he just seemed to enjoy it. He did it because he could. Everyone knew what he did, but no one, not even the sheriff, tried to stop him.

Freddie owned a weathered wooden trawler with unpainted boards and holey nets. Some days he would shrimp, some days he fished, some days he just ate and slept, but every night, he prowled. The amount of time he spent at home was in angry recovery from his latest bout with liquor and womanizing. It usually ended with him beating Jennet bloody. As Kitty grew older, sometimes his eyes followed her and his presence in a room filled her with terrified disgust. Kitty tried not to make eye contact, avoided him as much as possible and would seek a quick escape, sensing a day would come when he turned his full attention toward her and made her his target.

Fighting with Arcie had left her a little spooked. There was a cold steely knot in her stomach, almost a rising wave of panic when she thought of going back.

She had found herself screaming at Arcie as Arcie chided her to remember things she didn't want to remember. She wished they had never tampered with that stupid game. But that was exactly what they had done—the four of them, silly young girls, alone, a little drunk on stolen wine and smoking forbidden cigarettes—nervous, not wanting to appear cowardly and afraid—believing if they showed fear Yancy might later use it against them—hoping nothing bad would come from what they did.

Afterward, she thought they had participated in more than a simple game, and she hadn't mentioned it, but she knew something wasn't right. It was sort of like mixing together random chemicals. Most mixtures resulted in nothing, but there was always the off chance of creating serious problems. Had Yancy unknowingly done that?

Yes, they had promised to return when Yancy asked them. They said pacifying words and made a promise meant to be broken and forgotten. She'd never intended to keep the promise and felt Lacy hadn't either.

Talking about the fourth member of their group had made her stomach twist. She hadn't thought about Lacy in a long time. The situation with Lacy had been different from the one with Yancy. She had been tight with Lacy, until that last summer. Even though there had been rivalry and competition between them, Lac y had been the closest thing to her best friend. What she thought of as Lacy's betrayal had left a gaping wound that festered for a long time.

Lacy Kennedy disappeared from French Gap months before Kitty and Arcie went to New Orleans. No obvious reason, no explanation—one morning she was just gone. People said she ran away with a man. It wasn't unusual for girls her age, even younger, to do that sort of thing. Kitty never believed that. Belle Kennedy reported her missing, but somehow she didn't behave like a bereaved parent whose only child abruptly went missing without a trace.

About six weeks later the no-return-address note with a Baton Rouge postmark arrived. Lacy said he was fine, she would see them at Christmas. Her mother made her give the note to Belle; Belle passed it along to the sheriff, a man who had never much liked problems and did a poor job of taking care of them when they popped up. It made it easy for him to give up his search and write Lacy off as a runaway. Just that quickly, Lacy Kennedy became another teenaged statistic.

Lacy was a no-show at Christmas. Kitty waited for her to write again. Nothing. Absolutely nothing. She wondered if Lacy was dead, someone had picked her up, maybe raped and killed her. But Kitty knew, if she was still alive, Lacy wasn't ever coming back. She had found herself bitterly resentful.

Three years after they'd arrived in New Orleans, Lacy resurfaced in their lives.

Arcie's face had reddened with excitement, finger punching at the crumpled paper. Kitty had yanked the newspaper away from Arcie to read the article. It was a human interest column in the Metro section of the Sunday paper, a few inches with a fuzzy photo. The small headline read: ATLANTA RESTAURATEUR IN FATAL TRAIN ACCIDENT. An older man in the photo, standing in front of a massive plate-glass window, his hand pressed against a white brick facade painted with "STONES" in diagonal lettering. Unless someone knew him, was family, friend or a business associate, no one would have paid much attention to the damn thing, much less the brief mention of Lacy Kennedy.

According to the newspaper, Norman K. Fielding, 47, a prominent Atlanta resident and business owner, had been expanding his restaurant business into Louisiana and was only months away from opening his first New Orleans restaurant. His Jaguar had been struck by a freight train. The article stated the autopsy revealed he had died before the crash. Mr.

Fielding's cause of death was attributed to a brain aneurysm, not the crash. A memorial cremation service was held and his ashes were interred in the Lily-of-the-Valley Gardens mausoleum in Atlanta. There was mention of a son, William N. Fielding of Atlanta, an ex-wife, Abby Walker Fielding currently of North Carolina, and a fiancée, Lacy Kennedy, from Louisiana. Lacy had been barely twenty-one years old.

Kitty sat staring straight ahead through the windshield, fingers frozen around the steering wheel. Her heart fluttered and started up again with a frantic beat. A sprout of unease raced along her spine. Three of the four of them were unmarried. Was it a coincidence? Or was it just their karma, the destiny of them all to remain unmarried? Or maybe a simple twist of fate? She didn't think it was any of those things.

It was something carved from a deeper vein. Intuition told her with absolute certainty that no matter what had happened to Lacy Kennedy since she left French Gap, the one thing Lacy did not have was a husband. None of them had a husband. Was that her paranoia working overtime? Or was it a cover-up created by the mind, excuses for family cycles, life cycles, behavior patterns, good and bad choices, and all the things that were the real culprits of a person's course in life?

Another thought clawed its way to the front of

her mind . . . *this is our fault, we let her do this to us with her voodoo shit when we participated in that game* . . . and as the thought slipped away, Kitty realized it wasn't unrealistic to think whatever Yancy did had been done with intent to harm, and by accident or on purpose, by voodoo spell or coincidence or fate, had probably seriously altered their lives that night.

~15~

The Past

It was nearly 2:00 A.M., the street dark and quiet.

The moon had become a light-smear beyond the trees, almost full. Ground fog rose like a silvered shroud around ryegrasses and palmettos. A cold, sour smell drifted off the swamp. Small animals sniggered and snuffled in the dark. In the close distance, there was he hum of tiny wings as they skimmed the top of the water. Beyond that was only silence from the spot where a granddaddy gator would sometimes bring is body up from the dark mud to stretch his massive length in the late afternoon sunshine.

Most of the houses were empty. The occupied ones lay silent as their people slept.

The night wore a blue-black sheen, broken by the faint illumination of a working streetlamp under a canopy of oak trees. Moths fluttered and tapped against the broken globe.

Yancy scratched at a bug bite and slapped the persistent insect away from her face, its sound a rhythmic thrum against her eardrums.

A lamp left on inside the house provided a spray

of light on the serene face of a mounted deer head, the formidable rack of antlers casting irregular, dark fingers against a white wall. Open curtains allowed the interior light to cast a pale cone on the front porch, illuminating two drooping plants, a slat-backed rocker and the edge of a neglected flower bed where weeds struggled to remain upright.

The automobile's nose was edged into the oyster-shell drive, the rear bumper jutting onto the street. The driver sat slumped against the seat, head slung back with an open mouth. He snorted, occasionally grunting in his drunken sleep.

Yancy moved slowly forward. Her movements cast a wobbly, elongated ghost-shadow crawling up the side the car before disappearing across the roof. Reassuring herself that he slept soundly before she opened the squeaky door, she removed and untied the fabric knot she pulled from her pocket, and dropped the cloth over his face. A strong herb scent filled the car. For a moment, he batted ineffectually at the cloth, as if shooing away a troublesome insect, before sprawling sideways across the seat.

He didn't rouse during her struggle to push him over and get behind the wheel. She turned the key in the ignition, having forgotten about and unprepared for the engine's growl.

She froze, listening.

Nothing, only an occasional night sound, no

movement.

She backed the car into the street and rolled to a stop at the intersection. Flicking on the headlights, she pressed her foot against the accelerator.

It was a short drive to the place she had chosen. She stopped the car, and killed the engine, then she pulled him from the car with difficulty and began to drag him. He was over two hundred pounds of dead weight, his shoulders swollen with muscle. Moonlight edged the grooves where his boot heels dug a shallow path in the soft soil. After propping him against a tree, she leaned against it, her breathing hitched and heavy. Pulling him had brought a sharp ache to her entire body, taut muscle screaming.

She watched him while she rested. Reached out to touch his face and abruptly pulled back her hand. No tenderness, no affection, she told herself. She had to be cold and indifferent. This was a one-sided transaction. She shivered, impatient with need. It was difficult to ignore the quivers piercing her sex.

Catching a second wind, she began dragging him again.

In the small clearing, she lit a fire. When it burned fully, flames rich and scorching, she undressed him, then herself. She stood staring at his naked body. Her eyes gleamed with feral excitement. Nude, he was the most beautiful thing she'd ever seen. She had known he would be. Squatting, she leaned into him, her face not quite touching his, and inhaled his scent. Her nose twitched; her nostrils grew damp and leaky. He smells so good!

She knew what she was doing was crazy . . . but she was, wasn't she, a little crazy? Whether she believed it or not, everyone always said so. He wanted none of her. She had never accepted that—she wanted him, but most of all she wanted him to provide her with a daughter.

And he will, she thought, *he will, he doesn't have a choice.*

Consumed with need, she fumbled a small earthen jar from her discarded skirt, uncapped it, and allowed the potion to dribble into her mouth. The liquid scorched her tongue but turned to vapor within seconds. The mixture quickly clouded her mind, flushing an electric shock through her system. She knelt between his legs, swayed, filling a space in the silence with a soft chant.

She called out, her voice becoming a demand: *"Avancez, Maitresse Erzulie, satisfaire moi!"* as she tossed a handful of herbs into the fire. Flames hissed, a rancid vapor swirled upward. As if in reply, the moon's fullness seemed to contract, a leaping and skipping of light inside the shadow.

Lifting the jar again, she emptied it into her mouth, then let it slip from her hand and roll away. She struggled to her feet, and she began to dance. A slow sensuous dance, moving around him in a circle, over him, left to right, right to left, backward, forward, around and around, until her tight and tighter little circles brought her toes against his ribs. Dropping to her knees, she smeared a thick ointment over his body. Cupping his balls in her palm, she rubbed the ointment in slow deliberate circles, wrapped fingers around his member, gliding it on with long, gentle strokes.

His penis twitched, thickened, grew swollen in her hand. The crown blossomed into a mauve mushroom. A drop of seminal fluid gleamed at the slit. She finally straddled him, impaling her body on his erection with a moan. She rode him hard, pounding him, angry, needful, driving herself savagely against him and him into her, almost as if she wanted his shaft to penetrate her womb. Ignoring the bruising of her flesh, the crack of her bones, dissatisfied until she felt he was drained, only then did she stop.

His erection still firm inside her, she stretched herself down his length. She pushed her toes hard against the tops of his feet, pressed her face into his neck, sniffed along his shoulder, her finger following her nose as if she was sucking in his scent, savoring it, storing it up for another time. She licked at his sweaty skin, delighting in every hot, salty part of him. Her hand slipped between them, bringing wet fingers up and deeply inhaling the combined odor of their musk.

Later, she hardened him twice more and took him a second and third time. Then she slept.

The fire turned to ember, then ash. In the first streak of pale sun-gold, she rose and made her way back home. When the sun was hot and high, and the drug wore off, he would wake, achy, angry, and confused.

Yancy's eyes filled up with tears. Tonight made no difference. Their struggle would continue.

Nothing would change between them.

The hatred and indifference that filled him gave her bitter heartache.

16

Yancy leaned heavily against the scarred counter-top. Silence hung oppressively around her. She closed her eyes and thought about Euphrasine, wondered what she would think about the things her daughter was doing.

Even as a small child she had understood why white men came around with her their money and their hunger. Euphrasine had been special. She had been a quadroon, more beautiful than most white women in the parish. In another place, her lush body and masses of curling black hair would have made it easy to market herself and profit from it. Rich men would have paid a high price for her favors. She might even have married well. In this town, she was only a juju whore.

Oh, yes, they had loved Euphrasine, all those lusting white bayou dogs that paid for her favors when their fat, ugly wives locked them out of the bedroom and crossed their legs so there'd be no more babies. They were the same lying bastards that turned against Euphrasine; said terrible things about her when it was necessary to save their reputations or marriages.

Yancy stared into the candle flame that burned

near her elbow and imagined Euphrasine's face. Was she smiling at her? She poked a finger at the flame as if to touch her mother's cheek. The heat seared her skin. She jerked her hand away. The flame wavered, flashed blue, then Euphrasine's image was gone.

It was one of those sneaky, cowardly bayou dogs that had taken Euphrasine's life. In her heart Yancy knew it, she never doubted it. It took three days to find her scattered body parts, many lost to scavenging animals. She had no idea what happened and had never been able to find out who did such a horrible thing or why, but she hoped when she finished with her spell, somewhere the motherless sonofabitch died for what he'd done to her mama.

She had buried Euphrasine's remains under the sweeping branches of a willow and weighted the mound with rocks, the marker a wide, flat stone. Sometimes she brought a handful of wild flowers to the grave. Sometimes she cried and cursed Euphrasine because she'd let herself die. Other times she went and just sat, resting her hand on the stone as if it were a direct line of communication between them.

Yancy had never known who her father was, and had never worried about it until it was too late to ask. Euphrasine never mentioned him and she never dared ask about him, because Euphrasine never talked much to her. Most all her knowledge came from *Grandmere*, and as much as she loved her, she'd always been a little afraid of the old woman with her strange wandering blue-green eye.

Grandmere had important knowledge to pass to her, always eager to tell her about their side of the family; the fugitive French comte, the first dilution of their blood; the caul-born, older half-brother of her great-grandmother—a bocor, a creature fathered by pure evil, that cursed their family over rejection. And her duty, she was always reminded of her duty.

The bocor had claimed rights to *Grandmere's* mama when she was small. She had always tried to avoid him, believing he would find someone else and eventually lose interest in her before she reached maturity. She never listened when they told her he wouldn't go away, never believed what they told her he might do if she continued to refuse him. He had been patient and waited until someone chose her to marry, then he called down his evil curse and took his revenge.

"Call him! He will come to you. You and all those you love will die if you do not call him. His seed will fill your womb and rise up in the blood of another's child. Three daughters must sacrifice before the fourth daughter will end this hex!" *Grandmere* had breathed as she repeated the bocor's curse, fingers pressed hard against her lips.

That evening her great-grandmother found the statue at her door. That night her frightened mother stood watch as she called him.

Grandmere said most of their voudoun powers were a birthright, powers, and knowledge handed down for generations. But some family members inherited nothing, while most became voodoo practitioners, some even great conjurers of dark magic, like the bocor. Yancy might have abilities, but she might also never have the power or fully hold it. If it came to her, it would be long after puberty, only then would it be strong. And time for her sacrifice for the curse would also come when she turned eighteen and a day; when her body was fully mature, the statue waiting to be passed from mother to daughter.

Grandmere and Euphrasine had endured the sacrifice, and she, the third daughter, would endure it. Three generations producing a single impure female child. Her daughter would end the bocor's curse. After the birth, she was to destroy the statue.

Euphrasine always seemed to have her own way of doing magic, she called *Grandmere's* voodoo rituals "old country magic, nothing a child should mess with." She cautioned Yancy not to trust what *Grandmere* told her. And like her great-grandmother, Yancy refused to listen to what she was told, she had to do it her own way. She always felt sure, when she was much too young to try, her first spell brought her the friendship of the three girls, but she had never been as sure about the next one. It'll be easy, she thought. Tell them they can see the face of their future husband. What young girl wouldn't be interested? She had lied, of course. It had been a rejection spell that she cast, a controlling spell . . . and what she wanted to control was for all of them to stay away from Domeno

Something had gone wrong. The spell hadn't worked right. No one was supposed to see anything, but Kitty had seen *something*.

She told Euphrasine what she'd done.

Euphrasine's face twisted into something ugly, her voice threateningly low when she said, *"Viens pas foutumassser avec moi!"*—Don't mess with me!—and she glared at Yancy, expectant, waiting for a denial that never came. She fisted her daughter's hair, climbed her body like a tree, riding her to the floor with long legs in a ropy embrace, punching, and slapping until Yancy felt on fire. Euphrasine cursed her dead mother throughout the attack— *"Grand parleur! Elle sa lui revenait! Bete vieux chienne!"* Big talker! She had it coming! Stupid old bitch!

She finally released Yancy and walked away. *"Espesces de tete dure! T'es pas l'oeuf de la grosse poule. Sa fait pas rien, de tard, de tard,"* she mumbled, sadly shaking her head. You hard-headed thing! You are not as big as you think. It doesn't matter, too late, too late.

17

She had been raped.

Lacy had never forgotten the pain, burning angry pain so intense she couldn't scream. Or his whiskey odor and the crushing weight of him that bowed her spine, pushing her face into the ground as he threw up her dress. His hand that smashed her lips against her teeth until the skin cracked, his free hand ripping away her panties before he brutally shoved himself into her. When he finished, he left her in the weeds behind the diner where he attacked her.

Her grim-faced mother said they couldn't report it. No proof, no one to accuse, no one would believe her. People would stare, there would be ugly rumors. Neither of them could ever hold their heads up, the schoolteacher's daughter pregnant. Belle said people wouldn't trust her with their children, she'd lose her students, her livelihood. It was difficult enough to make ends meet, they didn't need another mouth to feed. They might have to leave town and she had no idea where they might go. They had to hide Lacy's pregnancy until they could give away the baby. Lacy knew she couldn't do it by herself. She hadn't worked a day in her life. Belle made the arrangements and they never spoke of it again until it was time for her to leave.

She spent six months in the Baton Rouge Catholic Charity Home for Unwed Pregnant Mothers. Belle dropped her off and never came back; never called, never wrote. Her mother had never believed her. She was just another girl who allowed some boy to take advantage and get her in trouble.

The nuns swept the baby away. Lacy never saw her newborn son. She thought it was easier to deny the reality of it that way. It might have worked better had she escaped the whispers of a few of the nuns who already knew.

She waited a week after the birth for Belle to come. Belle never came. The baby was gone, the home's post-natal obligation had ended. When the young nun handed her the envelope—only her name, no address, no past mark on the front—she felt herself go numb around the knot in her chest. She stared in disbelief at the two-hundred dollars in old, crumpled-but-smoothed-out twenty dollar bills Belle had enclosed, as she read the note. Her mother had abandoned her; didn't want her around anymore.

One of the old nuns told her the key to healing was to pray, to ask for forgiveness for those that did her injury. She couldn't. She felt only hurt and anger. She had no forgiveness for the man who had robbed her of her innocence, and left her with a baby she would never know. She had no forgiveness for a woman who felt shame more strongly than love, the most important thing in her life being her status in a miserable little community.

Lacy had never learned how to easily forgive, but she had learned to be a survivor in that barren little room off Plank Road with a soiled mattress and cockroaches for company. Where each day ended with exhaustion from being a waitress and dish-washer at a Chinese place behind a pool hall, and she was one of only two people who spoke English. And sometimes, no matter how hard she tried, it was impossible to not think about the baby boy she had never held.

And then there was Norman, whipping his Jaguar into the parking lot right before closing time and coming like a thunderstorm into her life. With a smile like a 100-watt light bulb, leaning casually back against the chair, sipping beer and waiting for shrimp egg rolls and beef-and-broccoli with noodles. He came twice a day for two days, always smiling, leaving a big tip.

The third day, he waited outside, leaning against the fender of his car.

She'd done well with the new life he gave her— until the phone call from Arcie Becnel.

That voice from the past tearing through her through her like a lightning strike, becoming a touch like clear cold contact with a ghost. It was a disturb-ing reminder that seemed more a command than a request for her return to French Gap. It left her with a creepy crawly sensation, filling her with nervous doubt that clung like the vapid burn of humidity—the twenty years were up.

She immediately hired a private investigator who unearthed Arcie and Kitty in New Orleans. Kitty had become a popular Louisiana fantasy artist; Arcie was a secretary for a large insurance company. Yancy was the problem. The PI had difficulty locating both the town and her. She still lived somewhere thereabouts, his report said, but the town was almost nonexistent, with inhospitable people. An almost-hostile sheriff would only acknowledge he knew of her, but never offered assistance in locating her. He sounded so unprofessional when he stated it was "creepy as hell" down there, she felt cheated.

She had no idea how Arcie found her, maybe an internet search of some sort. She didn't see her paying for a PI. Way too much information floated around out there these days, you could Google, Twitter and Facebook yourself right into hell. It was too late to worry, the damage was done. It was her own damn fault—a big mistake, never changing her name.

She'd grown up with the crazy stories that surrounded the Arceneaux family. She'd never wanted to believe what she heard about them, didn't want to believe it now, but she couldn't help wondering just how much truth really was in the gossip. She decided to do it, just go back and get it over with, pretend it was a perfectly normal request from an old friend. Some sort of sentimental adventure, even when that seemed over the top.

They'd been teenagers, for God's sake! Making promises was one of those silly things that teenagers do. It didn't make sense. It was a promise that should have been forgotten; if not forgotten, at least ignored. There were uncomfortable times between them as kids, but for some reason, they seemed to cling together. She had never quite understood that. Now the reunion cropped up out of nowhere, people trying to recapture something lost, bring it into the present instead of leaving it in the past. But it troubled her and made her a little angry that she felt as if her will-power to refuse was being held hostage, that she felt compelled to go . . . so she was doing exactly that.

How could she explain that to Gregg without sounding completely crazy?

Tomorrow she would meet up with women she wasn't sure she'd recognize if she passed them on the street. She was expected to participate in a reunion with people who hadn't shared a moment of her life for over twenty years, to revisit a past she didn't want to remember. She was going to subject herself to something that was likely as not to be unpleasant, and she couldn't come up with a logical reason for doing it. If she couldn't tell herself why, she certainly couldn't tell Gregg.

"Gregg?" she whispered.

"Uhhuum?" He was already drowsy, close to falling asleep.

"Will you stay?" There was a note of desperation in her voice. Was he awake enough to hear it? She waited, thinking him already asleep. She couldn't bring herself to voice the question again. She had never asked him to stay before. He sometimes fell asleep after sex, as men seemed predisposed to do, and she wouldn't wake him, so he stayed, like the previous night, without being asked.

He finally shifted, tilted forward over her, on full alert.

Outside, a soft moon had risen. She could see him study her in the luminous shafts of light. The blue of his eyes sparkled like expensive sapphires. A faint smile tipped one corner of his mouth. He laid his palm against her neck, turned her head so their lips were only an inch apart.

"I thought you would never ask," he said, rolling over and sliding smoothly into place on top of her.

18

Kitty climbed from her car, set the alarm and beeped the door locked. Fog curled in from the river, stealing through the Quarter, misting streets burgeoning with life and laughter, buoyant voices boomeranging off buildings.

She felt resentment gnawing at her toward Arcie, and what she considered a scheming betrayal. This new Arcie was nasty, insinuated ugly things, kept secrets, and had secret communication with people from their past. She'd always felt they left all that behind when they came to New Orleans. Why had Arcie felt it necessary to do that? How had all this behavior really come about, what started it?

As she walked, uneven pavers snapped as hungrily at her heels as her anger snapped at her mind. The evening had ended with nothing nice between them before Arcie walked out. She had demanded to know what made Arcie think she could make such a decision for her. With dark, angry eyes, Arcie had stared her down, and answered she made lots of decisions for her "because she never seemed to have enough time."

"Not that kind!" Kitty had screamed, frustration beating a wild tattoo inside her head. She had turned away, stood to look out the balcony doors. Lights twinkled in the distance, the brilliant crown of city night coming alive, the long bridge a disjointed hump superimposed against the lilac dusk. A car horn blaring in the street below had jolted her back.

Cold anger had solidified in her stomach, her throat tight, her heart thunder in her ears. Sounding like a petulant child when Arcie accused her of being afraid to go back, she had pivoted to face her, and stared into those burning eyes, knowing her denial a lie before the protest left her mouth. She was afraid.

The moment she'd started thinking about French Gap, fear started to build. Layer upon layer, it had attached itself, a fat interloper parasite. The little sucker feet tramped along her spine, drawing out fear like a syringe needle took blood. The shadowy, tattered memories surfacing almost smothered her. She had gasped air into her mouth, released it as a hiss through her teeth. She had read somewhere that suppressed memories never stayed that way forever, there always seemed to be a trigger that brought them back, no matter how hard you fought to keep them suppressed. She fought them harder, but memory shards, fragmented, disjointed images, slipped through. They came back like an old slide show, in separate frames, flickering a little, not quite forming a whole picture at once.

It had been a cold wintery night. Euphrasine had gone off and left them alone. They were bored, a little intoxicated from wine, a little lightheaded from cigarettes. Yancy issued the challenge out of nowhere. Kitty had never been one to back down from a challenge. So they played Yancy's game. But they shouldn't have, they should've refused, ignored her, simply left it alone. Why didn't they? She knew why. Because they never questioned Yancy about anything, always a little afraid of her and what she might do, making it easier to be around her by accepting what she told them with blind faith.

When the game ended, not a one of them said a word, they all left, and they never talked about it, as if it hadn't happened. An unspoken agreement not to remind them of that night. It made things she saw— or *thought* she saw—easier to forget. Made it easier to leave, because it was time, she couldn't wait any longer. She knew she had to leave. It was the only way to break free of the ugliness that filled her life like trash in a garbage can.

Now this spiteful new Arcie was pushing at her. As she calmed herself, an icy silence had stretched between them, a cold current of nerve washing up her spine, releasing a vague something, maybe a warning of some type, gnawing at the edges of her mind. She did not want to go back. She did not want to confront that part of her life again, but Arcie had made it seem so pointless to argue.

~ 19 ~

The Past

Domeno found it too difficult to breathe, chest heaving, face gone pasty-white, and his eyes wide with disbelief. "A *bebe*," he said, his voice a nasal whistle thick with emotion. He sounded slow-witted, only repeating what she had said, as he fought to comprehend.

She stared at him, nodded eagerly, touching the swell of her belly.

"A *bebe*," he repeated, eyes glazed. A sudden dullness crept into his voice as if his tongue was as thick as his mind. His hands twisted together, wrestling with each other in nervous anger. He became aware of the movement and shoved them in his pockets to quiet them as he desperately struggled to analyze his predicament. *"Mon bebe?"*

"Notre bebe." Our baby, she corrected, legs spread wide, her stance defiant.

"T'a menti!" You're lying! His face reddened, eyes narrow, cold and dark, lips pulled back in a snarl. An artery stood out, pulsing rapidly on the side of his neck. Tiny tremors whipped through muscle along his

forearms as his fingers clenched in his pockets. A low growl, the threatening inhuman kind, escaped his throat. *"Mon Dieu! Mais non!"* he shouted, pointing a shaky finger at her. My God! But no!

"Oui!" She nodded firmly.

"Mais comment ca s'fait?" he demanded. But how is that? A murderous fury blazed in his eyes. One long finger stabbed viciously at his own chest. *"Non! Pas le mien! C'est pas vari!"* No! Not mine! It's untrue!

The air charged with the ferocity of his anger. It would have terrified most people, but only caused her to cringe. *"C'est le votre!"* Yancy insisted, pointing an accusing finger. It's yours!

"Non, c'est pas faisable!" No, it's not possible!

She spat back: *"Oui, c'est!"* Yes, it is!

The shadow of confusion that darkened his eyes lingered a moment longer, then disappeared as quickly as it had come. Streamers of his unspoken rage crossed the distance between them, wrapping around her like cold bands. He moved on her, fingers opening and closing, and surprised her with his quickness.

He snarled, *"Chienne!"* Bitch!

She had never felt threatened by this man—fascinated, filled with desire and unrequited love, but never threatened . . . until now. There was a sharp flare of terror in her gut. Fear slithered through like a snake as she realized she might have underestimated him. He might try to kill her if he caught her. He was that angry. Her taunting seemed to have pushed him near the edge. The wild heat caused by his nearness had turned icy in her stomach. The saliva dried up in her mouth. She felt her bowels constrict and her bladder tighten. She thought she would soil herself.

She ran, screaming over her shoulder, *"Le tien, mon fils de grace!"* Yours, you bastard!

He took another step or two, halted, and no longer attempted to follow her. He stood curling and uncurling his fingers, overwhelmed, eyes staring into the plum-colored marsh shadows. Eventually, he turned away, thoughts tumbling over each other, his face a mask of frustration, revulsion, and despair.

She ran until she felt satisfied he wouldn't come after her, stopped and listened for pursuit. She panted her heart running ninety to nothing and banging her ribs so hard she thought something would break. Her eyes stung with tears as pains tore through her abdomen. With the rush of blood in her ears, she lowered herself to her knees, encircled her stomach tight with her arms and began to rock slowly. By the time her breathing had evened out, the cramping had disappeared, and the soft evening light had turned into a plum India-ink-streaked twilight . . . .

. . . the baby inside her kicked for the first time.

20

Lacy had disappeared and no one eemed to know what happened to her. Rumor had her running off with some man. Then Kitty and Arcie disappeared. No one seemed to know what happened to them either until that Lafourche shrimper came back to town. He told anyone who would listen about taking them to New Orleans and having his way with Kitty. How she had robbed him of every dollar in his pockets before they skipped out. He said he'd beat her within an inch of her whoring life if he ever saw her again.

None of them ever came back.

At first, Yancy thought the shrimper had found them and made good on his threat, but something told her that wasn't right. They were alive somewhere, and they were okay. So was Lacy, wherever she might be. She'd struggled to keep them close and control them—then, without a word, everyone was gone, leaving her behind. Her grief had been like a hot knife, slicing her through from the inside. They never considered how their leaving would hurt her. Caring so little about her, thinking only of themselves, they were so selfish. They probably still only thought of themselves.

She needed sleep without dreams, days without

resentment. She needed to know if they had stayed, would one of them have married him, given him children that should have been hers. It was time they knew everything, she wanted them to know. She wanted to hurt them, but would it? Would it make a difference? Would it mean anything now, would they even care?

Yancy hugged herself, humming as she stared at the wavering candle flame. *Damn you, Mama!* she thought. Euphrasine was long dead. Anger and verbal abuse served no purpose. No matter the bitterness and bad feelings she carried, nothing would change. It was too late for anything to change.

Had she made another mistake? She wanted the spell she'd cast to be a good one, but her powers had always been weak. She seemed to cast imperfect spells like it wasn't meant that she carry on family traditions. She had decided she was one of the ones who in-herited limited abilities as *Grandmere* told her about. The magic could die with her, the way the curse was supposed to die when she birthed her daughter.

Yancy pinched the candle wick. The flame died with a thin curl of smoke. She stared out the window where Spanish moss dripped off tall live oaks that formed a warped arbor against the bilious mushroom fungus of the moon. Thin branches resembled bleached and polished bone in the shadowed light. She closed her eyes and listened to the familiar drone of bullfrogs that took up their nightly chorus where the crook of marsh bled into the strip of bayou so shallow it was more mud than water.

Adrenaline made a wild loop through her body. She felt her mind wobble for a moment.

She had thought the spell an innocent binding. Instead, she'd bound Kitty closer to Domeno. Even with her leaving town, it wasn't over. Euphrasine said there had to be a sexual encounter for it to be over. All those years, the spell had rested dormant, now it could be forced into completion. It had to be completed. It was the last thing she wanted, but it had to happen. It was time for it to end, time she had peace of mind. It was time to move on.

She didn't think she intentionally meant them harm, then or now, but there was no guarantee. Sometimes she didn't know from one minute to the next what she wanted. As if each shift over the years left pinholes in her brain that sprang leaks, and each leak emptied tiny portions of her mind.

If the spell went wrong and something bad happened, she wasn't sure how bad it might get. She had no idea if she could do anything about it . . . or if she even wanted to. She could lose him forever. Was that possible, to lose what she had always wanted, had craved for so long, but had never been able to claim as hers?

21

Carson Crane's apartment overlooked the lower end of Royal Street. Inside was an atmosphere of racy elegance where crystal winked, silver gleamed, and rich dark wood glistened. Expensive Oriental rugs and erotic artwork added subtle touches of color. The sensual scent of spices hung like invisible drapery in the cool air.

Carson stood out from most of the other males in the room. Six feet four, black hair curled into his collar and over his forehead, framing hazel eyes that made his face rakish. His body seemed to throw off a continuous sexual heat, attracting male and female. He wore black leather pants like a second skin, melding the curves of buttocks and groin. An emerald silk shirt unbuttoned to the waist exposed a heavily muscled chest. A magnificent specimen: the Crane family had passed along stunning genetics.

He created eclectic and indiscriminately vulgar jewelry, a hobby turned into a profitable business. The look was for the fearless adventurer, the price for the affluent, and the waiting list was very long.

Creely stood in front of a massive glass étagère that held a priceless collection of antique cloisonné and Lladro porcelain, slightly to the right of the huge curved bar. An inch or two shorter, four years older and twenty muscular pounds heavier than Carson, Creely showed a flash of silver at his temples, his skin a deep bronze, eyes a brilliant topaz.

An anorexic blonde with purple-tipped hair, thrusting silicone, and enough face piercings to set off a metal detector, wearing a black leather bodysuit with matching reptile belt and over-the-knee stiletto boots, hung on Creely's arm as well as his words.

Kitty slid into the room. Creely's head turned as if he'd sensed her. Their glances locked. He smiled. She recognized that smile, confident, mischievous, almost wicked; a man who gave as much pleasure as he took.

The mirrored walls reflected her image as she moved toward him. Soft lighting slid off the navel-low, satiny green dress, the suppleness of hip, the ripe swell of breast, the flawless gloss of her complexion. No mistake, she was a prowling, lusty female animal a few inches above five feet, compact and sensual. With all his senses heightened, Creely thought she looked as delicious as he remembered. He felt as drawn to her as the first time they had met. A connection between them had never gone away, sometimes coming back so strongly it sucked his breath away. He felt a familiar jolt right down to his toes. His mind filled with every impure thought conceivable. He found himself tumid, realized his reaction was not appropriate but didn't care.

For a long moment, they stared at each other.

"Creely," she said softly.

"Kitty." He pulled her possessively against him, felt his penis jerk with contact. "What are you drinking?" he asked, pressing his lips into her neck.

"Vouvray."

Creely released her and she watched him pour the goblet of wine and his big hands were as she remembered When he handed her the wine glass, his touch made her warm, and the warmth insinuated itself into every deep unexplored place inside her.

The blonde, who might have ended up the house specialty of the evening, moved away with an indignant head toss, pausing beside a distinguished-looking older man. He acknowledged her by a lifted eyebrow and a brief glance without a pause in his conversation. Westerfeldt was a neurosurgeon at one of the New Orleans area's most prestigious hospitals; he was also Carson's significant other.

"To you," Creely said, tipping his own glass against Kitty's.

"To us," she corrected, as their glasses touched.

One heavy dark brow curled upward. "Back in circulation, are we?"

"Newly discharged from all obligations I might have had," she said.

They laughed, the way people do when they're comfortable, know each other well and are glad to see each other.

"Lovely lady," said someone with warm, peppermint-scented breath.

"Carson," she murmured, offering her cheek.

"We've missed you." Carson smiled and winked at her. "Don't stay away so long. Judgment errors are made and then strange things happen."

Creely frowned, fingers tightening around his highball glass. "Carson—"

"You should come around more often." Smiling, Carson drifted away, leaving behind a trace of his cologne and the significance of his words.

"I'm sorry." Creely's eyes resembled brilliant amber stones.

"We both know he likes to tease." For a moment the air had been rife with an unusual surge of testosterone. It was unlike them.

"He thinks my marriage is a mistake." Anger lay below the surface of his mild tone.

Kitty was tempted to ask: "Is it?" but she didn't. She had been surprised by Creely's decision to marry. She'd always thought he would never settle down. He thought himself a real badass, surrounded himself with a Skittle assortment of females, and usually hooked up with the first sexy ass that twitched the right way on any given night.

Glancing down at her, he whispered, "A few minutes alone? There's a beautiful moon tonight." He decided to change the subject before it got touchy.

"You could persuade me to look."

His hand pressed firmly in her back, he maneuvered her between people, directing her toward the terrace.

It was a beautiful moon, in its more-than-three-quarter phase, ghostly pale, hazed by a gray scarf of fog. Kitty leaned against the iron railing and looked down, breathing in the ambiance.

A transvestite on the opposite side of Royal moved slowly down the street on mile-high heels. A long column of neck, pale hair, knobby little breasts under a red mesh blouse; it could have been an incredibly tall and fleshless woman. Two young men in tee shirts and jeans walked by fast, gesturing angrily. One reached out and halted the other; they stared into each other's eyes for a moment, leaned into a kiss before they faded into shadow. A group of boisterous intoxicated men stumbled down the middle of Royal, pummeling each other with fists that landed without harm.

A black Lincoln MKS slid to the curb, the window glass so dark the occupants were invisible. A muscular young black, flashes of diamond in his ears, a heavy reflection of gold at his neck, climbed from behind the wheel and disappeared through a gate. He reappeared with a scantily-clad young girl, her head lolling against his shoulder. The rear door popped open. He stuffed her inside. The car disappeared with a squeal of rubber.

To the left, vapor lights on Canal Street were hazed with ribbons of misty fog; to the right, a street vendor pushed his cart to the corner of Royal and St. Ann. The smoky blur of rhythm and blues, the deep, rich tones of soulful jazz, drifted over from Bourbon.

"I went to your last exhibit," Creely said.

"I saw you—*and* her. I thought it best to keep my distance."

A moment of discomfort crossed his face. "I bought 'Winter Fairy' the next day."

"It's one of my favorites."

"I saw you when I looked at it. I suppose it was cowardly of me doing it after the fact by phone."

"Has she seen it?"

"It's hanging in my office."

"What happens when she sees it?"

He cocked an eyebrow and laughed. "She'll want to burn it."

"Where is she tonight?"

"She refuses to come here. She can't change the fact that he's my brother, but she won't socialize with him." There was a twinge of anger in his tone.

It was a big compromise, difficult to make and difficult to accept. A ticking time bomb. Kitty wondered how he planned on handling his upcoming nuptials.

His hands were on her shoulders, squeezing. Her lower body tightened. She turned, moved in closer to

him. He kissed her. A sigh built in her chest and slipped out as a breathy whisper. The time since being
together had melted away.

"That has never been a problem for us."

"No, it never was," Creely said.

"Carson thinks I should have put the ring on
your finger."

Me? Kitty thought. If he expected a response, she
didn't give him one. She knew his political aspirations.
She also knew she wasn't afraid of the political arena,
wouldn't mind trying but she would never be happy
always under scrutiny, playing the role of the politi-
cian's good little wife. They both knew it, even if Carson didn't. To reach the pinnacle of his ambitions, he
needed a wife like Barbara Mackey. If Creely elected
to remain on fast-forward in the political arena, he
needed to stay with Barbara. Her powerful connections made her the right someone, but the voice of
reason said it didn't make her right for him. She
hoped he wasn't sacrificing happiness for ambition.

"I'm glad you came tonight," he said into the
silence that had developed. "Friday nights haven't
been the same without you."

"So am I." She gave him her back again, sliding
her butt closely into him. "Are you still considering
the political bid?"

"I consider it often."

"And consider it more if you marry Mackey?"

Creely looked out over her head without answering. Sometimes Kitty drove him crazy. He couldn't think straight when in close contact with her. His blood sizzled and he felt greedily alive with need when she smiled. He didn't want to talk about Barbara, was aware only that he could smell Kitty, feel the sexual heat leaking off her body. All he wanted was to touch her all over, push himself inside her.

Kitty looked up. "It sounds like an advantageous formal arrangement," and she watched his jaw work, filled with a nervous wave of muscle. "Sorry."

"You find me that ruthless?"

"I didn't say that."

"You didn't have to."

"It's not the first time for something like that."

"I do have feelings for her." He seemed to have a sudden need to defend himself.

Innuendo had floated around Creely and Barbara from the beginning. A calculated relationship, rumors said. Creely had his eye on becoming District Attorney, Attorney General, and then Governor of Louisiana one day. Mackey family connections with local and state politics were well known. No one believed he loved her, or that she loved him, for that matter. People thought she was a politically convenient end. His enemies, like most enemies, whispered behind his back. A few friends had dared him to his face, but men had married wealthy, influential women for less honorable reasons.

Creely had a distinguished legal career. He was a super-charged criminal defense attorney who rarely lost a case, plus he had a long line of admirers. In and out of court, men respected him and women adored him. He was likable, a man of many charms, newsworthy, easily gaining favor with the media, getting their attention each time he entered the courtroom. He had everything material a person could want. What he needed was the perfect wife, educated and intelligent, politically connected and fashionably correct. Barbara Mackey was all those things, perfect to bring him a little higher up the ladder where wealth, friendship and ambition sometimes fell short.

Louisiana politics were hard and corrupt, not unlike other states, and corruption spread like rot. The manipulation of political power was frequently cold and ugly. It often had the vulgarity of pushing a woman's face tight against thrusting genitalia and holding it there until orgasm. Things were ever so much easier with connections. Even sleazy street punks needed and used connections. In the end, it all came down to money, connections, and power. Some were inherited. Sometimes enough money greased the right palms. Sometimes a person married them.

Barbara Mackey and her family had the necessary connections, influence and money. Those were the biggest part of the package for the higher rungs of the ladder. She, or someone like her, seemed an absolute necessity. It was a long way to the top, lots of rungs on the ladder, slippery corners and competition. Working to impress people with his ability, pressing palms, more long hours to invest, always selling himself, similar to a high-priced call girl. It was like adding extra coverage to an already unreasonably large insurance policy and wondering later how difficult it was going to be to pay the premiums. When had he decided marriage was a legitimate, easier way? It all came down to choices and making the correct one at the right time.

"But you probably don't love her."

"In my own way, I suppose I do," he said.

"She knows that?"

"It's possible."

"And she's good with it?" His heart rate had spiked against her shoulders, not much, just a little, enough to let her know she had made him uncomfortable. Sometimes honesty in friendship went too far. No need poking at him. Besides, his fiancée wasn't a stupid woman. She seemed savvy enough to know what was going on. If she didn't already know, she surely had her share of suspicions.

Mackey might be detouring around speed bumps, could delude herself with the pleasantries of romance and marriage, but she had to know what a womanizer she'd hitched to her wagon. Besides, it was rumored she had her own agenda. This could end up a marriage where the they shared the same space but not the same rooms, much less the same bed. They might stay together for the sake of propriety, with outsiders looking in on what appeared to be a good marriage because they had reached the stage where neither could afford the pain and scandal of divorce. As they grew older, maybe they would decide to be with someone familiar was better than being alone. Like his brother and close friends, Kitty hoped he knew what he was doing.

When Creely didn't reply, she looked up again and quietly asked, "What about the lost souls?" and watched as muscle molded against his jawbone. That was definitely another conflict between them.

Creely had visions he called his "Lost Souls." He didn't talk much about them, but she knew they came to him abruptly, without warning. He could never explain them to her, or perhaps it was Kitty who had never wanted to listen and fully under-stand. She wasn't too curious, but sometimes she listened with wary curiosity, but mostly, she blanked the vision stuff out. The unknown made her nervous, so she rarely discussed psychic stuff with him, but several times his visions helped locate a missing person, and had been instrumental in locating a cop killer.

A memory-shadow rushed in to touch her with searching fingers. Echoes of the past bounced around inside her skull. *Stop it!* Kitty scolded herself. *Don't think about it!* But she was thinking about it, she couldn't seem to stop. The shit with Arcie had shifted some unexplainably nasty stuff forefront in her mind. The more she thought about returning to French Gap and the confrontation with Arcie, who seemed to have some abhorrent program of her own, the more pissed off she felt. All those crazy thoughts were encroaching on her evening.

Creely felt her tense up, sensed her sudden detachment. One minute she was relaxed, the next unexpectedly stiff. Something was bothering her. He pulled her tight against his chest and nuzzled her neck. Was she unhappy about the direction of their conversation? He hoped it was just baggage she had brought with her, and if she decided to talk about it, he would be there to listen.

Kitty leaned back into him, torn between her anger and unease and the heat that flared up between them. It was so strong, elemental, sharp and basic; it always had been and still was.

"Something I said?"

"Nothing to do with you. It's an old problem that needs solving by tomorrow," she replied.

"It must be something distasteful."

"It certainly could be."

"Well, we could talk about, if you want."

Kitty shook her head. "No, I don't want."

"Okay, then don't let it bother you tonight." His thumbs stroked her nipples.

There was moisture between he thighs, a damp glaze over her skin. She turned into him, found his mouth, remembering the taste of him, all of him, every hard galvanizing inch of him.

"God, you're so beautiful!" he said. "I want you so much right now."

His hand slid up under her dress, and two fingers worked at her inside her thong. Her pulse rate increased. Each time his fingers moved, a sunburst of warmth flared. His teeth caught a nip of skin on her neck. Her knees almost folded.

Kitty closed her eyes against the long window squares across the street, where tall leafy trees grew in terra-cotta planters on either side of a screened door, and slanted flickers behind tilted shutter slats bounced off fern suspended from the iron railing. She allowed herself to drift with the slow pressure of his fingers as she reached around and squeezed tight his erection.

~ 22 ~

The Past

Yancy squatted in the corner, her back pressed tightly against the wall, digging at her thighs with cramped fingers. She was tired, so terribly tired, and desperately craving rest. She had never expected such terrible pain. It had been going on for hours, draining all her strength.

When the pain eased, she focused on her belly where something moved, causing her flesh to rise and fall, and her skin to ripple. Her hands fluttered like caged birds, unable to find a place to settle.

Then the pain was there again, growing in intensity, searing across her abdomen into her back. She screamed her throat raw, her pulse tripped too fast.

She panted, gasped air into her aching lungs, mewling to herself. The rough boards dug into her bare buttocks, into her shoulders through the thin material of her blouse. She pushed hard and quick, opening her legs wide, and pressed her palms against her knees until the knuckles of her hands blanched gray with effort.

As the pain subsided, she threw back her head,

breathing in short sobs, and she squeezed tears from her eyes that slid down her cheeks. It had been going on for so long, she was exhausted. She hadn't considered it would be anything like this. Her thighs ached from the strain of supporting her body in such an awkward position, her calves seized with cramps as if something big and ugly had taken bites out of her. Pain all over, sliding through parts of her body she'd never known existed.

The pain abruptly returned as burning twin jets racing up her spine.

She jammed herself tighter against the wall, and pushed again, hard. She heard a sucking sound; another sound, a popping noise. Her vision became a misty haze. Everything swam in shattered patterns of dazzling light as bloody water gushed and ran across the floor. The pain seemed to tear her apart, destroying vital organs, casting them aside like garbage. Fire blazed through her, catapulted her into foggy white noise, deep into nothingness.

Yancy slowly regained consciousness, allowed a moment of painless reprieve. The first noise she heard as she slid down the wall, hands balled against her belly, legs splayed wide, was the smack of her butt striking the wet floor. The second sound was the flies. Attracted by the odor, they buzzed and bumped against the window screen. Using all her strength, she pushed herself back into a squatting position.

The jabbing pain began again. She cried, panting between sobs.

The life inside her was so stubborn, refusing to come as if it were an alien weed rooted there to serve no purpose except to torment. She wanted to reach up inside herself and yank it free. But she knew it would eventually come, it had to come, or she would die. She must be strong. It was only a matter of time.

After all the pain had gone away, she told herself, it would be worth it when she held her baby girl and the family curse was gone . . . wouldn't it?

She must be strong and fight the pain until then. *It was only a matter of time . . . .*

She closed her eyes, clawed at her belly, pressing the heels of her hands deep into the hardness, as a stricken animal sound wrenched upward from her navel and bloomed into a violate scream.

The small body finally emerged.

23

Lacy Kennedy took the drink offered by the flight attendant, didn't pull down the seat-back tray and held the cup tightly against her chest. Flying made her nervous; the only thing she liked about it was the shifting clouds as the plane throbbed toward its destination.

The flight had been delayed. The plane left forty minutes late. It finally lifted smoothly into mists that evaporated, leaving behind wisps of pale cloud and a soft dove-blue jewel of sky. It whisked through an artery of mauve breaking through streaks of dull gray into a brilliant sunrise.

She found herself uneasy, a little irritable.

They had ridden to the airport in silence. Gregg had pulled to the curb at the terminal entrance, killed the car engine, turned to face her and said: "I'm thinking maybe this really isn't a reunion with old girlfriends."

"You're wrong."

"I want to believe you."

"You're jealous."

"No!" he protested, but it was obvious his feelings were lodged like a fist in his throat, as he said, "Well, perhaps . . . maybe, just a little." His forehead had puckered into a frown. "Damnit, Lacy!" but it wasn't mean, just frustrated, defeated. "Yeah, I'm jealous, and more than a little." His eyes flickered over her face, a boyish touch of color in his cheeks, as if he were embarrassed, had never had to handle a situation such as this and was floundering. a thin, tight smile touched the corners of his mouth. He was hurt, but he'd have purchased a ticket and left with only the clothes on his back if she'd asked him to.

He lifted her hand, kissed her knuckles. "I got a bad feeling. Can I at least have a phone number?"

"No phone," she said. Even if there was a phone and she had the number, she wouldn't have given it to him. He had a friend in communications who could track the location before the plane left the ground.

"Nothing I say will persuade you not to go?"

"No." His persistence was as strong as his sex drive.

Gregg reached in his jacket pocket, held out an object in his palm. She looked but didn't touch it.

"I thought you might have accidentally forgot it."

"I didn't."

"I've never known you to be without it." He slipped the Blackberry back in his pocket and his face scrunched up tight. He grabbed both her hands.

"Okay, what's this really about?" She broke his death hold grip on her fingers. Her refusal of the Blackberry had probably doubled his suspicions, but the PI's reports said there was no cellular service within forty or so miles of French Gap. As a precaution, her ticket had been purchased under an alias and she had told him it was unnecessary he come inside and wait with her.

"I've got a bad feeling," he repeated himself.

"You're overreacting."

"Why would I overreact?"

"You're jealous and no getting your way." He stiffened, color creeping up his neck. She leaned over, pressed her face close to his, and allowed her lips to linger against his unshaven cheek. "Think happy thoughts. You won't have time to miss me."

He turned away, climbed out, pulled her bag from the back seat, set it on the concrete and kissed her on the cheek without another word. As she walked away, she could have sworn she heard him say, "I love you, Lacy Kennedy."

Lacy sighed heavily. She wasn't thinking straight. She seemed to have lost her objectivity and couldn't put things into perspective. There was nothing sinister about this trip, even if Gregg was thinking—and making her think—along those lines. She just needed this trip to be over because, between her imagination and Gregg's intuition, she was getting antsier by the minute, and a logical explanation for her unease seemed unavailable. There was nothing important waiting for her in this place—no family, no real friends, nothing . . . except for painful memories.

Was she being paranoid, stressed over confronting her past? She did have a choice, of course, she did. She could simply board another fight from Kenner to Atlanta, head straight back home, and act like this never happened. No face-to-face with anyone. She could simply . . . .

No, you can't

The thought came out of nowhere, slammed into her head like a fist, raked across the surface of her skin like shards of glass. She had no idea where it came from. Was she exaggerating the situation? She felt as if her life was unraveling. A couple times she had thought their affair was moving too fast. Would this trip end up an inadvertent test of their relationship? She felt certain she hadn't misunderstood him. He might not have said it directly to her, but she was positive he'd said he loved her. Was that the root of his jealousy? Did that mean he was ready for the next step? Was she?

She thought what she felt for him might already be love, but wasn't sure if she was ready to explore more. People lived years loving each other without jumping into marriage. It was just a paper. Did she want their relationship rock-solid permanent? He'd want marriage when he declared his love. He would want the whole ball of wax, wouldn't settle for less.

Gregg was a wonderful person, an intelligent and

shrewd business manager, a terrific lover. No doubt he would be a thoughtful and caring husband. On all levels, she was lucky to have him. She had to make damn sure she made the right decision, otherwise, she might create an irreparable mess in both her business and personal life.

Men had come and gone over the years. She had never allowed herself to get too close, never considered any of them a great loss after they were gone. There had always been something missing with each of them. She had excelled in throwing up barriers to avoid serious romantic entanglements. She often thought she'd become too picky, but no one had ever captured her heart like Norman, until Gregg. There had been immediate recognition things would be different with him.

She still thought of Norman often and with love, and her memory of the day he died still lingered. The police, her pain, her empty heart, the lost feeling, as she struggled to cope with the devastation his death left behind. Wondering what she would do without him and where she would go.

Lacy would never forget the call from Norman's attorney, her sitting in his massive office the next day, feeling smothered by burgundy, brass-nailed leather, thick carpets, and heavy dark wood; staring self-consciously at the big man with the shaggy hair and shiny white teeth under an impressive black mustache. Stunned, not fully comprehending.

She had known Norman had money, there never seemed a lack of it; he had always been generous . . . but rich, beyond rich—*filthy rich*—was a word she'd never applied to him. She hadn't been with him for the money.

The others had sat around the long, shiny boardroom table, the four of them. The fat man, sweat glistening on his bald head, had represented the beautiful blonde ex-wife. She had been so furiously vocal, slapping her palms so hard against the table the vibration shook the water glasses. *"That bastard! She's not much more than a child!"* The malnourished-looking black man with teeth like a beaver representing the son; a thin young man with thick glasses, only a little older than Lacy, wrapped solidly in his bitterness and embarrassment, never looking directly at her. Norman seldom spoke of them and she had only known they existed somewhere in his past. It hadn't seemed im-portant that she knew more. Norman had done straightforward, strategic planning, and had a current, iron-clad will.

Later, with the formalities over, the attorney gave her a large, wax-sealed manila envelope and left her alone in his office tomb. She held on to the parcel for a long time, afraid to open it.

Inside: ten thick, banded packets, and a single sheet of embossed stationery.

"If you're reading this, it means something has happened to me and we'll never have the chance to grow old together. You should know you've been the love of my life from the moment I saw you . . . ."

He should have said those things while he was alive when it was most important for her to hear them. Instead, he had left her with a sick emptiness, the Atlanta condo, beachfront property in Myrtle Beach, a loft in New York, a black Mustang convertible, expensive jewelry, two thriving restaurants, each with a million dollars in operating capital. There was also a more than adequate trust account to pay taxes, an untraceable one-hundred-thousand dollars in hundred dollar bills and an overwhelming sadness that never quite went away.

Lacy pressed herself hard into the seat and realized her hands were trembling. She had never returned to French Gap, even when Norman encouraged her to do so. She couldn't force herself to go back. Over time, when resentment cooled, she had sent cards on holidays and birthdays, trying to repair the irreparable. Belle never responded, but she kept the cards. The sheriff found them and used the return address to contact her when Belle died. She never claimed Belle's personal items; could think of nothing she really wanted. She had sent funds for the burial, but she had never asked where they buried her.

Now, after all these years, she was going back,

responding to something trivial.

What does that say about me? Lacy wondered. If anyone had confronted her about her behavior, she knew she would have been deeply ashamed. She wasn't sure she liked herself much right now but decided there would be no explanations. She would give no explanations to anyone. It would be easier that way.

24

Kitty was floating, deliciously warm.

A frosted skylight filtered moonlight. A huge soft round bed, fat candles emitting a rich exotic scent. His big hands stroked down the length of her body, coaxing a response.

Heat climbed her skin, riding her entire body, and she shuddered with the sensation.

Creely suckled her breasts, teeth nipping at her. Her flesh thrummed, hot with a strong ripe need that took her breath away. He moved down, buried his face between her thighs, nibbling, lapping at her. She struggled to hold on as everything inside her tightened. Her legs trembled, and she bucked upward, clutching at his hair, driving his mouth hard against her. His voice was raspy as he whispered, "Wait." A whimper deep in her throat never came out. Moments later she screamed as her orgasm exploded.

He abruptly pulled her legs up around his neck, held her suspended on her elbows before he pierced her, slipping into her as his hands pulled her ass tight against the thrusting muscle and bone of his groin.

"Oh, dear God!" she moaned, as his weight pressed her knees back against her shoulders, his movements deliberate, sweet torture, more demanding with each thrust.

A hoarse cry filled her throat and a shudder began to build again somewhere deep inside as he ground himself into her.

Eventually, he rolled away, pulling her tight against his body and curving her into his length, his face nestled between her breasts. As she slipped into a light sleep, she sensed the movement of his tongue, lips tugging at her nipple almost infant-like, as . . . .

. . . a voice came from a great distance, tinny, angry sounding, annoying her.

She clung tenaciously to the delicious sensations that filled her.

There seemed to be something urgent in the voice as it penetrated her sleep, repeating her name. "Kitty . . . *Kitty, wake up!*"

A sobering purposeful hand shook her. The delicious warmth vanished, but the pressure of the hand remained, shaking and startling her awake.

Overcome with impatience bordering on anger, Kitty shouted: "Leave me *alone!*"

"It's getting late," Arcie said.

The drapes had been drawn. Only a sliver of brightness penetrated the bedroom. She opened one eye, glanced at the clock, closed her eye. It was only a little after ten.

"I wanna sleep."

"You can't."

Of course, I can. What the hell is she talking about? Kitty didn't open her eyes but made an effort to turn over. Her legs felt heavy, her feet almost numb. Something stirred, edged forward. Dusty, poking her head out. She tapped at the warm wet nose. The dog sneezed and made three slow circles that twisted the sheet in a knot.

"Stop!" Kitty ordered, yanking the sheet back up.

The dog obeyed, snuffling down tight to her shoulder, nose pressed against her neck.

"Damn, my head hurts." Exhausted, still high on booze and sex, her temples seemed to vibrate with the sound of her own voice.

"Here, take these." Arcie thrust three tablets and a glass of water at her.

Good old thoughtful Arcie, Kitty thought, with a trace of bitterness, as her nose caught the delicious sent of Mocha Nut fudge coffee. Determined not to be so easily persuaded, she hugged Dusty, muttering into soft doggy fur, "A couple more hours of sleep needed here."

"You can't!" Arcie's tone was sharper now, almost panicky. "Lacy's plane will be arriving soon."

A brilliant flash of anger hit her with such force Kitty thought the top of her head had blown off. "I told you last night I wasn't going!" Fully awake, she pushed herself up against the headboard, backhanding tangled hair from her eyes.

Arcie didn't reply. She sat on he edge of the bed, body stiff, expression sullen.

They stared at each other, waiting. When Arcie didn't blink or lower her eyes, Kitty closed hers. Dusty trembled, burrowing under Kitty's left arm. Since losing her sight, the dog didn't respond well to loud noises or raised voices. Kitty whispered *"Sshhh,"* and stroked her. She thumped her tail.

"Don't do this," Kitty murmured. "I'm tired."

"Hungover is what you are."

"Okay, hungover. I still don't want to fight. You meet her plane. We'll go get that great buffet brunch and talk about this."

"There's nothing to talk about."

"There's a lot to talk about."

No response.

Kitty opened her eyes. Arcie sat rigidly, her skin gone waxy, a thin sheen of perspiration across her upper lip. Her hands were balled into fists, pressed hard against the mattress. Her eyes looked stone-cold, dark and dead.

They continued to stare at each other, each waiting on the other to give in.

Kitty knew she could give in, knows she probably should, but she hung on to her anger. Arcie exasperated her. "Get pissed if you want. You can't force me to go if I don't want to," she said with petulance, finally breaking the silence.

Arcie still didn't respond. She offered only a mulish stare.

Kitty felt her breath hitch deep in her chest. A sudden dull humming sounded in her ears. *"Fuck you!"* she spat, curling her fingers tightly in doggy fur. Dusty licked at the side of her face. She slid down and pulled the sheet over her head, realized her re-action was immature, but couldn't help it. She wanted to scream, felt the sound crawling up her throat, struggling to get out. Kitty pressed the heels of her hands hard against her eyelids as she fought to calm herself.

"Be reasonable, Kitty."

It was her turn not to respond. Another deep silence developed.

"I packed your things." Arcie's voice was low, filled with icy condemnation.

Kitty threw back the sheet and jammed herself against the headboard again, crossing her arms across her naked breasts and glaring at Arcie. "Then you can *unpack* for me!"

Arcie stared at her disdainfully and, her voice tight, she said, "Do you know how mad I am at you right now?"

"You think I'm not mad at you?"

Arcie lowered her eyes. "We promised her."

"I don't care."

"Why are you being so stubborn?" The pleading tone in her voice pissed her off. She hated herself for it, but it was necessary. "You *have* to go . . . we *all* have to go."

"We don't *have* to do *anything.*"

"We have to do this," Arcie insisted.

"You might, but I don't. It was a stupid promise. Now it's twenty years stupid. Stupid promises are meant to be broken."

"Please," Arcie breathed. "Don't do this."

Kitty felt a nudge of uncertainty. She definitely didn't like this pushy new Arcie. Where was the old Arcie? Why had this reunion become so important? She wondered if Arcie really knew the reason herself.

Arcie stood, walked to the sliding doors, and roughly pushed aside the drapes. Kitty winced against the brightness. "You have to go, Kitty," she said over her shoulder.

Kitty could barely hear her, she spoke so low, but it didn't matter. Vague wisps of memory stirred. Twenty years was a long time, not that it mattered now, but it was Yancy who dictated the time frame of their return. A little buzzy on wine, they had agreed. In retrospect, like playing the game, she supposed they'd all been a little afraid to disagree. It was hard to disagree with Yancy. Yancy must have thought they would still be together, hadn't expected anyone to leave, or who might go if someone did.

"Tell me something."

Arcie turned to face Kitty, her stare frosty. "What?"

"What if something happened to one of us?"

"Nothing happened."

"It could have. Would it make a difference? Would it still be so damn important?"

Arcie frowned, studying something over Kitty's head. She stared with such concentration Kitty could have sworn something had materialized on the wall. She was almost tempted to look.

"You can't change things to suit yourself, Kitty." Arcie's glance dropped and flitted away. "We have no choice but to go."

Kitty snorted. "Excuse me? Do you realize how crazy that sounds?"

"I don't know what'll happen if we don't go back—"

"That sounds even crazier."

Arcie said nothing.

"Are you afraid? Is that it? Do you believe after all this time she can do something to hurt us if we don't go?"

"Nooo . . ."

"Okay, what then? Why should I worry over it?"

"You just should. I feel it."

She feels it—what kind of crap is that? Kitty wanted to laugh, couldn't find a scrap of humor in the situation. Arcie almost had her believing something bad would happen if they didn't go back.

Somehow this mess had gone beyond a contest of will. Arcie had repeated herself so many times, over and over and *over*, making it seem there really wasn't a choice. What if she didn't go and found out Arcie was right?

~ 25 ~

The Past

The pain ran screaming through Yancy's head. With each thundering throb of her temples, her fingers tightened, clutching the bundle closer.

It was late in the season, but vines were still full of muscadines, the fruity scent thick in the air. Gnats and fruit flies swarmed, the sweat trickling down her back attracting them as much as the succulent grapes. Thick brambles raked at her as she pushed her way through the foliage, but she ignored the pain as her body wept drops of blood.

She sat on the cypress stump by the water's edge, staring at the eroded earth where water had attacked the soil like a buzz saw gnawing wood. The dense foliage was strangling, the air pulsing with its own turgid life. The ground beneath her feet remained wet from yesterday's heavy rain. Indirect light filtering through moss-draped branches softened the edges of everything like partially melted butter. The acid tang of molding leaves filled her nostrils; a soft wind moaned, dank with swamp scents. A cottonmouth slithered through the water in front of her.

She rocked slowly back and forth, sadness etching deep runnels in her face. There were no more heart-wrenching cries or little sucking sounds. The small body had grown rigid. She could sense cold flesh through the blanket.

It shouldn't have been this way. She hadn't wanted this.

Her heart was filled to bursting with love . . . but the tiny body inside the blanket was male. It was not the baby she was meant to have. *Grandmere* said one child—a daughter to break the curse. Something had gone wrong.

She must lie with him soon, to fix that wrong.

It would be difficult to get to him, he was more cautious now, but she'd find a way. She wanted him desperately with every cell of her wretched body. Having sex with him meant more than pregnancy—she had tasted him, craved the sex until it had become almost as important as breaking the curse, but she had to have the pregnancy.

Her heart beat crazy rapid tatting against her ribs. More months of not shifting, controlling her emotions, and keeping her creature at bay to avoid aborting the fetus. She would be in for another long hard labor, another painful birth.

She uncovered the small body and held him away to study him. Distended purple vein-lines marked his cold flesh like a map, running up from tiny curled toes, the flaccid nub of sex, the frail little fingers arched like miniature claws. Twin marbles protruded against translucent eyelids, wisps of dark hair stood up from a domed head like thin wires. She smoothed down the hairs, her dirty hands covering blanched skin with shredded leaves and dabs of mud.

She had closed the door against his cries for two days, until his whimpers had grown so weak she could no longer hear the sound. She knew he had struggled for his life, but he hadn't been strong enough to last longer.

Yancy caressed the bloodless flesh of his short spindly neck with a finger. She placed a kiss on his forehead as she carefully rewrapped him, placed the little body in the hole and covered it.

She had never felt so empty, as if her heart had been torn out, a big gaping void left behind.

"Cher bebe,"—sweet baby—she whispered, choking on her tears.

Lacy sighed heavily. Why had Belle been so ashamed of her pregnancy? Was it the rape contention that drove her or more a residual of her own tormented past? Belle Kennedy had been illegitimate, just as Lacy had been, just as her son had been.

The world had advanced a lot in thirty years, not always for the good, but especially with the way people accepted things. If she were pregnant today, there would have been no reason for shame to be attached to her pregnancy, even if it had been rape. Women without husbands got pregnant all the time, had children, and experienced motherhood.

Sometimes when patterns formed, they continued on in families. It had certainly proved true with hers. She had wondered then, as she did now, how much Belle had known about her father. Had her parents been long-time lovers or had it been a brief romance? Was he already married? Had he promised her marriage or had he run? Had her mother even told him she was pregnant? Had he moved on without knowing, forgotten about his tryst with Belle? Her mother had never known her own father, but Lacy wished Belle had told her something about hers. Except, maybe she couldn't. Maybe there had been more than one man in her life.

Belle had arrived in French Gap by way of an eighteen-wheeler. She'd come from Beaumont, Texas, where her mother had returned to her family to die of cancer. At nineteen, thinking herself a burden, Belle struck out on her own. She never meant to stay in French Gap, but seeing a need, she started a tutoring service that blossomed into a small school, mostly teaching kids forced to learn before falling into the family fishing or trapping business where book knowledge wasn't considered so important. She got paid by parents wanting better for their children, not much and not always with money. But somewhere along the way she got pregnant, had Lacy, never left the town.

Whatever the reason, Belle hadn't given Lacy away. Maybe that made it easier for her to give away her grandchild. Maybe Belle thought she was saving her daughter from the same kind of life she'd lived. Maybe by adopting out the baby and pushing Lacy away, she thought she could force Lacy into a world that could offer more. Lacy would never know.

She felt a sharp prickling behind her eyelids.

She would have liked to explain all that to Gregg, to tell him about the peculiar bond that had formed between the four girls that she had never fully understood. It might have been something as simple as being the same age, social awkwardness, or unhappiness—they were each of them a bit of a misfit in one way or another—that had brought them together as children, sitting across from each other in Belle Kennedy's tiny schoolroom. That, and maybe a little fear, had kept them together as children and into their teen years, at times barely tolerating each other.

She and Kitty had been tighter with each other than the others until Domeno Abadie moved to town. An uncle had passed, leaving Ray, Domeno's father, a small trawler and a fishing shack. When Domeno's mother died shortly after the inheritance, his bull of a father moved himself and his son from Shreveport to French Gap. That cocky kid had stepped into their lives and managed to tear them apart.

They had been so different, yet all mired in similar lives.

Beautiful Kitty Chauvin, lusted after by men young and old, the product of a worthless, drunken father and a mother who daily found the wrong end of his fist.

Shy, fat Arcie Becnel, no father around, a mother who sold herself, almost always first in line for food stamps and her welfare check each month.

Strange little Yancy Arceneaux, who people said was "tetched in the head." The charity case who didn't want the schooling her mother never paid for, the one who seemed most knowledgeable about life. People called her grandmother and mother voodoo conjurers, and her exotically beautiful mother sold her body as often as she sold her spells.

And me. We were a strange foursome.

A tear slid from beneath her lashes. Her chest tightened. Very close to the surface she sensed that young girl again, the one pregnant and barely sixteen, sent away scared, lost and angry over the cards she'd been dealt in life. Her level-headed self wasn't sure the purpose this trip served, for her or them, but she seemed to have no more control over what was happening in her present than she'd had in her past.

What if Gregg was right? What if this turned into something more than a simple reunion?

27

Without sun most of the morning, the noonday wasn't warm. The air was interrupted by a sporadic chilly wind, and dry lightning occasionally sliced across the gray sky. Rain was coming in, bringing with it a light cold front. The wind had stirred up bayou water, turning it a brassy emerald. Several *poule d'eaus,* cruised through the water lilies. The dark-plumaged coots bobbed through the foliage picking at the water plants looking for insects. A pair of cranes walked on the opposite side of the coulee, avian eyes fastened on an egret moving through the disturbed water. One crane abruptly launched a furious attack of wings and cawing. The smaller bird fled, lifting effortlessly into the air.

Yancy slipped the nutria's webbed hind feet into the loop and drew the knot. Muscles in her forearms corded as she gave two strong pulls, suspending the muskrat a foot or so above the ground. The long rat-like tail of the rodent flopped down the width of its back. It was a big auburn-brown male with feet bigger than her hand. He barely moved. His eyes already had that glassy stare, but she knew he was alive. When she checked her traps early morning, he was there, a spitting distance from one filled with crawfish. *The start of a good day, fresh meat and seafood,* she thought, as she slid the knife into him, slipped its sharpness the length of groin to shoulder.

Feces slid from his rear, urine from his genitals. Air escaped his throat in a long wet sigh, lips curled back in a grimace revealing yellowed teeth. She reserved his blood for sausage in a bucket, reached inside, jerking the entrails from their hiding place, squeezing down the length of them, like one would a cow's teat, removing what the final defecation had left behind.

The insects came, flies and gnats, attracted by the blood and entrails waste. Feeding time. Yancy waved them away. They lifted and swirled like snatches of lint in the air. A few swift strokes separated the skin from the meat. Cutting the pieces she wanted, she left the carcass where it was tied. It would be gone in the morning. She severed the scrotum, palmed the testicles, drew back her arm and threw them high and wide across the water. The sac disappeared with a soft *ploop!* The cranes scurried to investigate.

She'd make jambalaya or *boulette*—meatballs—or maybe a meat pie, better to disguise the tangy flavor of the meat. If they realized what it was, they wouldn't eat it.

28

The sky was brilliant, a huge pale gemstone, reflected in the turquoise surface of the swimming pool. Midday sunlight blended with the lush growth of shrubbery and the colored hue of flower blooms.

Barbara Mackey stretched, lifting her legs away from the chaise's canvas. She glanced over at Creely: asleep, a frown pulling together his brows. He had looked a little haggard when he showed up. Arms wrapped around his neck, hips pressed tightly into him, she had back-walked him into her bedroom. Responsive, but not as quickly as he should have been, they managed sex anyway. Afterward, Annie, the housekeeper and cook, had served them salad, baked chicken and garlic bread on the patio, enough to sop up what Barbara knew was excess alcohol.

A mutual friend in Kenner had scheduled a casual dinner party for nine. Barbara sensed he didn't want to go, but he would, if for no other reason than she hadn't made a fuss over Carson's ludicrous Friday night gathering. She had spent another evening alone so he could surround himself with enough pussy to make his dick fall off. There were lots of rumors, but she didn't know how many women he really had, if he kept any of them or simply fucked them when it was convenient. So here they were, no conversation, him sleeping off his obviously eventful night, and her thinking too much.

Used up, she thought nastily.

They hadn't seen each other in three days, except for dinner the previous evening. The sex was usually excellent. It had been lousy this time, by any scoring standards. She was surprised he got it up. She would have preferred him to put more effort into it or skip the entire process. She had almost told him so. But he was no fool, if there hadn't been sex, he knew what she would be thinking. She was thinking about it anyway. It made her mad as hell.

Barbara was well-maintained, fleshy in the hips with nice breasts and long legs, and a haphazard tumble of auburn hair with a rusty dusting of freckles accenting her green eyes. With imperfect features, she knew she wasn't beautiful, but it didn't matter. She thought there was too much emphasis placed on beauty, and it was often overrated. Barbara considered that intellect, breeding, and money balanced most physical shortcomings, not particularly in that order.

The only child of affluent parents, a domineering mother and pliant father, she was almost forty, and she had never married. There had never been a shortage of suitors or escorts in her life, all amicable encounters frequently ending with what she considered an unimportant romp in the hay, but there had rarely been a substantial romantic interest. Her clock had never clicked on a family, so she had decided maybe she didn't have such a clock.

Children had never been her thing. She didn't need diapers, drool, and the patter of little feet to complicate her comfortable life. So she had never considered that much domesticity, at least until Creely Crane came along. Since the subject had never come up between them, she figured he felt the same. If he wanted children, he would have done something about it by now. He would have to be the one to produce another generation of Cranes; his outrageous brother never would.

Barbara had fallen in love with Creely, determined to have him—and became immediately aware that loving him would never be enough. Sometimes that troubled her a lot because she associated love with weakness, not strength, and she had never regarded herself as weak. Crane, like his dead father—her mother admitted she had once fucked the arrogant bastard in a kitchen pantry at a political fundraiser where he was working a security detail—and his churlish gay brother seemed to thrive on infidelity. A part of him seemed to belong to every seductive female who crossed his path. She did her best to ignore his various affairs as they churned out of the rumor mill, but she hated having to deal with it.

Be logical, she frequently reminded herself, but a woman in love wasn't always logical. The mind quite often listened less than it should.

She was well acquainted with infidelity. Her mother had survived for years the numerous amateurish affairs and frivolous flirtations in which her father had indulged. Deciding to keep her marriage intact, she never stopped loving him, even after he died in another woman's bed. She had taught her daughter, if a person wanted something badly enough, in order to get and keep what they wanted, certain concessions had to be made. Barbara had reconciled herself to sharing Creely, but it was difficult.

Creely abruptly catapulted to the edge of his chaise, shaking, his eyes squeezed shut. Startled, Barbara's heart slammed into her throat as the bottle of sunscreen slid from her hand, flowering in a slippery pool on the ceramic tiles.

"Creely?" She knelt in front of him. Hot tiles began to burn annoying crooked ridges into her knees. When there was no response, she repeated, *"Creely,"* her tone more urgent.

Creely's eyes were glazed and distant when he opened them.

"What's the matter?"

"A—a dream."

"What sort of dream?" She knew about his so-called visionary abilities, but nothing had ever occurred in her presence. Once or twice she had asked questions, but his placatory answers had irked her.

She had never asked again.

Barbara didn't believe in reading palms or tea leaves or tarot cards. She especially didn't believe in ghosts and séances or any type of psychic crap. She had decided to accept what had been told to her about him as an eccentric oddity. It marred him, gave him a flaw she saw as a character weakness. It was distasteful. She tolerated it as she tolerated everything else she didn't like.

She didn't doubt he knew how she felt, so frequently she had to remind herself what might be the motivating factor of his side of their relationship. . . . and then a small corner of her mind would gently nudge her—and remind her of hers.

"What sort of dream?" she repeated. She was good at doing polite, she found it wasn't as easy trying to do concerned and nice. She was curious, and at the same time uncomfortable with her curiosity. She also wanted to get off her knees. She felt kneeling, for any reason, was beneath her.

Creely's glance moved slowly toward her face and settled with concentration somewhere on her forehead. "A dream about a friend." He looked away.

"What friend?" she pressed.

His glance drifted back. After a long moment, he said, "Kitty Chauvin."

Barbara drew in a deep breath, stunned. A fiery fist closed around her lower intestines, but it wasn't the time to let her resentment surface. She thought it would have been better if he had lied. Women constantly ogled this chiseled, handsome man she had claimed as her own. She knew about a lot of his women, but they came and went, most short-lived, except Chauvin. The Chauvin bitch seemed to have more staying power than a tick on a dog. There seemed to be something special about her. Barbara wished she knew exactly what.

Jealousy strangled her. The fact that he was a serial womanizer and his tainted reputation preceded him had appeared to be only another hurdle in their relationship. Chauvin's name had never before crossed his lips in her presence. From the moment an attorney friend introduced them, she had anticipated a day like this might come but hadn't thought it would arrive so soon and hadn't dwelled on it. She had been determined to keep him against all odds.

"W-what sort of dream about her?" Her voice sounded choked.

"She's in trouble."

"What kind of trouble?" She had little doubt Kitty's trouble owned a penis, hoped it wasn't the one she knew they occasionally shared.

"I don't know." He ran his hands through his hair and over his face.

"Well, if you don't know, how do you know she's in trouble?"

"I just know she's in danger—she's going to need help soon."

Barbara said with great effort, "I'm sure she can take care of herself."

Creely shook his head. "She's in serious danger—and she doesn't suspect it."

Barbara attempted a smile but failed. She thought him a little crazy. His tone told her how seriously vested he was in whatever he thought he'd dreamed.

"You look flushed." She pushed herself up, rubbing at her crinkled, aching knees, trying to divert his thoughts. "It's cooler inside, Creely. Maybe something cold to drink and a couple of aspirin will help. You probably had too much sun on top of too much liquor last night—"

"Don't patronize me," he interrupted. "I know you don't believe in my visions."

The harshness of his voice startled Barbara. She backed away. "Oh, Creely, don't be ridiculous—"

"Ridiculous?" He snorted, cutting off her protest. Frowning at her, he demanded, "Well, *do* you?"

"I don't think the issue here is whether or not I believe in your visions."

"No?" Creely stood. His bathing trunks slipped, riding low above his sex. "What is the issue?"

"Creely—" she began tentatively, brushing her fingers against his upper arm.

"Don't," he warned, his voice dangerously low.

Barbara withdrew her hand, fingers curled in. A silent rage dilated her pupils. It was ridiculous of him to allow a hangover dream—a fucking *vision* as he insisted on calling it—to carry such importance. This had gone too far.

"You don't have to believe. I never asked you to believe."

"Where are we going with this, Creely? Are you looking for an argument over your belief or your dream? Over your *vision . . .* or your *friend?*"

Creely didn't speak. His eyes held hers. Her glance was frigid.

"I won't give you the satisfaction of arguing over another female. That is exactly what this is about. Perhaps you should leave until your priorities are straight."

Creely's eye color had changed to deep amber, his jaw a sharply angled line, his lips pulled tautly. "Finally we agree about something."

Barbara was at a loss what to say. She had thrown down the gauntlet. She had expected regret over the disagreement, maybe a little embarrassment, but definitely an apology. It hadn't occurred to her he would call her bluff. A little spat, that's all this should have been.

She had underestimated Chauvin's power over him. If he had dreamed about anyone else, one phone call to his buddy, Sal Impastato, a lieutenant or captain or someone equally as righteous—she'd never paid much attention to his rank—with the New Orleans police department would have looked into it for him.

Barbara turned away, wounded, disappointed and coldly furious, swallowing hard around the knot in her throat. She rarely cried, had never done so in front of him, but she could feel his stare scorch her skin. She thought for a moment she might be unable to hold back the hot raging tears.

If they both worked at it, it was possible to rectify what had happened—but somehow she didn't think they would. This felt different. It felt disturbingly uncivil. She was dancing too vigorous a line of distrust and jealous uncertainty to back down.

This wasn't just a normal disagreement. This was more of a warning, a prelude to failure. A destroyed engagement, a prestigious three-hundred-guest-list wedding wiped out, more distasteful, ugly gossip, embarrassment, humiliation, the governor's mansion gone from a possibility to a nightmarish dream—*all gone* because of an argument over one of his whores.

He might have already gotten his priorities straight—and maybe they didn't include her. She might have wasted months of effort and energy on something that could turn out to be a profitless investment.

29

Kitty wasn't sure at what point she realized she would give in and go. Stop fighting it, she had decided. *Just make the damn trip and get it over with.* Yancy and French Gap were the past that represented the troubled childhood she had left behind. Why couldn't she make Arcie understand that?

Silence had fallen during a frosty drive to the airport. They had discovered the flight delayed. It gave them plenty of time to sit in the noisy airport terminal not speaking to each other.

After Kitty had scrubbed herself red in the shower, Arcie had brought her coffee and juice while she had jerked on soft old jeans and a white men's shirt over her reluctant body. She drank both, but they sank to the bottom of her stomach with the aspirin that hadn't started working. She was a mess.

And, to make things worse, she was pissed over leaving an anxious dog. It wasn't like Dusty to be rebellious. She was used to being left behind when Kitty traveled. When Dusty wouldn't follow Arcie from the ondo, she had yanked the leash from Arcie's hand, and taken the dog herself across the hall to her sitter, Dusty whimpering and tugging back. Kitty felt as if her world had been turned upside down in a little over twenty-four hours.

The terminal noise only increased her irritability. The loud people, cell phones chirping out ridiculous trendy burps and jingles, the tinny steel of baggage cartwheels against the concourse floor. Babies crying, disobedient children, their feet like thunder. It seemed every sound was doubly magnified.

Kitty sighed heavily. Acid in the back of her throat, grumbling bowels; whatever was inside didn't know which way it wanted to go. She hated stress and pressure. Her body and mind never responded in quite the same manner and neither ever responded well. She was furious with herself for allowing Arcie and indistinct memories to manipulate her so easily. She was afraid to go back. How ridiculously juvenile and paranoid did that make her?

She glanced at this new Arcie person who went in an eye blink from helpful and compliant to argumentative and combative to sullen and silent. "This is crazy, Arcie."

"Yes, it is," Arcie agreed, staring straight ahead through the glass at the tarmac.

"Why is this so important? It was only a game." Or was it? Was it possible it had been something else entirely?

Arcie's eyes flickered toward her, then away. She didn't reply.

It was said Yancy's mother and grandmother were capable of powerful voodoo. There had never been an end to the stories—hexes and rites, love and death spells, potions, and powders, oils and talismans and charms; even a few rumbles about their ability to change into something non-human. Some spells were performed to help people, make the sick get well bring good luck; others were used for revenge, *fixed* people, bad *gris-gris* done to hurt or injure or even kill. It was said when someone died suddenly or disappeared and never came back or was never found, someone had paid for a curse. Kitty had tried not to believe those stories, but she knew she had. Was Yancy capable of all those wicked things people accused her family of doing? Had she decided to use one of those spells on them? If so, for what purpose?

Kitty had tried to close the door on everything related to French Gap. She thought Arcie had also, but she was too eager to go back, as if there was a special reason to return. Apparently, Arcie didn't think her childhood had been as wretched as Kitty's. Stress seemed to have succeeded in opening her door to that dark place inside where people closeted away memories they didn't want to acknowledge. That place where they always seemed able to hide hurt and pain, shame and embarrassment. Now it seemed her door had been cracked open, old memories beginning to slip out.

Kitty guessed Arcie didn't look on her experience that night the same way. Never bothering to ask, running away, Kitty was always rushing head-on with her life. She should have asked. It seemed maybe there were a lot of things she should have asked and never did. They'd had twenty years to talk. They should have talked more. Now they hardly talked at all. Sometimes life really could be a hard-assed bitch.

She wished she could see this trip from a different perspective and make Arcie do the same. Everything was different now, they were different. Whatever Arcie expected to find after all these years wouldn't be there. Or, if it was, it wouldn't be as she remembered it. Nothing stayed the same. Christ, she couldn't imagine Lacy wanting any part of this. Her abrupt disappearance, never coming back, meant she didn't want to have anything to do with them or French Gap, didn't it?

Kitty had always thought the mind a cluttered place, like an old attic. No matter how well you tried to clean, some of the corners would always be dusty, filled with years of ugly broken pieces like sadness and hurt, fear and pain, anger and disappointment. Sometimes a person wanted to give the clutter away and couldn't, so it built up, it wasn't always easy to maintain. Life sometimes trapped a person and sped away. It didn't offer a chance to do things differently. There was never a do-over, life just wasn't that accommodating. Let those people try who wanted to recapture their past, but she certainly didn't. Surely

Lacy felt the same, no matter what Arcie thought. Why come back now?

She felt a wave of instantaneous anger, a hot flare, a deep quick burn, and had tried to be patient when Arcie kept insisting they had to go back and see each other. So she had agreed, tired of hearing the same thing over and *over*. Just this once, she decided. No going back another time. No room for argument, no guilt, no accusations. She went, she participated, and she got the hell out of French Gap . . . *again*. Obligation over. Arcie wouldn't have a damn thing to bitch about. Arcie could stay there, forever, if that was what she chose to do, but one or two days would be more than enough time for her. It was only a reunion, same as any reunion, right? Smile, make friendly, impress and judge each other. Right?

Nothing more.

. . . *nothing*—

—a faint, indistinct flutter in the back of her mind . . . .

What?

Aggravated, Kitty had managed to work herself into such a depressed mood that she seemed to have ditched her common sense. She felt as if she was wallowing in misery, no longer sure what caused the itch along her neck.

"We aren't going to be comfortable with so much togetherness, Arcie," she said when Arcie stayed quiet and continued to ignore her. She guessed it wasn't because Arcie didn't have something to say, just that she was pissed. Kitty knew her words were sensible, but she sounded like a whiny little kid. Inside her head felt like someone had packed it with compost and dumped rocks on top.

Arcie said nothing, but Kitty saw her entire face tighten from the restraint of words she was unable to say aloud.

Stop it, wait for Lacy, Kitty told herself. Lacy would be the leverage she needs to get Arcie to see how ridiculous the whole situation was.

30

The Past

Air puffed from her open mouth in small, violent expulsions—as if she'd been running and running and running—taking her breath away.

Why, why, why? Yancy silently screamed.

It drove her crazy. Domeno had been gone for days. She had no idea where he went, or if he intended to come back. She wondered what she'd do if he didn't come back. There hadn't been another chance to get to him.

He did finally come back . . . but not alone. That girl-child came with him. He had just gone away and found this girl-child stranger. She had no idea where he'd found her or how long he'd plotted to do it, knowing it would make her crazy. She was a skinny little creature with pale hair, big eyes, and a serious face. The thin gold band on her finger sparkled in the sunlight. His ring flashed as brightly as hers. And Yancy angrily thought: *a wife!*

It ripped out her guts seeing them together. Bitter anger turned into a flame, searing her from the soles of her feet to the crown of her head. Howls of anguish rose in her throat and turned into choking sobs of despair.

Something was wrong with her, Yancy knew it, or she had made a terrible mistake with her spell, done something wrong. Something simple—something . . . *something!*—or else everything would have been okay, and the baby would have been female.

Now she had to deal with this—this *stranger,* this *child,* this . . . *this wife!* She had no baby girl, and she was still cursed. Now he'd gone and married some damn child. Her soul felt dark, shriveled, parched, and empty, like her arms. The blood hammered in her throat, deafening inside her head. Yancy dropped to her knees, her stomach painfully clenched. She ached all over, inside and out. But she would fix things, she would separate them, tear apart their lives, destroy whatever happiness he thought he might have found.

It didn't take long for the girl to get pregnant.

At midnight the night of the full moon in the girl child's sixth month, Yancy built a small fire in the clearing, anointed the flames with herbs, unsheathed the finely-honed bone knife, and carefully laid the small doll tied with hairs from the girl-child's head on a black cloth spread on the ground.

Yancy sat naked, the first bit of winter air raising gooseflesh on her body. Her hair wrapped her shoulders, a greasy veil clinging to her gaunt face. She rocked backward and forward with a slow hypnotic rhythm, mouthing sibilant incantations. A swift nip of the knife drew blood from the vein inside her elbow. She mixed her blood with the contents of the earthen bowl and drank. The vapors instantaneously swirled in her head.

"By all that is unholy, be you gone Tansie Abadie, die and rot in the grave," she whispered. "By this fire at midnight, I curse you. By the dead black hen, by the bloody goat, you cannot hide from this hex! May you have no peace! Tear you and rot! Tear you and rot, Tansie Abadie!"

She moaned, whimpered, and called out as if she were in pain. The wind seemed to answer her. It blew with a rattling sound through dry leaves, tall swamp grasses and tree branches; hissed through long manes of Spanish moss, and palmettos wrapped in curling ribbons of ground fog. The tainted smell of muck and fish roe rose from the reeds and lilies where the water was low. The sound of a heavy splash in the distant water. The sickly squeak of some furry creature caught off guard. A winged shadow crossing above her head offered the night a piercing cry. The moon skulked in and out of cloud, its light touching broken amber fingers to the impenetrable dark bayou curves.

Yancy raised her face to the night sky, her eyes squeezed shut, and moaned her blasphemous words, over and over, as the vapors wrapped her mind.

She lifted the bowl and drank again.

Her breath came rapidly, in wheezing puffs, as if her lungs were collapsing. Numbness crept through her to terminate in her fingers and toes. She lifted the knife, tweaked her skin below her navel until she bled, passed the knife blade through the blood, and smeared it on the doll in the same place from which it came. Grabbing up the faceless effigy, she sliced through the doll's middle with a single swift stroke of the blade, and whispered: *"Saigner! Mourir, chienne, mourir!"* Bleed! Die, bitch, die!

Not so far away, the girl convulsed in her sleep.

She awoke abruptly in the middle of devastating pain. Her eyes grew large and round with terror as she clutched the mattress with one hand and gripped the bed's headboard with the other, seeking leverage to pull upright. Her face contorting, she screamed, her body twisting and bucking.

Domeno Abadie jerked awake, calling out her name, grabbing for her, his voice thick with confusion and sleep. *"Quoi? Quoi c'est?"* he demanded. What? What is it?

Her sobs were wet and choking. Her breath came in heavy dog pants that brushed hotly against his face. He tried to pull her close, turn her into his arms and hold her. He could only press her head and shoulders tight against his chest and hug her between her breasts and the hump of her belly. Her hands had come together, her arms cupping the swell of her abdomen like a balloon. She finally stopped screaming and went limp against him, her head tilted back as she gasped for breath, eyes wild with fear as they searched out his face. A mewling sound came from deep in her chest.

His fingers dug into her arms as she wilted against him. He shook her, clutched her tight, but Tansie Abadie's eyes were glazed and her mouth hung open and she no longer moved. Horrified as the blood gushed and the small body pushed from between her legs, he sobbed, *"Non! Non!"* and threw back his head and screamed, *"Le bon Dieu mait la main de bebe!"* God help the baby!

As the words left his mouth, he reached out to touch the tiny body, knowing it already too late. If God had ever been there, He had deserted all of them.

31

Creely left the Mackey house in Chateau Estates, frustrated and mad as hell, and took a final glance back. Barbara stood on the sidewalk, sunlight striking her from behind, her hair a flower of flame across her shoulders. As she turned away, he knew three things with certainty—they had managed to leave too many unsaid things between them, she was enraged and wounded, and he felt a sad disappointment. This wouldn't be an easy fix and, at the moment, he wasn't sure how to fix it. The one thing he was sure of was his premonition. It was a clear message of danger. He was seriously worried about Kitty. He needed to do whatever it took to help her. Her safety was most important, he would figure out the rest later.

He got stuck in tangled traffic creeping east along I-10, impatiently clutching at the leather steering wheel of his Porsche 911 Carrera S convertible. He reached for the car phone, hesitated, dropped it back in its cradle, and slammed his fist against the dashboard in a frustrated punch. Sometimes women like Barbara had tunnel vision, they doubted anything they didn't understand, were never satisfied, and seemed to find all men lacking in something. She would always expect a man to alter a *little* something, erase or adjust some little something she considered an imperfection.

Creely had known for a long time what he wanted in his future. Marriage to Barbara came as part of the package. She was the type of wife his ambitions needed, so he had made an effort to please her. For years he'd enjoyed the excitement of the moment, and the various women that supplied that moment. He'd enjoyed sex and time spent with them, but he had never pretended to understand them and had never worried much about it either. After he made his decision about what he wanted for his future, he had searched for a woman to share that future with, but most never fit the guidelines he had set, so he never hung around a particular one very long. It hadn't mattered. He knew what most of them wanted from the moment he met them. They'd strip away their clothes, eager to be with him, and he obliged, making sure he gave them an orgasm or two each time they met.

Recently he had started having some doubt about choices he had already made. He hadn't intentionally meant to hurt Barbara, was sorry it happened the way it did, but if she wanted this marriage, she would have to be content with the current status of their relationship. He had a priority list and some things weren't negotiable. His brother and certain female friendships—never negotiable. Obviously, she hadn't realized until today the totality of non-negotiable.

Their relationship had seemed dry and edgy of late. If he felt it, he was sure she felt it. Maybe they could still make the marriage work if they redefined their battle lines before it turned into an all-out war. For starters, they could try being friends; they had never been friends. Kitty was his friend, they were always comfortable with each other, in public or private. She was just *there*, wonderfully warm and touchable. She had been away too long. He was glad she was back.

People who knew them thought it was the sex—only the sex—between them. It wasn't. The sex was good, hell, it was great, but he had never looked at their relationship as just great sex. He had a dozen words to accurately describe Kitty and how he felt about her, but mainly he enjoyed her. They seemed to have a connection he had never had with another woman. They were unconditional with each other. They didn't judge. She had never tried to change him. Had never asked anything of him he hadn't been willing to give. With Barbara, things were different.

Creely had spent his youth not understanding his visions, where they came from or why, but realized they were partial glimpses of tragedies that had occurred or were going to happen. The dreams, visions, premonitions, whatever someone chose to call them, popped out of nowhere, during sleep, idle moments or in the middle of some mundane activity. They were just there, images and thoughts that would sneak up on him. He never told anyone about them, even Carson, believing people would think him a little crazy. When a particularly worrisome one came, he decided to confide in Sal. That vision enabled police to find the body of a kidnapped young girl, brutally raped and strangled, her broken body curled inside a cardboard box and dumped near Bayou St. John. Afterward, he embraced his visions. They became as much a part of him as his height and eye color.

This vision was different. It was the first one he'd had about someone he knew.

Kitty had already gone when he awoke this morning. He had expected her to be there and was disappointed she wasn't. He thought about their night together, remembered the addictive smell and feel of her. He had awoken wanting to hold her again, be inside her, breathe her in until her scent filled him up like air in a balloon. Now she could be in danger and he wasn't sure he could fix whatever was wrong.

Creely felt a touch of guilt that he didn't have those kinds of feelings for Barbara. Today wasn't the first time he had performed like a trained animal because she expected it of him. Last night and today had been an awakening, maybe a little long in coming. Now he found himself faced with the stark possibility of losing Barbara and everything their marriage would represent.

A permanent relationship with Kitty wasn't likely to lead directly to the DA's office or the Senate or, eventually, the governor's mansion. She was an unlikely candidate for First Lady of State. Barbara knew that. She and her family had a huge amount of political contacts. Louisiana and other places; a lot of favors owed. Provoked, Barbara could spitefully use her knowledge, and this entire mess might end his political future. Hell, he was no fool. He had gotten himself into this shit pot of a mess, and he would find a way out, but right now Kitty was a priority.

He reached for the car phone again. The phone on the other end rang six times. An answering machine said: "Unavailable right now, you know what to do."

"Kitty, it's C, call me," he said.

An empty feeling tightened his chest. Something was troubling her last night. Not him, she'd said, an old problem to be solved by today. He had distracted her instead of asking more about the problem. Now he could kick himself. If he had pressed her, she would have told him what the problem was. It was imperative he hear her tell him everything was okay. He wouldn't be satisfied until she did.

32

"The illustrious Bill called this morning," Arcie said, her tone thick with sarcasm.

The statement caught Kitty off guard. For a second her heart leaped from surprise to hurt. She hated to ask, but she asked anyway, "What did you want?"

"He wanted you call, like there wasn't anything wrong. *Duh* . . . as if you'd do that!" Arcie cocked an eyebrow. "You wouldn't, would you? Call him?"

"No." Kitty saw Arcie's hands ball into fists in her lap. "You don't believe me?"

"What difference does it make what I believe?" She righteously turned her face away.

Kitty was thinking that any friendship should have some boundaries. Whatever was going on between them appeared to be much more than simply returning to French Gap, and she didn't understand exactly why, but whatever it was had taken a sharp turn toward unfriendly. It had turned into a crazy kind of a pugilistic mess. Why had something as ridiculous as this reunion been the thing to bring out all this animosity? How long had Arcie been harboring such anger and bitterness? She couldn't remember seeing it, but if it had been there, why hadn't she recognized it before now? And why did she keep berating herself? This was an Arcie problem, not hers.

Arcie was abruptly on her feet, as the passengers disembarked the plane, a bulldozer pushing her bulk across the waiting area, unmindful of anything or anyone. Her hands patted the air as she called, *"Laceee! Hey, Laceee . . . over here!"* All eagerness, enfolding Lacy Kennedy in a bear-hug before the other woman had time to recover from the attack. Lacy was startled, a frown pulling her brows together. Arcie's hands kept at Lacy, patting and touching, slapping at her arms. Lacy stood stiffly as if she were overwhelmed, maybe a little embarrassed by the attention of passersby brought to them by Arcie's behavior.

So there she is, Kitty thought. Lacy Kennedy, an adult version of the teenager Kitty remembered. No longer a tall, gangly girl, now an elegant, well-kept woman: high hollow cheeks, willow-thin body, full breasts, long legs, with dark-blonde hair streaked lighter. Hammered gold hoops in her ears, a gold-and-diamond Rolex on her left wrist, impeccably dressed in an expensive striped tunic, black leggings, and heeled sandals the exact shade of leather as her shoulder bag.

A snippet of memory flashed, an insignificant little something.

Clair de lune . . . *moonshine.* Kitty's maternal grand father had called Lacy that one day, in the middle of old men that gathered Saturday afternoons on

Schexnaydre General Merchandise's front porch for a card game, and to share local and parish gossip. *"Merveilleux,"*—magical—*Grandpere* Duplantis said, glancing up from his bouree game and pointing across the street.

Not a beautiful child, but something about her— *some little something*—that suggested cool brilliant light. Maybe it was a type of magic, magnetic quicksilver. An inside glow that made unattractive women appear beautiful without even being pretty. Whatever it was, wherever it came from, there was no doubt Lacy had moonshine.

A brief cautious shadow flickered in her eyes. It came and went so rapidly, Kitty thought it might have been her imagination, but felt certain it wasn't. Lacy Kennedy was being gracious, but she was uncomfortable with a lot more than Arcie's gauche attention.

33

The Past

Moonlight shone translucent, veiled with cloud as it embraced the silhouettes of cypress, water oak, and the creeping phantoms of nocturnal creatures. Water hyacinths formed vague little floating islands on dark water. The air was thick and wet, chokingly humid, with water from the afternoon rain dripping from leaves and fronds. The swamp looked soft and shadowy with ground fog. Mosquitoes buzzed. Fireflies glided through the moist dark, winking pinpricks of greenish fire. Somewhere an owl screamed.

Yancy paused in her digging, her nostrils flaring as she sniffed the mist that crept across the bayou. The heavy air carried the rich musk of his scent, made her want to *touch* him, *fuck* him. All the years she'd studied him, yearned for him, he had now become like an infectious disease, a tumor she'd learned to live with. A glimpse of him was so disruptive to her daily routine, afterward, she would obsess for days.

She lay flat, wearing shadow like a cloak. As she inhaled the scents close to the ground, for a moment her eyes flashed scarlet. She crawled forward on her elbows and knees, her stomach and thighs pressed against the ground, spongy soil cold and wet against her belly. *Why is he here? He* wants *something, wants it real bad.* Was it time for revenge? There had been so many other opportunities for revenge. It had been over a year since she performed the ritual that took the life of the girl and baby. More than six months since she'd been within touching distance of him.

He stood frozen as one with the tree, but his heat spread outward. She could feel it, smell everything about him: anxiety and anger, revulsion, doubt, and indecision. The emotions leaked from his pores like syrup from a bottle . . . and beneath that, she could smell him, the rawness of his sweat, the strong pulse of his blood, the mutable stench of his genitals.

Yancy's appetite for him crawled through her, swollen and alive. She'd often wondered if it was that way with other people, if it had been that way for her mother with the man who fathered her. Had her mother wanted that man as much as she wanted this one? She sat up, the sudden movement bringing her into a shaft of moonlight.

His eyes widened with surprise. Their glances locked for a mesmerizing moment. She smelled the stink of his panic. A glimmer of malice darkened his stare. His fear evaporated so quickly it startled her. Filled with the sharp edge of danger, Yancy's heartbeat increased to a wild, tight thumping in her throat.

He came at her with purpose, knocking her backward. Fear surged along her spine. She could taste sour terror in her mouth. She found herself unable to get up. She had underestimated him and the madness that energized him. She had to protect herself. She scrambled to lift her body from the ground, her mind grappling with the need to shift. It didn't happen.

His hands were on her shoulders, a knee slamming into her belly. One huge hand held her throat while the other buried in her hair and savagely yanked back her head. Pain flared across her skull. It felt as if he'd ripped a handful of hair and skin away from her scalp. He bore down on her, the raw pressure of his weight terrifying. Yancy dug her heels into the ground, scrabbling away an inch or two, seeking leverage to lift her body. She clawed at him, making contact, could smell blood as his skin peeled away.

Yancy pounded with her fists and continued to claw at him. He gave a small grunt with each blow, but his grip only tightened. He was so close to her, she could only see his eyes, huge and black with fury, against the pale angles of his face. Hot liquid fear shot up her spine. Her beast stirred, then slipped away, retreated without rising. Her screams drowned into a high keening choked off by his fingers.

"Pourquoi?" The sound a vicious, muted chest growl, and his spittle flew across her face. Why? "I should kill you for making my life so damn miserable!

For killing what I loved!" He straddled her, breath hot and fetid, thick with alcohol fumes, pressing her into the alligator grass with his weight.

His nose almost touched hers; fear lit fire in her blood. His fingers crawled up to dig like a vice under her jaw. *"Fou chienne! Sa fini pas!"* Crazy bitch! It never ends! His arm was across her throat, driving her head up and back. *"Mal chienne!"* Evil bitch!

Gathering her strength in a final effort to free herself, Yancy brought her knees up hard against his ass, ramming them directly behind his testicles. She'd expected him to release her as air whooshed from between his lips and a deep groan rose from his chest, but he only stiffened and came down hard with his full weight, using his butt like a pile driver. She heard her kneecap pop. Her other leg went limp and numb, jammed into the ground.

Yancy tried to unjumble her thoughts to summon her beast. She felt feel the force of power just under her skin, just out of reach. She tried to call it again. It didn't come. She didn't understand why.

The moonlight slid in a silver flash across the knife blade in his hand.

Yancy closed her eyes, sank into the gray that engulfed her, anticipating a painful death. She went limp, without a single thought of deliverance in her mind as her bladder emptied.

Salvatore Impastato looked up from paperwork, surprised to see Creely. He stood and offered his hand, then crossed the room and poured coffee into styrene cups. He passed Creely one before dropping his lanky frame back into his swivel chair. The man had been deputy chief of detectives, NOPD Homicide, for eight years. His dark eyes saw everything and revealed nothing, but had seen too much of the city's bad. Like his lined face, they rarely registered surprise.

"How you been, big guy?" he asked.

"Busy."

"I know. I read the papers, listen to the news *and* watch TV."

Creely chuckled. "And you?"

Impastato shrugged. "Cops are like criminals and lawyers, always busy." His long fingers rubbed at the worn vinyl of the chair arm. Whatever brought Creely to the squad room was important enough to rate a visit instead of a phone call. Maybe another vision.

Sal looked tired, a little pale. "The old ticker doing okay?" Creely asked. Impastato had already had quadruple bypass surgery. The purple-red blotches running along his forearms indicated his use of blood thinners. He had always been closed-mouthed, infrequently volunteered information about his health and he wasn't someone you pressured for answers. You had to be patient, slowly dig everything out.

"I'm considering retirement."

"You're too damn young."

"So says you. You get the easy part, you know. I get the hard part." Impastato shook his head, sighed heavily. "The horror of kids dealing drugs and blowing out each other's fuckin' brains. Damn pedophiles and the dead or destroyed innocent they leave behind. The rape victims that end up with shredded lives. Innocents gunned down because someone crazy thought he got looked at in a funny way. Old people beat and killed, robbed for their Social Security checks. The senseless gay bashings—and all the bureaucratic crap. The world has gone crazy. It's too much sometimes."

"Longest speech I ever heard you make. You thinking of running for office?"

Impastato offered a faint smile. "I'm fuckin' jaded, pal. I used to love this job. Now sometimes I wonder why."

"You've got lots of good years left," Creely said.

Impastato grunted. "My ray of sunshine, are you?" He swished his coffee, took a sip, and stared thoughtfully into the cup. A couple of moments of silence before he raised his eyes. They focused on Creely. He had already noted the nervous impatience running through Creely like electricity. "You want something?"

"I could be just making a social."

"Long time since just socials." Impastato had known the Crane boys since they were babies. Simon Crane had become his rookie partner when Creely was four and Carson was a newborn. Tall and massive, Simon was a rich, handsome, arrogant bastard that liked the ladies. He came from wealth going as far back as the Percys from the Mississippi Delta. Impastato never understood why Simon chose to put his life in danger of being an underpaid cop. Lorraine, Simon's wife, had never understood either. One night she tucked her boys in, kissed them goodnight, and told Simon she was taking the dog for his evening walk. When he awoke on the sofa at midnight, he found Lorraine gone and the 200-pound Neapolitan mastiff curled up on the front porch.

Simon insisted she'd skipped, Impastato thought she'd been abducted. He argued they search for her, even after the official search ended. He couldn't believe he would leave her boys like that, even if the marriage stank. Simon was right. They eventually traced her to California, found her living with the manager of a Volvo dealership in Los Angeles. Simon never went after her, never told his sons he'd found their mother. They grew up believing her dead.

After his pride healed, Simon moved in and out

of affairs with younger women until he was killed at a bank robbery when Creely was fourteen. Impastato told Creely the truth about his mother when he turned eighteen. As far as he knew, Creely had never told Carson or attempted contact with his mother.

Creely nodded. "I got a personal problem." Impastato's dark eyes were like obsidian marbles staring at him across the desk.

"I figured that."

"How's that?"

"You don't work weekends."

Creely chuckled. "I need background info on Kitty Chauvin, far back as you can go."

"The infamous Kitty Chauvin." Impastato offered up a grin, but his thoughts were humorless. Creely was treading dangerous ground. "Thought you already knew all there was to know."

Creely said nothing.

"Guess the two of you haven't spent much time talking."

Creely scowled. "That's unnecessary, Sal."

Impastato settled back in his chair and listened while Creely explained, giving him the details he could remember of his vision . His expression remained neutral, eyes dark slivers behind dropping eyelids, almost as if he was disinterested or fighting sleep. Creely knew better. "I need to know everything you can get," Creely finished.

"Uh-huh." Impastato sighed. "And how did that go over with Mackey?"

"Not so good."

"I figured as much."

"She told me to get my priorities straight."

"Apparently you have."

"Pretty much."

"And you don't want my advice, but gonna give it anyway. Let it ride until Monday."

Creely's stare went stony. "I think she's in serious trouble, Sal. I need to help her."

"Hardy works the weekend." Impastato rubbed his eyes with his knuckles and rocked slowly. The old chair squeaked. "He won't like it."

Gus Hardy, a handsome computer geek researcher, was one of the best. He could do traces in the blink of an eye, and find out pretty much all there was to know about a person in minutes. He also hated Creely's guts. Creely had escorted Kitty to the French Quarter Society's Adopt-A-Pet fundraiser one year. One of her paintings, some kind of weird kinky three-eared, five-legged dog creature, was in a silent auction. Pet lover Hardy had been there without his wife. Creely had introduced them. Kitty, her usual exuberant self when way over the limit of tipsy, had flirted outrageously, leaned in close and stroked his crotch before Creely had maneuvered her away from Hardy. Word had filtered back to Hardy's hot-headed Italian wife and Hardy had blamed him for the fiasco that followed.

"You seem a little short on memory."

"That was over four years ago."

"Resentments last a long time."

"Make it an order." Going against policy, breaching ethical boundaries and using a chain of command didn't disturb Creely, whatever necessary was acceptable to him. It was just another technical jump-through hoop.

Impastato didn't answer immediately, as if thinking about what he would say. Finally: "Not comfortable with that, Creely."

"You doubt my vision?"

"It's not uncommon to have a bad dream sometimes. This sounds crazy to me, Creely. She's a nice person, a great artist, but she's an alley cat. You know that. Not returning phone calls doesn't mean anything. She's probably just shacked up somewhere. When she gets enough of what she seems to like best, she'll come home."

"That's insulting."

"But truthful."

"She's not." Creely spoke softly, but the heat of anger rose up the back of his neck, making his shirt collar tight against his skin.

"Not what?"

"Shacked up someplace."

"And you know for sure how?"

"She was with me until around six this morning."

"And?" *Oh, dear Lord, you're more like your old man every day. Even now, only a couple of months away from getting married, you can't keep your dick in your pants,* Impastato thought, eyeing Creely shrewdly, knowing he needs to back off, but wanting to say more. He knew he had already stirred up enough righteous indignation in his friend. He liked Chauvin a hell of a lot more than that icy bitch Mackey, but that didn't mean he thought Chauvin was better for him. She might be what Creely really wanted, she just wasn't necessarily what he needed.

"I don't think she'd go looking so soon." Creely spoke with the certainty of a man without rejection.

Yep, just like his old man—testicles as big as cannon balls. "What makes you so sure she wouldn't take on two cocks in the same day?"

Creely didn't reply.

"Why are you really doing this, Creely?" The chair groaned in protest as Impastato rolled from one buttock to the other.

"What exactly do you mean by that?"

"You're putting your upcoming marriage and future career in jeopardy. There has to be another reason aside from Chauvin's a great fuck."

"There is." Creely dropped his glance, stared doggedly at the styrene cup in his hands, his grip so tight he thought it would pop. "I *like* her."

"Obviously quite a lot."

"Yeah."

"And Mackey?"

"What about her?"

"Does she have any idea what you're doing?"

Creely looked away and didn't answer. Maybe it was the way he sat driving his butt sharply against the wood of the uncomfortable visitor chair, but his ass had gone numb. He was so pissed it took all his control to keep from stalking out. He hadn't expected an interrogation or listening to derogatory remarks about Kitty. Sal had known about her for years. He needed Sal's help, but he wasn't up for this crap.

"Not going to tell her, are you?"

"It's a need to know basis."

"You're just going off on a wild goose chase."

"Not thinking of it that way."

"What's gonna happen when she finds out?"

They had rarely discussed Barbara . Sal understood his relationship with her was complicated. It was freakish how their affair and engagement had created so much gossip. He'd thought it would eventually stop. It never had. It irritated Creely to think their marriage would probably garner and stay under as much scrutiny as their engagement.

"Barbara is *my* business."

"Have you gone pussy-stupid, Creely?"

"What the hell is that supposed to mean?"

"Women are rarely forgiving about another woman. She knows about Chauvin. She might know
about all of them. She doesn't trust you, probably
never has, probably never will. You've never been
particularly discreet, counselor." Impastato pushed
himself out of his chair, refilled his coffee cup, and
motioned with the cup to Creely. Creely shook his
head. "She's waiting to see what you do next. She
knows lots of people who could be detrimental to
you, big man."

"I'll deal with it," Creely snapped. It didn't
matter that everything Sal said was true.

Impastato returned to his chair. *Like father, like
son, stubborn as mules,* he thought. "I know you will. I
just know where you'd like to be in a few years. Hate
to see you fuck it up."

Creely tried to stare Impastato down, his shoulders tight , his neck swollen with heat. "Something
troubled her last night. 'Old problem,' she said. Could
be something from before she came here. I should
have asked what it was."

"What you should've done was hold off fuckin'
her. It would have made things less complicated."

Creely bridled his anger, stood, and placed the
cup on the edge of the desk. It tipped over. The last
drop of coffee slipped toward the lip and he snapped
up the cup and tossed it in the wastebasket.

"A simple yes or no is good, Sal." Their glances locked, held for a painfully long moment.

Impastato looked away first, nodded solemnly. His counsel to the Crane boys had always been to make the best possible choices, not that his words usually made an impact. They might have listened, but rarely felt obligated to follow his advice. Both almost always went in their own directions, and Creely could be relentless when it came to something he wanted. "You know I won't refuse."

"Thanks." Creely backed away and paused at the door. Sal wasn't looking at him, he'd gone back to his paperwork. He hesitated a second, but when Sal didn't look up, he left without looking back.

Impastato watched his departure across the squad room without lifting his head. He felt a special closeness with Creely, had liked him as an energetic, intelligent kid, had liked him, even more, as a boldly ambitious adult. Having no children, he had often wished he had a son like him but found it troublesome that Creely was his father's son. He was sometimes hardheaded, he sometimes pissed people off, so he probably had near as many enemies as friends, but it didn't seem to matter to him. He had always liked doing things his way. Between his legal career and his trust fund, Creely might not even know his net worth.

Egotistical and promiscuous, sometimes narcissistic, he had always shared the same relentless urge for womanizing as his fatjer and his Uncle Danny, Simon's twin, the man who raised the boys after Simon's death. It seemed all the Crane men belonged to the Club of Traveling Dicks. Impastato wasn't sure if the trait was learned or inherited. He couldn't help wondering if, in the end, this situation was going to put him in a lot more hot water than Creely anticipated.

35

The Mercedes purred down Airline toward LaPlace. By the time they crossed the overpass spanning Lake Pontchartrain, Arcie's excitement seemed to have cooled to lukewarm. Conversation in the front had gone from friendly "Did you have a nice flight?" to lulls and gaps, monosyllables lacking enthusiasm.

Kitty's chest tightened from the arrival of repressed memory. Flimsy images, long buried in her subconscious, unfolded in the back of her mind. Old resentment bloomed to the surface.

Downhill slide to sixteen . . . she was madly in love with Domeno Abadie.

She begged her mama to let her go to the dance if she saved the money to buy that cheap dress at Schexnaydre General Merchandise. She had wanted to be the only girl he danced with at the *fais do-do* . . . .

. . . where the moon was gossamer, a flicker of pewter, ribbons of ebony between distant trees. A pale hazy mist glowed in the light of colored paper lanterns, and smiling couples danced in the shine of kerosene lamps hung on nails. With a soft collision of bodies, they twirled, and the throb of Cajun French vocals poured out "Jolie Blonde," "Allons a Lafayete" and "L'amour Indifferent," drifting through the warm Louisiana night, as feet tapped in time with the blended music of fiddle, guitar and steel.

She'd been furious watching Domeno whirl Lacy Kennedy through the sawdust, around bales of hay stacked high with wire crab traps, kicking up wood shavings at every turn. He had held Lacy too tight beneath the fishing gear and trawl nets hanging from the rafters, dancing her closer to the barn doors. Lacy went outside with him. He'd pressed her against the barn, his hands dragging her in dangerously close.

Lacy broke away and went back inside, leaving him mumbling. He took a pee next to an old pickup. Kitty walked up behind him, standing as close as her thundering heart would allow, anger flowing off her like a heat wave. He shoved himself back in his pants and zipping up, he turned into her, almost knocking her down.

She hit him in the chest with her fist and screamed at him, her voice somewhere between a whine and a snarl. She hadn't wanted to cry, didn't want him to see her cry. As she swiped at her tears with a trembling palm, he'd given a shrug, as if her feelings were unimportant, and chuckled, a deep sound that weakened her knees, and he walked away.

Later that night, she took her mama's scissors to that ugly dress.

36

Arcie was still a little dizzy with the excitement and heavy adrenaline rush that overcame her with greeting Lacy, but now she was coming down from that high, and she was pissed. Lacy seemed uncomfortable, ambivalent about being with them, and as unhappy about the reunion as Kitty. It was a bitter disappointment. Lacy wasn't the person she'd thought she would be, so stiff and cold when she hugged her, like an ice cube melting against Arcie's skin. Sure it had been a long time, sure, they were never as close as Lacy and Kitty, she understood that, but still . . . .

She hadn't known exactly what to expect, but she'd expected more enthusiasm, a nicer, friendlier person; she definitely had. Now she was as disappointed and upset with Lacy as she was with Kitty.

Kitty's stinky attitude made things worse. She was downright surly, even toward Lacy. No reason for it, except Kitty had been angry when Lacy disappeared, so maybe she was still angry at her. Kitty was selfish and hurt people's feelings. She wanted to tell her that, but she didn't; just kept her mouth shut, teeth clamped together so tight her jaw began to ache.

This was definitely not what she had anticipated and now she was losing focus. The effort to keep her thoughts straight was almost painful. She could feel the black funk poking its head out of its hiding place, snickering at her. Her palms sticky with sweat, her stomach flipping over itself, there was a burning, like a bad case of indigestion, high up under her breast-bone, and a sour taste in the back of her throat. For a minute she thought she might have to pull over and throw up.

She had figured on handling Kitty, but not Lacy. Not both of them at the same time. Too late now, not so important. It was two against one, but she wouldn't let them fill her with doubt about this situation; she wouldn't let them win this. She needed to focus remain calm—*Concentrate! Concentrate, Arcie!* She would do it, and try not to think about the number of pills it might take to keep her calm and focused. She had to figure out the best way to handle this because she could feel it—things were going to get worse.

Yep, they are, black funk said.

They were going to gang up on her, she knew it.

Yep, they are, black funk said again.

37

It was after midnight.

The sky was filled with star-tinsel and a slender, quarter-moon crescent. The first cold spell of winter had descended with frosty air.

He trudged through the ghostly gray-white mist rising over the bayou, snugged tight by the early morning chill. He pulled his flannel jacket's collar up under his ears and hitched the 30.06 rifle up higher on his shoulder. The steadily dropping temperature made him curse for not having worn heavier clothing. In the heat of anger, he had felt it would slow him down. He wanted to be able to move fast. He had anticipated a short track. Just kill the bastard with a single shot. He had underestimated its cunning and stamina. It had outsmarted him. It seemed to have known all along he was tracking, seemed to like the thrill, got off on the rush of the chase.

He heard a whisper of sound, nothing more.

The animal was a blur until it struck him solidly in the chest, placing him spread-eagle on his back in the oozing swamp grasses. The 30.06 slid over an outcropping of mud and weeds, almost falling into the bayou. By the time he'd found his feet, recovered his senses and the rifle, the bastard was gone; nothing but moon, cold wind, and trees in the night.

It was playing with him.

His eyes strained for movement. There was none. He began tracking again, agitated, his clothing soggy, his nostrils filled with animal foulness and the sour odor that emanated from the swamp. He was furious, more determined than ever to kill it.

The animal doubled back twice. The hours of tracking made him jittery. He was moving more slowly, feeling the hunger pangs deep in his stomach. Three times he'd caught a glimpse of it, gigantic, shadow-dark and fog-shrouded, but it moved too swiftly for him to get a shot. It was intelligent, in its prime, its belly filled with meat, and its movements slow and calculated, almost lazy, filled with patience.

He kept moving, breath frosting the air, fingers growing stiff with the cold, pissed with himself as much as the animal smart enough to evade him. There was a chill from his neck to his ass where his wet clothing hugged him. There was a blister on the heel of his left foot where he'd never mended the hole in his sock. A whisper of dampness crept through his boots to wrap his toes until they throbbed with each step. His stomach complained again and he cursed aloud, his temples pulsing relentlessly with impatient and angry thoughts.

The bastard might be running him in circles, but he was going to end it tonight. Tonight that son of a whoring bitch was going to be his. He was tired of people jumping up his ass over chickens and ducks gone missing, a hound, a pig, a cow, a sheep with a throat ripped out and a belly emptied of innards.

Until the child was killed.

It was one damn animal . . . with a taste for human flesh.

A damn *big* animal, species of undetermined origins, no one had seen. People weren't sure what it was, were terrified, locking themselves and their families in their homes before dark. They watched their children more closely, and whispered behind bolted windows and doors . . . *devil-dog!*

Now they whispered something worse—*diable. Evil spirit.* And he thought: *How the hell does anyone fight something like that?*

He had lived here most of his life, knew all the superstitions, and had heard all the tales. A smart man was suspicious of and questioned what he couldn't see, but didn't always believe what he heard. He didn't believe in spirits or a huge crossbreed feral dog, even before the first partial print was discovered. Even if it looked canine. From the beginning, he had thought outsized, much larger, and wondered where the bastard came from, what it really was. Large predatory animals weren't native in the backwater. A hunter passing through had mentioned a pair of big gray wolves, but they were farther north, near the Louisiana-Arkansas border. He'd heard about, but never seen black bears, cougars, and coyotes. He felt whatever it was had been brought in from someplace else and turned loose; some sort of bastardized hybrid someone had as a pet until they couldn't handle it as an adult. Sometimes people were just crazy, breeding two species to produce something bigger and different, for attention and money, never considering the consequences.

But there was something different about this animal. It seemed smart beyond natural instinct. It had appeared abruptly, crafty, capable and strong. Wild game and livestock were plentiful, yet it switched from animal kills to human almost immediately. It left no signs, except ravaged flesh and, if it had rained and they were lucky, a peculiar partial print or two in the soggy earth. Huge prints, two times wider than an adult man's hand. He agreed it was extraordinary, but he still refused to believe it was anything more than a monstrously large predator that had claimed his town as its territory. He just had to be smarter and quicker.

With the death of the boy, he had decided to listen more closely to the old people's whispers— whispers that said it was a haunt, unnatural and evil, that no one could kill. He didn't believe in the supernatural. It could be killed—and he was going to be the one to prove them wrong and kill the damn thing.

A deep rumbling snarl echoed in the quiet.

A brief flash of gunmetal-silver as twin beacons

launched toward him. The ground squished like quicksand under the heels of his boots. He stumbled and fell back. The furry torpedo lunged straight at his face, dislodging the gun from his hands. He had no idea where it landed. The cold early morning seemed to magnify the smallest sound, now filled with bottomless, deep-chest snarls, a heart-stopping threat. He rolled away, caught a glimpse of his huge attacker through the white steam rising from the disturbed grasses and mud.

He rolled again, his fingers grabbing at everything in search of his rifle.

He wasn't quick enough.

For only a second, he saw the entire creature for the first time as the full weight of it took him to the ground. A stream of fear jetted through his body as fangs sank into his shoulder. Fabric and flesh tore away, as pain and shock stole his breath. His nostrils filled with a cloying stench, hot and mephitic. The animal straddled him, solid, wet and foul, mockery in those huge, wild eyes.

His shoulder blazed with fire lancing to the bone. Blood ran freely inside his clothes. Fetid breath steamed in his face and red-amber eyes flashed as thick strands of bloody saliva dripped from a huge, gaping muzzle. Its hackles raised along its crest, like the long feathers in a peacock's tail, thick and silvery-black. Scratchy pads and sharp toenails broke his skin as a massive paw raked hard down the side of his face and neck. Bile rose up the back of his throat as the fangs descended again . . . . .

. . . and Domeno Abadie rolled off the bed and banged his temple against the nightstand, the familiar scream still lodged in his throat.

He slowly sat up, pushing himself against the bed frame, wiping sweat from his face with the heels of his hands. He had been having the same dream with such frequency for such a long time, he knew it well. Images that came in his sleep, he had trouble dealing with during waking hours. It made him hate the thought of sleep. Sometimes the horror visiting him in those dreams was almost too difficult to cope with. He sometimes thought offing himself would be best but had never reached that point. Instead, he had started measuring the amount of time he allotted to sleep, knowing the dream would return if he slept too deeply. He formed the habit to sleep only when exhausted, a couple of hours at a time, usually during the late morning or early afternoon. And each time he closed his eyes, he prayed to a God he wasn't sure existed—prayed and begged—to undo what happened and keep him from dreaming. But it never happened. He knew it was real, always dreamed, and when he came awake, the dream mercifully fading, all he could think of was revenge.

His pulse quickened to a rapid tapping. He rubbed at his shoulder. The stinging, fiery sensation passed through him until it flooded his entire left side, swept down his leg, stopped with a tingling thud that curled the toes on his foot. Domeno glanced at the bedside clock. Little more than an hour's sleep left him irritable and tired.

Domeno's thoughts fastened on what he missed: the love of his old dog. The dog had chosen to live away from him, inside the lopsided building that had once been the gas station. The sign that had fallen from the roof was leaning to the left of the opening, leaving it barely wide enough to admit a car; threadbare tires nearly blocking the entrance. Inside was dark and damp, even on sunny days, and as he lay shivering, the animal still offered a fight challenge he knew he could never win. Like his almost toothless mouth, his snarls and growls were no longer a threat.

The dog was very thin, sick and starving, with rheumy eyes, protruding ribs, and hairless, bony hindquarters that wobbled when he walked. He seemed to have accepted the reprieve of death and waited for it. Domeno left food, but the dog snarled until he walked away. He stopped eating what Domeno left. He figured the dog could smell a scent he carried, the underlying odor so strong it clung to everything he touched. Whether through fear or no tolerance of him, the dog was having none of it.

Domeno got his feet under him, his body tense, all his senses pulsing and agitated. He flexed his shoulder, rubbing until most of the pain had eased. Disgusted with his damaged flesh, he despised the bitch that had done this to him more each day.

Yancy had stolen everything important in his life. She'd always seemed to have an inability to understand the suffering she imposed on others. He wanted her to die. He wanted so badly to kill her, had planned to kill her. He had plotted it, dreamed of it for days . . . but, given the opportunity, he couldn't do it. He had only left her with a reminder he could have easily taken her life, and hoping she could no longer execute her spells. He had wanted her to know he could be cruel, but he still was and always would be, more human than she ever was.

Each time he touched anything that had belonged to Tansie, he drowned himself in his loss. each time he ran his fingers over the collection of tiny clothes she'd lovingly sewn for their baby, he thought of what had been taken from him. Each day when he looked at his reflection in the mirror and fingered his scarred body, he recognized the shadow of hatred in his eyes and thought he would be physically sick. Each time a shift tore his body apart and turned him into something hideous, he despised himself a little more for the weakness that hadn't allowed him to kill her. Suffering through lapses of memory, waiting for their return, feeling a deep sense of loss after he realized some memories never made it back, he tried to figure out which ones got lost. The ones he recovered, he saved, scrunching them together until the empty spaces were filled so he wouldn't be bothered as much by the missing ones.

Occasionally, he would be surprised by one popping back. It was part of the horror he'd learned he had to accept. There could be no going back.

38

The infatuation fling with Lacy was short-lived, but the damage was done, and it had definitely put a big kink in their friendship. Domeno moved on in less than a month to the daughter of the diner owner. If Lacy sensed Kitty's anger and the betrayal she felt, the other girl never let on. If Domeno had hurt Lacy, she was stoic enough to never show it. Maybe it had been only a moment of flirtation on her part and she'd been using him as much as he used her. Kitty knew she should have forgiven Lacy. If she hadn't loved Domeno with such faulty proprietorship, she probably would have.

None of it matters anymore, she thought. It was childish then, immature now, to fixate on any of it. It had been damn foolish to blame Lacy for the loss of what she'd wanted most at fifteen.

Somewhere after Destrehan, when Kitty still hadn't spoken a word to either of them, she realized her resentment was not as much over Domeno as over Lacy having left without saying a word. Unable to keep her thoughts to herself any longer, Kitty demanded, "What happened to you?" breaking the silence that had gone on too long.

Lacy started, turn in the seat, and pinned Kitty with her eyes. "Excuse me?"

"You heard me."

Lacy flinched, surprise reflected in her eyes, then looked away. Arcie glanced from one to the other, reached up and adjusted the rearview mirror. She stared hard at Kitty with the look of an adult scowling at a disobedient child.

A touch of color darkened Lacy's cheeks. "I did, but I'm not sure what you mean. I wrote—"

"Yeah, sure, you wrote a miserable little note . . . then nothing!" Kitty sat up, chest swelled with the return of her initial hurt. Her attack might be un-reasonable—Lacy probably thought she was a raving lunatic—but this woman had been her best friend and she had unanswered questions. Maybe it wasn't the appropriate time, but she had endured years of silence. She had let the current silence last as long as she could, so if she pissed Arcie off and made Lacy uncomfortable, screw it. She wanted to let go of all the old crap that no longer mattered. "You just dis-appeared! What kind of friend does that? You could have been dead. Your mother lied. She knew the entire time where you were."

"Kitty—" Arcie admonished, staring at her in the rearview mirror.

"Kitty, what?" she snapped.

"No, you're right, I did disappear." Lacy cleared her throat, the flush receding; an uneasy expression had settled in its place. "I met someone and started a new life. I was a kid and he was an adult. I was afraid it would cause trouble. I apologize."

"I'm not asking about that rich dead guy."

Lacy's eyes bored into Kitty. "You know about him?"

"Of course we do."

"I found an article in the *Times-Picayune,*" Arcie admitted, and Lacy's eyes flickered toward her. Arcie wouldn't look at her. "Your name was mentioned."

"Mentioned how?"

"That you were his fiancée."

"Now you can fill in everything else," Kitty said.

"She might not want to talk about it," Arcie said.

"She can tell me that herself."

Arcie stiffened, palms sweating against the steering wheel, fingers tightening until her knuckles resembled small white knobs against the black leather.

"Please . . . don't fight," Lacy said. "I've put my past behind me, Kitty. It was never my intent to come back here and talk about it."

You had to know someone would ask."

Lacy shrugged. "I didn't give it much thought."

"So why did you come back?"

"Not because I wanted to."

"What exactly does that mean?" Kitty asked.

"I felt I didn't have a choice."

"You sound like Arcie! Of course, you had a choice, you could have refused."

"It didn't feel that way. Arcie made it sound like I couldn't."

"Why?" Kitty stared at a silent, sullen Arcie.

"I don't know, I suppose it could have been my imagination," Lacy said.

"You realize how crazy that sounds?"

"I do." Lacy nodded. "Yes, I certainly do."

Everything sounded like not quite a lie but not quite the truth. Kitty waved a dismissive hand. "Okay, I get it. You didn't want me to know before, you don't want me to know now. Forget I asked." She was so damn tired. She thought how pleasant it would be without the arguments and lies. She slid back down into the seat.

As silence again filled the Mercedes and eventually the repetitious tire slap against asphalt soothed her, Kitty found herself lulled into a restless and troubled sleep.

39

A glint of pale moonlight on water . . . a thin mist, lazily shifting and swirling through a dense growth of trees . . . pale angles and indistinct lines materializing, a disembodied globe turning into a terrified female face, beseeching eyes filled with fear.

Something else lingered in the mist, something waiting— something huge and dark, a glimmer of silver, a shimmer of red.

The woman's eyes swam with terror, lips twisted in a scream. An arcing spray of scarlet . . . .

. . . and Creely jerked awake so abruptly the back of his skull banged sharply against the heavy headboard. He was momentarily stunned; a flash of pain exploded behind his eyes. His breath clogged far down in his throat, blood roaring inside his head. Darkness surrounded him, and it took a minute to remember where he was. He sucked in a mouthful of air and reached out, fumbling for the lamp switch. Light slashed through the bedroom, bright and intrusive. His tee shirt drenched, jockey shorts plastered against his skin, he thought someone had doused him with water. He glanced at the clock on the night table he had been asleep damn near three hours. He had lain down to rest and think about everything that was happening. He remembered closing his eyes but not falling asleep . . . and he'd had another vision.

Creely swung his legs over the side of the bed and hunched over, placing his face in his hands. He hadn't gotten a clear picture of her face, only a slice of it. The woman was a stranger to him, but his gut told him she was connected to Kitty. Who was she? Was she dead? He was positive she was, or was going to be, soon.

The telephone shrilled, startling him. He jerked upright and his heart made a double somersault and landed heavily inside his chest.

"Hullo," he croaked, jamming the receiver against his ear.

"Creely?"

"Yeah."

"Sounds like you're dying," Impastato said.

"Fell asleep."

"I tried your cell three times."

Creely snatched up his cell. Three missed calls. Still nothing from Kitty.

"Cell was on vibrate. What you got?"

"A bad afternoon."

"What happened?"

"Three nutzoid fags cut the bloody hell out of each other with knives."

Creely ignored the slur, immediately thinking of

his brother and the shady characters in his past. Carson had managed to get by unscathed until age and a successful business found him part of a different crowd and more discriminating in his choice of companions. Less high-risk lifestyle now, but it could still happen. The world was full of crazies. "Are they all dead?"

"Two are sushi, The third resisted arrest. He's in ICU on the short list."

"Don't need another worry right now, Sal."

"You think I don't think about him every time shit like that goes down? He was always a sweet kid."

"He's a good man, he's just following a different drummer. That doesn't make him less, just different. Could have easily been two guys over a woman." Impastato didn't reply and Creely added, "I had another vision." He peeled off his wet underwear and kicked it away.

"Same?"

"No, but they're related. I feel it. What you got?"

"Not much. Born Katine Bejou Chauvin in French Gap, Louisiana, December 12, 1977. Parents were Freddie and Jennet Chauvin, fisherman and housewife. Father is deceased, found dead in a local pond in '95, whereabouts of the mother unknown since '98. Mmust have changed her name, remarried, something. DMV didn't turn up a license or a registered vehicle. Social Security doesn't show an employment history, no wages reported, no income tax records with her name, no death certificate. Kitty has no siblings, never married, no kids. She's been in New Orleans since around seventeen or eighteen. Was a stripper for a couple of years, got discovered by some rich artsy guy who made her artwork popular. French Gap's a tiny place, deep in Terrebonne Parish. Somewhere off a little strip of bayou that doesn't seem to have a name. Never more than a fishing camp on good days. Why would she up and go back there?"

"No idea, but I feel it's connected with whatever was bothering her last night."

"You can't be sure that's where she's at."

"No, but my gut tells me it's a good possibility."

"Best of luck with it."

"I never heard of this place before."

"You, me and ninety-eight percent of the Louisiana population. It has been on a downhill slide for years. No info or directions on the internet. Hard find on what we got. Town sort of evaporated. It's kinda like the place just isn't there anymore."

"But probably still is."

"Weirder things have happened."

"What else?"

"Mostly trappers and fishermen, some employed with a pulp mill or seafood canning plant about twenty miles down the road. Those closed down years ago. Things got rezoned. Utility and postal services discontinued. That's probably why she left. She's got a successful life here. I can't imagine she'd want to go back unless it's for her mother." Impastato paused to clear his throat. A slurping noise followed; he was sucking up something through a straw.

"I need to find out. How do I get there?"

"You got feathers?" A touch of rare Impastato humor.

"A little short on feathers, Sal." He wasn't interested in humor.

After one of his infamous silences, Impastato said, "Car or seaplane. A boat. maybe, if you can find a cooperative body that knows their way around down there. You get lost in one of those fuckin' little swamp holes, you'll lose more than your plumbing to an unfriendly gator. Still determined to go?"

"I am."

Another throat clearing. "This place is unbelievably remote, Creely. It's buried in the swamp, somewhere inside dozens of little bayous. You got three choices. One: a plane into Houma-Terrebonne airport, and rent a car. Two: seaplane drop, rent a car. Three: drive that hot Porsche of yours. It might take longer, but it's safer. You won't be assured of gas. Keep a full tank. Take Highway 90 into Houma, keep going south. After that, you're on your own. Make frequent stops, ask directions of any friendly face." Impastato heaved up a sigh. "Oh, hell, this is fuckin' crazy! You don't really know she went there. You don't have anything to go on."

"Just a hunch and my fabulous psychic powers." A snip of sarcasm.

"Try common sense. You don't know she's there. She could've left town on business."

"She leaves a message for business."

"Does she leave one if she's with another man?"

"Starting to get pissed now, Sal."

"If you find this place, you have no idea what you'll find there. Better pissed than dead." Impastato didn't press the issue, just added: "A day there and back, if you get lucky. You might not even find the place. You know very little about her past, Creely, not everything about her present. She wasn't more than a kid when you met her. She's been in the city for a long time. Why go back now, when there isn't a lot to go back to?" Impastato stopped talking, as if he had run out of breath.

"That vision I mentioned?"

"Yeah, what about it?"

"A woman I didn't recognize was killed by something. If she's connected to Kitty, I don't want to see that happen to Kitty."

"What's that mean, 'by something'?"

"I couldn't see. It was too dark."

"But you're positive they're connected?"

"Yes."

"If someone got killed, I should notify the state police. Officially request they send a couple troopers to check it out. Say you're on your way. Maybe get you better info. You aren't going to a vacation resort, Creely. No phones, spotty cellular, if any. Help will be hard to come by if you're in need."

"They probably won't like it."

"Fuck that, cops are duty-bound to check."

Creely was silent for a minute, then said, "Let's do this my way."

"Your way makes me nervous."

"Appreciate the concern, but you don't believe me, Sal, why should they?"

"They don't have to believe you. It's their job. They know more about the area."

"Thanks anyway."

They lapsed into a strained silence. Sal was probably mulling over something he wanted to voice, Creely figured he knew what it was.

"You're sure about Mackey?"

"I'll call her before I leave." Knowing it was a lie.

"Generous of you."

Creely felt his pulse race, a flash of anger sparked heat in his neck. "I told you, I can handle it. I have too many people poking their nose in my business. I don't like it much."

"Yeah, well—" Impastato coughed up an audible sigh—"hate to see you be a toilet flush like yesterday's lunch."

"I get it."

"Truth is the truth. Sometimes it hurts."

"You've made your point." It wasn't right to be angry with Sal, but he was.

An awkward pause had developed between them.

Impastato finally spoke, his voice gruff, "Don't be a hero, Creely. Be cautious. I'd watch my ass if I were you. Some bayou folks have an unhealthy reputation. Unfriendly. They don't like strangers. People disappear in those swamps."

"You forget I have a generous helping of Cajun blood."

"Cajun and bayou are not always interchangeable."

"I'll remember that." Then, very quietly, "I really am sane, you know."

"Don't doubt your sanity," Impastato replied, voice somber. "Just your motive."

"And that means what?"

"That the lady in question is more than an occasional piece of ass. You're a lot more than just liking her. You could seriously fuck up your future."

Creely against felt a curl of anger, but before he could speak, Impastato hung up.

40

The Past

The ground was thickly covered with pine and magnolia that stunned the air with fragrance; the inky sky frosted with stars. The moon, pale and sheer behind the branches of live oak, seemed to give off a transparent ghostly aura, the night kissed by a chilled wind murmur as it shuffled through the treetops. Wood snapped and popped in the heart of the fire, the wavering flames brilliant against the dark.

As Domeno swam back toward consciousness, the penetrating heat blazed through his body, bore into his skin. All his senses were unaccountably dulled. His thoughts felt hazy, his body paralyzed. Heavy sweat covered him, making his skin slippery. He tried to lift his eyelids; they wouldn't respond. He knew he had been drinking, though he might have gotten disgustingly drunk again, somehow that didn't seem quite right. He'd been drunk too many times before; this wasn't the aftereffects of alcohol. This felt different. This was something stronger.

Confusion washed away, disbelief followed by an incredible surge of anger.

Gris-gris, he thought, the sluggish link between mind and body connecting.

He tried to turn over, couldn't. He tried to force open his eyes, but he only managed slits, just enough to recognize the figure as it passed across his line of vision.

Yancy was building a higher flame on the fire, pausing every so often to sniff the air. She stopped and cocked her head, listening, snuffling, listening again, as if the swamp whispered a melancholy language only she understood.

Domeno lay frozen in the flickering firelight, his skin a burning torment, his nostrils filled with a peculiar odor. She'd used her voodoo ointments on him, their strange perfumes releasing as his skin grew hot and slick from the fire.

She'd outmaneuvered him again. He commanded himself to sit up, his gut twisting with disgust and rage. His body didn't respond. He tried to scream his outrage, but his voice made only a whisper of wind in his throat. There was no denying it, he was afraid of her, hating himself for that weakness.

Yancy sensed he'd partially awakened. She could smell his fear in the strong pulse of his blood, the musky stench of his body odor overlaid by the opium of the ointments. She watched him, her eyes bright and birdlike as they moved down his length, from face to ragged scar to flaccid sex. She ran two fingers over him, slowly, from throat to groin, then brought them up and stuck them in her mouth, tasting him.

She turned away and he could see the fine coating of sable and silver hair shadowing her cheek and neck, along with her shoulders and down her spine. At some point, her beast had surfaced and not completely retreated. Or maybe it was the opposite, her shift was trying to come and hadn't yet.

He felt only numbness, but some part of him must have stirred. She sprang away, eyes wary, filled with flickers of scarlet, a pronounced tautness around her lips. He recognized the sharp, painful ghost of hunger swirling behind the red. Basic animal need surfaced; she was struggling with instinct. She hadn't fed recently, and the appetite of her beast was crawling through her.

Fear jetted along his spine. He moaned, tried to curl his unresponsive fingers, his fight instinct trying to kick in. She was doing it again, taking him against his will.

She smiled at him.

Mon Dieu! Domeno thought. *This time, she wants me to know she can do this to me!*

He'd watched the progress of her pregnancy. For months she had that huge belly; when next he saw her, her stomach was flat. She'd had the baby, but something wasn't right. She never tried to show him the baby. He continued vigilant watch for signs of a baby, listening for cries, some telling sound . . . *some-thing* . . . but when there was nothing, he knew without a doubt the baby was dead. Something had happened. A strange stirring troubled him for a couple of days, like a vague paternal tie tinged with anger. Later, he decided whatever happened was for the best.

Was this another attempt at pregnancy? Or was it simply a sexual urge? How many times had she done this that he hadn't awakened and couldn't remember? *Mon Dieu!* He had no way of knowing; it could have been dozens. Drugged and raped, he might not have come awake. It sickened him to there might have been countless times.

He had always heard a man couldn't be raped. They didn't know what they were talking about, the people that said such a thing. They didn't know the power of voodoo and the witch that controlled it. Now she was doing it again, and this time the application of ointments weren't as strong; she wanted him to *know*.

Since the attack when he tracked her before he knew what she was—it would have been better had she killed him that night—he had started drinking himself into stupors that took days from which to recover. And now . . . *this*—*again?*

Domeno managed to curl his index fingers. Stabs of pain bit the knuckle joints as his skin tightened and his flesh pulled taut against bone. She had doped him inside and out. Ointment lay in his mouth, heavy on his tongue. He could taste it. A thick grainy substance, slightly salty, like lard mixed with sand or soil, or maybe the hard grit of crushed oyster shell. Tongue glued to palate, he tried to swallow, but it took great effort.

Yancy squatted beside him. He saw the dark triangle guarding her genitals, a long thick slit spreading outward toward her thighs . . . and her sexual scent overpowered him. She ran her hands up and down his body, her mouth hanging open, her face twisted with primal desire, both animal and human.

He'd underestimated her again. He had made another mistake. Why hadn't his attack upon her been a strong enough deterrent? She seemed to have total disregard for injury. His brutality seemed to have only enhanced her desire. It would have been better for both of them if he'd been able to kill her . . . or, when he failed with her, killed himself.

Domeno tried to pull away from her touch, struggled to move his frozen muscles. His body betrayed him, responding to her touch and scent, blood hot, pulse heightened. Fear rocketed from his head and slammed into the soles of his feet, bending his toes. He didn't want to look at her, tried to turn his face away. His organ filled with raw sexual need, he couldn't take his agonized eyes off her. He groaned, filled with revulsion. *An erection! Doux Jesus, he had an erection!*

Her fingers encircled and began to work him, coaxing him into an incredible granite hardness that allowed her to mount him. The air suddenly filled with a blur of noise, not moans or scream, just scraps of sound he took to be her pleasure.

Fighting against his arousal, he was able to think of nothing else. He was so hard; the powerful surges of his heart, the blazing heat in his balls as they drew up tight. He could see the eager human brightness in her eyes, as well as the hard, black animal shine shadowed with scarlet. The animal part of him was responding to her, and for a moment, he lost himself in those eyes.

Mon Dieu! Help me! Domeno thought as he squeezed his eyes tightly shut. His muscles corded as she rose up a few inches and turned her back to him, sliding down over his engorged organ again, seeking a deeper purchase. Her buttocks pumped hard up and down. Her wetness surrounded him as her whole body seemed to be sucking at him through his cock. The opening and closing of her sex around his shaft stimulated him to and over the edge as he responded to the base and primitive violence of sexual need, thinking himself as much an animal like her. His orgasm burst from him, coming from some deep bottomless dark. It poured into her, wet glue that seemed to fuse them together. His testicles turned to stones drawn up right against his body as she continued to ride him, muscle movement squeezing every drop of his essence.

When she finished, she didn't move off. She just stopped, making a careful turn to face him. Head threw back, eyes closed, she sat him as a rider on a horse, her palms flattened and pressed against his chest, her thighs tight against his ribcage, her heels sharply jabbed against his hip bones.

He felt crushed by the weight of his orgasm, the heady overpowering scent of their sex, and the exertion of it all had snatched his breath away. He couldn't seem to pull enough oxygen inside his lungs. He struggled again to move, couldn't, listened to the frantic screams of outrage that raced through the tormented depths of his mind.

She opened her eyes, leaned forward and watched him, her elbows digging hard into his chest. He watched her: the quiver of her nostrils, the part and tremble of her lips, the pleasure and satisfaction mirrored by moonlight in her expression.

Domeno closed his eyes, waiting for his cock to wilt and drop out of her, praying it would be over soon.

41

The car tires rolled over the gas pump's rubber bell cord as Arcie pulled the Mercedes into a mini-mart. Kitty came groggily awake, with cramped muscles and a full bladder. She untwisted her body and followed Lacy inside, leaving Arcie to pump and pay. When Kitty came out of the restroom, Lacy was holding a brown paper bag and a six-pack of canned Cokes. As they pulled away from the station, she passed out bags of greasy cracklins and drinks.

They ate in silence, Arcie occasionally frowning at Kitty in the rearview mirror. After Lacy crumpled her cracklin bag, she was the first to speak.

"I'd forgotten how much I enjoyed those things. No place make cracklins like the little stores in the deep South," she said. "I'm sorry if I've caused any problems between the two of you."

"You haven't," Arcie said quickly.

"I guess I'm confused about what's going on."

"Why don't you tell her, Arcie?" Kitty snapped.

When Arcie didn't respond, Lacy said, "What's going on here, Kitty?"

"I'd rather go to hell than go back to French Gap—"Kitty tapped the side of her head with the heel of her hand—"Oops! Seems it's slipped my mind, hasn't it, Arcie? French Gap always was hell!"

Lacy looked at Arcie; she felt trapped, disliking. her behavior more every minute. Arcie refused to look at her. "I'm not happy about this either, Kitty. It isn't pleasant being forced into doing this."

"*Forced?* Y-you—you weren't forced!" Arcie sputtered. Her voice came out a squeak as if someone had stepped on her throat.

"It feels that way."

"She keeps insisting we all have to be together again," Kitty interrupted.

Lacy nodded. "That was sort of the way she put it to me." She looked at Arcie again. "Why is this so important, Arcie?"

"Yancy said . . . she said we should keep our promise to come back."

"And you felt you had to do exactly what Yancy said?" Lacy asked. Arcie's eyes flickered quickly to Lacy, then back to the highway, and she didn't speak. "Being conscientious is admirable, but it doesn't always mean it's right, Arcie. I never expected to keep that promise."

Kitty hadn't meant to keep it either. Why had she given in so easily? Her mind felt itchy thinking about the Arceneauxs. Had Yancy forced them back with a spell of some sort? Was she capable of that? Had she inherited the family traits of being able to practice voodoo? Was she capable of using spells to force people to do things against their will?

"There might be something more at work."

"Meaning what?" Lacy asked.

"Remembering stuff. Just a thought."

"Some kind of spell?"

Kitty nodded slowly. "Maybe."

"You're a believer?"

"I just remembered some things she did."

"I always thought it kid stuff. You actually believe she can do something like that?" Lacy asked.

Kitty shrugged. "It's possible. All those old stories about her family could have been true."

"From so far away?"

"Distance probably doesn't matter in a spell."

"You don't know what you're talking about," Arcie protested.

"Maybe not, but it's something to think about," Kitty snapped, never doubting Arcie knew more than she was telling.

"I'm not comfortable with this, Kitty. Thinking about Yancy putting a spell on us—even considering it's possible she *could* and *would* do that—it scares the hell out of me. Why would she do that?" Lacy said.

"She wanted to have control over us."

Lacy nodded. "I guess she felt we wouldn't come back on our own."

"That's my thinking. If we had wanted to come back, we would have already done it."

"This silly reunion couldn't mean that much."

"Arcie seems to think so," Kitty replied.

Lacy looked at Arcie. "Have we been forced back? Is she capable of that—a *spell*—to control us?"

Arcie didn't answer.

"Arcie thinks she's been waiting for something," Kitty said as if Arcie wasn't there.

Lacy frowned. "Waiting for what?"

"Arcie thinks it might be us."

"*Us?* Why?"

"To make sure we keep our promise. She just waited for the twenty years to be up, I guess."

"Why do you think she would worry so much about that?"

Kitty shrugged. "I don't know, but I think we might be stepping into a big pile of poop by coming back here." Kitty saw Arcie wince, her face flaming red, but Arcie said nothing.

Lacy shook her head slowly. "I wanted French Gap to stay in my past."

"You got that right."

Arcie felt dizzy, felt a tongue of nausea curl in her belly. *You're sitting right here! They're talking about you, over you, around you, as if you're not here!* that nasty little voice inside her head cried out. "You shouldn't have come!" she raged. "Neither of you should have come!" And she wanted to staple her mouth shut. Why had she said that? It was a stupid thing to say. She felt so wretched, fighting against the funk, trying to keep it at bay and there it was, tormenting her.

Kitty struck the back of the front seat hard with her fist, startling Arcie enough to jerk forward. "Pull over! Turn around! Take us back—right now!"

"*No!*"

Kitty reached over the seat, but Lacy blocked her hands. It angered her to be placed in this position as if appointed to act as a mediator between them. "That's enough!" Her tone carried a flinty edge. "We need to stop acting like children. Maybe this has nothing to do with a spell. It might just be us, we were meant to be together again, one last time. Sort out the way things were left between us. Talk about things that should've been said years ago. Our friendship was not always good. I think we all know that. Maybe it's necessary to say that in person."

"Ghosts," Kitty whispered.

"What?"

"We all have ghosts we need to get rid of."

"Yeah, I think maybe we do." Lacy stared at Arcie. "You and Yancy need to understand, no matter how this arrangement came about, I will not return here, Arcie. Don't contact me again—*ever.* Consider me dead."

Arcie remained silent. She kept her eyes trained on the road. At that moment she wanted exactly that, death for both of them. She couldn't speak. Her mouth had gone dry. It felt as if someone had poured sand down her throat. She fought hard for control, to keep everything destructive in the back of her mind, but her rage had swept her from hot to glacial in seconds. She was rushing headlong toward the dark side, almost hopelessly ensnared in that deep black funky place she knew so well. When Lacy touched her shoulder, she jerked violently away.

"Whoa!" Lacy pulled back her hand as if threatened with a dog bite. "Why are you so angry?"

"My sentiments exactly," Kitty said, finding it easier to like Lacy again. Arcie probably thought Lacy would be more pliable. What was going to happen when Yancy was thrown into the mix?

Arcie felt heat scorch her face like a blow torch. She was so agitated, so mortified, and had no ready answer for Lacy's question. *See, I told you how it would be,* whispered the voice inside her head. They kept talking *about* her, not *to* her, as if she wasn't there. Her fingers flexed against the wheel, wishing it was Kitty's neck.

"Okay, *okay,* you've made your point!" she said, not exactly sure which of them she was talking to, and tossing Kitty a resentful look in the mirror. She was having serious trouble holding the black funk at bay, wondering if she can control it when it breaks loose because she knows it will, and when it does . . . .

Lacy said, "I'm thinking this is getting too weird. I thought this was just the two of you having a disagreement and I ended up in the middle. It's more than that, isn't it?" She waved her hand between them. "We shouldn't have done this. We don't know each other anymore."

Arcie said, "We can get to know each other."

"Maybe, but I doubt it. We aren't the same little girls." Lacy's voice was a little sad. "Why bother? I've always felt we never really liked each other in the first place."

"Felt that way myself at times," Kitty admitted.

Arcie said nothing.

The Mercedes seemed to suck in a deep breath as if closing itself tight around them. None of them spoke again. The clank of an old truck passing in the opposite direction briefly penetrated the silence. At some point, they exchanged asphalt for pot-holed, two-lane blacktop. Arcie's foot nudged the accelera-ator. The speedometer needle jumped up. The car swayed, bounced on its suspension, traveling way too fast.

"Slow down," Kitty warned, a nasty dip tipping her head against the roof.

Arcie ignored her.

"Slow the hell down, Arcie!"

The speedometer needle dropped to 50, settled on 35, and the silence in the car resumed.

42

Exhausted and wound tight as a spring, once again Kitty had drifted off to sleep sitting up, and she awoke suddenly, a nasty crick in her neck. She had found herself sliding in and out of a troublesome dream she couldn't quite catch the jest of. She listened to the rapid *swoosh* of tires, painfully aware of the strained silence.

Bayou landscape had almost magically appeared while she slept. Passing through the small populated areas, the Mercedes zipped past a Brown's Thrifty Drugs, a weathered Texaco station, a Danny's Fried Chicken with dubious pricing (Fried Gizzard and Liver Dinner $1.89). A curve brought a few houses and the crumbling, unpainted entrance arch of Morris Cemetery into view. A gravel semi-circle fronted a seedy motel painted orange.

And suddenly there was recognition, and she was flooded with steamers of memory.

The huge metal-and-wood structure set back from the road, one side caved in on itself, wooden chutes collapsed under rot: L.E. Wood's Slaughter House and Meat Market – Wholesale and Retail. Remembering the stockyards caused her nose to wrinkle up.

The rendering plant had been a nasty place when

she was a kid, the scent of blood, the screams of
death, but *Grandpere* had loved his meat. She got a
treat for riding with him every month, but she always
had to pinch her nose closed against the thick, raw
smell of blood and feces as she looked through the
slatted chutes at those huge, brown terrified eyes. She
had always been nervous around that giant man with
his blood-splashed apron as he loaded the wrapped
beef into the trunk of *Grandpere's* pink '57 Olds.

The silence inside the car buzzed against her
eardrums as they passed through Boudreaux, still not
talking. Arcie stopped the Mercedes next to one of
two gas pumps at B. Dillon's Gas Stop, where Kitty's
grandfather had always gassed up the Olds, brought
her a glass-bottled Coke and a Hershey bar with
almonds on their way home. Same name, but a mod-
ernized convenience store now, a Shell logo on the
pumps, but the same pitted and rusty Phillips 66
shield hinged to the roof.

The old two-lane state road ditched down into a
rough, single-lane blacktop and finally into oyster
shell, running down the middle of wide, deep, cattail-
filled ditches, green water thick with lily pads.

Kitty remembered this godforsaken area, what it
was like to be a young girl with fear and desperate
want in her eyes. The sameness of unpainted wooden
houses where bright window curtains or a bed of
flowers and a twisted chinaberry tree, a malnourished

old hound and a few scrawny chickens in a weed-choked yard made a subtle difference.

Different from the Arceneaux house.

A big, plantation-style house, built by slaves in the 1800s, sold to Grandfather Arceneaux for a dime on the dollar by the owner's wife before she left town after her husband's death. It was inherited by Grandmother Arceneaux after the old man died when Yancy was an infant. It sat commandingly by itself off in the distance, close to a deep curve in the bayou, shaded by massive live oaks and magnolias. It was a big, lofty, stilted house, with a narrow-railed gallery covered in weeds that had flourished into vines from lack of upkeep. Up high, under the tin roof, were birds' nests over boards turned the rusted color of old dried blood. Down lower, the weather-bleached wood glowing with mildew where swamp water rose at certain times of the year, intertwined shade and sun always forming intricate spider web patterns.

Talk about the Arceneaux family always revolved around their strange powers, the old woman a little *fou* and Yancy's mama a juju woman and a *putain*. Not the town whore—Arcie's mama had been a whore, too—but Euphrasine was a white man's whore. It was said she never went with men of her own race. Maybe she didn't like them, but most likely none of them could afford her. No one trusted the Arceneauxs, most were frightened of them, but they all—men and women alike—eventually went to them for charms and spells and sex. Some dared to whisper Euphrasine was *bete comme une oie*—crazy as a goose—and all were always careful to never anger her, scared of what might happen if they did.

Family members talked openly about the Arceneauxs over meals, brave enough to say things in their own home they wouldn't say in public. Kids learned a lot around the dinner table, but they always gleaned more from the old men grouped together on porches as soft gray light speared around the dark-green edges of coulees and a blush crept through the skyline, shades of sepia tinted the water and boards creaked under the pressure of cane rockers, the glow of old men's cigarettes shining as lightning bugs in the twilight.

The old woman Arceneaux died mysteriously one night, not a mark on her body, found a few yards from the front of the church she'd never entered in her life. When the sheriff delivered the news, Euphrasine spit on his shoe and closed the door in his face. There was never any proof, she could've died naturally, but most town folks figured Euphrasine had *mettre un conjo*, put a curse on her, over a disagreement.

No one wanted to touch her body. A parish priest was called in to help bury her outside the churchyard cemetery. There was never a headstone, never a cross, only a wooden post that eventually fell down. When more than a year passed without trouble, and the area overgrew with weeds, most folks sighed with relief . . . and figured she was one less dangerous *fou* to worry about. Less superstitious folk guessed it was just the cycle of things, part of the way things were supposed to be, like when someone got careless and a gator got him, or a fish finned a man and he lost his hand to gangrene, or a hurricane came through and the weather went *fou*, destroying everything. Eventually, the mystery of her death became like most everything else: a story that changed with the teller, a crazy tale, imperfect history, part of how legends were made.

43

Lacy seemed content to not talk anymore and stared out the passenger side window. Arcie had adjusted the rearview mirror so she could watch Kitty sleeping. She stared at her and tried to swallow the anger that rose up, but the more she watched, the angrier she got. Her chest swelled tight, her mind clouded with nasty funk. When Kitty awoke and noticed her watching, she hastily looked away.

And suddenly the animals were there.

Horrified to see them—only vaguely aware of Lacy screaming out her name—Arcie pulled her eyes back to the road and tried to slam both feet against the brake. The Mercedes' tires skidded across the oyster shells. She missed, catching the pedal with the toes of one foot, as a wail of fright seized in her chest. Her seat belt pulled tight under her throat, each jolt of the car a knife blade under her ribs. The thuds of the animals hitting the front tires disoriented her. She hung onto the wheel, struggling to regain control, trying to go with the spinning curve of the car's motion, but the wheel abruptly twisted from her grip, the tires bouncing over potholes, and sliding through the oyster shells.

The vehicle finally stopped spinning, swerved hard right, nosed through two massive humps of shell, then slid and jerked down an embankment before tunneling into the swampy roadside ditch. Muddy water and algae sprayed across the entire car. The Mercedes didn't stop; it stormed out the other side of the ditch, the impact of the tires a harsh vibration in the frame. It came to a halt, rocking and shuddering, threatening to roll onto its side before settling in a semi-rearing positon straddling rows of thick green sugarcane stalks.

The airbags exploded, throwing Lacy back hard into her seat, and sandwiching Arcie against the door, screaming as her head hit the window glass. Kitty tumbled from the back seat, her shoulder hitting hard against the console, face pressed tight against the back of the front seat. Their ragged breathing competed with the ticking heat in the car's metal.

Lacy whispered in a fright-choked voice, "Hey-—*hey* . . . e-everyone okay?" as she fought the airbag, fumbling at the seat belt release. The harness retracted with a hiss.

"Y-yeah," Kitty murmured, lifting herself shakily upright on an elbow and tasting blood. She had bitten her tongue.

"Arcie?" Lacy asked. When Arcie didn't respond, she said again, *"Arcie?"*

Arcie moaned and stared at Lacy with dazed eyes, but she nodded. A cut bled at the corner of her mouth, a large lump was forming at her temple.

"What . . . what the hell *happened!?*" Kitty yelled.

"*H-h-huge* . . ." Arcie sputtered as she wiped away blood with the back of her hand.

"What was huge?" Kitty shoved back onto the seat, feeling like she was sitting in the tilted cage of a Ferris wheel.

"They were h-huge" Arcie repeated

"Armadillos . . . we hit a pair of armadillos," Lacy gasped.

"You hit a fucking *armadillo?*" Kitty snarled, slamming the back of the driver's seat hard with the heels of both hands.

White smoke drifted up from under the Mercedes' hood, ghostly veiling the windshield. The sickeningly sweet scent of crushed cane filled the air. The downward-angled trunk of the vehicle could be seen through the rear glass; beyond that a sea of destroyed sugarcane stalks.

Kitty tried to open the rear driver's door. It wouldn't budge. She scooted back and kicked. The third kick popped it open. The car protested the movement by dropping an inch. She climbed out, stumbled, caught her balance on the armrest, and managed to shuffle a foot or so away from the car. Fingers curled hard into her hip bones, she sucked in air and stared with smoldering eyes at the damage. She felt sickened.

Lacy's door wouldn't give either; so she climbed

over the seat and got out the rear door. The Mercedes protested with a ground-level drop of its front end. Lacy was covered with airbag residue, looking a little like a mime. Arcie tumbled out and stood swaying against the car's side, wide-eyed with fear.

When no one spoke, Lacy eyed the vehicle and said, "It could have been worse."

"How you figure that?" Kitty asked.

"No one hurt." Lacy squinted at Arcie's face. "A minor cut. You got nothing broken, right?"

Arcie shook her head.

Kitty snapped around. "What the hell were you *thinking? Huge?* What daydream were you having? We could have been killed!"

"I didn't do it on purpose! I didn't! They looked huge!" Arcie's voice was shrill, electric with shock and fear. "I didn't see them until it was too late!"

"Of course not—driving so fast you're lucky to see the damn road!"

"Maybe you could have done better!"

Kitty advanced threateningly toward her "Bitch!"

"Don't touch me!" Arcie screamed backing away.

Lacy placed herself between them. "Hey, *hey . . . easy*, you two." She reached out and touched Arcie's shoulder. Arcie flinched away. "No one said you did it on purpose. It was an accident, wasn't it? An inconvenient one, under the circumstances, but still an accident." She turned toward Kitty, but Kitty had already moved away and stood to stare down the long stretch of empty road. "Where you suppose we are?"

Kitty looked at her, her eyes bright with an anger spark that waited to be ignited. "Somewhere close to hell."

"You think we might have a long walk ahead of us?" When Kitty snorted and shook her head disparageingly, Lacy added, "Just asking."

Kitty shielded her eyes with her hand. She hadn't been paying much attention. Wildly overgrown land lay on one side of the road, fields of sugarcane on the other as far as a person could see. Wherever they were, it was unpopulated and disrepair shrieked a road rarely traveled. But somehow it seemed familiar. She had traveled this road years ago with *Grandpere*, had made her last trip down it on her way to New Orleans with the shrimper. It had once been the main artery leading into French Gap, stretching between small populated areas, through miles and miles of swamp and sugarcane. Did anyone but cane growers use it anymore? Had the state forgotten that people lived out here?

"There used to be other towns around here, didn't there?" Lacy said.

"Nothing close," Kitty replied.

Lacy found herself frustrated, not sure what to do or say. For a moment she did nothing, said nothing, feeling as if they had fallen back through a hole in time. The PI had said there was skimpy phone service, no cellular for miles, but she would have felt better with her BlackBerry. It had been foolish leaving it behind, even when she knew Gregg could and would trace her through it.

"We need to report the accident to the police and get a rental car. The insurance company will probably total Arcie's car."

Kitty stiffened, hands balled into fists. "*Mine! My damn car!*" she snarled.

"Sorry, I just assumed . . ."

"If it had been her damn tank of a Lincoln, she would've burned the rubber off her tires trying to stop, or run over the bastards and never looked back." Kitty tossed Arcie an accusing glance as she walked to the front of the car.

Oil and water leaked in steady drops, with a continuous ping from under the hood. "It's just a piece of junk now." The angry roar of blood in her ears, she kicked out at the front fender. She left a heel-sized cave-in mark on the slimy surface. "Stupid, stupid, *stupid!*" Blood beat a hot tattoo under her skin, as she reached inside and turned the key. The ignition ground, but the car didn't start, even on the third try. "They were stinking wild animals! If you'd run over them and kept going, at least we'd still have the car! Now we have nothing, it's late and we don't even know exactly where the hell we are."

"It happened so fast!" Arcie screeched.

Kitty stepped toward Arcie, fist uplifted, ready to strike out. Lacy placed herself between them again.

"Don't," she said, clamping her fingers around Kitty's arm, pressing it to her side. "That won't help."

Kitty resisted, jerking her arm away. "It would certainly make me feel better." Her glance locked with Lacy's, and they faced each other in a combative stance. Kitty gave Arcie a withering look over her shoulder.

"You would be sorry later," Lacy said.

"Don't bet on it." Kitty bent forward, placing her palms flat on her thighs, fingers curled over her knees. She tried to calm herself. Lacy was right, of course, but at this moment she thought knocking Arcie flat on her big ass would make her feel great. She was sure of it. Nerves like jittery beans hopped around under her skin as she whispered, "She makes me so angry."

"I see that. I'm not even going to ask what is going on between you two or why—it won't make any difference." Lacy squinted down the road into the sinking sun. She was trapped out there with them, no possible recue in sight. She didn't know how much longer she would be able to keep Kitty off Arcie. "Do either of you have a phone?"

"No. I was angry and she shuffled me out so fast, I didn't think to pick it up. Arcie refuses to use one."

Lacy sighed. "I left mine. I figured it wouldn't work out here."

Kitty sank down in the dirt, suddenly drained. The silence seemed to hug her tight. The scent of the crushed cane was nauseating. She thought she might vomit. She placed her elbows on her knees, and propped her forehead up with the heel of one hand, rubbing at her temple with the fingers of the other. She had one hell of a headache starting up.

Arcie sidled over to Lacy. "Will they hold us responsible for the field?"

"What?" Surprised, Lacy could only stare at her. In the midst of all their other problems, Arcie was worried about the damn sugarcane field.

"The damage to—" Arcie began again.

"I heard you, Arcie," Lacy said, cutting her off. "Sorry, not high on my worry-about list right now."

Kitty cocked her head and snapped, "Who the hell even cares?"

"Then what should we do?" Arcie asked.

"Walk," Kitty snarled.

"Or wait for someone to give us a ride," Lacy muttered, more or less under her breath, with an intensity in her words that caught Kitty's attention.

"Uh-huh, you got it . . . yep, people tripping over themselves to rescue us," Kitty said, flipping her hand in both directions.

Lacy's eyes narrowed a fraction. "Have a little

faith. Give it a few more minutes."

Kitty smirked and shrugged. "Sure. Why not? Sounds like a plan to me."

Arcie started to speak and seemed to think better of it. Her eyes glistened, shiny with unshed tears. Eventually, she inched closer and said, "I'm sorry about your car, Kitty."

Kitty looked at the ground, ignoring her. She didn't trust herself to look at the other woman. She didn't know what upset her more, Arcie's stupidity or the loss of her car. "God only knows how long we're going to be here." She stood and dusted off her jeans.

Night was only a couple of hours away. Would they be safe out here after dark? Suppose no one drove by? If they started walking, how far would they have to go before they found some sort of civilization? Of course, they would be held responsible for the damaged field. With the Mercedes sitting there like that, come morning someone was sure to find it.

"Maybe not much longer," Lacy said, pointing.

Late afternoon sunlight reflected off metal in blinding light flashes. A moment later came the deep bass rumbles that could only belong to a very large truck.

44

Not even a bird sound, only mosquito whine and an occasional whisper movement of grass or leaf or tree branch.

The stillness sometimes said danger, but this time it said, strangers.

They had arrived. They were somewhere near.

Yancy expected car sounds. When there were none, she stood on the gallery and sniffed the air, breathing their scents in deep.

Three distinctly different scents . . . they *had* all come back.

Yancy smiled and went back inside her house to wait for their arrival.

Domeno was also alerted by the sudden quiet . . . and the scents—unfamiliar, but sharply female.

He slipped out the door of his house, making himself inconspicuous in deep shadow, watching as they came down the road. They shouldn't be here. Who were they? Where were they from? What was their purpose? He would have to be cautious about what he said before he sent them on their way. He didn't want to speak with them, but he had to, he couldn't avoid it. He wouldn't hide from anyone in his own town.

Domeno squinted against the evening shadow

and his frown deepened.

His chest went tight, his blood hot, adrenaline surging like an electric current. His lips trembled and moved without sound.

For a moment, he thought he was mistaken—he had to be mistaken!—but *non*, no, he wasn't. When she turned in his direction, he knew her lovely face. No longer girlish, fully matured . . . but it *was* Kitty.

Mon Dieu, she's so beautiful! Domeno thought.

Recognition brought with it shock and pure primal heat. She'd been gone from his life so long. How could all that *need*, all that *want* still be there? How *could* it? Out of his life more than twenty years, yet frequent thoughts of her dominated his mind. She had always been older than her years, no longer a child, not quite a woman, attracting men like bees to honey, he remembered, with a vivid flash of pain. He had been so in love with her, had treated her so badly, thinking she would always be there.

Kitty. *His* Kitty.

Non, she wasn't *his* Kitty. He had given up that right a long time ago. There had been no second chance. He had no business harboring thoughts like that. He should have staked his claim when he had the chance. She had stopped caring for him, but twenty years hadn't come close to extinguishing his feelings for her. She may not be his, but she was certainly *someone's* Kitty; she belonged to someone.

Beauty like hers was always claimed, sometimes misused, but always claimed by someone.

Domeno had replayed those days in his mind time after time, year after year. He could recall every detail of his stupid macho bullshit games. He'd thought, no matter what, she would be there when *he* was ready. *Why did I think such a thing?* It had always been his intent to marry her, fuck her until she went blind, keep her pregnant with his *enfants*, adore her as she grew big and round, and hold tight to that roundness each night he went to sleep.

He'd never stopped loving her, only buried the emotion when he realized how useless it was to fantasize that way. It was destructive, harmful to a person's mind. He'd done such stupid stuff; he'd even used Lacy, her closest friend. He thought Lacy would be easy, as some of the other girls, never figured she'd refuse him or tire more quickly of him than he did of her. Then Kitty disappeared, never giving him a chance to repair the damage.

He felt he completely understood loneliness now. Emptiness, need, love, hurt. The pain of no longer catching a glimpse of a treasure you adored, wanting to suck in her light and unable to do so. Kitty's leaving had torn straight through his heart, leaving a gaping hole. The physical ache had returned.

Domeno slipped his hand inside his shirt, rested his palm against his scars. The misshapen skin did a slow burn. He flexed his shoulder, winced with the pain. His jaw tightened, swollen hard with his bitterness. He was broken now, no longer good enough for her. She had believed there was nothing here for her then, so there was nothing here for her now . . . why has she come back? Was it possible she'd come back to find him? That she never forgot him? Of course not! That was a crazy thought. He wasn't thinking straight. Desperation screwed with people, fucked up their thoughts, and made them look for answers that didn't exist.

He studied each of them; recognized them all. Lacy Kennedy. She had always reminded him of a thoroughbred racing filly, long and lean and a little shy. Arcie Becnel, always fat and homely—*Jesus, look at her size!*—she had swooped down on him like a vulture that time. He'd never indicated any interest, never once paid her any attention. What made her think he'd be interested? He'd never imagined they would be back together after twenty years. He needed to know what brought them back.

Walking. No car. What happened to their car? There had to be one somewhere, there was no other way to get here, except by water. Not even a consideration; he knew they hadn't come that way. So each toted a travel bag. Was that an indication of a lengthy stay? He couldn't imagine for what purpose. There was no reason for them to come. French Gap was no longer an easy trip, even from the closest town. It was dead and buried now, a difficult place to find, a place where no one wanted to come. A person had to have a truck or a car, maybe a cane harvester, a vehicle of some sort.

Domeno's eyes moved back to Kitty.

He had mourned his loss for so long, it was an extension of him, like a useless deformed limb. He had accepted a replacement in Tansie, and he'd loved her, but it was never quite the same. There was a sudden stirring in his groin that hadn't been there for a long time. His stomach seized with sharp little arrows of pain.

"Minou," he said, reaching down and cupping the mutinous hardness of his erection.

~ 45 ~

Their salvation was a big rig hauling hogs. Big five-and six-hundred pound, black-and-white porkers. The stench was disgusting, the noise deafening. The driver heaved his bulk down from the truck cab and re-moved his tattered, denim ball cap to scratch his head as he eyed the Mercedes. He was bald on top, his oily ponytail hung down the middle of his back. A salt-and-pepper beard spread across his massive gut, and he smelled a lot like his cargo.

"Sure did a job on it," he said, then asked where they were headed. He said he was running late on his delivery, he'd give them a lift as far as Cutoff Road.

Arcie sat up front, pushed against the door as hard as she could away from the driver. Lacy and Kitty crunched together with the luggage in the sleeper area. Giving them quick appraising looks over his shoulder, he smiled, showing empty spaces where some of his lower front teeth were missing.

It was an uncomfortable ride, bunched together with the overpowering smell of body odor and sweat, tobacco and feces, the squeal and thump of hogs against the sides of the truck each time they hit a pothole. When they reached Cutoff Road, he didn't move from behind the wheel, he idled in the middle of the road and waited for them to climb out. He had done his Good Samaritan bit and was gone with rumbles and grinds and belches of nasty diesel exhaust just as quickly as he had appeared. They watched him and the hogs disappearr and after the truck noise died away, they stood in the silence staring at each other beside the tilted metal road sign with only two visible letters.

"He couldn't wait to get rid of us. What was that about?" Kitty asked.

"His eyes were bright as a light bulb with a sexual gleam," Lacy said.

"He could have taken us into town."

"Not too enthusiastic about that idea, was he?" Lacy glanced up. The sun was melting, blending in with the horizon. Daylight was fading fast, with shadows beginning to creep in to embrace tree branches. "Besides, every little bit helps save wear and tear on the feet." She picked up her travel bag. "I think it's time to walk now."

Cutoff Road was thickly rutted, split by an almost useless old metal bridge with rusted-out girders and rotted plants spanning a dry, cracked coulee. It ended in a weed-choked, shell-covered dirt path. Utility wires hung low to the ground, some completely down, others severed and twisted around odd-angled, creosote-dipped power line poles. Their first glimpse of humanity was Ben Jolly's junkyard. Another thin shell road fed off to their right through wooden posts strung with rusted barbed wire and faded "NO TRESPASSIN'" signs. Beyond barren ground lay a few rusty car frames, dozens of discarded tires, stacks of rotted mattresses turned into twisted coils and warped wood, and a couple of mangled old appliances. Off to the side, where the shell ended, was charred wood that had once been a building.

A lopsided old weathered sign: TURTLE POND ROAD, and silence hanging over the remains of the pond. Locals had almost depleted the pond's large snapping turtle population years ago. Now the water was too low and dark for anything but turtles, maybe minnows or some other small fish. A pair of egrets, their yellow beaks bright against snowy feathers, and a smoky-blue heron, wading on long thin legs, stood at the far end. The birds twisted their necks around at the sounds of their approach, then they took flight.

Kitty stopped, felt her heart lurch against her chest as she stared deep into the murky jade. *This must be what amnesia feels like,* she thought. Emptiness, everything buried, pushed aside to become indistinct memory for twenty years and—*wham!*—it was there again, as clearly as if it happened yesterday. Mislaid, inconvenient memory from the past that had remained fragmented for far too long, abruptly coming into full focus.

Lacy moved up beside her, gently touched her elbow. "Come on, it was a long time ago," she whispered as if reading her thoughts.

Kitty allowed herself to be directed away. She didn't want to think about any of it but she'd tried to forget for way too long. She should've had the courage to come back at least once, and confront all her demons. Now she was here, no matter how painful or angry it made her, and that was exactly what she was going to do.

A month after she turned seventeen, Freddie Chauvin's body had been found in that pond. Wildlife had already made a meal of most of him. She had her, her heart beating too fast, her blood a little hot in her veins, relieved they would no longer have to be afraid of him. A bastard, but he was still her father. She thought she should have loved him a little, but she never had. She felt no pain, no remorse or sadness. He had met an end bad people like him deserved. She had reached for her mama's hand, but Jennet shook her off and moved away. Jennet had no comfort to offer and wanted none in return. Those types of emotions had been beaten out of her. For the remainder of her time in French Gap, Kitty never again looked to her mama for much of stood beside her mama as her mama made the identification, not quite touching anything.

Authorities called it an accident—just a drunk who drowned after falling in the water—and there wasn't enough left of Freddie to dispute that decision, but Kitty knew it hadn't been an accident. She wondered a few times if her mama had something to do with it when she had finally had enough. The next day Jennet threw his belongings outside, doused them with gasoline, touched a match to them, and everything burned until there was nothing but ash. A week later his old trawler was sold . . . and her mama held the cash in her hand and smiled for the first time in years. She was still smiling the last time Kitty saw her on the day she let the old shrimper take her away.

She felt strange, a cold whirl of emotion, and she knew what it was: the sharp edge of sorrow. She thought, *I didn't cry then, there's no reason to cry now,* as she swallowed hard around the lump in her throat and blinked against unwelcome tears that formed but never left her eyes.

46

They rounded the last curve and broke through knee-high underbrush into an oppressively heavy silence. A creepy dead quiet that made Kitty nervous. A belch or a fart would have been louder, more welcome, than the lack of noise. They turned to each other in dismay, wondering if they were in the wrong place.

Spooky. It was French Gap, no doubt about it, but no longer a place for human habitation. The farther along a person walked, the more sinister the area, the ground covered with blue-violet traceries edged by silvery ghosts of haunted-looking dusk. Catfish Street, once the main street, was no longer; it was heavily lined with an invasion of live oak, cedar, and hackberry, nothing more than a rutted, wide path.

The town was wracked with terrible deterioration, weed-choked and tree-infringed as if the town had rotted from the inside out. Old wood washed charcoal in the ubiquitous twilight, collapsed walls and roofs, sagging porches, missing doors, plywood-boarded and cracked or glassless windows. It appeared deserted, seemed to have nothing that walked or breathed.

The old man startled them. He sat wrapped in shadow, rocking on the remainder of a porch that fronted what had once been Schexnaydre General Merchandise. His head didn't move, but his eyes followed them from under the brim of his tattered straw hat. As they approached, he limped inside and slammed the door. The chair continued to wobble back and orth. The long-forgotten yet familiar sound of bare porch boards under creaky chair rockers seemed to thrum and swell in the air.

An involuntary shiver raced up Kitty's spine, as bitter, impotent fury overtook and burned through her. Arcie had forced her back to this wretched, empty place, and if the sharp sting of so much anger begot hated, then at that moment she hated Arcie.

During good times French Gap had rarely given claim to a population of more than a hundred or so. Most of each younger generation stumbled along until they could drift away. They wanted nice houses, fancy cars, electronics, and expensive clothes, not the hard life of twisted backs and gnarled hands from hauling trawl lines. Businesses closed as licensing fees and federal regulations made it harder each year to bring in a decent catch and take home enough money to feed families.

For a moment Kitty's expression was blank and her eyes empty. Then she softly said, "Welcome back to hell, Arcie."

47

Creely's temples filled with the dull splitting pain that sometimes followed his visions. His shoulders felt stiff, a pulsing crick in his neck that crisscrossed his scalp with needles. His nerves were jittery, his body still damp with sweat, a chill caused by the whisper of air from the ceiling ducts.

Remnants of his vision had become patchy particles of fuzz along the edges of his memory. He sat on the edge of the bed, listening to the nuances of his house. The distant hum of the fridge, the tick of his grandmother's old clock in the hall, the annoying little drip in the bathroom sink he kept forgetting to get fixed. The familiarity was comforting, settling his jumpy stomach with a little calm.

He lit a cigarette, the tip a brilliant nub as he drew smoke deeply into his lungs. He'd called Kitty three more times, sensing it would go straight to voice mail before it did. If nothing was wrong, she would have checked her messages. If she had retrieved his other messages, she would have called by now. Unless she was somewhere she couldn't. Somewhere that had no telephone or cellular service.

Relenting to hunger and thirst, he had slapped ham and Swiss with mustard and pickles between almost stale bread, devoured the sandwich, washed it down with Coke, managing to format a plan. A few hours of sleep, leave at daylight, hoping to be alert and quick-thinking. He would drive, comfortable with the familiar power of the Porsche under his antsy ass. By the time he finished his cigarette, he had changed his mind.

Calling his office, he left messages for his assistant and his secretary concerning a personal emergency. He said he would be out of the office a few days, they should reschedule all appointments they were unable to handle, he would a check in occasionally. He stuffed two changes of clothes into his black sports bag along with toilet articles and underwear, again sat on the edge of the bed, rubbing at his eyes with his thumbs, thinking about what Sal had said.

He grabbed up the phone but replaced the receiver without dialing. Barbara would be at the dinner party. He wouldn't leave a message. She was probably still furious and wouldn't listen to what he had to say anyway. He didn't want to set her off again. She needed time to cool off. No matter what Sal said, it was best not to touch that part of his life until he figured out what to do about this part.

Creely felt he needed to get moving, stop pissing away time thinking about things he had no control over right now. If he left soon, traffic should be lighter, he could narrow the miles between here and wherever that French Gap place was. After a quick shower, staring at the heavy stubble on his cheeks in the bathroom mirror, he found no need to shave. He slipped into his favorite old jeans, torn at the knees, washed soft and almost white, a blue polo shirt and sneakers without socks—travel comfort—he checked his wallet for cash and credit cards. Decided he needed to stop at an ATM for a few extra hundred; he just might need it. He glanced once more at the phone, knowing he wasn't going to use it. No need to over-think and put a guilt trip on himself, even if he did feel an uncomfortable nip of conscience.

Barbara had probably already listened to gossip and speculated about his affairs, but she had never caught him. She couldn't prove anything, so she'd never confronted him. What she couldn't prove couldn't hurt her. Couldn't hurt him either. Right? Yep, right. It was just that simple. He doubted she would go so far as to call off their marriage, but if she did, he had to think about how much it was going to impact his future plans. It could be a lot. Was he willing to chance it? Maybe. Was he willing to accept that if it did? Maybe not. He had to give it more thought.

What the hell was he thinking? Was he trying to talk himself out of going after Kitty" Seemed like it, and that was ridiculous. Kitty was important to him, he needed to find her. when he knew she was safe, he would settle matters with Barbara.

48

Maybe the old man could tell them something about the way the town looked and why. They descended on the porch in a rush, calling out, bumping into each other. They banged on the door, heard the hinges creak, the wood shaking under their fists. No one answered. Lacy tried the doorknob; it was locked. Kitty looked through the dirty cracked windows. The store appeared empty and the old man had vanished. Where? It was a crazy thing for him to do, but somehow it didn't surprise her. Why he had done it was what troubled her.

"Forget him, whoever the hell he is. Let's go. We're wasting time. We need to get to Yancy's while there is still enough light to see by," Kitty said, jumping down from the porch. Over her shoulder, she asked in a tigh t whisper: "What do you suppose happened here?"

"Everyone left," Arcie offered.

"No shit."

"This is terrible," Lacy murmured. "Maybe if he'd talked with us we could find out something."

"Maybe Yancy can fill us in." Kitty's jeans had worked their way up her crotch and in between the cheeks of her ass. Mosquitoes feasted on her, leaving itchy bloody welts where she scratched. The more she thought about the old man and his disappearing act, the angrier she found herself. He could have at least acknowledged them. How many people still lived here? Certainly, Yancy and the old man weren't the only inhabitants; there had to be more than two people in this wretched place. What if they discovered Yancy wasn't here and all this had been for nothing? What would they do? Stupidity on Arcie's part! Why didn't she think this through better before bringing them back here?

Arcie was having a hard time. Her temple bruise had fully materialized. She stumbled along and seemed to have trouble breathing. Kitty hoped she wouldn't trip and fall or have a heart attack. With the animosity she felt, if something happened, she would be tempted to leave Arcie's sorry ass where it fell.

They chose a footpath they thought was the right direction. They were followed by the annoying whine of mosquitoes, fought through needle-pointed palmetto fronds, thorny vines and Spanish moss that crawled across their faces. Kitty fell back a couple of steps, but Lacy pushed ahead through knee-high weeds and a thick tangle of vine-choked saplings, and they found themselves staring up at the old Arceneaux house.

Sections of the side galleries had collapsed under the abundant weight of foliage. The dried phosphorrescent slime of receded swamp water coated the stilts. An old gray van, encrusted with dirt and tin-seled with green, was parked under the giant magnolia tree. It had a long-expired Louisiana license plate hanging from one screw, one axle on a cinder block and three flats. All its glass was cracked and film-coated.

As if an alarm had sounded, a woman stepped from the house.

They stood frozen in place and stared up at the person on the gallery.

49

"What the hell?" Kitty breathed, horrified, more to herself than anyone else.

"This doesn't look good," Lacy whispered. She had thought she would know what to say and do when the time came and found she didn't.

Arcie stood with a bewildered look on her face and none of them seemed to be able to make their feet move.

Yancy Arceneaux stopped on the bottom step, mouth curled in a strange smile. She had a short gash under her left eye and a busted lip. She was stick-thin, without shoes, wearing a denim skirt faded beyond color, and a cotton blouse once red, her breasts visible through the thin fabric. Her crinkly hair, knotted at the nape of her neck, had gone completely gray.

Arcie recovered first. She rushed forward, pulled Yancy into a hug. Yancy's arms hung limply at her sides. No hug back.

They stood, several feet apart, in two awkward groups, unable to say much.

Eventually, they gravitated toward each other. Yancy didn't speak. She brought with her a fetid odor. Kitty felt heat rising up her neck. Unsure where the heat came from—nervousness, embarrassment, or awkwardness, a queasy stomach with nothing but the remnants of fried pork skins, or maybe just the effort she put into not gagging—she found herself over-whelmed by the stench. Yancy seemed to have doused herself in some kind of cheap perfume, and the underlying odor was raw and vile, like decom-position. Kitty's stomach lurched into her throat. Everything in front of her began to swim. Unsteady on her feet, she backed away, stumbled, collapsed to her knees, and threw up. When nothing remained by dry heaves, she opened her eyes and wiped snot away with the back of her hand.

Oh, my God, what have you done to us, Arcie? Kitty thought as she stared at the three pairs of feet form-ing a semi-circle around her.

Lacy dropped down beside her. "You okay?"

Kitty shook her head.

"Can you get her some water, Yancy?" Lacy asked.

As Yancy turned and hobbled away, Kitty dis-covered her voice. "Oh, shit! That . . . god-awful *smell!* She stinks!"

Lacy nodded. "I know. It's really bad."

Kitty tried to spit away the sour taste in her mouth. Her tongue was a strip o f sandpaper. Thin tendrils of nausea frolicked through her stomach.

"What do you suppose happened to her?"

"Something horrible," Kitty answered.

Arcie stood in a sulk, staring over their heads.

Kitty felt a flare of anger and managed to unglue her tongue from the roof of her mouth long enough to snap, "Did you *know?* Did you know and not *tell* us?"

"*No!*" Arcie protested. "No, I didn't know."

"You had no idea?" Lacy asked.

Arcie shook her head.

"Don't believe whatever she says," Kitty said.

"I-I didn't know . . . I just figured the years had changed her as it changed us."

"*Changed her?*" Kitty gasped. "Change is cutting your long hair short, or a brunette becoming blonde. Gaining fifty or a hundred pounds. That's change!" She waved her hand in the direction of the house. "Whatever *that* is, it's not a change, it's—a-a disaster!"

Arcie tensed. "What difference does it make?"

"Dear God, can't you *smell* her?" Kitty asked.

"Of course, I can." A look of sadness moved across Arcie's face.

Kitty felt an involuntary shudder. "No wonder she doesn't have a man."

"What a hateful and insulting thing to say! You don't know why she's like that."

"No water here? She needs a damn serious bath, that's one reason she smells like that!"

"Stop it!"

"It sounds ugly, Arcie, but Kitty's only being truthful. A good bath would certainly help."

Arcie turned on Lacy. "You're as bad as Kitty.

She hasn't been as fortunate as us. It could have happened to any of us if we'd stayed here."

"I doubt it," Kitty snapped.

"Can't either of you show a little compassion?"

Yancy had returned unnoticed, holding a blue cup double-fisted against her breasts. Her face looked pinched, with a bright saffron gleam to her eyes. Arcie made a grab at her, but Yancy side-stepped away. The cup tilted and water spilled down her front. She stood staring at the wet as if she had no idea where it came from.

Arcie moaned, "Oh, Yancy, it's just talk! They didn't mean it!"

Yancy said nothing.

Kitty stared into Yancy's glistening eyes. Her mind flashed on another memory.

Rats.

They were big, fat, grayish-brown rats, with long, whip-like tails, and gleaming little eyes that peered around a woodpile or from between the shadows of a stilted house. But never at their house, her mama wouldn't have allowed it. They had never been without at least three cats and a litter of kittens; huge and almost feral, the cats never ate a packaged meal. They had only served one purpose.

It was a cool summer afternoon when Yancy caught the rat, bashed its head with a heavy tree branch enough for near-consciousness. She tied the squeaky, squirmy thing's feet together with string, hung it upside down by its tail with a clothespin from the Arceneaux wash line, and tortured it with matches. The rat tried to crawl up itself, chewing at its own body, screeching its terrible death dance until the air reeked with burned hair and flesh. Yancy finally let the rat drop to the ground, not quite dead, but too weak to struggle, then stomped its head flat with as little effort as wind shifting leaves across the ground. The smell brought the two Arceneaux cats slinking in, hair raised along their spines, low hissing growls deep in their throats.

Before she slipped abruptly into blackness, Kitty remembered the same unsettling spark of insanity in Yancy's eyes that day.

~ 50 ~

Domeno followed the three women to the Arceneaux house. He hid behind a tree and watched as
Kitty got sick and he clenched his hands tight to
control himself and his urge to rush to her side. He
wanted to hear their brief exchange with Yancy before she went back inside the house, and the others
stood talking, but he wasn't close enough; the rush of
blood in his ears made it impossible to understand
their words. Instinct told him everything was not
right between them. They were angry with each other
and Yancy. Did they know about her, what she was,
what she was capable of? Had they come back on
their own to be with her? Why would they do that?
No, he knew better. One of her spells had brought
them back. But why would she do that? What did she
want with them? Did she aim to hurt them?

He felt his gut tighten as a hot flare of anger
crawled up his throat. He tamped it down, couldn't let
anger get the better of him, that wouldn't be good.
He knew what would happen if he lost control. He
had to fight so hard, so very hard, against it.

Sacre fou chienne! Damn fool bitch!

Had she sensed him? Did she know he was
watching? Of course, she did! She could smell him; he
was close enough that she could pick up his scent.

She was enjoying herself, taunting him, knowing he wouldn't make them aware of his presence. The thought flooded him with anger.

He rubbed his itchy palms together. He could imagine Yancy silently laughing at him.

Comment te elle y moquer de?—how dare she laugh at him?

He knew she always enjoyed tormenting him, mocking him.

Comment te elle y moquer de? Sacre fou chienne! he thought again, knowing he had to find another way to even the score between them.

51

Kitty surfaced to groggy half-consciousness a couple of times only to fade back both times. The third time she opened her eyes, she felt a tinge of lightheadedness as if a giant hand was squeezing the life from her lungs, and she discovered she lay on a bed. Lacy sat on the edge, pressing a wet washcloth against her forehead.

"What happened to me?" she asked.

"You passed out without saying a word."

"How did I get in here?"

"We carried you." Lacy removed the washcloth and sat back, folding it carefully.

"Where are the others?"

Lacy shrugged.

"They just dumped me and left us here?"

"They did. Arcie is angry. Yancy still hasn't spoken a word. I felt lucky they helped me move you inside before they disappeared. I wouldn't have gotten you inside by myself."

"How long have I been out?" Kitty struggled to sit up, trying to throw her legs over the side of the bed.

"Not too long." Lacy shoved her back down. "Don't. You need to rest."

"What I need is to get away from here and never

have come here in the first place."

"I agree, but we're here now and we have no transportation, so we need to remain calm and solve our problem." Lacy shook her head. "Arcie isn't going to be any help. She doesn't seem to find anything wrong with Yancy or this situation."

"She wouldn't. Is it dark yet?" Kitty glanced toward the thick, closed curtains.

"It is, and I'm tired. I think I've had enough for one day. Yancy assigned us each a bedroom, so best we sleep on all this. Maybe in the morning, we'll find a solution." Lacy stood up, waving her hand toward the bedroom door. "I'm right across the hall. Yell out if you need me. I don't imagine I'll get much sleep tonight." Then she walked out, closing the door softly behind her.

Lacy leaned against her bedroom door, pressing fingertips hard against her temples. She felt a little guilty leaving Kitty like that, but she was drained. She had developed a nagging headache, throbbing fiery feelers of pain that made her scalp tender. She was so tense, her muscles knotted, her body achy. She found Advil in her purse and dry-swallowed two tablets.

A little mirror on the wall revealed a small cut over her eyes. A large bruise had appeared under it. She felt beaten up, mentally and physically. Too much weird stuff, she didn't know what to expect next, all of it had her mind whirling. Years in the restaurant business had taught her how to handle stress, and she was usually pretty good under pressure, but this situation was definitely getting to her. Her mind was telling her to get some sleep, but she was nervous about sleeping.

They had placed Kitty on the bed and the others left. Just walked out and left her alone with Kitty. She had no idea what was wrong with her. Kitty had thrown up for no obvious reason. Yancy's smell had been awful, but she felt sure they had all smelled worse at one time or another. Then Kitty just blacked out. Maybe she'd hit her head during the accident, or she had an illness. Checking her purse hadn't produced any type of medication. She had lied to Kitty about the amount of time she had been unconscious. She had sat with her twenty minutes, watching her drift in and out of consciousness without fully awakening. She'd checked Kitty's pulse a couple of times but found it steady. She could think of nothing else but to watch and wait.

The longer she sat without Kitty fully awake, the more pissed she got at Arcie. She wanted to grab Arcie by the throat and force her to tell what she knew before she squeezed the life out of her. When telling them where to put their bags, Yancy had merely pointed at each of them and indicated the room they would use. She had no idea what was going on with her and not speaking.

If Kitty needed a doctor, Lacy had no idea where to locate one. French Gap hadn't seen a legitimate doctor since before she'd left. There definitely wouldn't be one around now. Yancy might know where to find one, but getting her to tell—what the hell was wrong with her, anyway?—would be like pulling teeth. Getting Kitty there was an entirely different matter.

Lacy was plain spitting mad, at them and herself. The situation was getting worse by the minute. She was letting emotion get in the way of common sense. *How do smart people get themselves into a situation like this?* she wondered. *How could I let this happen to me?* A few more hours and she might find herself turned into a blithering idiot. It was going to be difficult to ride this nightmare out until morning.

The quiet was astonishing, except for not far outside her window came some kind of chugging noise she thought she recognized. Some type of generator, gasoline- or kerosene-powered. When the noise stopped, the lights flickered out, and Lacy was surprised to find she was alone in the dark with only insect noise.

Her head jerked back so sharply her neck popped when she looked up. She could have sworn she heard something move above her, stealthy footsteps. Was someone in the attic trying not to attract attention? Each time she thought she heard a noise, she held her breath, listened, and heard nothing, but couldn't quite put it aside. She *felt* movement rather than heard it. She told herself to stop thinking the worst. Probably her imagination and nerves, both working overtime. It was likely Yancy or a rat, maybe a squirrel or simply the moan of the wind in the rafters.

She hadn't figured out what was wrong with Yancy. Surely Yancy wasn't refusing to speak to them on purpose. It was ridiculous to think she would do such a thing after they had come back to see her. This anger stuff between them was only good for so long, as far as she was concerned. They couldn't possibly spend an entire weekend that way. Was it possible she could no longer speak? Anything was possible, of course. Something might have happened to her and she lost her voice.

Yancy had been a peculiar kid, a little dull-witted, maybe not certifiably crazy, but definitely disturbed. People always said all the Arceneaux were crazy. Maybe it had been true.

Back then she had ignored it. She guessed everyone had, for whatever reason kids ignored certain things about their friends, but she couldn't ignore it now. Being near Yancy filled her with a sadness difficult to describe.

Trapped here with a pair of head cases, she was feeling way too vulnerable. She hadn't known what to expect but had certainly hoped for something better than what was happening now.

Hell, they were *complete* strangers. They didn't know squat about what had happened in each other's lives over the last twenty years. Even the most sociable strangers took time to warm up to each other, put some effort into finding a minimal comfort zone. What was happening here was absurd. Kitty was right, had Yancy forced them back with some kind of spell? If she had, why would she do that? And then not talk to them? How much more unreasonable could this situation get?

What had happened here, to the town and its people? It seemed illogical that everyone in a town just left, except for one old man and one demented woman. It didn't make a smidgen of sense. No local traffic, not even a workable road left. Were people only coming close enough to plant and harvest cane or check on livestock? Did they stay away because something had happened to make the area unfit for human habitation? It was possible, of course. Since their last fuel stop, she hadn't seen another person before the trucker. Sugarcane fields, black-faced sheep or ghost-colored Brahman cattle, a few battered uninhabited trailers, dilapidated shacks, and disabled broken boats. No people, just creepy emptiness.

French Gap had never thrived, but she hadn't expected it to turn into a ghost town. It had always been just a small backwater community of fishermen and trappers. Now it was a deteriorated capsule, devoid of humanity, as if embarrassed by its own existence. Something terrible had happened. Yancy might be the only one who knew what it was, but it seemed unlikely she would tell.

Lacy was sorry as hell for being the least bit curious about this place after so many years. She should have put all her embarrassment behind her before coming here. It had been foolish to tell no one where she was going, stripping herself of all forms of communication. Why had she done such a thing? She really should have trusted Gregg enough to confide in him. She cursed. *What if Gregg was right, what if this wasn't just a simple reunion?* Thinking of him brought moisture to her eyes. He was a good man, the best she had run across in a long time. She should have been more honest and taken her chances by telling him about her shame of her past.

Lacy cursed softly again, as a shudder ran through her. A light cool rain started, blowing a fine mist across the gallery, sifting through the window screen. She turned away from the window. She decided to not undress, removed only her shoes, and pulled back the musty quilt. The sheets were old, a bit musty, rough and scratchy from too much washing. She smoothed the quilt over her stomach, pulled the top sheet up under her chin, folded it over, and patted it in place. For a long time, she stared at the blades of the old-fashioned ceiling fan that hung unmoving from its long metal rod above the bed, making sinister shadows on the walls.

Lacy finally closed her eyes and thought: *One step at a time, just need to make it through the night.*

52

Arcie lay awake, flat on her back, arms pressed tight against her sides. Her fingers dug tightly at the wash-worn, slightly musty sheet. It was too early for sleep, especially with twisted nerves and creepy black funk close at hand. The bed was too narrow, her body touched each side of the mattress, restricting all movement unless she got up to lie down in a different position.

She was sore from the accident, her face bruised and painful. The lump on her forehead was huge, a peculiar ugly color. Her lip was swollen. They thought the accident was all her fault. It was Kitty's fault, too. If Kitty hadn't been so damn nasty and made her so angry, she wouldn't have driven so fast, she would have seen those horrible animals in enough time not to hit them; it wouldn't have happened.

She had taken more meds, scooping water in her palm from the bathroom faucet, sat on the edge of the bed, waiting for the drugs to kick in. When the electricity went out, she had finally lain down.

She was as angry at Lacy as she was at Kitty. It was like when they were kids, always so tight, agreeing with each other about everything. They'd embarrassed her the horrible way they treated Yancy, talking about her like that. Now Yancy seemed disinterested in being near them. She had vanished. Where had she gone? She wanted to talk with her, spend some time with her, but she was a guest, it didn't seem appropriate to snoop around looking for her. She hadn't gone to check on Kitty, figured whatever was wrong had to do with too much booze and sex the previous night. She knew it wasn't right not checking on her, but didn't really care. Lacy siding with Kitty had really chapped her ass.

A wildfire blazed through her body. She was too hot. It had rained a little and there had been a breeze, but the rain had stopped and so had the breeze. She couldn't use the fan and she was uncomfortably sweaty. Her thoughts were like ping pong balls, bouncing, bouncing, *bouncing* . . . but the pills were taking hold. A soft buzzing deep in her brain crept slowly forward, tugging at her, attempting to quiet her tortured thoughts.

Arcie watched the flashes of color behind her eyelids, a sure sign her blood pressure was way too high. It infuriated her, she couldn't remember if she'd taken *that* medicine. She wanted to scream, curse, punch, throw something—do something!— anything to feel better. Nothing was going right. *Damn, damn, damn* . . . .

Suddenly her mind was racing, running full tilt, swinging from one thought to another like some uncontrollable zoo monkey. It was moving too rapidly for her to fully grasp exactly what she was thinking. Every muscle in her body screamed from the accident, the walk, the tension. She felt creepy crawly things under her skin. Her mouth felt stuffed with cotton, like at the dentist's office. She was more than a little hungry. Yancy hadn't offered dinner, but she didn't want to accuse her unjustly. She might have thought they had already eaten. Now her bladder was uncomfortably full.

Feeling trapped, Arcie realized it was her own fault. That car was Kitty's new baby, sleek, powerful and luxurious, with only three thousand miles on the odometer. Had she wanted to hurt Kitty by wrecking the Mercedes? If so, she should have done something else, it had been a stupid stupid thing to do. Now they were without transportation.

So many confusing thoughts rushed around in her mind, she felt on the edg e of panic. Why hadn't Yancy told her about this place? Where were all the people? Where was Domeno? Yancy said he was here, but that had been a few years ago. Had that been a lie or had he decided to leave? Just thinking about him made her wet and tingly.

The funk snickered. *Oh, God, I'm scared!* Arcie thought. *I'm doing my best not to overreact, but I'm struggling, it's so hard to act like there's nothing wrong* .

The sharp pain of the cramp in her calf struck like lightning. No, no, *noooo* . . . .

She shifted her legs over the side of the bed. Heaving herself up, she put weight against her foot to ease the pain. She stood like that for a long time, her toes curled under and pressed into the cool floorboards. She walked gingerly to the window. Where moonlight highlighted a dark section of bayou, the water surface shimmered with a dull -gray luminescence almost like mercury.

If only her life had been different. Sometimes she wasn't right in the head, but she'd drifted with it, had learned to live with the inferior feelings. In that single-room school, she had attached herself to Kitty, because Kitty was everything she wanted to be.

She'd had a miserable home life, where her mama had rages, coming and going in a flash, striking out at her. Her mama slept most of the day and spent her nights with various men. They had survived on food stamps, welfare, and money dropped carelessly on the nightstand.

Her mama never mentioned her daddy. Since he'd never been around, Arcie occasionally wondered but never asked about him. There had been one man she'd thought might be her father. He came around late at night twice a week for a few years, then he stopped coming. She no longer had a clear picture of him in her mind. She had struggled to remember his face, something special about him. Eventually, she decided he wasn't who she thought so he was unimportant. If she couldn't remember his face or his height or weight, not even his voice, there couldn't possibly be anything special about him, except he occasionally brought fresh seafood and other treats— and one night he might have left enough sperm behind that she was conceived. She supposed, if by chance that was true, that made him *sort* of special.

After that man stopped coming, the endless procession of men began: some who beat up on her mama, some who pissed all over the floor instead of in the toilet, one who threw a heavy work boot and hit her upside her head because she'd walked in and caught a glimpse of his pitiful little wiener. One man who brought a Hershey bar he would give to her upon entering the house, before sending her outside, but if she didn't eat it immediately, he would ask for it back when he left, probably intending to give the same one to her again the next time he came.

Most weren't town folks, like the drunk that stumbled into the chicken house and slept past dawn. When she saw him a few days later, he pressed his finger against his lips and hurried away, not wanting the sheriff to find out what his brother-in-law had been up to.

Miserable scraps of humanity, drunks and cheating husbands, but they all had two things in common: they left behind their money and they didn't want anyone to know they had been there.

Arcie eased herself back on the bed. She was so tired and edgy and worried—thinking and thinking, and *thinking* . . . .

She thought she might sleep, she wanted to sleep, hoped she could sleep. She needed to sleep to block out the entire wretched day. Her eyelids felt heavy . . .

. . . and then everything was red—and she was on the kitchen floor. The first thing she saw was the red, an ocean of it, all over the floor, all over her. And then she saw the butcher knife. She screamed and screamed, trying to push herself up off the floor, but her hands kept slipping in the red stuff, smearing it all over, and her feet kept sliding out from under her. She kept falling on her face. It was sticky, so thick and nasty. She could smell it, taste it, and she thought she was going to be sick.

She screamed for her mama, needed her to explain where all the red came from, but there was no answer. Finally, getting her feet under her, she stumbled into her mama's room. Her mama was on her knees by the side of the bed as if she was praying, her head turned away, with her cheek pressed into the mattress. She grabbed her mama's shoulder with both hands and shook her, calling her name over and over. Her mama's body wobbled like a broken chair, then fell over sideways and lay sprawled on the dark red floor . . . .

Domeno stood in the rain on the peninsula at the edge of the coulee not far from the Arceneaux house. The rain was light, a wind-whipped mist, not a solid downpour. A storm was coming. It was still a ways off, but he could feel its approach in the shift of the air currents, the salty tang and briny fish odor in disturbed water that always settled in before a storm.

He'd stared at the lighted windows, watching the shadowy movements, wondering which shadow belonged to Kitty, until the generator stopped and the lights went out. Now he stared at the silver riffles in the water.

His nostrils flared, catching a whiff of Yancy. His pulse spiked. He jerked around; his gaze searched the dark. She was prowling. Not close enough to see, but he could smell her, and knew she could smell him. He should have known having them in her house wouldn't make a difference in her patterns.

He hated she couldn't accept either her own fate or his rejection, and always took matters into her own hands. It was horrible to have control of your body taken away like she had taken his. Her bite had done that to him, making him into a cursed something that was not totally one species or another.

Kitty came awake with the startling realization she was having trouble breathing. She was sucking in moist recycled air. Something was over her head, covering her face. A bolt of pure animal panic seized her. Sounds burbled in her throat. A blind reaction, kicking her feet, punching with balled fists, striking out at the unknown assailant determined to smother her.

Coolness suddenly washed over her.

Kitty stared in confusion at the offending bedclothes and untangled herself, releasing a nervous giggle, as she remembered where she was. Most of what happened was coming back. She pictured Yancy as she hobbled down the steps and she grasped the gallery railing for support. Her fingers had gripped the wood so hard her knuckles paled to the cold gray color of clay as ropey veins like fat worms exploded and swam under her skin up the inside of her arms. The unexpected smell of the woman had annihilated Kitty's senses, her head becoming muzzy. She had vomited through blinding pricks of light behind her eyelids. There had been a warming hum beginning in her brain, a gentle whirring of a distant motor, razor-edged little teeth ripping at her temples. And everything tilted, like a broken seesaw. At the top end, she could feel herself sliding, the ground rushing up to meet her. She remembered being touched as she drifted in and out of the gray fog, never quite surfacing back to consciousness. Finally making it, talking to Lacy, and pulling the quilt up under her chin, seeking warmth, falling asleep without realizing it. How long ago had that been? Had it been minutes, hours? She had no idea.

Fain t silver-white light edged around the window curtains. Above her head the fat body of an antiquated metal fan, distorted shadow dancing across the ceiling. She could almost feel the old house breathing around her.

Only traces remained of the dream that had awakened her, nothing substantial. She couldn't remember much except being chased, running hard. She tried to focus. Panic attacks, nausea, fainting—now, what seemed like a really bad dream. So much unease and anger, ridiculous crap, none of it good. All this nasty shit since she'd come back to this miserable place.

It felt like she was working her way toward crazy.

55

Yancy lingered under Kitty's window before leaving on her hunt, her ears picking up the small sounds Kitty made in her restless shifting in sleep. She had an angry pulse of blood in her veins. She was furious with herself. What had she been thinking? Why had she thought bringing them back would help? They wanted nothing to do with her, had never cared enough to come on their own, make her a part of their lives. Did they really need to know the things she wanted to tell them? It was too late to make a difference. Even Arcie was unhappy to see her. Arcie had only used the reunion as an excuse to cover the real reason for coming back: Domeno. He drew her —all of them—like a magnet.

A crooked little smile touched her lips. No need wasting fuel to give them light, fuel was getting harder to come by. She hadn't cooked or offered dinner, so they'd be hungry in the morning and wouldn't hesitate to eat what she served. Everything inside the house had become quiet, so she supposed they eventually slept.

The adrenaline burn had blazed inside her, the urge to shift and feed. The change slid through her, almost as smooth as silk. The rain misted her, the breeze whispering through the guard hairs of her pelt as she shook herself and raised her snout against the dark and into the hazy moonlight. Her ears twitched and she felt the slap and snap of tiny winged things against her muzzle. She   shook her head, warding them away from her eyes, dislodging some from her whiskers.

When her stomach growled, her lips curled back, fangs flashing like ivory stakes.

A moment later she disturbed sleeping things and made the night air shiver with a long thunderclap howl.

56

Get up! Get moving! Don't be such a chicken shit! Kitty scolded herself.

The soles of her feet tightened against the chill of bare wood as she slipped her legs over the side of the bed. The temperature seemed to have dropped and the room felt cool and damp. She shivered, wrapped the quilt around her shoulder, and clasped it to her as she hesitated, inhibited by her own cowardice. No lock on the door. She finally tip-toed forward, turned the knob, cracked the door, poked out her head. The hallway was empty. She listened, thought she heard a shuffling noise, slow and stealthy, a hesitant motion of feet brushing against wood, but was unable to determine from where the noise came and it stopped as quickly as it began.

Closing the door, she stood with shoulders pressed tight against the wood, realizing she was holding her breath. She released it and took shallow puffs of air as she tried to calm her racing heart. Her imagination was running rampant again. The only sounds she heard were the dry whisper of her legs rubbing together and the faint but distinct click of her teeth coming together.

The sounds she thought she heard before didn't come again. Since when was she scared of the least little noise? She thought to call out, opened her mouth, and discovered she couldn't find her voice. She was behaving miserably, like some squirrelly basket case, frightening her own self. Much more of this foolishness, and when she got back home she'd be looking for a shrink. Would a shrink believe her? It didn't matter, she supposed, shrinks didn't have to believe you, they got paid astronomical amounts of money to listen. Arcie should be the one going, not her. One look at Arcie in one of her moods and he would want to commit her to a maximum security psychiatric facility.

All because of this stupid, *stupid* reunion!

Kitty stumbled over the edge of the quilt, cursed as she righted herself and yanked it up so she could walk to the window. She pushed aside the curtains and found she was housed at the back of the house. In the moonlight, she could see vines grown heavy, climbing the length of trees, sending out hundreds of thin tendrils like some mystical creature. Lower down, the vines were twisted and thick and hung toward the ground like an old woman's knotted unkempt hair.

An old metal Airstream trailer sat in shadow, gunmetal dull in the moonlight, partially concealed by an overgrowth of foliage. It had been an expensive trailer in its day, left behind by its owner. Yancy had probably salvaged it. She thought it might be the one that belonged to . . . *what was that old bastard's name?*

She couldn't remember, but the kids had always been afraid of him. He hadn't shown up for church for the first time in years, was found inside his trailer that Sunday afternoon the summer before she left. Dead for a couple of days. Heat and insects had taken a toll, but he had outlived three wives and four of his fifteen children, a crippled sour lump of a man with a pair of mean-looking cypress canes, a bad temper and a glass eye always oozy around the edges.

The sudden streamers of memory with blurred edges surprised her. Things that happened and had seemed like natural occurrences, unimportant at the time, were coming back to her. Maybe things in French Gap had always been a little sour, like that mean old man, painfully bad, like a decayed tooth. Was that possible? Could a town be bad? Make its people bad, poor beyond poverty and ignorance? Maybe something in the marshy soil or the swampy water made some of them a little crazy from the moment they were born. It was scary to think people slipped from the womb that way.

She winced with the assault of each memory.

Suze Simoneaux had been her mother's only friend. Suze was a big awkward woman with a husband of twenty-five years named Togene. He was another mean man that used his wife for a punching bag. He left her childless and penniless when he died, with nothing more than an old box of a house in disrepair, a twenty-year-old automobile leaking oil and blowing smoke out the tailpipe, and a great, blind hulk of a dog named Horace. A week after Togene died, Suze shoved a suitcase into that rattletrap of a bar and drove away. No one heard from her again.

The sheriff found Horace wandering aimlessly through the swamp and took him home. The dog immediately drifted away and returned to the Simoneaux house. Hunkered down under the porch, he died a couple weeks later, but people swore they heard his mournful ghostly howl for the longest time, drifting through the stillness on nights of a full moon.

The pulp mill cut its employees and staggered its shifts when Kitty was around ten, but people were already moving on. The following spring the cannery almost closed. It managed to stay open another seven months, they closed its doors without notice or giving its employees a final paycheck. Another population decrease.

There had never been a hospital, but they'd had a doctor for a while. Most locals treated themselves with herbal remedies passed down generation after generation, so his practice never thrived. The affluent section of town had always consisted of a few businesses and six or seven better houses, but from what she's seen earlier, none of those remained. The people with any kind of money were wise enough to get away early. The general store and diner might have hung on for a while, but she guessed eventually not enough people remained to keep them open.

Two churches, both on the outskirts of town: The Solid Rock Church of Christian Fellowship, non-denominational, and the Catholic one, but there had never been much of a congregation for either. The priest belonged to the parish, wasn't permanent, and only came twice a month of Sunday, or when needed for a wedding, or burial or christening.

The Solid Rock preacher had been a widower past middle age. His usual Sunday sermon was about fornication, sin, and every other wicked way of man, alternating between the wrath of God and the coming of Judgement, while bored adults sat on hard benches in the heat or cold with irritable, restless babies, and a few adventurous teens got their first taste of sex in pickup trucks and the backseat of their parents' cars. One day he seemed to have left for parts unknown, but it was whispered he never made it out of town. He had been caught in the parsonage with his pants around his ankles, poking Sheriff Oubre's oldest daughter from the rear. The sheriff's oldest was sent away to Catholic school in Baton Rouge. No mention of a new preacher. Not many prayed regularly or ever much cared for messages about wickedness and sin anyway, so he really wasn't missed.

Five miles beyond the center of town, plopped right in the center of the largest cane field around,

was FROG'S FLATROOF BAR, a mainstay of existence, where Friday and Saturday nights drunks drove
off-kilter, mowing down rows of cane. It had a pitted
metal pole in front, where a flag had once flown,
later supporting a couple of plastic beer signs. On the
porch, men sat on a metal glider under a roof of several layers of arched rusted tin that had never been
flat. Inside stood a small wooden bar, a scarred pool
table with most of the baize missing and a cubbyhole
bathroom with a dirty toilet and a little window
mailed shut, panes painted dark green.

No one knew Frog, but someone named Joe
came by once a week to bring a fresh supply of liquor
and collect receipts. The bar help was a female, with
large breasts under a thin scrap of material she called
a blouse. She chewed gum vigorously, wore her
bleached hair teased high, stiff with hairspray, drank
straight whiskey in large amounts if someone bought
it, and all the regulars had sex with her at one time or
another. They all called her sweets or babe, not by
way of endearment, but because most of them just
didn't know her name. It was Onie. It was rumored
she had visited a doctor in Port Allen early on in her
employment, discovered she had a bad case of
gonorrhea and left without treatment or paying.

Onie's body was found dumped in Iberia Parish
after she didn't show for work. The state police
arrested a half-witted teenaged boy. When he strug-

gled, they beat him and he died unattended in jail from a brain hemorrhage. Everyone knew the boy was innocent, probably even knew who had killed Onie—a local who brought home a nasty dose of Onie's gonorrhea—but they let it go. It was soon forgotten. It was just part of the way things were. The way they took care of their own problems.

Kitty's young years had been spent in misery, with a dislike for the town from the moment she became aware of the bad things that went on. Maybe living within the confines of a bad town made bad, miserable people. Like toxic waste dumped on the unsuspecting, generation after generation, and babies were born bad because all the generations before them had been bad and it was in the blood. Something a little twisted buried in her and Lacy? If so, they had managed to escape before it was too late, but Yancy and Arcie hadn't seemed to make it. She had sworn she would never come back and now she had. Why hadn't she fought harder to stay away?

Kitty moved slowly down the hallway. She stood in the living room, looking with equal parts curiosity and trepidation at old furniture that had seen too much wear. She listened for any noise. She heard nothing except a sleepy house, and the sound of her own breathing, harsh through a throat closed tight with nerves and a mouth desert dry.

The clock on the mantel made a series of dull,

soft clicks. Kitty smelled old odors: cooking, a musti-
ness of dust, sweat, and herbs, and things she
couldn't name. An unclean stench lingered, almost
the insidious sweet smell of death. She walked into
the kitchen, aware she couldn't seem to stop listening
at the dark. Whatever she was listening for didn't
come to greet her. She felt pretty paranoid.

The moon raised high, a rich gold-white bayou
moon. Luminous light tendrils filtered through the
kitchen window, touched on the scared old table and
chairs, a hutch without glass tucked in a corner,
dishes and jars and bottles, colored glass items like
droplets from a rainbow with wavy textures but no
particular pattern. Colors ran together like someone
had poured a caustic solvent over them. Moving tree
branches, undulating with a hypnotic reflection in the
window glass, cast a slender shadow across water-
stained walls and worn white linoleum.

Opening the refrigerator, Kitty discovered a
plastic water jug, half a dozen eggs, some white, a
couple brown, and a bowl filled with potatoes and
other shriveled unrecognizable vegetables. The freezer was empty. Her stomach clenched in mild com-
plaint. She hadn't realized how hungry she was. She
would have gladly killed for a cheeseburger and a
double order of fries.

Kitty dropped into a chair, propped her elbows
on the table, and rubbed wearily at her eyes. It was

the middle of the night. She shouldn't be doing this. She had never fainted in her life. She was still feeling muzzy; she should go back to bed. Lowering her head on her arms, she continued to listen. She heard nothing beyond the steady pulse of her own blood in her ears, a rapid thump in her neck, the palms of her hands, and the soles of her feet. There was a dull ache down low, between her hip bones, a tenderness that couldn't quite be touched.

A memory twanged deep in her brain, her thoughts drifted and then she was far away in the past . . .

. . . as shadow crawled with the consistency of elongated worms, glittering in the random slashes of cold moonlight. Orange tongues of flame licked at the sooty fireplace stones. Glowing logs popped and hissed, shifting against the rick grate. The old house seemed to shiver on its stilts as a fretful wind made strange sounds between the wooden boards. It was raining, had rained most of that day and the previous day, a cold, driving rain. Everything was saturated. Now and then gusts of water surged against the windowpanes, rattling glass.

The four of them sat on the floor in front of the fireplace. Yancy's black hair was a skull-cap, crinkly, and sprouted from around her ears like broken, diseased grain stalks. Lacy folded her long legs up under her chin, her eyes shining in the dark. Arcie's cheeks flamed with bright spots of color as if someone had painted them there. She had unkempt hair and fingernails gnawed to the quick.

"Gonna play the game tonig't," Yancy said, face twisted in a foxy grin.

An uneasy quiet sprang up between them. They had discussed the game before, had disagreed, decided not to play. Now Yancy was pressing it on them again. They glanced at each other and looked away, uncomfortable, as if they expected an argument to erupt. Yancy, peeved, seemed to find their hesitation meddlesome, forcing her to be more persistent.

"Tu epouvante, Minou?" Yancy challenged. You scared, Kitty?

"Pas du tout!" Not at all! *"Nous peux faire quoi tu veux."* We can do what you want. She looked toward the other two, getting quick nods of agreement.

In the kitchen, they sat around the table. Yancy produced herbs and bowls and candles. Before she sat, she opened the front door.

"We'll freeze our damn asses off!" Kitty had protested, pulling her fatigue jacket tight around her. "It's too damn cold for that, Yancy."

"Tais-toi!" Yancy ordered. Hush up! "An open doo is a welcome to let him enter, to invite him in."

Gusts of nasty wind immediately filled the rooms

with wet cold. The fire flickered and danced, and the wood hissed, the embers and ash fluttering upward from between the popping logs.They hunched over the table, huddled inside their clothes.

Yancy prepared a small bowl by pricking her finger and squeezing droplets of blood into the bottom and mixing the blood with pinches of other things from a little brown jar.

"Why are you doing that?" Arcie asked, a look of disgust speeding across her face.

"Blood of the conjurer is powerful and important," Yancy answered, nothing more. She drank first and offered each of them the bowl. "Drink, and close your eyes."

They all sipped at the mixture hesitantly.

As icy air whipped through the door, rain played background music to Yancy's whispery chant. Kitty's tongue held the bittersweet taste of what she had drunk and she couldn't resist opening her eyes. The others had their eyes closed; they were scared and didn't want to see anything. Yancy seemed in the middle of a seizure, head thrown back, mouth gaping open, eyes rolling in a frenzied dance beneath squeezed shut eyelids. Her hands pressed palm-flat against the table, each of her fingers alive with movement, jerking and curling as if they were disconnected and had a mind of their own.

The clock clicked, chiming out the strokes of

midnight. The wind passed over, around, and between each of them, kissing out each candle flame.
Cold dark closed in.

Yancy's seizure passed, except for small tremors
in her face. Lacy sat stiffly, hands balled so tightly
against her chest the knuckles had whitened. Arcie
swayed as if buffeted from side to side by the wind.
And Kitty shivered, terrified, because something told
her they shouldn't have agreed to this, something
wasn't right about it.

A whispery sound . . . a staggering jolt to Kitty's
heart. A small noise that didn't belong, didn't mingle,
pitched high above the wind. Kitty jerked her head
toward the door.

A shadowy form slid through the open door, rain
glistening on its shoulders. It had a big, hairy naked
body, definitely male, all of him visible. Not exactly a
man, not exactly an animal.

Her throat closed tight, her stomach bolted
frantically up into that closed space.

He tilted his head and for a split second his
depthless eyes, without reflection, trained on her,
then, as suddenly as he had appeared, he was gone.

. . . and Kitty jerked upright from the table, gulp-
ing down air, clasping her hands together over her
mouth to choke her scream back down inside. No

longer a memory that stalked the perimeter of her mind; that night had come back full force. It was all there, the fright she had experienced, the uncertainty of not knowing exactly what she saw. No guessing now about that tiny shadow of fear she'd always carried deep inside since that night. It was one of the reasons why she hadn't wanted to come back to French Gap.

She tensed, jerked around, her eyes frantically searching the kitchen. Had something been in the room with her?

She felt sure something had brushed against her. Or was it only her imagination, fear, or paranoia?

There was no sign of an intruder in the dim room, but she was positive something had touched her—something had been in the room with her as she slept, flooded with memories, just like twenty years ago. Whatever it was—it had been there so briefly she didn't see it well, only felt the terror it evoked inside her—had it been only her memory of it that sprang to life, or had it returned, been the same abomination from that night come back to haunt her?

Kitty pushed away from the table, and felt it tilt, thinking it would overturn. She heard the legs settle with a soft thud against the linoleum. She barely made it to the sink. The heaves were so bad she wanted to rip her empty stomach apart to stop them. She hunched over the sink, fingers digging in hard as if as if trying to push the pain out through her back. Her knees wobbled, her head spun, her pulse raced, her blood made a throbbing drumbeat in her temples.

The heaves finally stopped. The pain drifted away, leaving her legs numb and shaky, as if all feeling stopped at her hips and she no longer had feet. A sweaty panic caught hold of her, bit in, held on as she stumbled back to her room, hugging the hall wall for protection against anything lurking in the broken shadows from the living room windows, still filled with the black crawling terror she had felt moments before.

Creely pulled up in front of Schexnaydre General Merchandise and killed the Porsche's engine. He yawned and rubbed at his eyes with his knuckles. He was tired, his muscles tied in knots. It had been a long drive. He had driven carefully, not knowing the level of local and state police surveillance. He had stopped frequently to fill the gas tank and always asked about French Gap. He got negative head shakes, peculiar looks, and misdirected once or twice. He got lost a couple of times. He'd had a few too many hours with impatient thoughts when all he wanted was quanimity. Stars speared the sky's darkness, and a ghostly moon shadowing endless fields of sugarcane and sleepy cattle brought him to a few abandoned houses off buckling asphalt.

Frustrated and uncomfortable, he wanted the sun to come up. Vaguely directed by a boy at his last gas stop, he found himself with nothing in his headlights but single lane blacktop bordered by swamp and sugarcane and the occasional shine of animal eyes in the dark. As the blacktop became oyster sell he knew put more than one ding and nick in the car's paint job, he drove until he realized he'd passed the turn the boy told him about. He found himself dead-ended by water visible through trees a few yards ahead, had to turn and back-track for miles.

The sun peaked over the horizon as oyster shell gave way to a dirt track not much wider than the Porsche. The place didn't seem to have a real road running to it. What was there ran about a quarter of a mile straight, then turned into what looked like was once the main street.

Creely cursed softly under his breath, easing himself from behind the wheel and glancing warily around. He stared ahead, and turned to look behind at empty streets   and gutted decaying buildings. A couple of roofs had collapsed, caved in and around desiccated boards and crumbly stuff that might have once been sheetrock. Doors twisted sideways on rusty hinges. Windblown trash was trapped inside entrances without doors and speared on shards of broken window glass. Weeds grew up as tall as his ass through the floorboards. It looked as if the town had been abandoned a long time. More than abandoned, he decided, closer to cursed, so no one would want to ever live there.

Town proper was only about three blocks long, oyster shell twisting off through trees. Walking paths head into thick, weedy oblivion. No stop lights, a couple of long-dead street lights, a stretch of dirt with potholes and huge patches of crushed shell veering left and right. Dilapidated buildings; an anonymous little diner fronted with jagged, broken plate glass. A tiny gas station, the paint on the single gas pump morphed to slate-gray years ago, what the elements hadn't eaten away the size of white quarters, gasoline grand unidentifiable. A glint of sun in the windshield of an ancient Chevy parked in front of a squat building with a "Sheriff's Office" sign over the door. How long had it been since this place needed a sheriff?

Stretching, pretending indifference, he studied the emptiness, his ears straining for sound, feeling a prickling along his spine. The pricks were the discomfort of being watched. He looked in every direction but saw no one, not a single iota of life. This was the kind of place when it thrived, if it ever did, kids were born, grew up, and ran away from with great speed.

Creely stepped with caution onto the porch of the old store. The boards creaked and bent inward under his feet. He treaded carefully across holes, paused, and scowled at the mannequin in the dirty display window. It was bald, a cavity the size of a saucer in the left side of its head, a three-fingered left hand, a missing right hand. What had once been hair was a mutilated little animal curled at its feet. It might have been female. Now it stood cracked and yellowed, comically without gender.

The store's door relented with a deep groan; stale and sour odors assaulted him. Busted cans, rotted contents hardened on shelves, empty cellophane packages curled in, gnawed through at the corners.

He stepped back as a rat scuttled across the warped counter within slapping distance of his hand. A pair of big cockroaches raced in circles behind the cracked counter glass.

Near the rear of the store, an emaciated woman scratched through debris with a sparse broom. She didn't look up, behaving as if she didn't see him.

He cleared his throat. She stopped sweeping and edged away, holding the broom out in front of her like a weapon. Creely couldn't fathom her age. Freckled parchment skin drew tightly across her almost-bald skull, a few wisps of white hair draped over peculiar inward-curled ears, and she had a toothless mouth.

"Good morning, ma'am." He tried a smile, felt sure it failed. He motioned over his shoulder with his thumb. "Am I in the right place, is this French Gap?"

She didn't respond.

"Ma'am?"

Small eyes darted slyly over him. She reversed the broom and stood it on its wooden handle, only the upper half of her face visible. She spoke through the straw, "Don't knowed nothin', mistah. Go see de man . . . go see Abadie." She wiggled the broom back and forth, pushing the straw at him, and waving her hand as if he were an annoying housefly.

When he didn't move or speak, she hissed, "Git! Git gone w'th y'all. Go see Abadie!" She backed away, putting the counter between them.

Creely took an uncertain backward step or two. "Where might I find him?"

"She'iff office," she snapped, pointing a shaky finger.

He closed the door behind himself, feeling as if she had physically ejected him. Was this man Abadie actually the sheriff? Why had she directed him there?

The quiet and emptiness of the town seemed to suck at him. If this was the environment Kitty came from, no wonder she had left. Sal was right, it wasn't much of a place, not enough remained to even call it a fishing camp, and in the best of times, it had probably been much more than it was. Where *were* the people? Why had everyone left? How long ago had that happened? Surely there were others, it was highly unlikely that old woman lived here alone. Lord knows anything was possible, but there didn't seem to be enough viable life to sustain a hungry flea in or around this place.

What could have been so urgent? He'd thought they knew each other well enough Kitty could tell him anything. Why would she want to come here? Sal said he couldn't find any family. Was there something more disturbing going on? Whatever happened, it had been a last minute decision, he was sure of it. She'd been upset, worried over it, but had almost brushed it aside, and hadn't told him because she didn't expect to leave. Did it really matter why she came back?. It didn't, as long as he found out she was okay.

Was he wrong? Maybe he'd been wrong. Maybe she wasn't here. No, he wasn't even going there. This wasteland of a place might cause him speculation about a lot of things, but instinct told him to throw away his doubt. He was more positive now than before leaving New Orleans—Kitty was somewhere close by.

Creely felt *exposed* and glanced surreptitiously around.

It was the best word he could come up with. He was being watched, but he couldn't figure out by whom, how many or from where. The only watcher he openly saw was a mangy old dog in the shade of a broken-down truck a few feet down the road. The dog appeared to be watching with cautious disinterest and only one eye.

58

As the man came out of the store, Domeno Abadie sized him up and found himself, just for a moment, seized by a bolt of pure animal panic.

This is not good! Not good at all!

It was the third time in a long time he'd had to confront outsiders invading his territory. First, it was the three women, now this stranger. What the hell was going on? Who was this man? Had he made a wrong turn? No, that hadn't happened. They were too far into the swamp. It was sometimes difficult for area locals to find their way around here. Outsiders hadn't come to French Gap in years, by accident or on purpose, except for that snooping PI he'd sent packing. He knew people from surrounding areas hadn't stopped whispering, but fear and the years had destroyed most of their curiosity. Someone curious enough to come around never liked what they saw, and left quickly without a problem.

This stranger was going to be different, not like that antsy PI with the shifty eyes. This man had quiet bulldog tenacity about him. He'd ome with a purpose. The tense set of his shoulders said he found his surroundings troubling and offensive. He wouldn't be easily deterred, wouldn't leave without a resolution. Domeno would have to be careful with him.

After Domeno confronted him, if this man wouldn't quietly leave on his own, and seemed determined to cause trouble, Domeno would have to take care of it. He was good at that. He wouldn't like doing it, but if he had to, he would kill him.

No one would ever find his body.

59

When the rooster crowed first light, Kitty didn't hear him. She had made her way back to the bedroom and sat huddled on the bed for an eternity. Finally, she fell into an exhausted sleep. What did wake her was the tapping on the door.

Lacy's cautious voice from the hall said, "Kitty, you awake yet?"

"Come in," she whispered, pushing her shoulders up against the wall.

Lacy stepped inside, her hand lingering on the doorknob. She offered a small smile. "Good morning. Are you feeling better?"

"Close the door." Lacy looked good in snug-fitting black jeans, a green shirt with sleeves rolled to the elbows, and Doc Marten brogans.

Lacy's eyes narrowed and she glanced over her shoulder. "Is something wrong?" she asked, closing the door.

Kitty slipped her legs over the edge of the bed, the heels of her hands pressed hard against the mattress, her voice a conspiratorial whisper. "Where are they?" she asked as Lacy sat next to her.

"I'm not sure."

"What happened to me?"

"You just passed out and took a while coming

around."

"I've never fainted in my life."

Lacy shrugged. "I'm not a doctor, Kitty. One minute you were with us, the next you were out."

"What happened after that?"

"They helped me get you in here and they both left. I haven't seen either of them since. After you and I talked, I went to my room. I've been there until about twenty minutes ago."

"You never talked with them?" Kitty asked.

Lacy shook her head. "No."

Kitty frowned at her. "Don't you find that a little strange? Why disappear and not talk with you?"

"Yes, I find it strange. Yancy never spoke a single word and Arcie was angry, so she wouldn't talk to me. I didn't press it. I was worried about you."

"I appreciate that." Kitty tugged at her bottom lip. "I'm really confused about her not saying a word to either of us since we arrived. Do you think she's spoken to Arcie?"

"I don't know about Arcie, but it's really strange, isn't it?"

"Do you think something is wrong with her? Maybe she can't speak anymore?"

"I appreciate that." Kitty tugged at her bottom lip. "I'm really confused about her not saying a word to either of us since we arrived. Do you think she's spoken to Arcie?"

"I considered it, but I think she's really mad at us, and it could be her way of getting even."

"Pretty stupid, wanting us to back all this way, and then doing that, don't you think?"

"I do, but she overheard what we said outside. Maybe that has something to do with the way she's behaving. She probably didn't expect that sort of reaction from us."

"Good Lord, I don't think I can take another day like yesterday," Kitty breathed.

"But you're feeling better?"

"Shaky."

"And you're still angry with Arcie."

"I'm certainly not happy with her . . . too much crap is going down. She coerced me into this."

"And not enough explanation about what is going on. This is quite an experience." Lacy made an uneasy little sound in her throat. "Did you sleep?"

"A little."

"I didn't get much sleep."

"Why not?"

"A lot of uncomfortable, weird thoughts. I thought I kept hearing something above my head, a noise like something was moving around in the attic."

"What was it?"

"Don't know, maybe a rat or a squirrel. The noise kept coming and going."

Should I tell her about the kitchen episode? Kitty wondered. No, not a good idea. She couldn't explain something she was unsure about, she didn't want to sound freakin' crazy. Maybe she had just drifted off at the table, and it had been the residual of a dream, a faded memory bouncing back because she had been thinking too hard, and remembering too much shit from the past.

"I had some kind of nightmare, I think."

"About what?"

Kitty grinned a little sheepishly. "I don't remember much, but I know it scared me."

"I know this was the first time I've gone without dinner in a long time."

Kitty frowned. "You're kidding, you didn't get any dinner?"

"I didn't see either of them again. So, nope, none was offered. I glanced in the kitchen before going to my room, but there was nothing there and no one was around."

"You're serious?"

"As a heart attack."

"How weird is that?"

"No worse than some of the other stuff."

Kitty studied Lacy for a moment, then said, "Thanks for helping me yesterday. I really do appreciate it." Right now she needed a friend, at least an ally. She couldn't let feelings from the past stand in the way of that. "I owe you an apology."

"For what?"

"I've been rude."

"Forget it. It wasn't a good day for any of us."

"No, it wasn't. Arcie and this miserable trip had my last nerve frazzled. And we need to do something about transportation, so we can get away from here a soon as possible."

Lacy patted Kitty's knee and stood up. "Yes, we do, but try a shower first. It works wonders on dead or overworked brain cells. I'm headed to the kitchen. I'm hungry and could use some breakfast, even if I have to find something to cook myself. I'm not an empty-stomach thinker." She reached out again, and patted Kitty's hand.

"Yeah, I could use something to eat myself, but—" Kitty began. She was interrupted by the bedroom door being thrown open.

Arcie stepped into the room without knock ing, a frown pulling her eyebrows together, her lips in a tight line, something close to anger in her eyes.

"What are you two whispering about?"

Kitty rolled her eyes and looked away.

Lacy walked to the window without speaking, pushed aside the curtains, and seemed to be gathering her thoughts before putting them into words. After a moment, she turned back, mouth pinched tight. Her tone was testy when she said, "It's a little early for this, Arcie. Yesterday was rough on all of us. I was certainly hoping for a better day today."

A tic had appeared in Arcie's cheek. She glanced warily from one to the other. Her hands worked at her blouse, pinching fabric nervously into pleats. "I don't want to argue," she said slowly.

"So don't start it," Kitty said.

"Seems as if you do," Lacy added.

"This isn't why we came here," Arcie whispered.

"Maybe you could explain a little better exactly why we did come," Lacy said. "I think we've tried, but neither of us can fully understand what is going on. From my perspective, things just don't seem to be working out."

"This is unfair. You two have decided to gang up on me."

"We just want the truth about what's going on," Kitty said.

Arcie took a couple of steps forward. "I didn't know . . . about her, I mean, or about the town. I never stopped to think twenty years could make that much difference. I thought it would have gotten bigger, not get deserted. I didn't think it would look like this. I've wanted to come back for so long . . ."

"Why didn't you come? You could have come by yourself. You drove here yesterday okay," Lacy said. "You didn't need us to come back here."

Arcie gave her a vacant stare as if Lacy had made an unrealistic suggestion. That returning by herself never occurred to her. "I—I guess I didn't want to come back alone. I always figured we would keep our promise and come back together." She sighed, offered a weak smile. "It's only a couple of days. That's all she asked for."

"Two too many," Kitty muttered.

"Not if we could stop fighting over everything. Maybe you'll think differently after some breakfast."

"No food for breakfast," Kitty said, remembering the pitiful assortment in the fridge.

"What does that mean?" Arcie jerked her body up straight, her posture tense again.

"No food in the refrigerator."

"How would you know?"

"I was in the kitchen last night."

"You went snooping?" Arcie accused.

"I went looking for water."

"You shouldn't have done that!" Rays of bright pink danced in Arcie's cheeks.

"I suppose I should have gone thirsty? Well, I did it, it's done." She glanced at Lacy. "See why I get so mad at her?" She directed her gaze back to Arcie. "What the hell's wrong with you, Arcie? You're always trying to make everything into something more than it is, just itching for a fight. Not snooping. I was thirsty." They faced each other in belligerent silence, their anger like bristles erupting from their skin.

"She's right," Lacy said quietly. "It might just as

well have been me."

"I-I didn't . . . mean for it to sound that way," Arcie said. They were ganging up on her.

Yes, they are, black funk whispered in her head.

"Really?" Kitty had thin patience now. The new Arcie seemed intent on provoking an argument, and she refused to allow herself to be drawn into one. She just wanted the crap to stop and go away. Why was Arcie suddenly so adamant about arguing? Was all this crap the beginnings of a nervous breakdown or maybe something worse? Lacy was doing her best to play friendly, to intercede between them, but she had lost most of the calm and polish she'd arrived with.

"Yancy's fixing breakfast," Arcie interjected, squaring her shoulders.

"With what?" Kitty demanded. "What do you think she intends to feed us?"

"Apparently the food you didn't see last night."

"Or maybe it's some kind of fresh morning road kill," Kitty snapped.

"You're so nasty, Kitty. Why do you have to be so nasty?" Arcie gave her a smoldering look before she turned away. "Breakfast will be ready in a few minutes. Try to pull yourself together enough to be civilized," she said over her shoulder as the door closed hard behind her.

In the kitchen, Yancy overheard every word. Anger brought her creature right below the surface of her skin. She fought against it, knowing what would happen if she it. There were other things that needed to be done. They were all so nervous about being back, snapping at each other like starving dogs. And Domeno was nosing around the house; she had smelled him nearby yesterday and last night. He knew the others were here, had probably recognized Kitty right away and the bastard was working on a way to get his hands on her. It was starting to make her nervous.

She turned the potatoes over in the skillet, scooped them out and slapped them on to a platter. Morning road kill? Yancy thought, with a small smile. Kitty didn't know how close to the truth that really was.

60

Creely pushed open the door without knocking, halting just inside when he found himself confronted by a big blond man behind an old desk, looking up and flattening his huge hands against the desktop, apparently annoyed by the intrusion. He had a look about him that said he quickly angered but wasn't usually offended unless doubted. He was one of those tall, muscular, big men not easily dismissed or forgotten, wide chest and broad shoulders, badly in need of a haircut. There was a youthful strength about him, but his sun-rough skin and the wrinkles around his eyes and mouth suggested late thirties-early forties. He appeared full of surliness and suspicion. His stare was direct, but his eyes were veiled, cold and flat. They were an unusual color that could have been a shade of green but appeared to be more a burnished copper, the time-caressed metal of an old coin.

"He'p y'u w'th somethin', mistah?" His lip curled insolently. He had clipped elocution, a thick slur on his words.

Creely wondered if it was done on purpose as a distraction ploy. "Are you Abadie?"

"Could be . . . who's askin'?"

"Creely Crane." He stepped forward, offered his hand. Abadie raised his gaze for a split second before his eyes flickered away. Creely had already had a good taste of attitude during his drive down, but this was the worst yet. Extracting a business card from his wallet, he extended it. Abadie the card, read it, and tossed it. It landed face-down in metal ashtray overflowing with unfiltered cigarette butts.

Okay, Creely thought, seething, eyeing cigarette ash that swirled and settled over his business card. "I was told you might be able to help me."

"Wha' can I do fer y'u, Mr. Attorney from New Orleans?"

Creely's jaw clenched, he felt the angry, rhythmic muscle throb in his cheek and the dull pulsing artery in his neck. A person met all types of people in his line of work. He had met a lot of people like this man, arrogant, insolent and uneducated, much too full of himself to recognize his own ignorance. There was violent propensity here, everything about this man yelled danger. He seemed to have established a paramount in this creepy place. Creely didn't like him any more than the others he'd met, but he didn't have to like Abadie, just be polite. It was difficult but doable. Impolite wouldn't get him very far; he was on Abadie's turf. He would have to play by his rules, like it or not. Creely needed to get lucky. Too bad he didn't much believe in luck.

"I'm looking for a friend. I believe she and two others arrived here sometime yesterday. There's been an emergency. I need to find her as soon as possible."

"We don't get a lotta strangers h're."

"She wouldn't be a stranger."

"*Non?*" The green-gold eyes narrowed. "Who migh' she be?"

"A native, born here." The language switch hadn't escaped Creely. Abadie wanted to toy with him and the play wasn't going to be friendly. The question was, how much was he going to play and how unfriendly would it get. *Okay, big guy, let's play,* Creely thought. "Her name is Kitty Chauvin."

"Kitty Chauvin, huh?" Abadie pursed his lips, plucked at them with long, thick fingers. "Name don't sound fam'liar."

"Have you lived here long, Mr. Abadie?" Creely inquired quietly.

"Mos' my life." The reply was succinct, his expression guarded.

"You appear to be about her age. You might have gone to school with her."

Abadie tensed. He didn't like his word disputed. Creely sensed his pure brute force as something shifted in his eyes.

"Kitty—like a cat," Abadie said softly, savoring the flavor of the name against his tongue. A faint smile touched the corners of his mouth as if he'd found a fond remembrance. He produced a crumpled pack of Camels from his pocket and lit one. Thin streams of smoke dribbled from his nostrils.

Creely took the time Abadie's pause provided to glance around the office. Everything looked old and tired. A space of rare usage, occupied only when a presence was necessary by a man probably unauthorized to use it. He looked at Abadie and waited. He knew how to do that. Growing up around Sal had taught him how to wait.

"Hell, yeah, now I 'member 'er," Abadie said. "She left h're a lon' time ago . . . uumm, what, twenty year or so back? She weren't no more 'an a kid when she left, if I 'member righ'."

"You haven't seen her since?"

"Non." Abadie chuckled, winked suggestively. A faint humorless smile barely tilted the corners of his mouth. "But if I 'member righ', I wouldn't mind seein' 'er aga'n. Y'all know what I mean? That one, she was a real looker." He sucked deeply on his cigarette, his eyes wary. "But, hell, Mr. Attorney, if I 'member righ', all she did was talk 'bout gettin' away from h're. Why would she come back now?"

"I asked myself the same question." Creely glanced through the small window where dust motes danced languidly in thin streams of sunlight. He liked Abadie's smile less each time it appeared. "There doesn't seem to be much around her for a person to come back to."

"Well, if she was h're, lookin' like I 'member 'er

. . . hell, lookin' *anyways,* fer that matter—" he leaned slightly forward, voice lowered conspiratorially, his expression almost a leer—"then I would 'member. Even as a kid, she as a fine piece of ass." He waited a moment as if expecting a male-bonding response; when he didn't get one, his face dropped into an immobile mask. His eyes shuttered over, dark pupils narrowed dangerously. "She y'ur woman?"

"A very close friend."

"Ca c'est triste."

"Pardon?"

Abadie's lips twisted in amusement. "I said 'that's too bad.' She runnin' from someone?"

"No, she isn't."

"Y'u workin' fer 'er husban'?"

"No husband." *Not smart, Creely. You shouldn't have said that. Giving out too much information.*

Abadie crushed his cigarette out on top of Creely's business card, leaned back in his chair. "Woman like that otta h've a husban' to care fer 'er, don't y'u think, Mr. Attorney? How lon' y'u say she been missin'?" He grinned, a derisive twitch of lip.

"I said she came here. That doesn't make her missing, does it?"

"Non. My mistake." He made a *tssking* noise. "She ain't y'ur woman, but y'u chasin' 'er down. Lon' way to come, lot to do fer jest a friend."

"I said there is an emergency."

"Yep, so y'u did." Abadie had a pensive frown, a shadow-flicker of something close to annoyance in those flat eyes.

"It's important that I locate her, Mr. Abadie, a matter of life or death."

"Sheriff," Abadie corrected.

"Sheriff," Creely acknowledged.

Abadie shrugged. "I see y'u th'nk so, Mr. Attorney, but how y'u say?. . . women are—*qui puet pas etre predit* . . . y'u know, unpredictable. Maybe got 'erself a new fella. Jes' took off w'th 'im fer a few days—seein' as y'u ain't 'er husban' or boyfr'end an' all, it sho'ldn't worry y'u too much."

Creely took one of the chairs opposite the desk without asking. Abadie frowned, but said nothing. Creely pulled out his cigarettes and lit one, taking a moment to regroup his thoughts. He felt a small tingle, a burn between his shoulder blades, a sixth sense bad feeling about Abadie that was more than instant dislike. No need for a sheriff in this pitiful excuse for a town. Here was someone who had assumed his position, not elected or appointed law enforcement. Abadie was intent on playing with him, trying to make him uncomfortable and irritated by not volunteering information. He didn't seem to care his behavior made the situation suspicious. How long since there were strangers, even residents, around here? How long had he sat in that chair with his inflated ego, preening around the badge pinned to his shirt?

Abadie rocked slowly, watching him closely with those strangely colored eyes. A muscle jerked in his left eyelid, almost in unison with the muted groan of the chair. The air was close, with slow-to-disperse cigarette smoke that hung above their heads. They sat listening to each other breathe for what seemed like an eternity, Creely watching Abadie as intensely as Abadie watched him.

After his last call to Kitty went directly to voice mail, Creely had made a few phone calls. Putting the word out on the street to those he knew who knew her. He had spoken with her building superintendent, an ex-cop who was head of security for the condos, someone he occasionally played cards with. He was told Kitty and Arcie left in Kitty's Mercedes around eleven that morning with a couple travel bags. She'd left her dog with the usual sitter, the old lady in the condo across the hall, but hadn't told the woman anything about where she was going, except she'd be gone a couple days. He hadn't spoken directly to her, had only seen them leaving the parking garage. They put Arcie's Lincoln in the spot usually occupied by the Mercedes, and he had no idea where they might be headed. He said he would get in touch if he found out anything. A taxi driver of his acquaintance called shortly after and said he'd seen her leaving the airport with two women, the Mercedes heading out toward Destrehan or LaPlace.

"They left Kenner yesterday, Kitty, Arcie Becnel, and another woman they picked up at the airport," Creely said, the heat collecting under his collar, his patience stretched thin.

"Wha' makes y'u sure they come h're?"

"Bayou people are a different lot, aren't they, Mr. Abadie?" Creely decided to stray from the main inquiry, catching Abadie off guard.

"And wha's that mean, Mr. Attorney?" There was a flicker of something deep in his eyes, a subtle change in his expression.

"They believe in weird stuff like witchcraft and voodoo, don't they?"

"We migh' be a bit supersti'ous, but y'u cain't alw'ys believe wha' y'u h'ar. Why y'u askin'? Jest 'cause she's from 'round h're? She's gone missin' a day and y'u thi'kin 'bout runnin' righ' out fer a chick'n bone throw or taro' card readin' or candle-burnin' spell? Maybe a séance? A little *gris-gris*? Somethin' like that tell y'u she come back h're? Or did y'u jest come h're first 'cause y'u figured we'd know all 'bout that sorta stuff? Maybe we'd whip up a spell or two fer y'u. Y'u coulda stay closer to home fer that. Sounds a bit *fou* to me."

"Pardon?" Creely was alerted to an undertone in Abadie's voice he didn't like.

Abadie smirked. *"Fou,"* he repeated. "Crazy."

"I see." Creely cleared his throat. "Don't really need any of that. You ever heard of an intuitive?"

"I h'ard it 'fore." Abadie propped his feet on the desk. Mud had collected in his boot heels, dark, spiky little burrs on his trouser cuffs. He nonchalantly began to pluck the burrs, and toss them in the waste-basket. "Y'u one of 'em kinda people?" His tone was edged with deprecation.

"I am."

"How often y'u h've 'em ghostly visions. Mr. Attorney?" Now his tone was sarcastic.

"Often enough." Creely stood and walked to the window, working at his blank lawyer face. The street had remained deserted. The old dog had merely shifted position, hairy muzzle resting on front paws. Flies buzzed him; he flicked an ear occasionally in discouragement. "You're not very helpful for a law enforcement officer, Mr. Abadie," he observed.

"'Cause what y'u tellin' me don't make much sense, Mr. Attorney."

"Crane," Creely snapped, turning to face him. "Crane, Creely Crane—*Sheriff.*" Dislike for this man was beginning to interfere. Their conversation had turned into a pissing match. He wanted to jerk the bastard up, knock him on his ass, break his nose, destroy a couple teeth in that mocking smile, but he had to be careful. He didn't want to lose his object-

tivity to anger. Anger clouded the brain, caused a person not to think straight. He had learned nothing; he was losing ground by the second. "I was warned that some bayou people aren't always friendly. I see that's true."

"We keep our own."

"I sense strangers aren't welcome here."

Abadie seemed to have a strong antipathy toward strangers and Creely wondered why. All strangers? Maybe not. Maybe just those that offered a challenge he perceived as a threat.

"Not 'specially." Abadie smirked, stood, walked around the desk, and entered Creely's personal space. "Look h're, Mr. Attorney, we wastin' time h're. If Chauvin and 'er friends show up h're, I'll tell 'er to get in touch w'th y'u. Best I can do." His biceps tightened and flexed under his shirt. He was making himself into an intimidating force, his posture a challenge, his tone a dismissal.

Creely snuffed out a surge of anger. "Does Kitty have family around here?"

"Non." Where Abadie had been evasive and bored, he was now impatient, a touch of mockery in his voice.

"Someone she might want to see after all these years?"

"Cain't th'nk of none."

"How large is French Gap?" Creely persisted.

"Don't blink y'ur eyes passin' thro'gh."

"I was referring to population."

Abadie hesitated. "Y'u migh' be a needin' to know that fer wha' reason?"

"I've only seen two people, you and the old woman at the store."

"Y'u takin' a census? Plannin' on movin' h're?" His voice was full of hostility now.

"Curiosity. Any reason you mind me asking?"

"Ask all y'u want. Towns die. People die. Places like this—young'uns move on. Not much to offer h're anymore."

"Did this place ever have much to offer?"

"A lon' time ago."

"Then why did you stay, Mr. Abadie? Not much need for a sheriff without people."

Abadie slapped his big hand hard against the desk. Dust flew; cigarette ash gushed up in a small cloud. His eyes had frosted over. "Y'u awful nosey. I don't th'nk that info'mation is any of y'ur bidness. I th'nk I been patient w'th y'u, suh. We got us a quiet little place h're. We mind our bidness, don't bother nobody. We like it that way." His upper lip curled in a nasty little snarl. "I tol' y'u I ain't seen 'er. That's 'bout all I got to say, Mr. Attorney."

"Crane," Creely corrected again. "Creely Crane."

Abadie didn't acknowledge the correction.

Their glances locked. Creely felt the furious rush

of his blood. No progress with this Neanderthal. He was uncomfortable second-guessing Abadie, he didn't want to think his emotions were skewing his judgment; he wanted to think Abadie was just the ignorant ass he believed him to be, but they were past the bullshit posturing. If he kept pushing, he would probably get himself busted up, at least a black eye or broken nose, but no closer to the information he needed. Getting injured wouldn't solve anything, but something definitely wasn't right. Abadie was hiding something he seemed determined to guard.

Creely grabbed the doorknob. "Someone could get killed here and it would never get noticed, would it, sheriff?"

"I migh' could su'gest a person be careful, if I had a half mind to, Mr. Crane." Abadie used Creely's name for the first time, offering a dangerously benign smile, his tone razor-edged. "Pe'ple dis'ppear 'round h're all the time."

61

"I knew nothing good was going to come of this trip," Kitty whispered. "It seems to get worse all the time. I don't know how much more I can take of this. I feel like I'm losing my mind."

"Don't be so hard on yourself." Lacy touched her shoulder, her expression sympathetic.

Kitty shook her head and swore softly. How could Arcie turn the tables so easily? She wanted to laugh, it was so absurd, but couldn't because deep down it was a little scary and incredibly sad. "I'm okay—really. Go on. I'll be along in a few minutes."

"Are you sure?"

"As sure as I'm ever going to be until I leave this damn place. Go on . . . don't wait for me. I just need some time to—what did she say?—oh, yeah. Pull myself together enough to be civilized."

"Let it go, Kitty. She's angry because things aren't going the way she thought."

"I think she wrecked my car on purpose."

Lacy hrugged. "It seemed to be an accident. She got scared and lost control of the car," she said, but there was uncertainty in her eyes.

"I'd like to think that . . . it's just hard for me to believe right now." Kitty pulled clean clothes from her travel bag. "I'll take a quick shower and catch up with you."

"Okay, we'll wait on you to eat." Lacy walked down the hall and Kitty followed her as far as the bathroom.

After Kitty showered and dressed and she entered the kitchen, there was a tense moment when everyone turned to look at her and said nothing. Lacy and Arcie sat across the table from each other, plates in front of them; Yancy leaned against the kitchen counter. The smell of fried food, particularly meat, assaulted Kitty's nostrils with a physical strength. she tried a smile on Yancy, but the woman looked away. Arcie puffed herself up like a young fighting cock when Kitty sat down next to Lacy.

"Feeling better?" Lacy asked, with a thin smile.

Kitty nodded, not sure about feeling better, but at least she was clean. She studied the two platters in the middle of the table over the plate in front of her. There were slabs of fried potatoes on one; runny scrambled eggs and thinly sliced, crispy dark meat on the other. She felt a wash of embarrassment as she sparsely scooped food onto her place. It had been stupid on her part to have mentioned the absence of food. Weird as Yancy seemed, it was ridiculous to think she wouldn't be prepared to feed them knowing there were no restaurants in town. She should have kept her mouth shut.

The shower had revived her, but she was still

tense. Surprisingly, there had been hot water and clean towels. Everything was close to immaculate in the bathroom, even the old toilet.

She sampled the eggs and potatoes, passed on the meat. It had a distinctly sharp, almost-musky odor that made her suspicious about its origin. Definitely not beef or pork or chicken, maybe some swamp creature. Eating wild things wouldn't faze Yancy. Would she be so bold as to feed it to them? Yeah, she would.

Kitty needed to eat, or at least try, and stop with the suspicious, nasty thoughts. They weren't helping to stabilize her wobbly mental state.

"See, I told you there was food," Arcie said.

"Yes, you did," she answered, struggling for agreeable in order to forestall another argument. She should have known Arcie wouldn't let it go.

Yancy stood with her back to them, looking out the window. The silence that hung over all of them felt almost cautious, as if a single wrong word would lead to another disagreement. Kitty took a couple bites of egg and potatoes, shoved her place away, and pushed herself to her feet. Her hand tightened on the back of the chair as she swayed a little, overcome with a touch of lightheadedness and the need to get away, her anxiety strumming her body like fingers on guitar strings.

"I—I need some fresh air."

"You want to take a walk?" Lacy asked.

"Yeah, I think I need a walk."

"A walk sounds great," Arcie agreed, but inwardly groaned. More walking was the last thing she wanted to do, but this might just be her chance to see Domeno if he was still here.

"No!" Kitty shouted before she could stop herself. They stared at her in surprise.

"No," she said again, more softly. "I . . . I need a little alone time."

"Why would you need to be alone?" Arcie asked.

The tight line of her temper unraveling, Kitty stared down at Arcie a long moment without speaking. She realized if she spoke, she would say something she might later regret. She turned and walked away.

"Bitch!" Arcie hissed, the single word low, dark, and a little threatening, her eyes following Kitty's departure.

62

Creely drove slowly, trying to avoid the ruts and bumps in the almost-non-existent road, mulling over his confrontation with Abadie. He still felt Abadie's eyes on his back, dissecting him as he walked away. Sitting uncomfortably across that old desk from each other, a nudge, a push, a shove, working on seeing whose dick was bigger. It hadn't worked.

To someone different, Abadie might have been threatening and intimidating, Creely gave him that. He wasn't the congenial type. He made no attempt toward playing that part.

What burned his ass about the situation was Abadie posturing as a sheriff of an unpopulated placed locate in the middle of nowhere, a place that looked as if a plague had overtaken it, and wiped it void of humanity with a single swipe. It was so isolated, the man couldn't help but know exactly what went on, but behaved as if he saw and knew nothing. Defensive and wary, less than truthful about everything, no intention of providing information, Abadie was hiding something. People died, people moved away. That was logical, probably as close to the truth Abadie had come during their conversation. People did what they had to do to survive.

Creely couldn't put the pieces together—yet.

People disappear around here all the time. The fine hairs on his neck had stood at attention, even the shortest ones. It had been a strong and carefully worded warning. Probably the second truth Abadie had told him.

Who *was* Abadie? Creely had been around too much law enforcement not to pay judicious notice to instinct telling him Abadie wasn't the official sheriff. He was likely an opportunist, a self-appointed citizen when there was no one left to defy him or question his authority. He'd pinned that badge on himself. No need checking back with the old woman. She had been nervous, anxious to get rid of him. She certainly wasn't going to divulge any information. Abadie probably had an understanding with her about how to handle strangers.

He could call Sal when he found cell service again; see what he could find out about Abadie, but he had to keep it simple, not put Sal into guardian mode. He didn't want to bring too many people in on this unless it was necessary. Sal could always contact the state police at any time Creely found he was unable to handle things. He needed to find food and lodging until he could find Kitty, for at least one night, hopefully not more, and Boudreaux was the closest town. He could try the local police in Boudreaux, someone with a badge and real authority to go back with him to French Gap.

Abadie could be a criminal, have a sheet as long as his arm. But if that proved true and they didn't locate Kitty, that move might only stir Abadie up and put her and her friends in jeopardy. He needed to give that idea more thought.

Oyster shell turned into one-lane blacktop again, then two-lane blacktop and finally asphalt. Daylight made all the difference in the drive. In darkness, it had seemed to take forever to cover the same distance. He passed THERIOT OYSTER AND SEA-FOOD COMPANY; dozens of crab traps, shredded trawl nets, and strips of tin. Two rusty trucks in a shell lot next to waist-high weeds, parked beside what appeared to be the main building. Closed, or functioning minimally. A few miles farther on, BAY JUNOP SUGAR REFINERY was boarded up. A small family business probably forced into closure by some big conglomerate.

The road was less choked with overgrowth, water more visible, in the distance a channel weaving its way darkly into the Gulf of Mexico. The shiny opal water seemed to touch the distant sun-blazed horizon. A flatboat and pirogues floated listlessly against S- and W-shaped banks of low water, where erosion had eaten the land. Mounds of oyster shell, rusted machinery, and discarded household items were verywhere. The vacant land had become a convenient dumping ground.

Boudreaux was northwest of French Gap. Not much civilization lay between them. The closer he got to Boudreaux, life seemed to rise up and sprout in little patches. Shanties extending over the bayou, pirogues in luminescent water, cane fields, Brahman cattle, a few dirty, butt-ugly sheep. Scaly half-sunken relics, survivors of high storm waters and past hurricanes, mingled with well-maintained fishing boats. He passed three large white boats nudged up to piers decorated with tire bumpers—*THE BIG CLAM, MISS LAURA*, and *WEEZER*. Several men on the decks glanced up from their work with curiosity.

Several houses in succession backed up to the bayou with their own wooden piers, flatboat or pirogue; clothes on rope lines, yard chickens, hunting dogs sprawled lazily around steps. *Thank God for civilization!* Creely thought, crossing into what seemed to be town limits. He stopped at Shakey Joe's Gas Stop and Mini Mart to fill the Porsche's tank.

The town wasn't particularly large, but it was neat and attractive, had a double-wide asphalt main street, four paved cross-sections of streets and more trucks than cars. A few people were on the street, ordinary people with chores to be done or church services to attend, natural Sunday morning activities. Curious, maybe even suspicious glances, in his direction. Checking out a stranger and his fancy car that was attracting attention.

Creely killed the engine in front of a wooden-walled tavern called THE MATING PLACE. A bold sign over the doorway: A buxom woman, a grinning man with one winking eye, one suggestively down-cast. Across the street, BURRELL'S AUTOMOTIVE REPAIR AND GAS had its bay door pulled down. *Josie's Luncheonette* was next door; a small restaurant with a striped, tattered cloth awning and an outside picnic table. It had a shell parking area occupied by a white Chevy van and a blue Ford F-150 truck. Sandwiched between *Josie's* and Boudreaux's Mercantile was a glass-fronted Rexall Drugs. A human relic with a misshapen hat sucked at a pipe, rocking in slow motion in the entryway.

Across the street were Batiste's Real Estate and Law Offices, an auto parts store, a liquor store, barber shop, a butcher shop, and the neon-lighted front of a small grocery with a dark interior. A church with a bell tower rose on the east end of town. Boudreaux City Hall stood next door, a boxy brick building with a square metal billboard outfront, loaded with tattered fringes of advertisements and notices, the soft breeze squeaking it against the narrow rod of an inverted U-frame. Boudreaux appeared small-town normal as if it had jumped out of a Norman Rockwell painting. If there was anything weird about it, what it was obviously waited for dark to appear.

Two kids on rusty bicycles, followed by a big,

black mongrel, abruptly whipped around a corner, passing alarmingly close to the Porsche. They rolled their eyes at Creely and snickered. He tracked them until they disappeared around another building, then he turned his attention back to *Josie's*. He could eat and recharge in the little restaurant.

A sudden rumble filled the air. A big man pushed up the heavy metal door on BURRELL'S. A pair of teenaged boys with threadbare tee shirts and holey jeans walked past and glanced inside. The man waved them away impatiently. They laughed, gestured with their fingers and moved on. He disappeared into an adjoining office space. Creely stepped closer, tried to decipher the dim interior, and could only make out shadowy outlines.

The kids noticed something out of place, he thought, squinting against the yellow melt of sun, and started across the street for a closer look, hunger forgotten.

Almost buried in shadow stood muddy dark-blue Mercedes, backed onto a raised lift, half its underside guts spread out on oily concrete. The smell of gasoline and motor oil hung heavy in the air. Creely walked inside, and moved around to the rear of the car, noted the empty truck space. Lowering the truck lid a few iniches, he studied the Louisiana vanity plate.

He was walking back up the driver's side as the man came out of the office. He had discolored bib overalls, a heavy beard, and smelled of melded sweat, oil, and whiskey. Surprised, he stopped short, forehead crinkled in a deep frown. Brown eyes narrowed under a shaggy overhang of black hair, glinting with suspicion and sudden anger. He stepped directly in front of Creely. He was at least six-feet-six of flab and muscle, a distrustful, ugly, suspicious mountain.

"Whatcha want h'r, mistah?" he growled, leaning back on his heels, shoving his curled beefy hands inside the overall's bib. Tension radiated from him.

"When you opened the door, I saw the car from the street," Creely said. "I was wondering where I would be able to locate the owner."

"How y'all knowed I ain't the owner?" The man's voice, deep and rough, seemed to crawl out of his chest with a life of its own.

"Just a good guess." Creely tried a smile, knew it failed. "Do you know where the owner can be located?"

"Cain't say I rightly knowed. Or ifn it's any of your bidness."

"Are you Burrell?"

"Dependin' on who's askin'."

Oh, shit, here we go again, Creely thought, as he pulled a business card from his wallet. The giant eyed the card suspiciously but never touched it.

Creely tucked the card in his pocket. "Creely Crane, an attorney from New Orleans. Car belongs to a friend of mine. I'm trying to locate her."

"Uh-huh, well—I cain't he'p you. My boy found it in a cane field last night a prutty good ways from h're when 'im and the dawgs come back from huntin'."

"Your boy usually go long distances to hunt?"

"'im and the dawgs go all over. It keeps 'em busy. He tole me 'bout it when he got home. I guess they jest left it there after it got busted up."

"And it got here how?"

"We hooked 'er up and brought 'er h're." He sucked at his front teeth. "Your frien' gotta name?"

"She does, it's Kitty Chauvin." Burrell already knew that. The first thing he would have done was check the car over, look in the glove box for identification, insurance papers, and whatever else he could find. The man was testing him.

Burrell eyed him shrewdly. "How you knowed the car belon' to 'er?"

Creely offered what he thought to be his most charming smile. "You forgot to remove the personalized plate." The man thought he'd found a windfall: removed the VIN, repair it, maybe repaint it, sell it; money enough to last a couple of years.

Burrell's swarthy skin darkened from the last visible inch of his thick neck to the roots of his black hair. Caught with his misappropriation, now he was seriously angry. His eyes flickered past Creely to the car, then back.

"Wouldn't h've to ifn I'm repairin' it. How come you don't knowed wh're to find her, ifn you knowed 'er so good?" Burrell snapped.

Creely felt his hackles rise. He was tired of a question answered with a question. Hell, he was tired of evasive behavior and no answers, period. Sal had warmed him and he had listened with half an ear, never believing he would find things this bad. "You're in illegal possession of an automobile, Mr. Burrell. However, if you have any useful information to locate Ms. Chauvin, maybe we can consider it a misunder- standing. She will be appreciative of the tow. Her insurance company will reimburse a fee and any other expense incurred. We'll just forget what might have happened to the car. Do we understand each other, Mr. Burrell?"

"I cain't he'p you." Burrell had relaxed a little; he shook his head from side to side like a big bear. "Don't knowed wh're she at. And ifn I did, I ain't shore 'bout tellin'. Jest cuz you a law'er, you could still be an ex-husb'nd or somethin'. She migh'a run away from you."

"You could be right, Mr. Burrell, Creely said, nodding and smiling induleently, then the smile slip- ped from his face. Muscle jerked in his jaw. "But you aren't. I'm her attorney and friend." He produced his business card again, held it out.

Burrell took the card this time, ran his thumb over the raised letters. He lifted the card to his mouth, began picking at his teeth with it, mumbling around the card. "'pensive, huh? Like that ride you got." Burrell half-turned, and looked at the Porsche with greed in his eyes.

Creely kept a tight rein on his temper. Accustomed to being in charge, having no authority here, he was finding all this difficult to accept, and didn't like it much. The man might be a short distance from moron, as well as an ass, but he was a clever ass and gigantic. Threats didn't mean much to him. If Creely left, Kitty's car would be gone by the time he got back. He knew it; Burrell knew he knew it.

"Look, Mr. Burrell—" Creely began again, pulling a hundred dollar bill from his wallet, and watching Burrell's eyes brighten. Money always talked.

Burrell took the bill, stuffed it in his pocket, grinned slyly at Creely. "Still can't he'p you," he said. "Tol' you I ne'er seen nobody."

"And your boy? He never saw anyone either?"

"Naw . . ." He tapped the side of his head with his forefinger. "He ain't got rights up h're all the time since he got back from the war. He rides all o'er in that old truck of his. 'im and dem dawgs jest wander 'round all day. He loves dem dawgs, treats 'em like fam'ly. But fer this—" he tapped his pocket—"I can tellyou wh're he found it . . .'tween h're and that place wh're folk don't live no m're—"

"Where might that be?"

"Use to be called French Gap. It ain't called nothin' now 'cept sometimes people call it No Name, Lou'siana."

"You're sure?" *Where folk don't live no more.*

"Shore as I step in dawg shit and git it on my shoe. Folks don't go o'er thata way no m're. Tol' that boy a hun'red times stay 'way, but he don't ne'er lis'en to me."

"Why don't people go there anymore?" Creely's curiosity was piqued.

Burrell's eyes shifted evasively. "You keep askin' a lotta questions."

"I need a lot of answers. Why don't people go there?"

"Jest 'cause they don't," Burrell snapped.

He had pushed and Burrell had pushed back, shutting down on him. "I see. Well, thank you, Mr. Burrell." He jerked his thumb toward the Mercedes. "And try not to forget about the car not being yours."

Creely ambled back to the Prosche. He felt Burrell's eyes tracing him, felt a zing of adrenaline in his blood. The car would be gone without a trace within the hour. Local law enforcement would be no help, probably kinfolk of Burrell's. If pushed hard, Burrell might take a notion to rip him in half. A little info was better than none. At least he was on the right track, but he seemed to keep getting a little too close to having his face rearranged in the process.

He paused with his hand on the Porsche's hood, lost in thought. Maybe the zing wasn't so great. Abadie had lied from the get go . . . and every tingling nerve in his body let him know he had been naïve. It was beginning to look like he had just walked himself unprepared into a shit load of trouble.

63

Kitty leaned against one of the remaining upright posts of an old animal enclosure that had relegated itself to dry rot. The chickens followed like hounds, squawking and running when she kicked dirt at them. Her sinuses complained a little at the morning scents. In the leaf-filtered sunlight, the whispery sound made by the brush of the fine wings of mosquito hawks turned to iridescent filigree touched her ears. The air was already getting heavy with humidity that misted her skin, making yesterday's mosquito bites itch again.

Honeysuckle grew rampant. A small brown bird flicked out from tangerine flowers along the tangled vines. The sky was clear, opal and cloudless, as if stroked by a paintbrush. A faint breeze, just enough to stir the pine needles and clusters f crinkly leaves, sending them in scratching flurries around her ankles.

Splintered sunlight glittered on the cloaked water of the pond. On the far side, husked-out trees raked at the sky with gray-white fingers. A rabbit scampered into the undergrowth. A squirrel bolted up a tree, red brush of tail twitching as it vanished into the upper branches. An egret at the far end leaped into the air and was suddenly gone, its splashing flight echoing in water ripples and the faint tremble of lily pads.

Kitty stared at her warped reflection in the water.

Her blood thrummed in quick beats, her thoughts running in a disordered pattern. She'd had no direction in mind when she left thehouse, she just knew she couldn't be around the others any longer. She closed her eyes and sighed. She was stiff and bruised, bone-weary, a little lightheaded, and hungry. She couldn't remember being quite this hungry in years. She should have forced down a few more bites of greasy food.

She'd moved too close to the pond's edge; the soggy soil sucked at the toes of her sneakers. She stepped back, turned away, and began walkin g again. Surprised and shamed to find she had succumbed so easily to the need to see the old house, she stopped in front of the rubble that had been her childhood home. Had that been her destination from the beginning?

The house had been burned. On purpose or by accident, she had no idea.

Leaf-shadow danced through the charred naked timbers. Tall grasses and weeds had sprouted beween the few remaining floorboards. The old cast iron stove was still there, the long disjointed pipe resting at an angle with the ground. A gaping black cavity was where the kitchen used to be, filled with rain water, swamp seepage and whatever else had been trapped down there.

It seemed ghosts circled overhead, shadows

taunted, the stress stirring up memories. Catching a glimmer of those memories, she felt herself sliding back into a place she tried not to recognize, but felt a pang of regret, a moment of unexplainable sorrow. That old house had been her home for a little over eighteen years. If there had ever been love in that house, somewhere along the way it died, becoming pain—*so much pain*—and misery and hatred.

Freddie had crippled Jennet, a woman that lived for years with psychological, emotional and physical abuse, battered into submission by a cruel thoughtless man. He had kept her pregnant; eight miscarriages in ten years; three full term pregnancies. She had given birth to two weak boy babies that died shortly after birth before Kitty came along. Somehow, she had survived. *Grandpere* said Kitty was hard as nails, tenacious like a weed. He said sometimes it was just that way with babies, they survived all odds.

A couple of big blue-green bottle flies buzzed around the floorboard hole. She stared at them, hypnotized by their movement. A sudden flash of pain across her forehead, stabbing at her temples, blinding her. She closed her eyes and pressed the heels of her hands hard against the side of her head, as another dreadful suppressed memory shot through her mind.

No! Please, no . . . .

In some amorphous valley of her mind, she had

buried but retained it, a snarling dog of memory that had given her nightmares in her youth and chased her into adulthood. Tears collected in her eyes. Her breath was a dry whimper in her throat as the breeze seemed to whisper sympathy against her ear.

Arcie's fault! It was all Arcie's fault! Arcie knew she had reasons not to come back to this miserable place, even if Kitty never told her what they were. It was impossible not to remember now, the pain and fear, the loathing, self-hatred, humiliation and sense of degradation. All those horrible, horrible things he had managed to block out. She shuddered, squeezed her eyes tight, and revisited the experience that came along with her memory.

"Joyeux seize fete de naissance, Minou, Papa's joli fille," he had whispered. Happy sixteenth birthday, Kitty, Papa's beautiful girl.

Fumbling back the covers, he had cautioned her with a finger against her lips to be quiet. She lay terrified, knowing not to fight, almost strangling on her own saliva, whispering like a wounded animal. Biting down on her tongue until she bled, she tasted her fear of him in th blood. His whiskey breath hot, hisunshaven face dry and scratchy, brusing against her cheeks. He had caught both her wrists in his fist, pushing them above her head as he unfastened his zipper, his knee twisting hard between her legs. He had jabbed at her, making several unsuccessful drunken attempts to enter her—then he was pushing himself inside.

Anxiety, shoved along by hatred, building to an unbearable level. Not a manufactured memory, real, it had happened. Back then she'd always thought it was all her fault. She had restrained the memory to help herself heal.

And Mama knew! *She knew,* Kitty thought. *Mama knew—how could she not know?—and she did nothing. Shouldn't she have tried to stop it? How could she let him touch me? She washed those dirty sheets from that night and every night afterward that he came to me until he died, and never said a word. Why did she protect that animal who was my father?*

The ground beneath her feet seemed to shift, left her unsteady. She dropped to her knees. The anguished whimper in her throat became a high keening that vibratd into a violate scream.

64

Is Kitty right, is there a spell? Is she capable of that? Lacy wondered.

"Yancy?" she said and was ignored. *Is she ever going to speak to us?* "Yancy?" she repeated and was ignored again. *I wonder if she might not be able to speak for some reason,* Lacy thought as she watched the other woman's throat working as she swallowed time after time, *but she can damn well hear. She could make some sort of attempt to communicate.*

Lacy abruptly turned on Arcie, as if Yancy wasn't in the room. Her voice was almost shrill when she spoke. "If she wanted us here so badly, she should speak to us, damnit! Is she ever going to speak to us?"

"I don't know."

"What *do* you know, Arcie? Why don't I believe you? Is she not talking on purpose? Or does she have a problem?"

"Yes, she has a problem," Arcie admitted.

"What? Just tell me. Why can't she speak?"

"Someone hurt her."

"Hurt her how?"

"Someone . . . cut out her t-tongue," Arcie said.

Lacy sucked in her breath, horrified. *"Cut out her tongue?"* Her pulse was tapping double time. "Have you known this all along?"

"She told me a long time ago, in one of her letters."

"And you thought to keep that from *us*? Why didn't you tell us?"

"And make things worse?"

"Make things *worse*? So you just decided it wasn't something we should know?"

Arcie shrugged. "Look how the two of you reacted when you first saw her."

"We were shocked, of course, but you could have prepared us for this." Lacy felt sudden blazing heat all over her body. "How could you do this, Arcie? How could you do this to us? You don't do that sort of thing to people you call friends."

Arcie tensed but remained silent.

"Who did such a horrible thing to her?"

"She didn't tell me."

"Are you lying again?"

"I never lied about it!"

"No, you didn't, you just omitted telling us the truth. And you know a lot more than you're telling us now. You need to start telling us the truth, all of it."

Arcie flinched, pink flaming her cheeks, and looked away.

"If you'd told us about it, at least it would have been one less bad surprise." Lacy glanced cautiously at Yancy. "I hate talking as if she's not here and she says nothing. She's got to hate it, too."

And with that, Yancy abruptly left the room. Their eyes followed her jerky movements, pink color turning red as it stained Arcie's face, but said nothing.

Lacy heard herself whisper, "Oh, dear God!"

They sat like that, staring over each other's shoulders, not moving, not speaking until the tension in the room increased to a viable entity. Lacy was furious, her hands balled into fists under the table. Their distrust of each other made their disagreement more wretched, the silence more awkward. The walls seemed to be closing in. Ugly old walls burdened with roped-together strings of garlic, dried herbs and other things Lacy didn't recognize.

The things human beings did to each other scared the shit out of her. Who had done such an atrocious thing to Yancy? Why had they done it? If Arcie knew, why wouldn't she say? She had been awake the better part of last night listening to every noise, each and every sound. She was tired, irritable, impatient and hungry. The food was terrible, what little she had eaten settled like a rock in her stomach. She'd decided Kitty's anger wasn't misplaced.

It appeared Arcie was more than a bit unstable. How could she not be, keeping so much secret from them when it was important they be told? She didn't want to believe it, even think it, but had Arcie wrecked the car on purpose in an attempt to keep them here longer? If she had, it was a terrible, terrible mistake on her part. It had been a thoughtless mistake that not only endangered them but her as well. Lacy couldn't remember how many miles it was to the next town or even its name. She should have paid more attention, instead of drowning in her own misery about being here and not being able to do something about it. Could they possibly walk to the next town? What if they managed to do that and found it as deserted as French Gap? What would they do then?

Finally, when she'd calmed down a little, she said, "Where did she go?"

A sad smile touched Arcie's lips. "To get away from us."

"You said she wanted us here."

"She's probably sorry we came back."

"She can't be any sorrier than we are."

"You're starting to sound nasty, like Kitty."

"Why did you have to involve me in this?" Lacy asked. "Surely you knew I'd built a life for myself away from here. Didn't you realize I wouldn't want to come back, either?"

"It was the four of us then. It had to be the four of us now."

"That's crazy, Arcie. If you were in touch with Yancy, why didn't you come back before?"

Arcie looked away with a flicker of eyelash. "We could have come back, you know? But Kitty didn't want to. She never wanted to."

"I meant you, Arcie. You didn't need Kitty to come for a visit. You have your own car." Arcie didn't answer. Lacy waited, but she said nothing, so Lacy stood, the chair scraping loudly against the kitchen floor as she stood up.

"Where are you going?" Arcie squeaked, her eyes widening in surprise.

"Maybe to look for Kitty. Just out of here."

"Why?"

Burning with the fury of her anger, Lacy stalked out of the house without answering. Now she found herself sitting in a rocking chair on the gallery, her heart rate jacked up, her throat dry and tight, her butt numb, wondering where the hell Kitty had disappeared to and how much longer before she decided to come back. She had been gone a long time. Lacy could understand her need for separation, but it had been unwise to let Kitty go off alone like that. She should have followed her, at least tried to stop her. It didn't feel safe here. Suppose something happened to her?

Kitty needed to know what she'd learned had happened to Yancy.

65

Kitty pushed down the anguish and flames of anger. She heard the car approach before it appeared, the stuttering noise shattering the silence, the sound of tires spitting shell against the underside of the car. Her pulse quickening, her heart jumped against her ribcage, and she hastily scrambled to her feet. *A car! Someone with a car!* She had no idea where they might have come from, and whatever amount they wanted to help them, it didn't matter, she would pay it for them to take her away.

The car rolled slowly down the road, billowing black exhaust. It was the old Chevy she had noticed in front of the sheriff's office and assumed inoperable. It came to a stop with the loud crunch of shell, its driver cast in shadow as the engine died with a whine and shudder.

The driver's door groaned in protest as a man pushed it open, unwound his body from behind the steering wheel, and folded his arms across the top of the door. A cigarette between his lips, he stood look-ing at her, squinting through the curl of smoke. He closed the door and walked toward her with an arrogant swagger, spine swooped into his hips. His blond hair brushed his shoulders, cheekbones high and hollowed, jawline rich with reddish stubble.

A quickening started low in her belly. She felt the immediate string of current between them, hot and sweet, a little erratic.

"Domeno," she breathed.

He stopped a foot from her, legs spread wide, placed his hands on his hips. His gaze was intense as it crawled over her, almost an appraisal. A quirk of a smile touched his sensuous lips.

"Kitty," he acknowledged, in a tone that seemed to caress her name.

He's not surprised to see me, she thought, as she studied his tall, hard body, his handsome face criss-crossed with leaf-shadow. A deep expectant quiver developed in her chest. She found she was stunned by the implication. She knew that feeling, had experienced it too many times not to know it. There was still a connection between them. *This is impossibly crazy, but he still has the same effect on me.*

"Hi," she said with faint breathiness in her voice.

"Hey," he answered.

"It's been a long time. How've you been?"

Domeno plucked the unfiltered cigarette from his lower lip, and threw it away, leaving a thin trace of paper. *"Bon*—fine. Good." He kicked the toe of his boot in the shell, almost shy, maybe a little nervous. "Hell, 'kay, that's 'bout all. Whatcha doin' back h're?"

"We're visiting Yancy."

Domeno's eyes narrowed, pansy-dark slits in the

middle of a deep ugly frown, lips curled in a bitter smile. "Vis'tin' Yancy," he repeated. "Why wo'ld y'u do that?"

"Do you remember Arcie Becnel and Lacy Kennedy? I came with them. Arcie calls it a reunion."

"A reunion," he repeated. "No kiddin'?"

"Yeah, no kidding."

"Wha' migh' y'u call it?" he asked.

"An experiment in torture." She laughed softly, more a nervous giggle, her throat a little clogged up. She found his gaze almost hypnotic. His husky voice touched her in places she wasn't sure it should. She could feel his heat, a strong pulsating animal heat, hot and powerful, disarming her. She was drawn to him on some crazy elemental level and, although deliciously sensual, she didn't understand it, felt certain it was something that shouldn't be happening.

Kitty envisioned him as a teenager, narcissistic, arrogant as if he owned the world. He had been inconsiderate and thoughtless, so quick to hurt someone's feelings. She had lost her heart—had wanted to lose her body—to him. He, without thought, had broken that heart. Looking into his eyes now, she suddenly felt the burn of that rejection. It hadn't seemed to matter to him.

Kitty wasn't that silly young girl anymore, so why did she still find herself so strongly attracted to him after all these years? It didn't make sense. It was as if she had only buried her want of him and it had never gone away, just waited until she saw him again to rise flaming up between them. Had she really never gotten over him? What about him? Did he feel it, too?

"Y'u look like a city gal," he said.

"I am a city gal. I have been for a long time."

"No one knew wh're y'u went. Wh're'd y'u go?"

"New Orleans."

He nodded. Muscle rippled under his shirt when he moved, a forest of silvered blond hair peeking out the open collar. He smelled so manly, of sweat and tobacco, faintly woodsy. Kitty resisted the temptation to touch him, feel his hardness under her hands.

Domeno's tawny-green gaze held steady, evaluating her. It felt as if he could read her thoughts. When he reached out and ran his knuckles gently across her cheekbone and tapped them against her chin, his thoughts seemed to run the same vein as hers, and the roughness of his skin caused an anticipatory quiver along her spine.

"Y'u alw'ys was the prett'est gal in the parish." His hand dropped back to his side. His look was speculative as he added, "I bet y'u done gone got y'urself marr'ed w'th a buncha young'uns."

"No, never married. No children." His touch had left her knees weak. "Are you married?"

He looked over her head, eyes flinty and distant, lips pulled into a bitter twist. Finally, he said, "Yeah,

I marr'ed."

"Did I know her?"

"*Non.* She was from up Houma way. Tansie Poche. She was youn'er 'an us."

"You and Tansie have children?" She had always thought Domeno would make beautiful children with someone. All those years ago, she'd thought it might be her.

"*Non.*" His voice had dropped dangerously low.

Kitty picked up on the disappointment in that single word as an angry shadow of hurt leaped across his eyes, canceled the brilliant green-gold and made them a muddy reddish color for an instant. *Something happened. He's angry over it. Maybe they lost a baby. Maybe she couldn't have any. Maybe she's gone, maybe she left him. Let it be.* She wanted him to say something— *anything*—to break the quiet that had fallen between them.

Clearing her throat, she said, "Well, tell her hello, maybe we'll get to meet before I leave."

"*Non,*" he said gravely. Icy anger, what might have been bottled-up rage, had relocated from his eyes to his voice. "She died nine years ago."

"*Ohhh, God . . .* I'm so sorry, Domeno."

Domeno's face became chiseled stone, eyes mutinous and pain-filled, and his eyelids lowered, tripped like a camera shutter. He looked away, gestured with his big hand toward the ruins of her old house, refocusing his thoughts, changing the subject.

"Th're ain't much to see anym're."

Kitty stared dispassionately at the skeletal remains. "What happened?"

"Burned down 'bout twelve years back."

"My mama got caught in the fire?" Her throat
tightened. No matter how much she resented Jennet,
she wouldn't have wished her such a horrible death.

He shook his head. "Gone lon' 'fore that."

"Died?" she whispered, feeling a hitch and tug in
her chest.

"*Non,* left town." His eyes flickered back toward
her. "Y'u didn't know?"

"I haven't seen or spoken to her since I left." She
couldn't help but wonder where Jennet had gone,
what happened to her. Was she still alive, had she
remarried, had she found peace, was she happy? Was
there a man who was good to her or was he another
Freddie? Did she have other children or had all the
pregnancies by Freddie left her barren, or not wanting
the burden of children again?

"Sorry," he said.

"It doesn't matter." Kitty shook her head. But
somehow it did matter, a little. "A long time go."

"Yeah, I was," he agreed. "Things changed
'round h're a lot."

"I noticed."

"Y'u changed, Kitty?"

"As much as most people when they grow up—" she said, and decided to push it a little—"but not as much as Yancy's changed."

Domeno stiffened, his jaw clenched. Just the mention of Yancy's name bothered him. There was definitely something troubling there. Given a little time, maybe he'd tell her, but best not touch it now.

Kitty smiled, tilting her head to te side as she playfully poked hi chest with her index finger. "How much have you changed, big guy?" She was shamelessly flirting and wondered if she should do that, if it was such a good idea, at the same time unable to resist doing it.

Domeno reached out and cupped her cheek in his rough palm, so swiftly and gently she was uncertain for a moment he had done it. His thick fingers traced down the side of her face, her shoulder, down her arm to her hand, a long slow burn. It brought tightness to her throat, her heart almost jumping out of her chest. She studied the pale hairs growing above his knuckles that seemed to glitter in the sunlight, not looking into his eyes. Her blood raced hotly through her veins, the abrupt sexual power that leaped between them with his touch galvanized in her lower belly.

The turning of their bodies into each other was a purely spontaneous response. His lips brushed across her mouth. Surprised, she heard herself gasp. For a breathless second his face retreated, but before she could catch her breath, his lips had descended a second time, hard and wet and possessive. She found it difficult to breathe. Her chest hurt from the wild tattoo of her heartbeat, knees so weak she thought she would fall. He rocked back on his heels, pressing her tighter to him, and she clutched at his arms for support. Everything blurred . . . there was only that moment, that one single moment—as she lost herself in the hunger of his kiss.

He's kissing me like he could eat me up, she thought, kissing him back with a passion that rivaled his.

66

Arcie watched Lacy through the kitchen window. Had Lacy noticed her, she would have seen the anger in her eyes, her face blotched with startling red color. Black funk was close, smirking. A spark of fire began to build in her chest. Beautiful perfect Lacy, beautiful perfect Kitty. All the good things in life happened to them. But Yancy . . . *what happened to Yancy?*

Her mind was that stupid ping-pong ball again, bouncing around and trying to keep the black funk at bay. She ached all over and was still hungry. Unlike what Kitty said, there had been food, but greasy and unappetizing, the meat peculiar-tasting. She'd scarfed down as much as possible, her empty stomach clenched tight, but she hadn't eaten nearly enough to satisfy her hunger before things exploded and Yancy had emptied the uneaten food into the garbage. Kitty had made such a big deal over the food, she would have eaten slop if necessary to prove her point— *nothing to eat, as if!* She knew Yancy wouldn't let them go hungry. Why had Kitty insinuated such a thing? It pissed her off.

The entire situation made her furious. Nothing was the way it should be. She'd done nothing wrong, only tried to bring them all together again. She had managed that, but she seemed to have failed at every-

thing else. She doubted she could hold herself together much longer. So stupid of her to believe they
could renew their friendship, they couldn't even talk
to each other. They had nothing in common.

How would they get home? If they had to walk
any distance again, she wasn't sure her body could
stand up to it. Arcie's back ached, her ankles felt as if
someone had bound them in barbed wire, the muscles
in her calves were pulled tight, even her toes hurt. She
wasn't skinny and fit like them. She hated to admit
they had been right. There was nothing here for them.
No town, no people, no car to get them back home.
She felt sure if they found a way to leave, they
wouldn't hesitate. They might not even ask her to go.
If I don't leave with them, what will happen to me? She
couldn't stay here. She knew now that she was here,
she didn't want to stay. It never occurred to her it
would be like this. Maybe Yancy could live this way,
but she couldn't. She wanted her little house and her
fish and flowers. What had she been thinking?

Ridiculous question, Arcie, she scolded herself. She
knew what she'd thought—the only thought that had
filled her mind for years—*Domeno* She'd thought he
would see how much she loved him, and it would be
just the two of them. The crazy world inside her head
would stop spinning after that. She would be happy,
make him happy. She could stay, they could live in
their own little universe; they wouldn't need anyone

else. Maybe he would come back to New Orleans with her—for real, nothing she imagined . . . but she hadn't seen him, didn't even know for sure if he was still here, couldn't even ask Yancy about him. Not knowing was tearing her up inside. None of the things she wanted were happening. It seemed none was going to happen. *What an idiot I am!*

Movement from the outside jerked her from her reverie. Lacy walked across the yard and moved slowly around the old van, looking through each dirty window, then stood to study it as if her thoughts alone would make it a working vehicle again.

Arcie came out of the house, closing the screen door softly behind her. Talking with Lacy was almost as bad as talking with Kitty. Lacy turned back toward the house. She raised her eyes and looked up at her, a little startled, surprise reflected in her expression.

"Hey," Arcie said.

Lacy looked away, but she answered, "Hey."

"What you doing?"

"Just scoping out things."

Arcie could tell it made Lacy nervous that she was suddenly there, her approach undetectable. Did Lacy suspect she had been watching her since she left the kitchen? She supposed Lacy had expected her to come raging out the door screaming about invasion of privacy for looking in the van. "What did you see?"

"Nothing much. Just a rusty old piece of junk

with no steering column, SKOAL tobacco and rusted food cans with shredded labels knee-deep littering the floor. A lot of empty cardboard boxes distorted by wetness and age. There's something like a big, hairy petrified nut hanging from the rearview mirror by a narrow leather cord, and a plant of some sort that has long ago died and become a stick in the dirt in a rusted bucket near the rear doors."

"Are you okay?" Arcie asked.

"As well as can be expected." Lacy motioned toward the van. "No transportation here."

"Can we talk?" Arcie edged down the steps.

"We aren't okay, Arcie, but I guess we can try to talk. Where is she?"

"I don't know."

"She's really good at disappearing, isn't she?"

"I'm sorry about all this," Arcie said, but the apology was glue on her tongue.

"Is that all you wanted to talk about?"

"I only wanted to keep our promise."

"You lied to us. You didn't tell us everything that you knew. You can't force people to do what you think is right."

"I didn't mean to."

"You knew what happened to her. You should have told us. Prepared us."

"I didn't think it would matter that much what happened to her. Just because she can't talk doesn't mean she isn't the same."

"Seriously? It scares me. She isn't the same, Arcie, and not just because she can't talk anymore."

"I—I made a mistake."

"Yes, you did. A really big one. Now we have no transportation and no form of communication."

"It could work if we pulled together."

"I don't believe any of us except you want it to work."

Arcie said nothing, but tears were running down her cheeks and she sniffled behind her hand.

"Okay, okay, cut the tears," Lacy said. Her lack of sympathy was in her tone and sounded mean. "What's with the tears? Is this some new strategy to win me over to your side? I'm not even sure if they are real or fake. If you're looking for sympathy, you aren't getting any. I'm and frustrated, and feeling as exasperated with you as Kitty is right now." On impulse, she reached out and caught Arcie's hand, but Arcie tensed and jerked her hand away. Arcie's rebuff caught her by surprise and Lacy threw up her hands and stepped back from the other woman as if she'd been struck. "I'm trying my hardest not to blame you for this mess, Arcie. You're just not making it easy."

"I-I—I thought I was doing good for all of us," Arcie whined.

"I wish I could believe that." Her voice and her expression indicated she was no longer as ambivalent about Arcie as she had been the day before. It was obvious today she flat out didn't trust her. "Maybe I need a walk. I don't like what's happening here. I need to try and clear my head."

"Lacy, maybe—"

Lacy waved her away. "Stop," she said. "Please, just stop. I don't want to hear any more." A single tear leaked from the corner of her eye. More came as she walked away. Lacy found she couldn't stop her tears. The slump of her shoulders showed she was disheartened, and her resolve to be the strong one was gone; the jut of her chin indicated she was more than a little angry about being lied to. She had decided the charade couldn't go on much longer without a real explosion between them.

Chickens scrounging the yard scattered about her feet. The rooster rushed her and, feeling frustrated, she kicked out at him and missed. She would never do something this foolish again. When Kitty got back, they would put their heads together on how to handle this mess, even if it meant a long walk to the next town.

But first Kitty needed to hear what Arcie had told her about Yancy.

67

Creely's stomach demanded food. His head jerked toward the small café he had spotted down the street, more inviting than Josie's Luncheonette. He whipped the Porsche around, parked directly in front and stood listening to a sporadic chorus of frogs intermingled with the cacophony of gulls beyond the banana plants.

The red lettering above the door announced: LA CUISINE. Before entering, he paused to read the hand-lettered cardboard signs in the windows. On the left-hand side was the breakfast list:

> *andouille*(pork w/stomach sausage)
> *boudin rouge*(blood sausage)
> *boudin blanc*(sausage without blood)
> *soucisse*(pork sausage)—*beguine*(bacon)
> *gru*(grits)—*jambon*(ham)—*oeufs*(eggs):
> *frit*(fried) or *mollet*(soft-boiled) or omelette,
> *crepes*(pancakes), *pain perdu*(French toast),
> *sauce rouillee* (roasted gravy) or *sauce piquante*
> biscuits with *beurre* (butter).

The lunch-dinner menu, in alphabetical order, on the right side read:

> *bisque d'ecrevisse*(crawfish bisque)
> *bouillabaisse*(fish soup)
> *bouilli*(internal organ stew-highly seasoned)

etouffee d'ecreuvisse(crawfish stew)
grenouille jambre(frog legs)
cocodril(alligator)—*poisson arme*(gar)
poisson rouge(redfish), *gombo*(gumbo)
patates frits(French fries)
salade de laitue &tomate(lettuce & tomato)
brioche(egg bread) & *pain de mais* (cornbread)

There was a placard centered on the door above the OPEN sign that offered a medley of fried, boiled and baked seafood, IN SEASON: *cheuvrette* (shrimp)—*zuits*(oysters)—*ecreuvisse*(crawfish)—*goujon caille* (yellow catfish)—*crabe*(crab).

The interior was cool, small and homey, with fabric tablecloths in bright colors. A couple of men in jeans, tee shirts, and heavy work boots ate po'boys at a rear table; a young woman with glasses and thick chestnut hair reading a book at another. They glanced up but went immediately back to eating. Thewaitress, older, thin, bleached hair with gray roots, approached his table with a glass of water and flatware wrapped in a cloth napkin. Her narrow face appeared friendly when she smiled, her front teeth in need of dental work. He figured he would stick with something familiar, and ordered seafood gumbo and an oyster po'boy.

The food was good; the gumbo spicy, filled with assorted seafood, the French bread hot and fresh, the oysters tender. Eating slowly, he thought about what he had learned and what he hadn't. People didn't go around French Gap anymore—No Name, Louisiana? It seemed appropriate. But what kept them away? Abadie? Possibly, but a little unlikely. There had to be more, something bigger than one man to keep them away, no matter how dangerous he appeared. Each time he thought of Abadie, he got pissed again over the way the man had wasted no time on pleasantries or cooperation.

The Mercedes was wrecked, which meant Kitty and the others were on foot. Did Abadie have anything to do with that or was it just an accident? No luggage in the trunk. He knew they had luggage, no one went away for a weekend without at least a change of clothing and a toothbrush, especially a woman. Had they removed their bags or had someone stolen them? Assuming they took it, they probably hadn't walked very far. Had there been bad blood between Kitty and Abadie? Did that have something to do with her leaving twenty years ago? Now that she had come back, was Abadie set on settling an old score? If so, what would he do to get even? Abadie had to know Creely knew he had been lied to. Would Abadie realize he would come back? Absolutely. It wouldn't make a difference with a man like that—enormous ego, private agenda—he was prepared to do the necessary to defend his territory. And it was his territory; he'd claimed it and he intended to hold onto it.

Creely didn't want to jeopardize Kitty or her friends in any manner. He would have to be cautious when he went back. He would have to be as unobtrusive as possible, be prepared for whatever came his way. He didn't know if Abadie would hurt Kitty, or any of the others, for that matter, but it was a chance he couldn't—*wouldn't*—take.

68

Kitty and Domeno walked back toward the pond where a willow tree formed a lacy green veil over the edge of muck, weak sunshine slipping through. It happened so quickly. Next, she knew his body anchored hers in the soft plumy grasses. He was nibbling at her ear, making her shiver, then slowly he touched his mouth to hers, and a rush of heat coalesced in the pit of her stomach. His tongue slid into her mouth, his kisses eager, more demanding. For a moment she couldn't think clearly, simply moaned and leaned into him, kissing him back with the same eagerness. Sinking her fingers in his hair, she clung to him, wet with wanting for him in a way she hadn't thought possible. Her fingers trailed down, felt the rapid stutter of his heartbeat; her hand settled on the hardness of his crotch. He groaned deep in his throat, pressed back hard against her palm for a minute, then he reached down and covered her hand with his, stilling the movement of hers. He pulled away, leaving her breathless, stunned, incapable of understanding what happened.

"*Non*—don't." He rolled away from her, but not before she saw the dangerous hungry gleam in his eyes that was a contradiction of his words. He sat up, edging away, not to be within touching distance.

Confused, she made no attempt to touch him. He pulled a pack of Camels from his shirt pocket, shook one loose, fit it between his lips. He touched the flame of a disposable lighter against the end, sucked on it deeply, the smoke drifting away into shadowy paleness where sunlight seeped through denser tree branches.

Silence, except for an occasional bird twitter or faint pond water ripple; thicker than she ever imagined silence could be.

Her skin was flushed from his touch, her lips abraded from the roughness of his kisses, her breathing rough in her chest. When she could no longer tolerate the silence, she whispered, "I—I'm sorry."

Domeno shook his head, dismissing her apology, didn't look at her as he said, "Not y'ur fault. Mine."

What did that mean? Had she misjudged his intentions? Was he teasing her again? She felt a deep hurt, overwhelmed by his rejection. Two decades, and he had rejected her again. Did he find the same thing wrong with her now that he'd found then? An empty ache hitched tight in her chest. *What the hell does he find wrong with me?* She had no valid explanation for her current behavior, only that she wanted him, but why? She couldn't figure out why. She had offered herself, no questions asked, no explanations needed— and he had refused her!

Kitty felt sudden anger. She knew it was in her

voice and didn't care. She wanted him to know he'd pissed her off. "I guess I've never been what you wanted, have I?"

"'actly what I wanted."

"Then why?" She waited a bitter moment for a comment. When there wasn't one, she asked, "Am I not attractive enough for you? Is there something wrong with me?" before her courage failed.

"*Non*. Y'u're *parfait*—perfect. *Belle*—beautiful." He shook his head and studied her, eyes gleaming, with what she knew was need and desire, but made no move to touch her. "Y'u alw'ys been *parfait* and *belle*. Don't be mad at me."

Don't be mad at him? Was he serious? Had he forgotten what happened between them over twenty years ago? She had every right to be mad. He needed to explain what just happened between them, not leave her hanging. Had it really only been her need she'd recognized and responded to? She thought he'd felt it too, but it happened so fast, her mind was a little unclear about their coming together. She felt sure he touched her first, but had it been her, not him? Had she assumed too much? Was she being too pushy, misinterpreting his touch and his kisses? Had her behavior been too slutty, taking him by surprise? Did she find her aggression offensive? It was easy to think it her fault, too late to take it back.

What had Arcie said . . . any penis will do. Maybe

she was right. She was filled with hurt from Bill that
even Creely hadn't healed, and when she hurt, for
whatever reason, she seemed to seek out and use sex
like a salve. Maybe that was one of her biggest problems. She always seemed to use one man to heal the
hurt of another. Was that ever going to stop?

Kitty felt tightness in her throat, a sting behind
her eyelids. She turned her face away. "I should never
have let this happen."

"*Non! Non*, no, don't do that," he said quickly.
"My fault. All my fault. Don't be mad at me."

"I'm angry with myself."

"Don't be, please—don't be."

"Is it because you have someone?"

"*Non*, no one."

"Something else?"

"No, it's . . . *mal.*"

"What did you say?"

"*Mal*—wrong." He looked uncertain, unhappy,
almost sad, but his tone said resigned.

"I don't understand what you're talking about."
They were adults, for God's sake, how could he
rationalize a spontaneous need as being wrong, especially since he said there was no one else? She could
understand if there was someone else in his life.

"I know, I know y'u don't. It ain't easy to 'plain."

"Try me."

"There's nothin' wrong w'th y'u. I want y'u," he

said, and he threw his arms wide, "But not h're—not like this."

Kitty glanced around. "It's beautiful here."

"I won't take y'u on the ground—like animals!"

Kitty was stunned, at a loss what to say.

"I sh'ulda waited, bu t I jest needed to touch y'u. It went too far."

Kitty felt laughter come bubbling up. So that was it? It all amounted to his new concept of morality? Sex shouldn't be spontaneous, should be carefully planned? Next, he would be telling her it required a marriage license. She knew he'd had plenty of sex, plenty of other girls—lord only knows how many through the years since she left. That couldn't have been the reason he never touched her years ago.

Domeno misinterpreted her laugher. He stiffened, cheeks flushed, eyes darkening to a copper color. *"Sa t' amuse moi?"* he snapped.

"Excuse me?" Except for a few simple words, all the *le francais de meche,* Cajun marsh French, she'd been taught was gone.

"Do y'u find me amusing" Am I funny?"

"No! Of course not." Kitty grabbed at his arm as he made a move to push to his feet. He attempted to pull away, but she held on tightly. "I'm not laughing at *you!* I'm laughing at *me!* I thought I made a fool of myself again. I thought you don't want me now like you didn't want me years ago."

"What made you th'nk such a th'ng?" His face pinched into a frown.

"I've always thought that."

"Y'u alw'ys tho'ght wrong." He took her shoulders in his big hands, pressed his forehead against hers with closed eyes. "I alw'ys wanted y'u. The minute I saw y'u I knew that ne'er changed." He pulled her toward him, held her tight against his chest, and touched his lips gently to her temple.

"You hurt me, you know." Her heart raced.

"I know. I'm sorry."

"Did you do it just to see if you could?" He smelled so good. He was so hard and warm, holding her so tight, her nose pressed deep against his chest.

"I was young and stupid, into the chall'nge."

"I was a challenge?"

"Yes."

"Was Lacy a challenge?"

"Yes." He sighed deeply. "Y'u ne'er liked it h're."

"I didn't." She had no idea to what he alluded. What difference did it make?

"I was afr'id."

"Afraid of what?"

"Afr'id y'u'd leave . . . and y'u did." He reached out, gathered a wisp of her hair, let it sift through his fingers. *"Comme ca baille,"* he whispered. She looked at him quizzically. "So blonde," he said. "I ne'er forgot the color."

When the last strand had fallen, his fingers brushed the hair away from her eye, trailed down, settled on the thundering artery in her neck. Passion seemed to hover between them, not quite full- blown, waiting. His hand grasped her neck, pulling her toward him again, eyes darkening as a shadow of indefinable something crossed his face.

"Moi Minou—comme ca belle," he said softly. My Kitty—so beautiful.

She hadn't known he was still here, she hadn't thought about him in years. She had never thought about igniting her old flame for him, but it still seemed to be there, had easily ignited itself. She still found him physically attractive, feeling a confusing need to investigate that attraction, but if he thought she had come back to be with him, might even consider staying, he thought wrong. She would have sex with him, not to get even for his past transgressions, only to scratch that long-remembered itch. But she had no intention of remaining here longer than necessary. Since he seemed to still want her, even if only under his own terms, and seemed to have the only operative vehicle within miles if there was no other way, if it was necessary for her to use sex to persuade him to get her out of here, she would do exactly that.

69

Creely left the restaurant and parked in front of the tavern. He had decided a cold beer would taste good, but it was more a gut feeling that pushed him there. In the local bar, all types of informational nuggets could be gleaned. Over a couple of drinks, men loosened up and became talkative. A few more drinks unleashed the tongue and, just this side of drunk, they usually talked a lot more. He had exchanged a few pleasantries with his waitress at the cafe and she had openly flirted with him. He'd considered fishing her a little, but when she lingered too long at the table, a tall bald man appeared from the kitchen and called out her name.

"My old man. He's the jealous type," she said, smiling apologetically as she wiped up bread crumbs and refilled his coffee cup, then left him to his meal.

He passed between two derelicts that had moved in on the front porch of the tavern since he arrived in town, both sipping from long-necked bottles. Their curiously inanimate eyes followed his movement without so much as a head motion or flicker of an eyelash. Creely nodded at them. Their eyes rolled away from him.

The bar wasn't particularly seedy, cool and a little bright at mid-day, sun seeping in around partially shuttered windows. It probably got inky, smoky and busy toward evening, especially when it wasn't Sunday. The only occupants were two customers and a bartender, the air beery smelling with a tinge of some fruity aerosol spray. A large, aged air conditioning unit in the rear wall hummed fitfully. The place had a wide bar inlaid with cheap Mexican tile, four scarred tables, with two chairs each, and a tiny dance floor. An old jukebox with a broken plastic front emitted the poignant final notes of an ancient melody and lapsed into silence with a click. A cracked back-mirror and unvarnished wooden shelves lined with liquor bottles, a couple racks of assorted chips and nuts framed the back wall. A few smoke-yellowed business cards and newspaper clippings hung thumb-tacked on either side of the bottles. He eyed one with the picture of a peculiar-looking, snarling wolf and the headline: *"Unleashing Legends of the Bayou's loup-garou."*

The bartender's eyes followed Creely from the door to the vacant stool one down from an old man with tufts of yellow-white hair and grizzled stubble. The old man looked at Creely with pale eyes buried in wrinkled flesh. When Creely nodded, he looked away.

"Hullo," the bartender said. "Whatcha avin?" He was a bull, mid-forties, bald, a beer-belly and double chin, his eyes clear and gray, his mouth thin, massive shoulders and arms and muscle that rippled with each measured movement. He had a hard, lethal

look about him, as if his gut might not be soft, reinforced instead with steel. Large hands with scarred
knuckles said he'd seen more than his share of fights.

"Draft," Creely said.

"Bottle only."

"Whatever you have is fine."

The bartender grinned. "You a salesman?"

"Do I look like a salesman?" Creely asked.

"We get salesmen passin' through sometimes
askin' for a draft. Ne'er had nobody else ever ask for
one." The man placed a bottle in front of Creely. "I'm
Louie." He extended his meaty paw.

"Creely." He shook the proffered hand that had
a grip like a vise. Taking a long swallow of beer, he
felt his energy beginning to rise up again. If he was
careful and played his cards right, there was something to be unearthed here, he was sure of it. He
finished his beer, tapped the side of the bottle.

Louie removed the empty, replaced it with a
fresh one. He felt the stabbing sensation of being
watched, turned his head, and found the old man
staring at him. He smiled, nodded again. The old man
didn't blink but continued to stare.

"Don't mind him," Louie said, resting his elbow
on the bar. He tapped an index finger against his
temple. *'Il a pas tout*—he's coo-coo. He drifts in and
out. He's been 'round so long he's part of the wood-
work. A little crazy, but harmless. Every 'spectable

town has one, you know."

Creely nodded.

"If you not a salesman, whatcha doin' down this way?"

"I'm looking for a friend." Tense, needle-fine pain in his shoulders ran up the back of his neck. Careful, go slow, he reminded himself. Come on too hard and fast, these people would close up tighter than an oyster. He didn't need another convoluted dance routine like Abadie and Burrell.

"Your friend lives in Boudreaux?"

"No, she's visiting in a town called French Gap."

Louie stiffened and his face closed up. His gray eyes frosted over, the color of storm clouds. He removed his elbow from the bar, and stood erect, thin lips compressed. "Let me know if you want 'nother," he said, an unfriendly edge to his voice, moving a short distance down the bar.

The old man began to mutter. Creely glanced over at him. The old man looked away again. The town's name seemed to have sprung like the disabling jaws of a trap on both men.

"Is something wrong?" Creely asked.

"That ain't a town no more."

"Why is that?"

Louie moved a foot or two back toward him, eyes narrowed. "It just ain't. Why'd she go th're?"

"Friends."

"Not likely. Not many people th're no more."

"Maybe those left are her friends," Creely said.

"Not likely," Louie repeated.

"Okay. Could you help me out with a little information?"

"Yeah, you're goin' the wrong direction." Louie jerked his thumb left. "Follow the road south outta own, 'bout fifty miles or so. It's a bad road, should get th're in 'bout an hour, give or take."

"I just came from there."

A shadow of displeasure undulated in the depths of Louie's flinty eyes. "Then you shouldn't have no trouble findin' your way back," he growled.

"That's not the information I need—"

"That's all the information I got for you."

At the far end of the bar, the tavern's other customer chose that moment to call out for another drink. Louie ignored him. He began to beat the tiles with his empty whiskey glass.

"*A la minute!*" Louie snarled. In a minute!

"*A cette heure! J'ai soif!*" the man screeched. Now, right now! I'm thirsty!

Louie cursed, made his way down the bar. He poured whiskey into the man's glass and hurried back, not quite quick enough. Creely had already changed seats.

"Excuse me, sir." Creely tapped the old man's arm with a finger. "Might I have a word with you?"

The old guy wrapped his hands protectively around his whiskey glass; enormous parchment hands distorted with enlarged, misshapen knuckles and horny, cancerous bird droppings, long fingernails, thickly ridged, curling under like talons. A bulbous network of veins seemed to have a life of their own beneath his skin. He cocked his head, bird-like, his eyes milky with cataracts.

"Leave 'im be," Louie snapped, thrusting himself almost bodily between them across the bar, a trace of alarm in his eyes.

They sat for an uncomfortable minute or two staring at each other. Louie didn't move. Creely didn't either. The old man's eyes flickered between them. Finally, the old man lifted his glass, downed the remainder of his whiskey, pushed the empty glass across the bar top, and used the same gnarled finger to poke Louie's chest.

"*A ca oui!*" he grunted. Go away! His voice was gravelly, creaky like a screen door left unoiled for a long time. "*A ca oui!*" he repeated.

Louie retracted his head a little, breathing harder, muscle spasms rippling through his big arms, a dark, dangerous glitter in his eyes. "He's crazy, I told you—*fou!*" he growled. "He had too many years under a hard hat in the oil fields and on the rigs. Sun's baked his brain, whiskey's eatin' away what's left. He ain't got nothin' to say to you. He's *bete comme une oie,* crazy as a goose."

The old man bristled. Anger flared in his eyes.

"He la-bas, ane assez!" Hey, you asshole! He stabbed at Louie again with his knobby finger. Louie's cheeks turned a brilliant red-violet hue. He lowered his eyes but didn't back away. "You stop tellin' folk I ain't got me rights upstairs. Got the same rights I always had. Got as much rights 'bout me as you got, you smart-alecky fucker." He scowled at Creely. "Whatcha th'nk, boy? Y'all th'nk I got me rights 'bout me?"

Creely smiled. He'd probably just lucked on to one of the only people in the entire godforsaken area who might be willing to tell him something of importance. He just needed to get him to tell whatever it was before Louie decided to jump the bar and beat him to a fucking pulp. Louie had worked his angry face between them again, doggedly intent on keeping them apart. His eyes silvered, glittering like starlight.

"Just a friendly conversation, Louie," Creely said.

"We don't much like strangers 'round h're."

"Why not?"

"Just don't," Louie snapped. "Maybe you oughta be goin' 'bout now, mistah."

Creely turned toward the old man again. "Let me buy you another drink."

The old guy tittered, grinning at Creely, revealing darkened nubs. He pointed his finger and cocked an eyebrow at Louie. "See, you stupid fucker, even this h're stranger can see I got me rights 'bout me," he challenged. "Wantin' to be conversatin' w'th me fer a bit and says he's buyin'. Gimme 'nother one, *ane assez.*" He waved his glass in Louie's face, let the glass drop against the tile with a soft thump. The anger Louie had provoked committed suicide in his cloudy eyes as Louie refilled his glass with Johnnie Walker Black. "Whatcha got on y'all mind, youn' fella?"

"A place called French Gap." Creely ignored the annihilating hostility in Louie's stare and hoped Louie could restrain himself. He didn't want to be physically ejected. "You know it?"

"We all knowed it." There was a shadow flicker in the depths of the old man's faded eyes. "Ain't got nothin' good to say 'bout that th're place," he replied solemnly, slowly waggling his head. "Bad th're—a bad place."

"Stop it, Jacques. You had 'nough for today," Louie said.

The old guy ignored him, a shaky hand fumbling his glass back to his lips. He swallowed the balance of the liquor and tipped his head toward Creely, one eyebrow cocked, questioning if his new friend was into buying him another round.

Creely looked pointedly at Louie. Louie didn't move.

"Ifn you smart, boy, you stay 'way from th're,"

the old man cautioned. His long fingernail clicked against the empty glass. *"J'ai soif!"* I'm thirsty!

"Now, Jacques—"

"Bouche ta gueule!" he said. Shut your mouth! He drew himself up, pushing out his skinny chest until it looked hard and tight under his faded shirt.

Louie poured another whiskey then discovered something of interest on the Mexican tile, polishing each tile vigorously, and worked his way down the bar from them.

"Bet'er you stay 'way from th're. You h'ar me, boy?" He waved a palsied finger like a metronome under Creely's nose.

"I hear you."

"You jest list'n and stay 'way." He poured the last of the whiskey down his throat.

"Can you tell me why?"

"You stupid, boy?" Pushing shakily to his feet, he stared at Creely with milky-white disdain. "This youn' gen'ration . . . all stupid youn' fuckers. Th'nk they the smart ones. Don't list'n when ol' folk tell 'em things. Think we ol'folk don't ne'er knowed what we talkin' 'bout. A body can shove it up their ass, jest won't list'n." He swayed, dangerously close to falling, caught himself, and pointed a shaky finger over Creely's shoulder. "See th're, boy?"

Creely turned and looked. The old man was pointing at the yellowed news clipping with the snarling wolf. From somewhere between his teeth-nubs, he hissed, "Loups-garous! That place got loups-garous! You h'ar me, boy?" He began shuffling a precarious path toward the door, pulling his baggy pants up tight against his crotch with one hand, and said over his shoulder, "Bet'er list'n to me, youn' fella. I knowed what I'm talkin' 'bout. People call it No Name fer a re'son. People don't come back ifn they goes th're. If you got any rights 'bout you—don't go fuckin' 'round that place, it ain't been safe fer years. Ain't nothin' th're no more but 'em loups-garous!"

70

Lacy didn't walk very far, halted behind a tree, and waited until Arcie went back inside. She hoped Arcie wouldn't bother her again when she returned to sit in the cane-backed rocker. She was there when Kitty returned, staring at the damn rooster strutting across the yard for such a long time she felt she had memorized every feather on his scrawny little ass. She had cried a little, but doing so hadn't made her feel much better, just lonely and more sad.

When Kitty crossed the yard, the rooster ruffled his feathers and made a crazy zig-zag toward her with outstretched wings. She kicked dirt at him and watched him run off, herding the hens in front of him. Lacy felt sure her face showed her relief when Kitty dropped into the rocker next to her.

"Crazy little bastard."

"Yeah," Lacy agreed. "Have a nice walk?"

Kitty shrugged.

"I was worried."

"About me?"

"Yeah, about you," Lacy said, a nip of annoyance in her tone. "I thought something happened to you."

"Sorry. Where are they?"

Lacy lifted one shoulder, tapped her toe against the weathered gallery boards and set her rocker in motion. "Have no idea. Yancy disappeared again and Arcie got pissed at me because I got tired of arguing with her and she went inside. I've been sitting here with the damn freaking chickens for entertainment."

"Having a pity party."

"Why should you say that?" Lacy frowned.

"Doing a little crying."

Lacy flushed. "It's that obvious?"

"Pretty much." Kitty pointed at her face. "Puffy eyes, smeared mascara, snail tracks on your cheeks. That's usually a good sign." She smiled. "But even with all that, you look great. Life must be good. You never married? No kids?"

"No." Lacy's eyes went sad.

"One or both?"

"Both."

"But you've got someone special?"

"Yes." Her eyes brightened a little, a sudden wistful look on her face.

"Does he know where you are?"

"I didn't tell him." Lacy's cheeks flamed.

"Why? You thought he might not like you so much if he knew where you came from?"

"It occurred to me."

"Some of the best people have the worst beginnings. If he's that shallow, he doesn't deserve you, and you don't want him anyway."

"You're probably right, but it's not him, he's

great. It's more about me. How about you?"

Kitty thought of Bill—felt a flush of anger—then thought of Creely and the anger washed away. "Some one special—sometimes," she whispered.

"He doesn't know where you are, either."

"No—I didn't know I was coming until after I saw him on Friday. It's sort of a strange relationship."

"He's married." There was no accusation in Lacy's voice, only curiosity.

"No, not yet anyway. We run in different circles, on-again, off-again, nothing permanent."

"Well, since no one knows where we are, sounds like we might have a bigger problem than having a car. I found out Yancy can't talk anymore, that's why she hasn't said a word to us, not because she's angry. Although she's probably that, too." Lacy ran her fingers nervously through her hair. Her Rolex flashed in the light. "Someone cut out her tongue." Just saying the words caused Lacy's stomach to twist a little. She could tell by Kitty's expression she had shocked and startled her.

"What?" Kitty said, a squeak in her voice.

"Arcie told me after you left."

"Cut out her tongue?" Kitty felt a cold blast of fear. "When? Why? Arcie knew all along?"

"She didn't think it should make a difference."

"She wouldn't. Sometimes she doesn't think right, like her brain disconnects."

"Why would someone do something like that, Kitty? That's cruel and inhumane. She could have bled to death and died."

"I don't know about bleeding to death, but maybe that's what was intended."

"For her to die?"

Kitty nodded. "Maybe they couldn't actually kill her for some reason. Or maybe they just wanted to hurt her badly, their way to leave her feeling helpless without speech."

"That's sick. *Who* would do that?"

"Arcie wouldn't tell you?"

"Arcie said she didn't know. I don't know if I believe her." Lacy looked at Kitty, her eyes too wide. "This scares the hell out of me, Kitty. I just want to get away from here as fast as we can. To hell with this crazy reunion. It was never necessary."

Kitty nodded. "No, it wasn't. You got any ideas on how to go about doing that?"

"Walk."

"Maybe not."

Lacy frowned. "What's that mean?"

"I can do you one better."

"How?"

"I ran into an old acquaintance of ours."

"I had doubts there was anyone besides Yancy and that old man left here. Who?" Lacy asked.

"Domeno Abadie."

"Domeno Abadie," Lacy repeated. "My God, I have to admit I'm surprised. I thought him long gone. Where did you run into him?"

"Near what used to be my old house."

Lacy frowned again. "Used to be?"

"Not much left of it. Domeno said it burned down around twelve years ago."

"Your mother? She wasn't in it, was she?"

"No." Kitty felt her throat close tight. "He said she left town not long after I did."

"You never heard from her?"

"I never contacted her after I left."

Lacy studied her for a moment. "Are you sorry you didn't?"

"I used to be, sometimes, late at night, when I was still a kid. Not so much for a few years now. What about yours?"

Lacy shook her head. She worried the cuticle on her right thumb, scraped at her thumbnail with the index nail, eyes downcast.

"She died," she said sadly. "Cancer. I wrote, tried to keep in touch. She never wrote back, but she kept my cards. The sheriff contacted me when she died. I sent money for the burial, but I never came back."

"I'm sorry."

Lacy nodded, her lips pulled tight. "So am I. Now more than ever since I came back for this." She stood, walked to the gallery railing. talking about

Belle made her uneasy, made her think about the baby she had given away, but she wasn't up for too many confessions, and being with Kitty felt nice. Much better than being alone. "I thought earlier about looking for her grave, but I have no idea where they buried her."

"Probably the old church graveyard."

"Yeah, maybe. You know, this stuff with Yancy really makes me nervous."

"We don't know whoever did it is still here. Maybe there is nothing or no one to be afraid of except Yancy. You know she's not right, don't you?"

"It would be hard to miss the signs."

Kitty came to stand beside Lacy. "If you want to look for your mother's grave, and you want me to come, I'll go look with you."

"Why wouldn't I want you to come?"

"Thought you'd be mad at me deserting you."

"You certainly did that, and, yeah, I was a little mad. But the longer you were gone, the more I was afraid something happened to you and I'd be left alone with the other two."

"Sorry. I couldn't take any more of them."

"I understand. I felt the same way. Especially with Arcie. I don't think she's altogether right either, you know." Lacy walked own the gallery steps.

"Sometimes she's not. She can be a little strange at times."

"Did it help?"

Kitty followed her. "What?"

"Your visit to the old house. Did it help get rid of some ghosts?"

"More like demons," Kitty admitted. "I had a screaming good cry, surprised myself. I wouldn't have done that in front of anyone."

"Yancy seems to have changed her mind about us, uncertain what to do now that we're here." Lacy kicked at a chunk of rotted wood. It leaped up, shattered in the air.

"You're more diplomatic than me. I guess I thought if you were left alone with them, you would find out more. You didn't spend much time with either of them?"

"No more than necessary. Arcie tried to play me by making nice for a few minutes."

And?"

"It didn't happen. I have the same problem you have with her. I don't believe her."

"Sometimes she makes it difficult to be around her."

"I noticed. Is she always so manipulative?"

"She has lots of mood swings, but this is the worse one I think I've ever seen. She has some kind of problem going on and has been trying to keep it from me. It seems she's lost her control over it. It could have been going on a long time. I guess I never paid much attention before now."

"What kind of problem?" Lacy asked. Kitty tapped the side of her head. Lacy shook hers. "I guess that makes two of them."

"I suppose I should be more sympathetic, but she makes it hard. I think she's taking meds for it, but Yancy's probably not. Where would she get them? How would she get them? I just don't understand why Arcie was so damn determined about this trip. If she just wanted to come back, she had hundreds of times to do so over the years."

"She wanted it for herself but was afraid to come alone, the way I figure it. Remembering our promise gave her an excuse to drag us into it."

Kitty frowned. "You believe that's all there is to it?"

"Only thing I can see. She felt pretty strongly about you never wanting to come back with her."

"You could be right. She knew I hated this place."

"What about Domeno?"

"He looks pretty much the same as he did years ago. I was getting over my crying jag when he showed up. I was surprised to see him, but I don't think he was surprised to see me. I don't think it was an accidental meeting. I believe he already knew we were here."

"Why would you think that?"

"It felt that way. Like he planned to meet me."

Lacy stopped walking. "Why wouldn't he come say hello if he already knew we were here?"

"I didn't think to ask." Kitty shrugged. "It felt a little awkward being around him after so long." She tapped her left breast. "Bright shiny badge. He's the sheriff."

"The sheriff?"

"Yeah, it surprised me, too." Kitty laughed. "Not many people here, so what do you need a sheriff for, right? Not anyone around to even pay him a salary. I didn't say that to him, but I thought it." She broke off a small tree branch, twirling it as she walked, swatting at weeds and wildflowers. "I get the feeling something bad went down between him and Yancy. They must just stay out of each other's way, probably why he didn't come to see us right away once he found out we were staying at her house."

"Where else would we stay? There's no place else to stay." Lacy sucked in her breath, a fluttery sensation in her stomach. "He told you something about Yancy?"

"He insinuated it. He seemed real tense whenever I brought her name up. I think a lot of bad stuff went down around here since we left." Kitty held up her hand, twirled her fingers around in the air. "Damn, look around, Lacy. There's more activity in a cemetery on a Saturday night."

"Yeah, it's awfully strange. With so few people around, you would think the two of them would have gotten together. Maybe got married and had kids. Become lovers, at least." Kitty was giving her wide eyes. Lacy realized what she'd said, gave a little laugh, and offered a small half-smile. "Oops, sorry, guess not—forgot myself there for a minute."

Kitty laughed. Lacy laughed with her.

"Well, maybe they were lovers and it didn't work out, but if that's true, I think it would have been a long time ago." Kitty was almost comfortable with Lacy, decided it wasn't so bad being friendly again. Funny how things worked out when you least expected them. Being friendly could be advantageous for them both. Later, Lacy might reconsider, but maybe when they got back home they could keep in touch. She thought she'd like that, maybe Lacy would also. She turned, walked backward. "Let's go see Domeno. He said to come to his office anytime. Let's just go and surprise him, you and me."

"Now?"

"Sure, why not? It might help us find out what the hell is going on here."

"You think he'll tell us?" Lacy asked doubtfully.

"Can't hurt to try." Kitty grinned. "Besides, I didn't tell you the best part of all of this."

"Which is?"

"Domeno has a car!"

71

The tiny hardware store was almost hidden by the banana plants it shared with the café. When the spring-loaded wooden door slammed behind Creely, an elderly man stood up behind the counter and closed a tattered Bible. He squinted at Creely, curling his thumbs under his suspenders, taking on the pugilistic stance of a much younger man.

"Whatcha wantin', son?" His voice was throaty, his tone a little unfriendly.

"Not quite sure. You have any big knives?"

"Nope, jest guns." The man cocked a curious eyebrow.

"Would you mind if I look around?"

"Reckon not." He released his suspenders, leaned on the glass-fronted counter, one hand hidden behind it. Inside the counter were handguns and ammunition. Behind him, on the wall, were several rifles and a big badass double-barrel shotgun.

Creely walked the length of the four cramped aisles, past overloaded shelves and bins. Chipped sheets of pegboard nailed to the wall held hammers and hacksaws, brushes and rollers. Cans of paint were stacked below. He wondered if the paint was so old it had dried up inside the cans. Most things were dusty, untouched for a long time. He found what he thought he could use on the last aisle, bottom row. The cardboard box was ripped, coated in dirt, its contents old and rusty. He hefted the object in his hand, deciding it might work.

"How much?" he asked, as he laid the item on the counter.

The man frowned, scratched his head, and squinted up at him. "Don't rightly knowed. Been h're a lon' time. You wantin' only the one?"

"Yes—and a file, the largest one you have."

"Top shelf rear," he said, pointing toward the back of the store.

Creely brought the file back, looked inside the counter, tapped at the glass. "Give me a box of those shells."

"Cain't sell you no gun."

"Don't need agun, just the shells." He pulled his money clip from his pocket. "How much do I owe you?"

"Forty oughta do it." The man stuffed the money in his pocket and bagged the purchases. "Whatcha gonna do with them th'ngs?"

Creely picked up the brown bag.

"Not quite sure," he repeated as he walked out.

72

Yancy sat in the thickest part of the undergrowth, where a dark, twisty channel spilled into a bayou, and everything living was shadow-tinted in the weak light. She'd become uncomfortable with her thoughts, with the restless stirring of her beast just below the surface of her skin, but it was tranquil here, an earthy place, a favorite place. The world slowed down here. She slowed with it, able to absorb the silence, her brain responding with a sluggish stirring like a big animal turning laboriously around within a confined space until it found a solace zone. She was aware of her heartbeat, liked listening to it, feeling it. It was strong, steady, a resounding duplicate throb inside her chest and skull as it pushed her blood around. Her nostrils quivered, sensitive to all surrounding odors. Her ears tingled deep inside, picking up sounds.

It had rained, but not for long, just enough to get things wet but not soggy. She loved the swamp after rain. She breathed deeply, pulling all the scents from the air, pushing them far down inside her. She could smell everything—water and fish, flowers and trees, all the animals—everything smelled fresh and delicious and made her hungry. It was times like this that made her glad she'd never left home. She belonged here. It was her world, a special world. A world the other women would never understand or be a part of. Theirs was the outside world. The two worlds were the difference between a caged and a wild animal.

Arcie's first letter came as a surprise, but when the others came, Yancy found she liked receiving them, had even answered a few, but the effort had been painfully long and tiring. She had never liked Belle Kennedy's school and had never learned much, so her writing and spelling were poor. When Arcie had asked about Domeno, she got the first sniff of why the woman wanted to come back. It had nothing to do with a reunion; everything to do with Domeno. Bu t sometimes she would open Arcie's letters and reread the pages, give herself glimpses of the outside, push away her loneliness for a little while. It was the letters that made her think more about the promise of a reunion and decide to bring them back.

After the post office closed down and they stopped delivering mail, there were no more letters from Arcie. To either send or receive mail, she would've had to get a box in Boudreaux's post office, take the pirogue most of the way through a brackish bay and walk the rest of the way. She considered it a hard day's journey for a letter, sent or received. And it was dangerous. One look at her and they'd know who she was and where she came from. They would be afraid. Fear was an open invitation to kill.

Yancy shifted her squatting position until her

butt touched the ground and her back rested against a tree. She cocked her head and listened. She could hear the night crawlers, fat rubbery bodies sliding and wiggling through the soil, hiding their movement in mulch when they surfaced as if sensing her as much as she sensed them. She pushed aside the leaves. There were three or four, twisted into a ball, crawling over and around each other. She held them in her palm, poked them apart with her finger, playing with them, watching them twist and jerk, doubling back on themselves, then dropped them back to the ground.

A large, hard-shelled beetle trundled from under a rotting branch. Its ebony shell glowed with thin streaks of green, its underside a delicate umber color. She caught it, held it between two fingers, and watched it struggle, spiny legs wildly seeking a purchase in the air. She used her thumbnail to split its belly down the center and scrape out its soft innards. Some insects were a treat, like candy, each with its own special flavor, like chocolate or cinnamon or peppermint.

The others thought her crazy, dirty and disgusting. If they saw her now, what would she thin? If they knew the truth, would they be scared?

She had a brief shift last night and caught and ate a rabbit, a tasty scrap to tide her over. She was hungry again, needing something more substantial. That hunt would take longer and might take her too far away from the house. She was determined to hold off, but her resolve was weakening. The thought of her fangs buried in tender flesh, a struggling body tight under hers, the blood rich and thick on her tongue, was hard to ignore. Having them here made things difficult. She smelled their blood, their individual skin scents, that settled deep in her nasal cavities, burning like a small fire. She could feel each heartbeat, sense each spike and surge of pulse—and it was so tempting.

Yancy was beginning to hate herself for bringing them back. She should never have agreed with Arcie to do it. Telling them about things of the past no longer seemed so important, especially since she lost her tongue and couldn't speak, couldn't explain things properly. She could find a way, she felt sure, but fancy, self-important, big city women that they were, she no longer felt they would care about any of it; it wouldn't be important to them. She just might keep everything to herself after all. She needed to be careful to protect what was hers and was already thinking how peaceful it would be once they were gone.

They hadn't done right by her, so there was still revenge in her heart. It didn't matter now, but she could've done better, she knew she could have if given a chance. She might have been somebody if taken away from here like Kitty had taken Arcie. If given a break, she might have been so much more. She could have forgotten about Domeno. Forgotten that he had found the others special, but never her. Maybe she would have met someone that would've wanted her, would've given her that precious girl-baby she needed. Maybe no longer worried about her curses that never seemed to work, or the things they might have done. Here she was just someone people looked away from, and was scared of, another fou . . . forced by obligation into sometimes becoming an animal.

74

Rain clouds bruised a sky that suddenly cracked open, a hard rain soaking Creely as he left the hardware store. The rain pounded, thunder crashed, lightning flashed in white lines as he sat in the Porsche, blinking water away, using paper napkins in an attempt to partially dry himself. Concentrating on the rain-drenched windshield as the rain came down harder, he seemed to lose his fix on time.

Loups-garous . . . *werewolves!*

The old man's words caused his pulse to speed. This was virgin territory for him. He had never really believed in supernatural creatures, and he didn't want to believe in this, but the old guy's warning echoed inside his head and wouldn't go away. It made him nervous, maybe more than a little scared.

Did such things really exist beyond books, television, and movies? Mythology was filled with such lore—stories, drawings, and paintings—but he had never paid much attention to that type of book. He had been born and raised in a city with an enormously colorful past and present enmeshed in voodoo and witchcraft. He knew there were cults of people who believed they were vampires and drank blood on a regular basis; people who believed they had animals' spirits inside, had lived another life as a animal and would return after death for another life as an animal. Just because people believed all that didn't make it true. Although in this imperfect, politically correct world where people killed for no reason, he had discovered almost anything was possible. Real life, humanity in general, was often more devastating than imagination and fantasy.

As a kid, he had never believed in monsters in the closet or under the bed, never been afraid of the boogie man. He didn't want to believe in them now. The old man had been a little drunk and he might be a little crazy to boot, but he seemed to genuinely believe werewolves really existed in French Gap. He, on the other hand, wanted to believe it was a hoax to dissuade strangers. Even if no werewolves, there was definitely something going on there that no one wanted to talk about, with the illustrious sheriff unquestionably keeping it under wraps.

The sky had turned an ugly slate color, full of dark clouds, and it was getting late, so he decided against going back until morning. He needed time to do a couple of things, to be better prepared, more confident in daylight. Already at a disadvantage with Abadie, he had no need to be foolhardy. What troubled him was the unknown woman in his vision. She had to be the woman from the airport. He hoped tonight wasn't the night she would die.

The rain had stopped or hadn't come that far

over by the time he reached the WHITE SWAN MOTEL the gas station attendant had directed him to. ETIENNE'S SWAMP TOURS AND GIFT SHOP was separated by a shell parking area from a small drive-thru hamburger-chicken place on one side of the motel, an old Exxon station on the other side. Across the parish roadway, set in the middle of a sugarcane field with a small shell parking lot in front was *The Purple Lady*. The boards were painted bright white and the trim was a deep purple, the door a lighter shade. No cars in the lot. Creely figured it was a whore house, slow in the customer department on a Sunday evening, or maybe just a really ugly bar with no customers. There was one vehicle in the parking lot of the swamp tours, none at the drive-thru food place, and one near the entrance of the motel.

The man behind the desk was grizzled, a patch over his left eye. He stared at Creely suspiciously with his good eye. When Creely pulled out his American Express, the man thumbed to the *CASH ONLY* sign on the wall. He paid cash for one night and took an honest-to-god key. Number 8 was the last on the left, almost on the parish road. He parked the Porsche in front of the door, removed his travel bag and activated the car's alarm.

The room was small and sparse. A double bed, an older model TV bolted to the ceiling, a scarred nightstand with a lamp screwed into the surface with a pair of big bolts. Across from the bed was a two-drawer chest with a plastic ice bucket and a single sanitary-wrapped plastic glass on top. The bathroom was a tiny cubicle. When you sat on the toilet, your knees touched the shower curtain on the left and the toilet paper holder on the right. It was a less-than-modest motel, definitely not luxury accommodations, lacking in most amenities.

Creely stripped and showered. The water ran barely hot, the shower stall gritty underneath his feet. He stood under the tepid water until it was cold, toweled off, slipped on a fresh pair of briefs, and sat on the bed to remove his purchases from the hardware store bag.

He didn't want to waste time on lack of knowledge. He had once read somewhere that a silver instrument through the heart could kill a shapeshifter, but something long and sharp through the heart would kill pretty much anything that breathed, wouldn't it? Still uncertain what he intended to do, he knew he needed to replace his anger and frustration with calm and work out some kind of strategy. He had always felt he could do anything that needed doing, and, more importantly, he always finished what he started. Most times anything was the pride of accomplishment; this time there was a lot more to it, but he would finish this, too, and would stick with it until the situation was resolved. What troubled him most was he had a feeling things were up for getting really bad before the situation would be over.

Maybe all he needed was his gun and bullets. Maybe not. He might not get a chance to shoot. Given the chance, he wouldn't hesitate. If forced to shoot, he wasn't looking to wound. He would be looking to kill. He might settle everything with one bullet—except for one thing. If what the old guy said was true, he could be facing something that might not be so easy to kill.

75

"You know what I find most confusing," Lacy said as they pushed their way through rough foliage back toward town. "There was no need to involve us in this at all. She could have come back anytime, why did she feel she had to have you with her?"

"I wish I knew."

"Are the two of you in a habit of doing everything together?"

"Actually, just the opposite. We're not that tight. We only go out to eat together maybe once a week. We lead totally different lives, except when she comes to my condo to help me take care of business. She's been my personal assistant for a few years. She's good at it, believe it or not."

They had taken shelter under an arbor of trees when the rain started. It hadn't lasted long but came down hard. Finally, it stopped, leaving them wet and uncomfortable.

"I feel like a drowned rat," Kitty grumbled.

Lacy laughed, stripping off her shirt and wringing the water out. "I'm sure we look like it."

Kitty unbuttoned her blouse and did the same. "Fine looking pair we make to go visiting someone we haven't seen in twenty years."

"Are you sure you want to do this?"

Kitty shrugged. "What difference does it make?"

"None, I suppose."

Falling into a thoughtful silence, they watched a pelican slide in from a thick gray sky and land in dappled water where weak sunlight, pushing through a misshapen cloud, slanted along the shiny dark surface. The bird drifted close to the bank, spotted them and took flight with a heavy flap of wings.

"Arcie thought something bad would happen to us if we didn't come back."

"She told you that?"

"She did." Kitty finished buttoning her blouse and started walking again. "I as much as told her she was nuts, then I got to thinking about the entire Arceneaux family and started to wonder if maybe she could be a little right."

"You don't believe that, do you?" Lacy asked.

"I don't want to, but—well, no, I guess not." She shrugged. "But stranger things have happened." Kitty no longer knew what to believe. They seemed to have been led into some surreal adventure that had turned sour. She and Arcie had been together for a long time. She thought Arcie a friend, even during bad times. Until now. Now she felt angry and betrayed. When they got back home, if their friendship survived, it would be tenuous at best.

The old man had returned to his rocker. They nodded at him. He didn't move, didn't acknowledge

them in any manner, but they could feel the weight of
of his stare. The dog was up, wet and muddied, limp-
ing in circles, lips pulled back in a permanent snarl.
Once massive, a combination of several large breeds,
now skin hung on his emaciated frame like a dark
dirty rug. His bones protruded at all angles. His
muzzle looked as if he had stuck his nose into the ass-
end of a porcupine. He didn't acknowledge them any
more than the old man.

"Crazy ol' dog," said a deep voice from out of
nowhere behind them.

Startled, Kitty and Lacy jumped, bumped into
each other, and turned simultaneously.

"Good God, Domeno, at least let us know you're
there!" Kitty admonished.

"Sorry, ladies. Thou'ht y'u knew I was h're."

Liar, Kitty thought, *you did that on purpose.* He had
intentionally snuck up on them.

Domeno grinned. "Got y'urself wet, huh?"

Lacy laughed uneasily. "You could say that." She
gestured toward the dog. "We were paying attention
to him. Is he dangerous?"

"*Non,* jest ol' and sick. Tho'ght he'd pass on by
'imself, but guess I gotta shoot 'im one day soon."
Lacy grimaced. Domeno grinned, his glance shrewd
and evaluating when it touched on her. "Y'u a-lookin'
mighty pretty, Miss Lacy. How y'u been all this time?"

"Doing pretty damn good until Arcie brought us

back here."

Domeno glanced over his shoulder, frowning. "Yep, y'u missin' one, ain't y'u?"

"We didn't invite her," Kitty admitted.

"Why's that?"

Kitty shrugged and Lacy said, "We had a few words with her."

"She's tight w'th Yancy?" His eyes flickered between the two of them.

"Maybe not tight," Kitty said, "but she's gone off on some crazy crusade when it comes to Yancy."

Domeno nodded, swiping the back of his big hand across his forehead where sweat had collected, then down his trouser leg, glancing up at the sky. The sun was back, climbing higher, pressing hard against their backs.

"Hot. It's alw'ys like this after a rain. No need us standin' h're in the heat. Let's go to my office? No air cond'tion, but its cooler inside." He didn't wait for an answer. He linked an arm through each of theirs, almost pulling them along.

Kitty instantly felt the heat of him, but if his touch had an effect on Lacy, she didn't show it. It occurred to Kitty again that something was wrong with the way she was responding. It wasn't normal. Even when he removed his arm, the heat lingered.

"Entrez," he said, pushing open the door and standing aside, tilting his head in a polite little bow.

The room was shadowy, definitely cooler than outside, with weak light from the single window. A scarred desk, metal folding chairs, crumbly corkboard bulletin board, yellowed memorabilia, battered file cabinets below a Mississippi riverboat print. A heavy leather holster hung on a peg next to the bulletin board, an old-fashioned revolver with a pearl-inlaid grip inside the holster.

Kitty said, "I remember that gun."

"It was Oubre's gun."

"What happened to him?" Rasley Oubre, the old sheriff, had been big and ugly, with a pudgy face scarred from serious acne as a kid. Pockmarks wrapped around the back of his head from ear lobe to ear lobe, the thick brass buckle of his belt digging into the overhang of his enormous belly, the sun reflecting in white flashes off the gun butt as he walked down the street. *Grandpere* never had much use for Oubre. Always said he was nothing more than a figurehead, a useless symbol of authority, a waste of a poor town's money when they could handle their own problems.

"He died 'bout 'leven years ago. I got the gun, like the job." Domeno gave a small, humorless chuckle. "They were both somethin' no one wanted." He brushed past Kitty to sit behind the desk, leaving a trail of outrageous heat, gesturing toward the chairs, his eyes following her movement.

"What happened here, Domeno?" Lacy asked

as she sat.

"Whatcha mean?" Domeno smiled, but his smile didn't quite touch his eyes.

"The town's gone. It looks to me like you're the sheriff of a ghost town."

"Whatcha said?" The remark had annoyed him, his friendly tone gone.

"It's broken down and abandoned, absolutely nothing here. Hardly any people, not even animals, except wild ones, only Yancy's chickens and that pitiful dog." A trembling challenge was in her voice, as if a little afraid of him, daring him to lie because she would know it was a lie. "Why didn't you leave?"

"Ne'er wanted to," he said, expression hard, eyes boring into Lacy. "Had no reason, nothin' fer me out th're."

"How can you live like this?"

"Only th'ng I know. Spent most all my life h're." Agitated, Domeno sat erect, shoulders stiff, rubbing his palm up and down his thigh.

Kitty had wondered about the same things, but she hadn't asked because her body remembered the feel of him pressed hard against her, his lips bruising her mouth. Another rush of warmth crawled through her. *What the hell? Why am I reacting this way?*

Domeno was almost a stranger; she didn't know anything about him anymore. She was acting like a horny teenager with these unreasonable feelings.

None of it was making sense. Like a bug bite, an itch in a spot she couldn't reach, she just kept scratching at it without relief. Something was definitely wrong with that. Was it the sex? Would she feel differently right now if they'd had sex? *Is that what it's going to take? Just do it—just so I know?* she wondered.

"I would have thought you'd want more." Lacy's tone was just short of antagonistic.

Domeno digested her words; definitely didn't like them. "I ne'er wanted much." He grinned, not a particularly nice grin, lips curling back over his teeth in an almost feral manner, leaving the impression he was no longer behind his face. "Ne'er needed much 'cept the swamp and freedom. I ne'er wanted a fancy car or house or a big bank account." He chuckled, but the sound was without humor. "Hell, I ain't ne'er had no bank account in my life!" He looked directly into her eyes, a long, considering look, voice coming from far down in his chest, the area from which a big nasty dog growled, and said, "Hell, money ain't everythin', Lacy." His words seemed calculated, a direct slight.

Kitty felt more than saw Lacy wince. He couldn't possibly know how rich she was. They were sparring with each other, dancing around some hidden agitation that wasn't new. She wondered exactly what had happened between them as teenagers.

"You're right, of course," Lacy said with a smile, like his, that wasn't quite a smile, "but it certainly helps buy the creature comforts."

"I ain't ne'er been one to give up what I had fer what I might git. Ne'er wanted nobody ownin' me."

"What about Yancy?" Kitty blurted out.

"What 'bout 'er?" he snapped, flinty eyes turning toward her.

"What happened to her?"

"Not my bidness. I don't talk 'bout 'er."

"Excuse me?"

"She ain't worth the tro'ble."

Kitty felt her heart leap and painfully collide with her ribcage. Something terrible happened between them. "How can you live this close and not know what happened to her? Why would you say that?"

"She done ter'ible things," he said flatly.

"What the hell are you talking about?" Her voice went a little shrill, a skitter of fear jolting her stomach. What kind of game was Domeno playing? Why not just come out and tell them what had happened? Lacy's hand applied pressure to her arm. Kitty fought down her wave of indignation and fear. This was not the time to get angry with him. They were going to have to use him. Finding out about Yancy was less important than getting a way out of town, but she was so frustrated and tired of being fed scraps of information. Plain tired of everyone jerking her around and lying to her. "Did someone hurt her? We think someone hurt her."

"Y'u th'nk that 'cause y'all don't know 'er," Domeno said, eyes icy. "She uses 'er crazy voodoo spells to h'rt and kill."

Kitty gasped. "So she really uses spells? I never wanted to believe it. So it's all true, everything they always said about the Arceneauxs?" And she thought of their night around the kitchen table, when they were supposed to see their future husbands. She had indulged Yancy, thought it a silly game; had never considered it a spell. At least, not until the door opened and whatever it was had come inside.

"It's true."

Kitty didn't want to believe what he said, but he sounded truthful. He seemed different from earlier as if their visit and questions had poured fuel on a deep, complex inner fire and he was fighting to keep his composure. She had absolutely no doubt this bitter, resentful Domeno, when displeased and provoked, would respond badly. He could be as deadly as the icy dark she saw lurking in his eyes. His big body seemed to exude raw heat, filled with repressed violence.

She knew their remarks had agitated him, and Domeno had a strange, fierce strength about him, that fascinated but scared the shit out of her. She struggled not to let it show. In this rotten little place, where they were at least temporarily trapped, Domeno was powerful, the ultimate authority, his word final. They had to be careful; he was probably their only way out of French Gap anytime soon.

"Let it go," Lacy said, quietly.

I believe him, Kitty thought, her blood singing. She stood and walked to the window. A wind had risen, nipping at the ground, kicking up a stampede of crinkly leaves, a whisper of oyster shell dust. The sun had disappeared behind a cloud again. A dark skyline rotated slowly, coming in their direction; another storm moving in. They needed to get back to Yancy's, but she didn't want to let it go as Lacy had advised.

Kitty whipped around. "She did something terrible to you, didn't she?" She already knew the answer, but wanted to hear him say the words.

Lacy flinched and pressed her shoulders hard against the chair, alarm flitting across her face.

"She did." His fierce stare bored into Kitty. "She killed my wife and unborn baby."

It had rained hard for over an hour. The storm had drained away the weak sunlight, pounding the roof, lashing so hard against the building the door to the motel room rattled.

Creely stood and stretched, rotating his shoulders. His back hurt, his neck ached, and his fingers were stiff and scraped, a couple bleeding. The plaid bedspread was covered with rust flakes, and the shiny remnants of his labor. His efforts had been successful.

If he needed one, he now had another weapon—a most impressive weapon.

A weapon for distance, and a weapon for up close.

If he was attacked, if whatever attacked was close enough and he was fast enough, his new weapon, rightly placed, should do the job. He picked it up, hefted it in his palm, and examined it more closely under the light from the single lamp.

It gleamed bright, shiny silver.

A thick, old-fashioned rail spike honed to about four blade inches and a lethal point.

Domeno sat on the edge of his bed, head resting in his palms, heels of his hands pressed tightly against his eyes. He had lost control for a minute, and that was dangerous. They had stayed until the second storm passed, and the office had turned gray with fading light. It felt as if they were trapped in the closeness of the small room and it made him uneasy. Kitty's expression was one of shock and sadness; Lacy's stunned, her eyes grave. He could tell they both wanted to get away from him.

They refused his offer of a ride as if the closeness of the office had been enough togetherness. They wouldn't be able to tolerate the entrapment of the car. He'd gone to his house, had been sitting like this for a long time, listening, waiting, reluctant to accept what he knew was coming, fighting against the need that surged through him. He was tense and hungry. Just being near them, sensing the pulse of their blood, their scents buried deep inside his nose, had stirred his own blood to boil and his beast had nudged closer to the surface. It had been over a week since he had shifted and fed. He needed to feed.

He didn't mean to say it. He hadn't meant to tell them. They didn't need to know about Tansie and the *baby*. He could still see the revulsion on Kitty's face, the horror in her eyes, and the fear spreading like a carefully laid cloth across Lacy's beautiful features. Lacy had tried to make her face expressionless, so he couldn't read her fear, but it was there, deep in her eyes, just the same. They didn't want to believe what he said, but they knew it was true. They were afraid of him now. He didn't know how to repair the damage. Would it keep Kitty away? Not if he could help it. She'd been so soft in his arms, so willing to . . . *what?*

Fuck me, he thought.

A strong, impersonal, emotional response that most times had nothing to do with love. The rage of hormones, a tempest of hot blood and excitement. It was a natural carnal need when there was a strong attraction between two people. He and Kitty had always been attracted to each other. She would've fucked him and walked away. He had felt it. So casual, like shopping for a new dress, trying him on for size.

What a fool he had been, always filled with adolescent dreams and fantasies, none of which worked out in reality. Conquests . . . youthful rites of passage, ego, that's all it had been about. He hated himself for thinking only of satisfying his needs, for using Lacy and all the other girls in town, when all he wanted was so much more from Kitty. It had always been Kitty. After she left, he'd wallowed for a long time in the misery of his loss. He'd been so angry, even hated her for a time, when that Bayou Lafourche guy told everyone about taking her away. Now, he had been given a second chance and he wanted to take it. Had he fucked that up, too, and lost her again?

Domeno thought of Tansie, his beautiful, wonderful little Tansie. The moment he laid eyes on her, he knew she was special. She had been such a sweet, innocent girl, not much more than a child mentally, but physically already a woman, with a woman's desires. She hadn't wiped away his love for Kitty, but she made him almost whole again. She gave him a reason to start over, made him *happy*, sometimes driving him crazy because he didn't want to stop touching her. All he could think about was being inside of her, of losing himself in her. Their days and night had been fierce. He'd been her first, but she'd been so passionate, willing to do anything he asked, always touching him, wanting him all the time. When she tore at him, he would get caught up in the pleasure of her tight, naked little body, and sometimes he'd forget about Kitty. Because Kitty wasn't real, he couldn't touch her, but Tansie was real.

And so was Yancy. In one vicious, jealous moment that crazy bitch had taken it all away. Her demented mind had taken away everything he'd grown to love, had wiped away his life, and signed away his soul. He knew she'd cast a spell, used her *gris-gris*. He had found the burned circle; the remnants of the doll with blonde hair tied around its faceless head, the black streaks of blood dried on its body, the knife hole in its stomach area. Tansie didn't deserve what Yancy did to her, and he didn't deserve the misery caused by her bite that slashed away at his humanity.

A tear slid down and dropped as a damp circle onto his khaki pants. He swiped angrily at his wet cheek. He hadn't cried in a long time, didn't want to now, but he couldn't stop. He'd gotten little sleep in the last twenty-four hours. It told in his behavior, the way he felt, so . . . angry, so empty.

It would have been a pleasure, a relief, to kill Yancy. He would have been satisfied by that, he could have killed himself afterward. It would have been so easy just to stick Oubre's old revolver in his mouth, and blow his brains out the back of his head. But he hadn't been able to kill her.

Domeno looked out the window, swallowing around the lump that had thickened in his throat. The second storm had been savage. It had grown dark early. Reed-like tips of swamp grasses bent double, heavy with moisture, attempting to straighten and offer their broken flowers to the twilight. In the distance, the moon rose, shadowing the treetops.

Almost a full moon, a virulent orange, shrouded by a thin vaporous veil, cottony mercury sliced through with thin lines of red as if leaking blood.

It was a mean moon.

A warning; an omen of bad things to come.

Domeno wiped his face, breathed deeply, the air from the open window filling his nostrils with after-storm scents, delicious pungent fragrances that touched him with fire.

The rampant surge of emotion on the last day had weakened his willpower. His body was impatient. He itched from his scalp to the soles of his feet. Darts of flame shot through him. He could feel the shift coming, overtaking him. He lifted his head. In his reflection in the window glass, he saw an uncharitable light flare up, and dance in his gold eyes, sheening them with scarlet. The energy of his beast was pushing out of him.

The emptiness first, then the twisting scintillate, the hunger—consuming him.

No one but Yancy could imagine the pain that came with it; no one but she could understand the madness that energized him. No one but she could smell the leaking odors that stirred the thirst, could hear the beat of the heart, feel the swell of the pulse.

Domeno stripped away his clothes, climbed naked through the window, and sat on the ground, wet leaves and damp cold soil under his buttocks, toes curling into the muddy puddles under his feet as he waited for his beast to rise.

The pulsing sense of power began its run through his blood.

The shambles of a pigsty stood in front of him. The broken wooden rails were like drunken little people leaning left and right. It had been a long time since he kept animals, but this was a place he knew well. He'd sat here like this so many times, he could identify each rotted gutter and wormhole in the wood.

The boiling in his blood, straining of muscle, throbbing of sound deep inside his chest as his flesh expanded and melted. It stretched tautly over misshapen bones never again to belong only to him as a human. An explosive festival burned every nerve, filled him with yearning beyond comprehension, and swallowed up most memory and conscience until he was no longer able to resist. The change came, surging through him as a hard electric rush.

He rose up, shook himself, and felt the night breeze ripple coolly through his fur. His vision cleared, his nostrils flared, acutely aware of everything around him. The crisp, sharp swamp odors were intense beyond ordinary. He heard and felt every sound, whisper, movement, color, and scent. Hunching forward on his long front legs, lowering his head, nose touching paws, body bent into a bow, his ears rotated side to front, back again, as he listened to the soft whistle of air rushing through his powerful, elongated snout. He took pleasure in his paws sinking into the wet earth, soaking up the textures of mud, leaves, and oyster shell in his pads. His taut leg muscles stretched, pulling back on his lean hips, detonating spasms of delight in his veins and along his spine as his body exploded in a ground-eating lope. His keen, consuming hunger came alive deep inside.

He came to a halt, his pelt a rich gold in the bath of angry moonlight. He planted his giant paws in damp soil, pushed his nose through plant fronds, blinking away the clinging rainwater from his eyes, listening. Shouldering from the shadows into the open, he offered the night a deep-chest chuffing, a simple warning of his location to any adversary that might cross his path.

78

After the brutal lashings of the storm had passed over, Kitty and Lacy walked through the deep gray daylight strung with ribbons of white like frosted holiday lights, the air as heavy and wet as their feet slipping through soggy piles of leaves. Domeno had offered a ride they refused, mutually sensing their need to be away from him. Dusk caught Kitty and Lacy in its gloomy dripping light, brushed against their shoulders, wrapped around them like a shawl. Overhead trees dribbled rainwater, great hunched old men leaning toward them in an unfriendly manner.

Kitty wrapped her body in her arms and shivered inside clothes not fully dried, cursing her cold feet and mud-covered shoes. Lacy marched at her side, saying nothing, absorbed in thought.

The shadows around them filled with movement, the gibberish of small things in the tangle of under-growth, unidentifiable sounds that startled and made them wince, raising the hairs along their arms. They picked up their pace. A few yards from the house, Lacy grabbed Kitty's arm, jerking her to a halt.

Kitty's feet almost slipped out from under her. *"What?"* she snapped.

For a minute, Lacy's eyes seemed focused on something in the distance. Finally, they shifted toward

Kitty. She pushed her hand through her damp hair, dragging it away from her face and behind her ear.

"What?" Kitty repeated.

"He did it, didn't he? Not talking about it doesn't change things. You know he did it."

Kitty's throat closed tight. The skin across her shoulders twitched, as if little bugs ran across it, sort of like an animal's hide that shimmied when it tried to dislodge annoying flies. Domeno's words tore at her, weights resting on her shoulders. Lacy had sat frozen, while the floor seemed to have shifted under her feet. She had moved her lips to say something, found she was unable to speak, her tongue fused to the roof of her mouth. She had stared at him with a stunned, bewildered look. Finally, her breath hitched inside her chest, fluttered up her throat, and escaped as a soft, "Oh, my God." Sadness overtook her as his tawny glacier stare held fast onto her face.

In that single dead silent moment that held the small room and the three of them in its grasp, she had known with absolute certainty . . . Domeno Abadie had been the one to mutilate Yancy Arceneaux.

Now Lacy wanted her to talk about it. There had been no outright admittance on his part, and they had no evidence, only their feelings. She didn't want to talk about it, didn't want to answer Lacy. She felt unsure about thinking it, much less saying it aloud.

79

Domeno lay in the dense tall grasses, licking his paws clean, his hunger barely abated. His long tongue curled around his jowls, clearing away the blood left behind from his meal.

He hadn't wanted to go far. He had to eat, his beast wouldn't let him go without eating, but to get something bigger than a rabbit or rodents, he would have to travel a short distance away from the area. Unlike Yancy, he had always satisfied his hunger with animals, and the bigger natural-dwelling animals had grown aware of him, always seeming to sense his approach before he was close enough for a kill. He had never killed a human, but after a shift, his hunger reflected little difference between the blood and scent of an animal and a human until he had fed. He couldn't deny the instinct, it was always there, clear and sharp and powerful, wrapping his mind like razor wire. The hunger had to be satisfied. It had become a daily struggle, never wanting to lose all his humanity.

The old dog was gnawing on a squirrel carcass, tearing it slowly apart with jaws and teeth that didn't work quite right. As Domeno approached, he looked up, eyes bright with knowledge.

The dog and the wolf stared long at each other, sharing a final memory flicker of better times. He dropped the squirrel remnants and bared his teeth through his grizzled muzzle, pushing himself up from the ground with effort. He made a feeble lunge, the gleam in his rheumy eyes in total acceptance of his fate. Almost as if he'd been waiting for the moment, he seemed to take quiet satisfaction in having survived long enough to force Domeno, in the form of human or wolf, to take his life.

Domeno sank his teeth into the old dog's throat, listened to his tired old lungs wheezed a last breath, and held on until his weak legs jerks stopped. There had been a moment of hesitation, of chaos deep inside, what his human side would later recognize as pangs of sorrow and regret. But at this moment, as the blood pumped down his throat and his teeth tore vital organs and sparse flesh from the dog's bones, he was aware only of his hunger.

The ground vibrated under him. A snap of a twig, the whisper of shell pushed aside or overturned by cautious footsteps. The flick of rainwater from tree branches, the odor of smashed leaves, wet and ripe, a stew of mold and bacteria that stung his nostrils—along with a sharp pulsing scent of human blood.

80

Kitty had decided even if Domeno had done such a terrible thing, it was not the time to judge him. It wasn't their business, even if they had ended up in the middle of it. It was something between him and Yancy. It was too late to fix the problem and whatever had caused it, and even if it wasn't too late, they certainly couldn't fix it. They needed him on their side. They needed his car.

She couldn't confide in Lacy her time spent alone with Domeno. No matter how much she tried to rationalize things in her mind, it frightened her to think this man who held her tight, that she'd been so willing to give herself to, could commit such an atrocity. Obviously, Domeno was filled with anger and hatred toward Yancy whether she had done what he accused her of or not; it was in his voice and in his eyes. It never occurred to her to consider Yancy beyond doing such that Domeno was accusing her unjustly. Violence seemed to lurk right below the surface. She didn't want to think of him as a monster, but she knew if he'd seriously injured someone once, he was capable of it again.

"I'd like to talk to Arcie about all this, see how much she knew before bringing us here, but it might just set her off again." She looked at Lacy, but couldn't see her face clearly. The last light had dipped beyond the trees, leaving the skyline a deep purple. The road's curve seemed to terminate in an an amorphous wall of charcoal that faded into black. The moon had began to rise, but it's light barely touched the dark. "What do you think? As angry as I am with her, I'd still like to believe she wouldn't have known all this and brought us into it without telling us. Should we try talking with her?"

Before Lacy could answer, the screen door banged open. Arcie stepped outside, hands fisted on her hips. Kitty felt a taste of bitterness. Arcie had brought them into this hostile unsafe environment that placed them in danger. How many more deceptions were to be uncovered?

Kitty couldn't stop herself. "Did you know?"

"Did I know what?" Arcie asked.

"All this nasty shit with Yancy and Domeno?"

Arcie stepped up close to Kitty. "I have no idea what you're talking about, but whatever you think you've found out, you need to leave it alone."

Kitty could tell by her expression she might not know how it came about, but she knew where they had been, and she didn't care about Kitty's anger or Lacy's disapproval. They had seen Domeno. Kitty didn't know why that was so important to her, but she now knew what Arcie cared most about was seeing Domeno, but it hadn't happened for her.

"*Leave it alone?* Domeno says she killed his wife and unborn child," Kitty said.

"I don't know anything about that. You couldn't let things be, could you?" Arcie pointed over their heads into the dark. "You had to go find him and get mixed up with him again. Now you believe whatever terrible story he told you!"

"Why would he lie about something that horrible?" A blistering heat rising up her neck, her heart racing full tilt, Kitty reached out and laid a restraining hand on Arcie's arm.

Arcie jerked away. "Don't touch me!" Angry, frightened, the same defensive tone she had at the accident site filled her voice.

Kitty removed her hand, lifted her hands, palms out, and stepped back. "Are you absolutely *crazy,* Arcie? Listen to yourself. Have you forgotten we're stranded here?"

Arcie made a move to turn away. Kitty grabbed her arm. She tried to pull away, bringing her arm up and jerking it back so quickly she caught Kitty across the jaw. The blow was hard enough to snap Kitty's head back. She lost her grip and almost her balance. "You *bitch!*" she snarled, thinking the hit was done on purpose. She reached for Arcie again.

"*Stop it! Stop it!*" Lacy screamed, stamping her feet as she stepped between them, planting the heels of her hands hard against their shoulders. She separated them by inches.

"It was an accident!" Arcie wailed, shrinking back, eyes wide.

"Yeah, like my car, like knowing nothing about this fucking place—to you everything is an accident!"

"Stop it! Right now! I've had about all I can take! We need to stick together. Things aren't nice here," Lacy said as Kitty stepped back and said nothing. Arcie's head moved in a barely perceivable nod, shame in her eyes. "Don't you realize we could be in serious danger, Arcie?"

"Why would you think such a thing?"

"Because it's true, there is too much weird shit going on here."

"Whatever he told you could be a lie," Arcie countered.

"What the—" Kitty began, but Lacy silenced her with an uplifted hand.

"You're right, it could be, but whatever we've been told sounds like the truth, all considered. And we're yelling at each other like raving maniacs," Lacy said, her voice tight and low. "You knew Domeno was still here, but didn't tell us that either?"

Arcie shrugged, lowered her eyes and nodded.

"Why not?"

Arcie shrugged again without looking at Lacy. "Why would it matter? It didn't seem important."

"Of course it's important! Don't believe her,"

Kitty interjected. "She's lied to us so much. I don't think she knows what the truth is anymore."

"Where is Yancy now?" Lacy held up a hand to quiet her. "Have you seen her since we left?"

"I don't know. No, she's not happy with us." Arcie offered Kitty a withering stare. "What did he tell you?"

"Not nearly enough," Kitty snapped.

"Enough to scare the crap out of us," Lacy said. "If you're trying to protect her, you need to stop. Things aren't right with her."

Arcie's eyes widened as her head swiveled between them. "You just believe him?"

"Of course we do," Kitty said. "We can't believe you. You haven't been straight with us since all this shit started."

"We also believe he was the one who cut out her tongue," Lacy said.

Arcie gasped, backing away from them, her butt bumping against the screen door. "You only have his word—you don't know what he said is true."

"You're right, we don't know for sure. He didn't admit he did anything to her. It's just what we believe. If it isn't true, Yancy needs to step up and straighten it out, somehow find a way to tell us what is true. What he said, as horrible as it was to hear it, makes sense to us," Lacy said.

"But you know, don't you?" Kitty said, pushing

her face closer to Arcie's.

"Kitty, don't—" Lacy began, grabbing her arm.

"She's lying." Kitty jerked her arm away and took a step back.

"I didn't know about the wife and baby. In one of her letters, she told me the wife died, years ago, nothing about a baby. She told me he tried to kill her, but he couldn't. She never told me why, only that he cut out her tongue."

"Why would he do that without good reason?"

"I don't know. I never asked."

"Why couldn't he just kill her? Why only mutilate her?" Lacy asked.

"She has a—power," Arcie whispered. "I think it must have helped protect her."

"A power?" Kitty snorted. "More lies."

"Like her mother and grandmother."

"Voodoo power," Lacy said. "That time she tried to use that spell, I thought it was a game. Some kind of trick to scare us. I never believed she knew what she was doing. I never saw a man's face. I never saw anything. Did you?"

Arcie shook her head.

"You're saying everything we heard was all true?" Arcie nodded slowly.

"Oh, *fuck!*" Kitty threw up her hands. She made another impatient, angry move toward Arcie, stopped, and stepped back. She turned away, too disgusted to look at her.

"I don't know about all of it, but I believe what *she* told me. Like you believe what *he* told you."

They stood in silence. A soft wind whistled around the edges of the tin roof. Icy feet tiptoed up Kitty's spine. Night had fallen thick around them to the backdrop of a tie-dyed sky. A few stars imprinted the dark. Shadow had lengthened to ebony between the house stilts. Chickens stirred, agitated movement, rustling feathers, disturbed from sleep by their voices.

These people are hurting each other . . . mutilating each other—*killing* each other. Doing things that only cold-blooded killers or insane people would do, Kitty thought. This wasn't a nightmare. This was *real.* Yancy dabbling in voodoo, just mixing up some spells and *presto!* getting rid of what she didn't want around, kill it off and be done with it. Was that the way she did it? It seemed so simple, almost economical, probably didn't even have to be premeditated, a spur-of-the-moment decision, depending on her mood. What Kitty couldn't understand was why kill Domeno's wife and baby? What had been Yancy's reasoning? Surely the other woman couldn't have done something so terrible to provoke such a horrible action. Did she consider them a threat for some reason or—yes, of course, Yancy had wanted him all to herself! Maybe he was the last man in town . . . maybe she actually thought she loved him.

"You put us in this terrible position," Kitty said, staring at Arcie with unveiled contempt. "You knew all these things and didn't tell us. You did this."

Arcie glowered at her. "I didn't do anything. She probably knew the two of you wouldn't come on your own. I think she did a spell to bring us back."

"If you thought that, you should've said so."

"She didn't just think it." Kitty stared at Arcie, her expression fierce. *"Us,"* she motioned between Lacy and herself. "Not *you*. Us. You knew we'd never come back willingly. You told Yancy. You arranged all of this. Whatever her reasons might have been for wanting us to come back, I believe you asked her to do whatever she thought necessary, whatever she could, to bring us back," Kitty whispered. She turned away from Arcie, exchanged a long look with Lacy, gut-wrenching afraid. After a moment, she breathed, "We need to get the hell away from here. I don't want to go back in there. If we are to beliee Domeno, she might decided to kill us off in our sleep."

The drive-thru burger joint was closed by the time the storm passed. Creely drove back to Boudreaux, found the café closed, but *Josie's Luncheonette* still open. He ate a BLT with a double order of home fries, two refills of Coke and Dutch Apple pie with a double scoop of vanilla ice cream.

Barbara briefly popped into his mind. He instantly dismissed her, as his thoughts strayed back to Kitty, remembering the first time they met. It made him smile. He hadn't ever given it serious thought before, but maybe that had been the defining moment when he first began to love her. Why hadn't he recognized it for what it really was before now? Why had it taken the possibility of losing her forever for his heart to give his feelings an identity, and his mind to figure it out? Carson had recognized it for what it was, and always teased them about it; maybe that made his brother a little smarter.

He had been so young, they both were so young when it began between them. That was just a fact, not an excuse, but he had known instantly Kitty was different from the other females he knew and had been with, so maybe he'd been protecting himself at the time, and ever since, not taking an emotional risk with her.

Kitty had brushed up against him leaving a restaurant. He knew immediately she had lifted his wallet. She obviously thought she'd succeeded and began
to slide away through the doorway. He had almost
yanked her shoulder from its socket and her feet out
from under her in a bone-crushing grip around her
upper arm. She yelped as he jerked her toward him,
lifting her high on her toes. Pressing his lips against
her cheek, he whispered: "Give it back."

She had gnawed at her lip, staring at him wide-
eyed, a shadow of fear leaping through her eyes, as
she slowly pulled his wallet from her bra and handed
it back. When he said, "Come with me," she balked
and struggled a little. A couple next to them exchanged glances and moved away. A boyfriend or husband
getting a little too rough? They didn't want to get involved, not their business. But the man stepping
through the door behind the couple thought it his.

"Everything's all right," he had said as the man
paused in front of them. "Just a lover's spat, nothing
serious, right, honey?" He had increased pressure on
her arm until she nodded, yanking her out the door
and almost dragging her down the sidewalk, aware
the man was watching. He had wondered if the man
would call the police.

Half a block down, he shoved Kitty into an
empty doorway, pushing her up hard against the door,
holding her hands behind her back.

"Let go! I gave the damn thing back! Let me go!" she hissed, kicking at him, trying to knee him in the balls, her face a bright red.

Creely had jammed his hand under her jaw, forcing her head up until they looked each other eye to eye. "You want jail time?" he had asked.

She had paled, breathing sharply through her mouth, her heart thrumming hard against his shoulder, while she studied him slyly from under half-lowered eyelids, weighing the odds. "I-I—I could scream, say you tried to rape me," she countered.

It had been a quick and gusty reply, he had to give her that. He wasn't much older than her, not much more than a kid himself. He could read the shrewd calculations in her eyes. He said nothing, holding her tightly by the throat until she relented and murmured, "N-no, I don't want jail time."

"Then listen to me—don't ever try something like that again. The next time you get caught, that man might not be so generous."

After a long moment, she had nodded, but had defiance in her stare.

"What's your name?" he had asked, releasing her arms, but holding her escape at bay with his body. She was probably desperate for money, had successfully picked a pocket a hundred times before without getting caught. It didn't matter. There was always a first time and he had been the lucky winner.

He had known he couldn't just let her walk away. He had wanted to see her again. She was beautiful, but aside from that, something about her intrigued him and made his blood sizzle. Just looking into her eyes had made him tumescent.

"Why?" she had asked suspiciously. "You want to chase me down some more, sic the cops on me?"

He had released his hold on her neck, took a step away, and shoved his wallet back in his pants. He had debated for a moment if he should give her some money, let the episode go and never see her again, then he decided against it. Instead, he smiled and said, "I thought I would take you to dinner."

That was the beginning of their relationship.

And twenty years later, Kitty was still as spunky as the day they met.

Creely used the remote to lock and alarm the Porsche in front of Unit 8. He was as determined now as he had been then. He would find Kitty tomorrow, get her out of danger, take her away from that god-forsaken place, and bring her back into his life where she belonged.

82

Lacy felt the queasy feeling lope up her throat, thought she might throw up, and wished she'd passed on the food. No Yancy, but the food had been on the table when they went inside. It had been a highly-seasoned meat pie with a thick, brown crust. Kitty took one bite and refused to eat more. She stalked off down the hall, muttering something under her breath about crazy people. Lacy couldn't blame her, but she worried how much longer Kitty could go without food. She watched Arcie fill her plate a second time, while she pushed the food around on her plate, and they hadn't spoken a word during the meal.

"Kitty and I are going to try leaving in the morning," she said as she collected dirty dishes. "Are you coming with us?"

Arcie glanced at her, then quickly away, a flush creeping into her cheeks, her hands making agitated movement as she washed flatware.

"Why would I do that?"

"Because if you don't come with us, you might have to walk out by yourself. The mood Kitty is in, I don't think she has any intention of begging you to come with us." She didn't mention Domeno or his car. It wasn't a sure thing, no need asking for more trouble. They might have to walk anyway. "Three is a safer number than one. Things haven't worked out as you wanted them to, Arcie. Even Yancy knows that. She doesn't want us here any more than we want to be here. This was a bad idea, spell or no spell." Mentioning the spell sent a shiver up her spine.

Arcie's flush turned a bright scarlet. "I'm not surprised you sided with Kitty."

"It's not a matter of siding with Kitty—" she started to protest.

"Yes, it *is!*"

Lacy was too tired and nervous to fight over something so superficial, too aggravated to deal with Arcie's mulish behavior. The woman didn't seem to have an ounce of common sense to understand they could be in serious danger. She no longer had the patience for Arcie. "What about you siding with Yancy?" she snapped.

Arcie backed away from her, dripping water and suds. She hastily grabbed a dish towel and began wiping the floor.

"Leave me alone, Lacy!" she cried angrily. "Just leave me the hell alone!"

"Arcie—"

"*No!*" In a fraction of a second, her voice had risen to an almost hysterical pitch. "*No!*" she screeched again, throwing the wet towel at Lacy and bolting down the hall to her bedroom.

After Arcie's bedroom door slammed, Lacy

stood in the kitchen, struck dumb and filled with resentment. She felt she had tried, really tried; felt she had done her best to be fair to Arcie in the situation. Nothing had worked.

She raised her eyes to the ceiling. Maybe she had accidentally discovered Yancy's hiding place, as good as any place to spy and listen to their conversaions—because Lacy could have sworn on her mother's grave, wherever it was, when Arcie screamed at her, ran and slammed the bedroom door, there had been a sudden sound of startled movement in the attic above her head.

It was a shuffling sound, almost like footsteps, but not quite.

83

The house was dark except for what moonlight seeped through the windows. No electricity again. The bedroom was warm and muggy, even with the open window. She had a sheen of sweat on her skin. Lacy had no doubt it was being done intentionally to make them uncomfortable. She lay on the bed, her head a little fuzzy. She dozed once or twice for brief periods, coming uneasily awake with each settling of the house, each strange whisper beneath the eaves, and each shuffling movement of some nocturnal creature outside the window. Cricket chirps, mosquito whines, and a bullfrog's croak made an occasional interruption in the silence.

Opening her eyes, she sat up, shoulders against the wall, restless and fretful, overwhelmed by frustration and wishing for a taste of cool air. Arcie seemed dumb as a rock at times, but she was right about Lacy siding with Kitty. Kitty was an almost sure bet for a ride out of here. She'd detected the sexual undercurrent between her and Domeno. She didn't understand it, not after all these years, but it could be useful. All the girls had wanted him back then. For a short time, she'd been no different, but he'd only wanted sex—another notch on his belt—and she hadn't liked him enough for that. When she refused, he moved on quickly enough. Once or twice she'd wondered if he'd been her rapist, but when she gave it more thought, memory served up someone older. She was unsure what had transpired between him and Kitty, but she didn't think he had succeeded there either. Maybe this morning when they met and were alone, as adults instead of hormonal kids, they had discovered and settled unfinished business. Whatever the reason, the attraction was obviously mutual.

She had been surprised that today she had found Domeno quite ordinary, nothing special; still handsome, but disappointingly dull compared to Gregor Gilles. There was no use denying he had scared her. Sexual attraction aside, she thought he had also scared Kitty. She'd again decided she didn't like him much. Of course, none of that mattered. What mattered was getting away. Come morning they would visit him again and persuade him to drive them to the next town. At least, she hoped Kitty would be able to do that. If Arcie refused to go, they would leave her. They had too much resentment between them to deal with her much longer. It would be up to Kitty to make arrangements to get Arcie back to New Orleans. She wanted no part in that.

Lacy paced and paused to listen at each turn. Her nerves felt jittery, like live cables. The house was quiet, but the stuffy room had become too confining. She began to itch with each circuit of nervous energy and decided she needed fresh air, to get out of this echoic old house, even for a few minutes.

Leaning on the window ledge, she tried to suck cooler air into her lungs, listening to the tap of insects against the screen, their steady whine in the grass below the window. She noticed the screen had no latch. It just snugged tight into the frame. She pressed with the heels of her hands and shoved, catching the wobbly old frame before it hit the gallery. A bright green little tree frog clung to the edge of the windowsill, flipping off into the dark as the screen dislodged. Mosquitoes immediately buzzed her.

Uncertain exactly what she intended, Lacy knew she was making a radical move, and in the back of her mind thinking it was probably something incredibly stupid she shouldn't do. She was going to do it anyway. *Smart people don't do this kind of thing,* she told herself, *especially when they know murders have been committed and they might know the murderer.*

She slipped her legs over the ledge and climbed out the window. It was surprisingly cooler outside. Wind whispered through tree branches. The air was almost crisp with night scents. The night was filled with musical sounds she'd only faintly heard from inside the bedroom. A crescendo of crickets, the chorus of tree frogs faint against the thick dull croak of bulls. She hung over the rickety gallery rail and looked up, inhaling deeply and deciding the air didn't smell so fresh, filled with the odor of something like garbage left open to the sun too long. She decided it was just the night smell of the swamp she hadn't remembered. The dark sky had a sprinkle of stars but blazed with the wash of a wicked-looking moon. In its peculiar reddish light, shadows abounded, and the tall grasses near the swamp's edge shimmered, alternating waves of pale and dark.

Beyond the trees, everything looked thick and black like tar. A variation of sound came from all directions, nocturnal creatures taking care of business. A little spooky, she decided, not exactly the conducive atmosphere for a leisure stroll. But she needed to stop scaring herself, being suspicious of everything.

Circling the gallery toward the front door, she walked slowly down the steps, the old boards creaking under her feet. She paused at the bottom, and realized she was lonely. Thoughts of Gregg caused a quick-silver rush, a racing warm tingle coursing a straight path between her legs. She pressed her fingers against her jeans that cut tight between her thighs and applied pressure, gasping as prickling mercurial tremors shot through her. The feeling made her dizzy and breathless. She slid down to a step, held tight to the railing, and caught her breath. Finally, she stood and edged her way into the dark.

Lacy walked carefully, not wanting to trip and fall on the obscure path, and jumped as something brushed against her arm—*a weed, a bush,* she thought, with a nervous giggle, *nothing more.* A sudden breeze rushed through her hair, whipped it across her face; she struggled to shove it behind her ears.

An owl screeched, startling her; a long single cry that trailed off into violated silence. Lacy glanced around, puzzled. It seemed too quiet, a deep silence down below where there had been softer natural night sounds only minutes before. There was no longer a cricket chorus, not a single tree frog song, only the wispy buzz of a mosquito near her ear, the string of its bite a second later. She slapped at it, glancing over her shoulder. She had walked farther than she intended. The old house was a vague shadow. It was time to turn around and go back.

The air seemed suddenly charged and it startled her. A chill crawled up her spine, changed into fearful cold across her shoulders. Her pulse quickened. Instinct told her something wasn't right.

What was that?

A fear pocket, curled far up inside, ripped a seam, let its contents spill out. She listened to vague sounds up ahead, floating on the air; a misplaced footstep, soft and stealthy, disturbing twigs and shell. The movement of a tree branch or leaves, maybe? No, more a soft shuffling sound—more like breathing, magnified by the silence.

Lacy turned a half circle in one direction, then

the other.

No doubt about it . . . it was breathing.

A tremor of fear whipped through her.

She gasped, a burn in her chest, as her breath went rapid and erratic. *This was incredibly stupid!* she thought, shifting into panic mode. *What made me do this?* She should have stayed put in the bedroom, uncomfortable or not.

She wasn't alone—*someone else is out here!* No longer in front of her, behind her now, someone was there . . . *between me and the house!*

Lacy squinted against the dark, but couldn't see anything. Too many shadows tried to hug her, pull her close. The moon had spiraled away, the sky inky camouflage for whoever seemed to be stalking her.

Think, Lacy! her mind screamed. *Think!*

An intense jabbing pain below her breasts snatched her breath away. Was this going to be another rape? She didn't think she could withstand another rape. Should she run? *Could* she run? She worked out three times a week, had long legs, but she'd never been a runner. Experts said don't run from a threat, it only made the danger worse. If harm was intended, running would only excite, making the chase and attack faster. But she thought she should try, whether it was the right thing to do or not.

Maybe she could get past whoever was there and make it back to the house, but her legs felt unsteady, no longer flexible, her feet seemed glued to the ground. Fear seemed to have immobilized her but electrified every nerve. Her breath was a wheeze, simultaneously burning out through her nose and mouth. Her tongue shriveled hard with dryness; her ears filled with the furious pounding of her heart.

Something big and solid moved in the shadows.

Lacy felt her heart lunge upward, her throat close tight. She gasped a thin snarl of fright, her knees almost folding.

Waiting, watching me! she thought, paralyzed, trying to distinguish the outline.

It was big and tall. But *human*—it was human, not an animal . . . *wasn't it?*

Her eyes widened, straining against the dark. *"Hello?"* she called tentatively, a nervous bubble of sound touching her lips, her hands clasped tightly against her palpitating chest. *"Domeno?* Is that you?"

She felt sure it was a man. But his presence was nonetheless frightening, slinking around in such an ominous manner. At least it was a *human*—wasn't it? She could deal with a human, but an animal—especially an animal *that* big—was a different matter.

"Hello?" she said. "Who's there? What do you want?"

Only an occasional scuff sound of movement. It had stopped a couple yards away, in deep shadow, motionless, but she could hear the breathing.

"Who are you?" Her voice was thin, whistling through her nasal cavity.

Lacy tilted her head, trying for a better view, filled with terror so acute she thought she might have a heart attack.

"Okay, damnit, whoever you are, come out and show yourself," she said, thinking, *Don't show how scared you are,* and trying to force genuine courage into her voice and cover her fear. The quaver in her voice told her she hadn't succeeded.

It moved toward her again.

Lacy's heart made a series of jittery, stuttering beats, her thoughts hemorrhaging fear, the dark a melancholy anthem. Details she didn't comprehend flashed rapid-fire in front of her eyes.

It was so *big* . . . whoever—*whatever*—because she wasn't thinking human so much anymore—was *so big.*

But something was odd, it was peculiar looking, it didn't seem to have a normal appearance . . . longer and lower to the ground now, as if it had crouched down. There seemed to be *two* of something—*eyes? Was that eyes?*—luminous gold discs that seemed to glow faintly red.

The breeze shifted and the stench of it assaulted her, all animal, thick and cloying.

Lacy's skin crawled tight against her bones, as she caught a glimpse of it moving through wisps of the phosphorescent dark. Her body instinctively shrank in on itself.

It was long and broad, taller than her head on four legs, and hairy. Thick dark hair black as coal covered its entire body.

The moon floated free of the clouds above the trees, casting light wedges the color of blood-orange into the shadowy tree branches.

Lacy Kennedy's eyes widened with horror. She threw up her arms across her face in a useless defense. Her scream clogged her throat and turned into a terrified mewling.

The last thought she had was: *I'm going to die!*

The last thing she felt was the weight of the huge body as it contacted hers, covering her completely.

The last thing she saw was saliva dripping from gleaming fangs before they fastened onto her throat.

84

Domeno surged upright on all fours and shoved his massive head through the undergrowth. A human was walking down the road toward him. The scent tingled his senses. His salivary glands began to work overtime. Saliva dripped from his jaws. His muscles gave anticipatory jerks, his beast's reaction to a beating heart. His ears twitched, picking up another sound, and his head jerked left. His nostrils quivered, filling with her scent. Tremors of excitement flashed along his spine.

Yancy was there, in the trees.

His heart beat faster, a resounding *thump thump* against his ribs. Deep inside, where his human part struggled to maintain itself even during a change, he felt anxious and sad and a sharp pang of fear for the unaware person on the path.

She had moved closer. He could hear her cautious steps, her snuffling, and soft *wuff* sounds of anticipation. She had targeted the person on the path. There would be no escape. It would be an easy kill.

As the moon floated free of cloud, Lacy Kennedy's long lean body stood in full view against the dark of the trees.

The attack came fast.

Lacy went down with a single terrified scream.

Domeno didn't move, but his heart made a powerful lunge inside his chest and he was on full alert, every muscle straining. the scent of fresh blood, deliciously rich and inviting, stirred his hunger. It was thick in the air, blood and death, heavy wet sounds of tearing and ripping. Hunger moved like thick syrup in his roiling belly.

He curled his lip, revealing his fangs. His muscles tightened and twitched, waiting hard and ready. His beast was impatient. It was pushing him. He fought against it.

Yancy paused, her bloody snout buried in the eviscerated chest cavity, ears flattened against her skull, and emitted a rumbling snarl, a combination of warning and satisfaction. She was taking pleasure in knowing he watched, in knowing the amount of restraint it took for him not to come closer.

She lifted her head and offered up a different sound . . . several sharp, quick *uummph* sounds, like choked-off barks—a challenge, daring him.

Muscle coiled and bulging, sinew straining, he planted his paws firmly against the ground and struggled against the need of his beast.

She turned, moving toward him. For a long moment, they stared at each other, then circled each other, ears flattened, fangs bared. Her tongue slipped out, swiping at the blood on her snout, her eyes flashing scarlet. She snarled a dare.

A deep bass rumble built in his chest.

He was larger and stronger, outweighing her by over a hundred pounds, but in a confrontation that didn't make for certain he could best her. If he advanced, she would fight. If he waited and she retreated, it wouldn't indicate fear.

Domeno couldn't help himself. He padded toward her, head low, ears flat, thick brush stiff and straight out from his rippling hindquarters. She whirled to her left, leaves and pine needles, mud and shell, flying from beneath her huge paws. The fur along her spine bristled, hair standing erect in the ruff around her neck, ears flattened against her head, stiff legs spread in a defensive stance.

He halted. If he challenged her, they could do severe damage to each other. One of them might die.

But it seemed it wouldn't be tonight. She wasn't ready, whether to surrender her life or to take his. He wasn't sure which.

Yancy snarled again, a thick wet rumble from way down deep. She spun around, sending up a geyser of debris, relinquishing her kill before sliding back into the dark with only a whisper of sound.

85

The vision began as a *glint of reddish moonlight . . . a thin mist . . . a glitter of red-gold . . . almost shapeless in the dark, breathing slowly, something huge and black spinning through air . . . a single muffled scream . . . blood! . . . splash after splash after splash of rich bright blood*—and ended as quickly as it began.

Creely woke with a start, heart hammering at his chest, his blood pulsing in his ears, unable to think or move for a moment. He'd been exhausted, mentally and physically. He'd pulled the pillow up behind his head, leaned back, and now it was morning, feeble sunlight slipping into the room through the thin curtains covering the single window. He glanced at his watch. It was almost seven. He'd slept, but not well; he was tired, fatigue pressing heavy behind his eyes. He lit a cigarette, walked to the window, looked out.

The sky was gloomy and obscured by cloud, but searching fingers of light attempted to push through. A pair of mourning doves spread their wings and skimmed the top of palmetto in the center island of the motel parking lot. They disappeared into the fog, looking as if the tips of their feathers were slick with freshly dipped chocolate. A battered red Ford F150 truck pulling a small boat on a trailer sat parked in front of the room across from his. The storm had bent a large portion of the cane stalks, and they moved restlessly in the wind around the building of *The Purple Lady*. A single vehicle was parked in the lot, a newer model gray Honda. If it was a whore house, maybe morning rates were cheaper. The lights were on in the motel office, a hazy saffron through the warped fog.

Creely's eyes sought out the rail spike. He touched it, running his fingers along the cold blade-smooth surface. He felt a certain sense of urgency but knew he couldn't allow it to control his actions. He still didn't have a stable plan. He felt sure his most recent vision indicated the woman had regrettably lost her life last night. He hadn't seen her face, but he knew it was the same woman from his previous vision. He felt sad he hadn't put everything together fast enough and been unable to save her.

The more he tried to put the pieces together, the more they slid apart. He still had trouble believing in werewolves, but he couldn't so easily discount the old drunk's story. He didn't want to go in blind with only a stranger's solemn angry affirmation. Maybe it was only a myth locals perpetrated to keep away strangers. But whatever it was, human or animal, it was real enough to have killed the woman in his vision.

Of course, he thought, *it might only be a man . . . a big, strong man who considered himself the ultimate authority in a dead little town in the middle of nowhere.*

86

Arcie hadn't undressed before going to bed. She woke at sunrise, hot and sweaty, staring at the toes of her Daffy Duck slippers. Usually sleep protected her, but not so last night. She struggled to pull herself from a dream whose fragments clung to her like static chicken feathers as the big man held her down with one hand, face squished against the mattress, sheets crammed tight against her mouth until she thought she would suffocate. He used his other hand to throw up her dress, strip off her panties, then direct himself in between the cheeks of her ass and finally into her rectum. She screamed, continued to scream, in mind and voice, through the pain and humiliation, the sound an echo inside the smelly sheets on her mama's bed. It seemed forever, but she knew it hadn't taken him long, and when he finished, he patted her butt almost affectionately, zipped up and left the bedroom. He stuffed crumpled currency down her mama's bra as he squeezed passed her in the doorway.

Arcie shivered and covered her mouth with her hands to avoid screaming. She went to some dark place in her head for a minute, remembering her pain and humiliation. It had all come back from the deep hole she had buried the memory in.

She could recall how the floor seemed to tilt

under her feet as she walked around her mama into the kitchen and stared out the kitchen window before she picked up the butcher knife from the drain board . . . .

. . . and turned toward her mama. Then, she drove the knife into her belly, across her throat, slashing, again and again. She just stood and stared at her mama as she lay on the floor, hating her, happy with her effort of erasing her from her life, knowing what her mama allowed done to her for a few dollars would never happen to her again . . . .

And that is exactly what happened, Arcie thought. Kitty, without ever knowing, had taken her away from the horror that bitch allowed him to do to her.

It had been a long time since she'd remembered that terrible day. She had suppressed the events until they were a blur, once or twice in the past coming in dreams, but never in waking thoughts. Now the memory had returned and stayed. And she knew why it had come back—because she had come back.

The screams came from down the hall, an endless stream of noise like a tornado warning, and tore through her mind like a razor. Arcie bolted upright, threw herself out of bed, stumbled and almost fell as she threw open the bedroom door and ran into the hall.

She twisted the doorknob of Kitty's room and shoved open the door. Kitty sat huddled on the bed, her eyes closed, her entire body shoved up against the headboard.

"What is it? What's happened?" she shouted and realized Kitty must have been dreaming and woke from her dream screaming.

When Kitty continued to scream, without hesitation, Arcie slapped her as hard as she could. She heard the vertebrae crack in Kitty's neck as her head snapped sharply back.

Kitty gasped and her eyes popped open. She stared at Arcie without comprehension for a second. Arcie could see Kitty was stunned by the way she sucked in her breath, and she could see the imprint of her fingers on Kitty's cheek. Kitty was furious.

Kitty found her voice, choking on the sharp edge of her rage as she said, "Don't *ever* do that again."

Arcie lost her color, her mouth falling open like a floundering fish's. Backing away from the bed, she murmured, "The way you were screaming, I thought someone was killing you, that you were dying."

Kitty continued to stare at her, venom in her eyes. She gingerly cupped her cheek.

"I had to do something to stop your screaming. I didn't know what else to do," Arcie protested.

It might have been the only sensible thing Arcie could have done to break the hysteria that erupted from her dream, but there had been a lot of intentional hurt in the impact of Arcie's hand. Kitty couldn't help herself when she snarled, "You were a little too enthusiastic."

"You scared the hell out of me." Arcie inched closer.

Kitty slid her legs over the side of the bed. "I scared the hell out of myself."

"Why were you screaming like that?"

Kitty fumbled for an explanation that seemed just out of reach. She knew she had been dreaming, but she couldn't remember the dream. Not a single snatch of it. Whatever it had been had scared the crap out of her.

"Why were you screaming?" Arcie repeated.

"I had some kind of horrible nightmare, but I can't remember it."

"I thought for sure someone was hurting you."

"Would it have mattered if that was true?" Kitty snapped.

Arcie flushed an unbecoming shade of red. "Of course it would."

"The last few days make me think otherwise." Kitty stood up and walked to the window, stood with her back to Arcie. "I—I think I saw it . . ." she said.

"That must've been one hell of a nightmare. Saw *it*? What is *it*?"

"Yes, it was a nightmare tonight, but last night—

I was awake. Tonight, it was in a dream—maybe. But last night—in the kitchen, it was real . . ." She realized she was babbling, her thoughts rushing ahead of her tongue. "I *felt* it. It touched me. It was so close—right next to me . . . I-I couldn't see it, but I could have reached out and touched *it*."

"Touched *what?* What are you talking about?" Arcie's tone was testy.

"I thought it was a s-shadow . . . but it was something else. Just like twenty years ago, when we played that horrible game." Her voice cracked and trailed off.

"Just like twenty years ago?" Arcie said. "You saw *it* twenty years ago?"

Kitty nodded, but her thoughts were all snarled up inside her head.

"I *knew* you saw something! What was it? What did you see? What did it look like?" Arcie's eyes glittered with excitement. She was consumed with the need to know. All else could be damned. "Was it a face? The future husband Yancy talked about?"

"I don't know what it was. I wasn't able to tell exactly what it was . . ."

"What do you mean you weren't able to tell exactly what it was?"

"I think it was a man, but it didn't look quite like a man. There was something different about it, something strange."

"I didn't see anything. Why was it only you that

saw it?" Arcie demanded.

"You don't know it was only me. How can you be so sure of that? Lacy could have seen it."

"No one else saw anything, no one but you, I know. What I want to know is why it was just you?" Arcie's tone was terse. Whatever Kitty thought she'd seen years ago, thought she saw again last night and tonight, had scared her shitless, but Kitty was finally talking about it. She had waited so long to find out, she had to make Kitty tell her what she'd seen.

"We never talked about that night afterward, at least I didn't. If that's true, I don't know why just me." Kitty honestly didn't know. "But one thing for sure, whatever it was, I know it wasn't my future husband!" She stared at Arcie with disdain. Arcie, pressing her for answers she didn't have. Arcie, not in the least worried about her. She only wanted to satisfy her curiosity. She could feel the slow curling tendrils of anger again. She didn't want to get angry. She wished that having Arcie in close proximity didn't make her angry so often. It just seemed to work out that way.

Kitty whipped around. "What time is it? Where are Lacy and Yancy?"

"I'm not sure—somewhere between six and seven, I think. I guess they slept through your banshee wailing."

"Say again?" Kitty stared at her, incredulous.

"Banshee wailing?"

Arcie's eyes flashed. "Well, that's what it sounded like."

"If I was that loud, Arcie, how come they didn't hear me?"

"I don't know, Kitty, you need to ask them." Arcie's eyes flashed her impatience and she planted her hands on her hips.

Oh, God, not again! Not another fight! Kitty thought, feeling her anger spike. Her heart had already been beating too fast. Now it picked up speed again. She wasn't ready for another altercation with Arcie, but if Arcie kept pushing her, she didn't know how she could avoid one. Their eyes melded; Arcie looked away first.

"Don't you get tired of fighting, Arcie? Can't we call a truce and talk about all this crap?"

"All what crap?"

"Everything, especially about Domeno."

Arcie's face went bloodless, fireballs of scarlet developing in her cheeks, and her eyes went cold and flat. "What about Domeno?"

"We need to know what is going on here, Arcie, especially between him and Yancy."

"It's none of our business."

"It is—now that you've brought us back here. Whatever is going on, we're up to our necks in it."

"You don't know what you're talking about."

"Yes, I do. We can't leave here without help."

"I didn't bring you back . . . *she* brought you."

"Whatever, Arcie—we're still here, without a decent prospect of leaving. You knew what she might do to get us here and you went along with it," Kitty snapped. "You helped her by forcing us back here."

"Why do you want to know what happened between them?"

"Aren't you the least bit curious?"

"No, I'm not. Whatever is going on between them is their business."

"Or maybe you know already," Kitty suggested.

"I don't know anything."

"Okay, maybe you don't, but you're not scared?"

"Of what?"

"You know what I think, Arcie . . . this is all bullshit! You don't want us to know what's going on here. Especially between Yancy and Domeno. What I don't understand is why. Why, after all the years we've been together, are you taking her side against me in this?"

"I don't know what you're talking about. It's more like Lacy taking your side."

And in one abrupt, startling moment, it came to Kitty on some half-conscious level—Arcie believed herself to be in love with Domeno. It was ridiculous, but she felt it was true. It was the only thing that made sense. "Let's leave Lacy out of it for now. This is more between you and me. I believe you know the answers to everything I'm talking about, and I also have a very strong feeling about something else."

"What might that be?"

"It's only a guess, but I believe you think you're in love with him. You wanted to come back to see him, didn't you? You needed to find out for sure about your feelings. You didn't have the guts to do it by yourself, so you dragged us along. But it hasn't worked out right for you, has it?"

"You don't know what you talking about," Arcie said again.

"Oh, yes, I believe I do. And you can stop the nonsense, Arcie. The denials won't change my mind about this." Kitty nodded slowly. "All the girls, including me, thought he was so special back then, so damn hot, so why shouldn't you?"

"Meaning you don't think he's special anymore?" Arcie growled.

"Meaning we were kids. What I felt for him wasn't love. It was hormones. I just wanted to have sex with him."

"And you did." Arcie looked down at the floor.

"No, I never did."

"You don't have to lie to me."

"I have no reason to lie. It never happened."

Arcie sagged, every line of her body, hairline to toes. A glimmer of tears appeared in her eyes as she hastily averted her face. She put out her hands, gripping the edge of the dresser to steady herself as she turned away. "Do you think I'm stupid enough to believe that?"

"I don't care what you believe, but you should believe me. I have no reason to lie to you. I'm telling the truth. It was a long time ago. If that's what's been bothering you all these years, it's time you drag yourself from whatever romantic fantasy world you've been in and realize Domeno was just a guy all the girls wanted. Some of the girls had him, but he never *belonged* to any of us."

"Easy for you to say," Arcie whispered.

"Okay, find out for yourself. Go tell him how you feel, see what he says. I think that's part of the problem with Yancy and Domeno. She felt the same way about him and all these years in the same town didn't make a difference for her."

"I'm not Yancy—or you." Arcie's voice was a tumult hiss, filled with bitterness. Tears slipped down her cheeks as she turned to face Kitty, hands clenched into fists. Her eyes blazed with unmistakable fury. "He always wanted you, just you." Her rage felt like a rope of fire, twisting and burning; she was wrestling with all her terrible dark thoughts again.

"Damnit, we were kids, Arcie. It's stupid to keep thinking that way, for us to fight over something that never was and never will be."

"All these years I've seen everything you have. I just wanted something like that—some of what you had, but no matter how fast I ran, I was always a mile behind and I couldn't catch up. So damn easy for you . . . you get any man you want, even that disgusting old creep that took us away from here. They fall all over themselves to get at you. It doesn't matter who or what they are—young, old, single, married, gay, straight . . . all of them. Without a thought, you just spread your scent around. They come after you, dogs after some bitch in heat!" Arcie brushed at her leaky nose with the back of her hand, wiped her hand on her jeans.

It was unexpected, the hysterics, the rage. Kitty stared into Arcie's wild eyes, could see the swirling dark there, so black it seemed to come from a bottomless depth inside her. All that anger and resentment, bitterness and hatred, had finally broken loose and was flowing out of her. Where had it been hiding for so long? How had Arcie managed to keep it so well hidden? She caught a glimpse of the mad and lonely soul of her friend, feeling a small guilt. Bubbles of pity started a carbonated rise through her chest. There was nothing normal about this. If Arcie had said something, given her hint, she would have tried to understand and help her, because what Kitty now saw was nothing more than frenzied madness.

Broken, Kitty thought. *She's just broken. Wanting*

someone to want her, desperate to belong to someone, anyone, looking for a fix, and she's blaming me for breaking her. She couldn't fault Arcie for her need or her want, but for the first time since she'd known her, Kitty found herself a little frightened by Arcie. An icy dread rose in the pit of her stomach and instinct told her it wasn't the time for pity.

Arcie seemed to have moved into a deep dark space inside her head, her eyes narrowed, her lips twisted into a knot. "Lacy wasn't beautiful like you, not like now, but there was always something special about her, too," Arcie said.

"Moonshine," Kitty breathed, attempting to distract her, at the same time feeling a twinge of old jealousy.

"What?"

"Moonshine," Kitty repeated. "*Grandpere* said that. Sometimes kids imagine stupid crap. I thought *Grandpere* loved her more than me when he said that, when he thought she was special, and she wasn't even his kin. It was petty, but I resented her. I resented her for the attention Domeno gave her. It wasn't her fault." Her heart beat fast again. She had a tight, painful burn in her chest. "Yesterday I realized how trifling it all was. None of it was Lacy's fault . . . no more than it's mine what you're accusing me of. If anyone's at fault, it's Domeno. He played us against each other. It's unimportant now. It was just part of growing up."

"*Stop it!*" Arcie screamed. She could feel it rising to the surface, powerful, in control, that dark twisted thing that inhabited her mind and soul. A nebula of black, swirling like a cloud of ebony cinders inside her head, as it pushed vicious spiking pain along her spine. "*Stop it!* It is important. It wasn't just part of growing up." There was chilling contempt in her voice and her face contorted with pure animal rage. She was suffocating, felt like she couldn't breathe, couldn't suck in enough air. The power of the funk threatened to blow her head apart, hate rising and squeezing at her heart.

Arcie moved in close enough to infringe on Kitty's space, paused, and looked around the bedroom as if trying to remember why she was so angry. Inside all she found was the years she had suffered as a shadow and the need for retribution. She could feel the zing and sizzle of blood in her veins, boiling her inside. Her pupils had shrunk to pinpricks. Her mind was roaring, skidding, sliding to a halt, starting up again, spinning, roaring . . . .

"He wanted all o f you . . . but he *never* wanted me!" she raged. "I was the one that loved him, really loved him. I always loved him so much—but he—he *never* wanted me!"

Irregular burgundy-colored stains . . . bruised, shredded flesh . . . translucent rope gleaming against ashy gray . . . the steady hum of flies, a single fly walking across the empty green landscape of an eye, its fat, glossy body a phosphorus-bronze. It paused over the pupil, lifted its spiny legs and cleaned itself . . .

. . . and Creely found himself thrown back against the car seat, seat belt pulled rigid across his throat. For a moment he lost control of the Porsche. Slamming his foot on the brake, he brought the car to a shaking halt. He was drenched in a cold sweat, his fingers wrapped like steel around the steering wheel, breath lodged tightly in his throat. When he was able to focus, he sat staring wide-eyed at the wavering green of cane, trying to gather his wits. He closed his eyes, tried to pull the vision tatters in closer, making them more precise. They fluttered and fluctuated. One moment they were there, the next they slipped away.

But no doubt about it, he'd just seen the ravaged body of the same woman from his previous visions.

Kitty fell into the stunned silence that filled the space between Arcie and her; she didn't know what to say to her. She knew Arcie had serious issues, but she never imagined Arcie felt that way. She stared at her with mute fascination, no longer doubting Arcie was having some kind of psychotic break. It was time to end their conversation, she didn't want to hear any more. She grabbed up her toothbrush and toothpaste, and walked toward the door, stopping when a flitting insight made her scalp prickle.

At some point in the past, Arcie had initiated contact with Domeno and he'd rejected her. Now, Arcie seemed to believe she could change that if given a second chance. That was what had brought her here. That was what had been so necessary and urgent about this visit, not a reunion of childhood friends, nothing to do with keeping a promise to Yancy. She wanted them all there for when she thought she would win the prize, when Domeno would choose her over them.

It was amazing how all of them had wanted the same man. Like there had never been another male around. The choices might have been slim, but there had been others. Yancy, the only one remaining behind, was the one with the best chance of getting him, but look what it cost her. Kitty had no right to judge Domeno too harshly. What must it have cost him, losing a wife and unborn child, living every day in proximity to the woman that he felt certain had done such a horrific thing? Too damn much. It cost them both too damn much.

Yancy might be able to do nasty voodoo spells that controlled and killed people, but that hadn't caused her mental problems. She had inherited those. They had obviously spiraled out of control over the years, and fueled by her inability to catch Domeno, had driven her over the edge. She needed to be locked up some place, away from others she could harm. She would talk it out with Creely. He would know what should be done. He could get the ball rolling on picking her up and getting her committed.

She would have to give the Arcie situation more thought. She'd suggested Arcie speak with Domeno, but she was almost positive Domeno wouldn't have anything to do with her now any more than he had back then. It was something Arcie would have to find out for herself, not be told by someone she already had a vendetta against and wouldn't believe. It sickened Kitty to think of the years Arcie had allowed all this to fester. She had always thought Arcie a little strange at times, a lot of dark days. But Kitty had also thought Arcie a rock.

Arcie stared at Kitty with open hostility. Kitty

could tell the taste for blood was pumping through her. She took a step sideways. Arcie took one with her. Her eyes were black with torment, her face a peculiar shade of red. Fear darted down Kitty's spine, and instinct told her to run, but she felt if she ran something bad would happen.

The attack came so suddenly, the hairs along her neck prickled a warning a fraction too late.

Arcie launched her bulk forward, like an angry dog hitting hard on the end of his chain, and slammed the heel of one hand into Kitty's chest as her fist flew up and struck Kitty across the bridge of her nose, squarely between the eyes.

Kitty stumbled back, the toothbrush and tooth-paste flying out of her hand, her feet almost going out from under her. Disbelief widened her eyes. The impact's resonance became burning agony inside her skull. Brilliant lights flashed as the room wavered. She moaned and her knees buckled for a moment. She thought she was going to black out. Catching herself against the door frame with one hand, her first coherent thought was furious: *the crazy bitch broke my nose!* She caught the blood flow in her free hand and stared at it for a second.

One look at Arcie's face made her forget her pain. Absolute terror set in. She swayed sideways, hung on the door frame, and slipped around the corner into the hall. Her shoulder struck the wall. She caught herself and stumbled forward.

"You fuckin' *bitch!*" Arcie hissed as she spun through the door. "You think I'm *stupid*, don't you? Fat *and* stupid! All these years making me feel less about myself!"

Kitty bumped the door to Lacy's room. It swung open. The room was empty and, considering all the noise, she had difficulty understand what that meant. A brief, jumbled thought: *Lacy! Where is Lacy? Why hasn't she come to see what the commotion is about?*

"*Stop it, Arcie!*" she screamed. "Have you lost your mind? I never hurt you. What the hell's wrong with you?" Her vision blurred, her breathing turned into a heavy pant, and she was unable to control her wobbly legs and get them to work right. The blood from her nose kept coming. She stumbled and almost fell. Pressing herself tightly against the wall, she managed to shove her body forward again.

"What's so awful about me?" Arcie screamed. "That's what I want to know, what I want you to tell me—what's so *wrong* with *me!* All these years, never good enough! Never pretty or important or smart or talented enough. Just *fat!* Always the fat girl no man wants—fat, fat, *fat!*" Her tone was vehement, her voice a high, frantic screech, the words just spewing out. "What makes you the expert? Tell me, bitch! What makes you the expert on love after all the men you've fucked? You still don't have anyone permamanent, do you?"

Blood ran down the back of Kitty's throat, out the front of her nose, across her lips, the blood staining her camisole. *Run! Run!* her terrified mind screamed. She couldn't run. Her legs wouldn't work right. She glanced back. Arcie had gained on her, breathing the loud deep pants of a big overheated dog, her teeth bared in a snarl. *"Stop it!"* she shouted. "I won't let you do this to me!"

"You won't let me?" Arcie screamed back, her voice lost for a moment in almost maniacal laughter that choked off in a delighted twittering burble. "Try and stop me!"

Kitty wheeled around, unable to bear the thought of Arcie behind her, and edged backward, one arm thrust out in front of her. She was breathing through her mouth, her nose clogged with blood, her tongue coated with the taste of metal.

Arcie had managed to get closer, her face twisted grotesquely, eyes dancing with luminous insanity, a deprecatory smile tilting her mouth. Kitty's eyes darted around, looking for something to defend herself. She saw nothing within reach. Her eyes were swelling closed, and she was having trouble maintaining her balance. Her butt contacted the front door.

Yes! she thought, as sh e fumbled the doorknob and jerked on it. It slid around in her bloody palm, but it opened. She bumped through the screen door onto the gallery. Her feet connected with something yielding, throwing her completely off balance.

She tripped, heart pounding like a jackhammer, and fought to remain upright. She failed and sprawled headlong across the gallery. Her face collided with wood. New pain slithered through her face and head. Splinters pierced her cheek and the soft tissue below her left eye. She wanted to scream, but the scream lodged in her throat. All she could think of was getting her feet under her and running. Her arms were shaking like a bowl of gelatin, and it took all her strength to push herself up. She could hear Arcie coming, the soft *swish-swish* of her sliding feet in those silly Daffy Duck slippers.

Halfway to her feet, she hung there and gasped, staring through one half-closed eye at the shoe only inches from her fingers.

There was a badly mutilated leg inside the muddy brogan—beyond the leg lay the evisceration of Lacy Kennedy.

And for one crazy second all Kitty thought was Lacy needed to be covered up, she would be embarrassed, even in death, exposed like that for strangers to gawk at . . . then she was up and running.

89

Rage washed over Arcie. The taste for blood was pumping through her. *I'm here, I've finally arrived,* she thought, knowing she'd finally lost her tentative grasp on control over the funk. She had fought back the black funk so hard, for so long, but she couldn't fight it any longer. She had reached that very dark bottomless place she'd struggled so hard to stay out of. It was too late for pills, pills wouldn't help anymore.

Funk had taken over. It swirled inside her head, thick and solid and hot, pushing so strongly at her tormented mind all her anger and bitterness came pouring out. She was vaguely aware the woman in front of her was of some importance in her life, but somehow it no longer mattered, because the funk didn't think it mattered, and what the funk thought was the most important thing. She wanted to hurt someone. The funk told her it was okay if she hurt someone. She was having trouble making sense of her thoughts beyond the need to hurt someone.

As Kitty stumbled through the door into the hallway, Arcie hesitated, catching sight of a nightmarish version of her face in the dresser mirror. Her face was changing colors like the rotation of a color wheel, her features twisted, her eyes wide and wild, and her lips pushed back in a snarl showing almost all her teeth. She no longer felt inferior, she had never felt so agile, so light, so energized, in her entire life. Her rage was like a buoy, lifting her up, carrying her forward.

You're in charge here! Make her know it! black funk roared inside her mind. *Get her, go get her!*

I will! her mind responded. *I'll get her, I'll show her!*

"You need to be punished, you whoring bitch! I need to punish you!" she shouted down the hall.

Get her! funk urged, egging her on. *Get her good!*

"I will!" she squealed aloud as something dark passed through her eyes, making them feral. *"I will!"*

90

It appeared to Creely that without question anything could happen around French Gap. Abadie was either at the bottom of whatever happened—or he damn well knew who or what was. Creely felt like he was banging his head against a wall and ending up with nothing except a substantial headache. This might be some kind of game to Abadie, but it certainly wasn't to him. Being extra cautious seemed the only way to stay alive and keep his skin intact. Somewhere in this unholy mess of things, someone was already dead. He decided he didn't much care if his adversary was animal or human, he just wanted to get Kitty away without incident. If someone else died, as long as it wasn't Kitty or himself, he might feel bad, but he would find a way to overlook it and learn to live with it. Nothing would be reported. Abadie wasn't the type who would run to another authority to file a report or ask for assistance.

He packed his sports bag and checked out of the motel, where the sleepy-eyed clerk watched him slide the key across the counter with only a nod. The fog had lifted and he wheeled the Porsche into a crisp clear dawn, the air heavy with swamp odors as he stopped in Boudreaux and found the café closed. He drove to *Josie's Luncheonette* again and found himself alone except for one other customer, a big man in a khaki delivery uniform. The man glanced up briefly over the edge of his coffee cup when Creely entered.

The same waitress was filling sugar canisters. Creely took a booth toward the rear. She dusted sugar from her hands, picked up a cup and saucer, and brought him a glass pot of coffee.

"Mornin'," she said, slipping the cup and saucer on the table, lifting the pot in a questioning gesture.

"Mornin'," he answered, and ordered French toast with blackberries, two eggs over-easy, hash browns, bacon, and grits with extra butter. She tore off the ticket, clipped his order to the metal turnstile for the cook, and refilled the big man's coffee cup before going back to her sugar canisters.

Creely ate quickly, finding he was edgy. The werewolf thing bothered him a lot. He found it difficult to wrap his mind around a human that changed into some large hairy creature. Something like that didn't—*did it?*—exist, it could only be make-believe. People just didn't change into *an*y kind of animal—*did they? Could they?* What he knew about myths and monsters would cover his thumbnail. If it really was a werewolf, he still had to worry whether he had the strength to defend himself and kill it. He had one powerful, efficient weapon, the second one shiny and bad and ugly. Shiny and bad and ugly was good, wasn't it?

He wanted whatever—whomever—it was to be Abadie. He hadn't liked the bastard the moment he laid eyes on him. He was just a tough-guy piece of shit. He hadn't been able to figure out what motivated Abadie, or why the few remaining people in that little crap hole of a town considered him so powerful, but it was what it was, and he guessed figuring it out no longer really mattered.

Creely wasn't a fighter. He had never considered brawling, drunk or sober, sophisticated, only injurious. Hopefully, it wouldn't come to that, but if it got physical, he would attempt to hold his own.

No, he reconsidered, *maybe it will come to something worse than just physical.*

He climbed back into the Porsche with a full stomach and headed back toward French Gap.

Twenty minutes later, the vision had taken him by surprise. Pulses, like a huge finger tapping in his mind. Image flashes, like odd-shaped puzzle pieces falling from someone's hand, not much left of her to see, but it was no doubt the same woman.

When his head cleared, he unclenched his hands, his heart slowing its slam against his ribs, and jammed his foot against the accelerator. The Porsche's tires hissed wetly through the potholed water.

91

Kitty's fear was almost a pulse on the air, but somehow her feet kept moving. Panicked, shot through with adrenaline and terror, she couldn't stop running.

She had to get away. The need for survival had kicked in and she was panting, her muscles trembling, wanting to seize up, but her brain was running full tilt.

She had managed to get turned around, discovering paths she hadn't been on and didn't know were there, or where they went. They swerved in all directions, none of them the right one. Everywhere she looked seemed new and different and threatening, each swampy serpentine path and twisted shell trail seemed to dead-end in thick foliage and brambles, trees or swamp. The soft, wet ground squished up between her toes, like mashed potatoes. She was lost, running in circles and thinking: *Oh, dear God, don't let me die like Lacy, not like that!* Her sanity simultaneously screaming—*don't think about it! Run, just run!* So that's what she did, at the same time thinking if she didn't find her way out of the swamp's maze soon, she would die there and never be found.

She struggled for breath, her chest filled with a brush-fire burning, lungs laboring harder with each pump of leg muscle. Sticks and oyster shell scored the soles of her bare feet, her robe flapping open behind her like wings. Blood and snot dripped from her injured nose, staining a bright path across her camisole. None of this made sense, except she seemed to have fallen into a deep hole of madness. Lacy was dead, the other two fighting insanity or already insane, totally, completely insane, *crazy, crazy, crazy*. Would being in proximity to them allow them to pass along their incredible insanity disease? Could she end up like that? *No, no, nooo*—she couldn't let that happen.

Had Arcie brought her here with the intent to kill her? She had said "punish", but without a doubt "punish" and "kill" were interchangeable in Arcie's inflamed mind.

And Lacy—*ripped apart, slaughtered, like an nimal.*

Had Arcie done that? Or Yancy? Someone, or something else?

Domeno! She had to find Domeno. But what if he'd been the one to kill Lacy? No, she couldn't believe that of him. She didn't want to believe him capable of such savagery. It wasn't good to think that. There was no one else, no other place to go except to Domeno. There wasn't time to question that decision, even if it turned out to be a mistake. She had to take her chances, she mustn't be afraid of him. She had to keep reminding herself of that, she had to believe he would help. She needed him; she had to trust him. It seemed better than the other alternative.

With swollen eyes, her vision impaired and unfocused, she struggled along, each breath a stabbing torture. Her feet screamed with pain each time they struck the ground. She was positive she was leaving an easy-to-follow blood trail. How long before Arcie caught up with her?

She didn't see the pothole, even as her foot hit it. But she felt it, straight up the bones in her leg, into her teeth and out the top of her skull. Her ankle twisted and her knee buckled. She went down on both knees, arms straight out in front, pushing her hands out palm-first in a futile attempt to break her fall. A single thin, terrified wail slipped out as she pitched forward, a frontal face strike with the ground, her temple colliding with a rock. For a second she grappled with the glittering blast of pain, then her brain seemed to implode and there was only black.

Creely slammed on the brakes as another vision overtook him.

Blue robe slick with blood, face twisted in pain and fear—she was running, screaming—tripping, falling, smashing into the ground . . . .

The vision surged out of nowhere, stronger than the ones before. It hit in waves, sending shivers through him. His foot reflexively stomped the brake and he briefly blacked out, the Porsche fishtailing in a halt in the roadside shell. When he came around and opened his eyes, his head pounded like the muffled thump of a big drum. Something wet on his upper lip. He touched it, and his fingers came away bloody. It was a nose bleed.

Kitty!

It was Kitty this time, he'd recognized her before he blacked out.

He didn't understand what was happening to him. A headache, yes, but the nose bleed, never. That was something new, and there was no time to think about it. If he wanted her back alive, he had to find her quickly.

Arcie was chasing Kitty. Yancy didn't know why. And Domeno was there, stepping from the shadows. He'd shifted and brought Lacy's body to the gallery. He moved in behind Arcie and knocked her out with one solid blow of his fist against her temple as she came through the screen door. If it was his intent to kill her, he wouldn't do it immediately. Yancy knew he found it difficult to kill another human.

She watched him try to lift Arcie. He couldn't, she was too heavy. Hefting her under her arms, he dragged her on her ass down the steps, across the yard, and toward the old Blanchard house.

There was a cellar there. Edval Blanchard had been a hunter and trapper. His wife had grown a garden, for protection against bad times. Reinforced with mortared cinder blocks and wood against rising water, the cellar was cool and damp. In the heat of summer it preserved; in winter it was a freezer.

She should never have listened to Arcie. Had she meant to hurt them by bringing them back? She wasn't sure, but one was dead, one captive, the third unaware she was about to finish a long-dormant spell that would become complete before the day was over.

Kitty struggled toward consciousness. *Where am I?* she thought. Hazy dimness swam before her eyes as she tried to move, but the pain was severe and none of her body parts responded. *Where am I?* she thought a second time. Unconsciousness made a reclamation.

She struggled toward consciousness once more, but it was difficult. So much pain.

Where am I? She vaguely remembers thinking that before.

She's aware she lost consciousness, but has no idea for how long, where she is, or who might be with her—because someone *is* with her. She senses them nearby; has no idea where they are. All her body parts ache, her thoughts cloudy, her mind swimming in molasses-thick ooze. Everything is in slow motion, like flickering snowy images on a bad television set. A brutal spreading pain held captive everything above her neck; a terrible throbbing in her head. She tried to open her eyes. Her eyelids seemed glued together.

There was a whispering sound, almost a caress, as if someone was talking softly close to her ear. It worried her. The sound seems so close, but still distant. Bewildered, she takes a running leap toward the sound, tried to grab it, wanting to touch it, but she lost it, it slipped away. Something cold pressed against her face. She jerked away, the movement causing excruciating pain savaging her entire head, and she struggled to open her eyes. When she couldn't open her eyes, she screamed, and her arms automatically rose to strike out.

"*Non! Non!*" said a voice

She thought she recognized it, as a pair of big hands restrained her, pressing her back against something soft.

"No, *Minou* . . . don't, stop 'fore you h'rt y'urself worse."

The hands continued to restrain her. Her injured body screamed in outrage. She ceased to struggle, listening to the soft, continuous murmur of the familiar voice.

Was that Domeno? Still unable to open her eyes, she whispered, "D-Domeno?"

"*Oui . . . Oui, mon bien-aime.*" Yes, my beloved.

She fought to pull herself up, grabbing at whatever might be in front of her. Her fingers, screaming with pain, found material, curled into it, bunched the fabric together.

"I-I can't see! *I can't see!*" she sobbed. "Why can't I see?"

His big hands wrapped around hers. He made soft *ssshhhing* noises.

"*J'connaitre, j'connaitre,*" he murmured. I know, I know. "It's ' kay. Y'u're not blind. Y'ur eyes swol'en shut. I put tape on y'ur nose, stuffed toilet paper in it to stop the bleedin', and pulled the splin'ers out of y'ur face. H're, let me—" the cold touched her, she flinched away, but he held it steady against her skin and after a moment she relaxed into it—"good, good, this will he'p w'th the swel'in."

They were the last words she heard. She didn't know if she fainted or slept, or for how long. When next she reached for consciousness, the first thing she was aware of was she couldn't breathe through her nose. She experienced a wave of panic, her hands flying up to her face. Flesh against something hard brought brilliant flashes of new pain, but she managed marginal slits with her eyelids.

Domeno was there, leaning toward her, holding an old-fashioned, blue-rubber ice pack pressed against her face, eyes stormy with worry.

"Hullo, *p'tit Minou,*" he whispered. He smiled and his entire face seemed to melt, all the lines becoming soft and gentle.

Kitty clutched at his arm, knocking the ice pack from his hand. "Arcie is trying to *kill* me!"

"I know, *Minou,* I know," he said, disengaging her fingers and folding her into his arms. He stroked her like a cat, running the flat of his hand up and down her back. "But y'u're safe. Nobody can h'rt y'u when y'u're w'th me." His lips gently pressed against the swelling on her temple. *"Sauve."* Safe.

Kitty sagged against his chest, and he engulfed her with those big arms. She found herself crying, deep wrenching sobs, tears that burned her ravaged face. He let her cry until she had cried herself out, then he held her away from him. He carefully wiped the tears from her face with gentle kisses.

"I-I—I was so scared," she whimpered.

"J'connaitre, I know, *Minou,* I know."

"How did you find me?"

"I was out walkin'. Messed y'urself up damn good, y'u did." He tentatively touched her temple. "Got y'urself a nasty knot th're. A couple black eyes comin' out. Y'ur face is pretty messed up."

Kitty winced. "Where are we?" Her glance flickered around the room.

"At my house."

"Where's Arcie?"

"Don't know."

"Did she follow me?"

"I didn't see 'er." Domeno gently pushed her down. *"Sshhh . . . prendre son aise."* Take it easy. "Y'u don't want to see 'er anyway, do y'u?"

"No! She caused this, she was chasing me!"

"Why wo'ld she do that to y'u?"

"She suddenly went crazy, blaming me for all sorts of things."

"'kay, it's 'kay. Wherever Arcie is, she cain't do anyth'ng to y'u now. Y'u need rest. Nothin' else impo'tant right now. Rest."

Kitty nodded, but when he leaned out of her line of vision, her breath quickened and she grabbed for him, digging her fingers into his arm. *"Don't go!"* she panted. *"Please,* don't go!"

Domeno broke her grip. *"Sshhh, Minou.* Not goin' 'way. I'm h're fer y'u, *mon p'tit Minou.* H're *boisson*—drink. *Tisane*—herb tea." He pressed the chipped white cup to her lips. She sucked in a few drops and turned her head away. *"Boisson,"* he urged, pressing the cup against her lips again.

'I-I can't breathe and drink," she protested.

"'kay." He set the cup aside, gently pulled the wads of tissue from her nostrils. The paper was almost black with old blood, but nothing fresh followed the exit. "It's 'kay now. Not bleedin' any-more." He lifted the cup again. "Drink."

Kitty obeyed. It was hot, with a distinctly bitter, almost-flowery flavor. She didn't like it, but her mouth was dry, so she drank.

"What is it?" she asked, turning her face away, as suspicion blossomed. What was he giving her? What-ever it was left her tongue sticky with an after-taste.

"Pied de mamou. The mamou plant, a herb that grows aroun' h're. I don' h've anythin' else to give y'u. It'll he'p the pain." He pushed the cup against her mouth again.

She had to trust him, didn't she? She swallowed

another sip.

"Un petit peu a la fois." A little at a time. "Good, good," he said. He patted her shoulder and pulled the pillow up higher under her head. "Y'u rest now."

Kitty felt woozy and beginning to feel warm, as if somewhere inside she was melting, and her vision had grown fuzzy around the edges. Had he given her some sort of tranquilizer? He had a logical reason for giving it to her; to ease her pain, he'd told her that. Why was she scared and thinking the worst of him? She tried to fight it, listened to the thump and flutter of her heartbeat, but it overtook her. Her body seemed close to paralysis. She was having trouble thinking straight; her mind seemed to be shutting down.

In her core, she felt a soft melting sensation. She was floating, drifting away fast. The emptiness was sort of nice, comfortable, seemed to push back some of her fear. Her body felt boneless, floppy, and the pain seemed to have gone far, far away.

The inside of her nose felt crinkly, stiff with dried blood, she supposed, but she could breathe again, the air making a tinny whistling sound inside her head, and she could smell him—a powerful scent, woodsy, masculine, underlaid with another odor she couldn't identify—but his smell made her feel safe.

He told her she was safe. She had to believe him, didn't she?

95

When Arcie surfaced from darkness, she opened her eyes to a dull, slow pulse in her lower molars. An almost unbearable throbbing tenderness, like the spreading of a very large bruise, lay at the base of her skull. She had an icy sensation in her fingers and toes. She struggled to lift her head and look down. Her wrists and ankles were tied together with thin, plastic yellow rope. Her hands were white and cold from lack of circulation, her feet bare. She had lost her slippers.

She could remember snatching up the butcher knife from the kitchen counter, the feel of it heavy against her palm—and being furious . . . *so angry*— filled with such uncontrollable black rage to kill.

Think! She had to think—*think, think, think* . . .

She blinked against the dimness, tried to concentrate, tried to focus.

Yes, *yes* . . . she remembered—the dark funky thing had gotten out; she'd been hanging onto it by her fingernails, desperate to control it, but it had been like a bomb going off when she turned toward Kitty.

Yes, *Kitty* . . . Kitty making her furious—crazy *rabid* furious. Kitty running away—and she chased her, wanting to kill her.

Suddenly Domeno was there, calling out her name, halting her in mid-step as she pushed through the screen door. She had pivoted toward him, surprised, thrilled, Kitty forgotten for a second. She had stretched out her arms, reached for him, desperate to touch him as she breathed his name . . . and found herself hit hard. Her head exploded with bright light, the knife clattered from her hand, the gallery boards sprang toward her face. She collapsed, felt her eyes roll back in her head, and everything went dark. Domeno had struck her, knocked her out! She didn't understand. Why had he done that?

Arcie turned her head and saw only blackness.

When she came back to herself, opening her eyes and blinking to adjust them to the dimness, unfamiliar forms slowly took shape. Overhead hung thick tangles of cobwebs. The rotted slats of what might have been a floor admitted pale gray fingers of light. She felt damp, cold earth under her. Behind her was the rough solidity of irregular rock and rotting wood.

Underground, she was in an underground place. Some type of underground room. Broken kegs were stacked directly in front of her. Shelves full of mason jars, above the kegs; old vegetables and fruits a shriveled grayish-green, the jars not properly sealed. Behind the shelves was the sagging timber of steps.

A fetid odor assaulted her, a wave of nausea washed over her. Next to her, half-turned on its side, was a badly decomposed deer. Flies and strings of maggots tumbled through bloated, bloodless tissue like glistening cord passing through the holes of a giant gray sponge. Gnats hovered inside empty eye sockets. A spider spun a web from the small antlers to a niche in the wall. Big and black and hairy, it walked the strands of the web like a tiny high-wire aerial performer.

Arcie cringed away and gagged, squeezing her eyes closed, and sucking air in through her mouth. She was terrified of spiders.

A skittering noise.

Her eyes flew open and she jerked her head around to find herself confronted with a rat half the size of a house cat. Sitting up on its hindquarters, nose twitching, it squeaked, whiskers jerking as it sniffed at her. Grunting and whimpering, she kicked, flopped away, fell sideways against the deer carcass.

The web shivered and the spider moved a fraction down the silken strands toward her face. The rat bolted, scuttled up a cracked support beam, darted to another, and sat there looking down at her, its dark little eyes sparkling in the diluted light. A moment later it disappeared in the dark somewhere above her.

Arcie struggled until she turned herself onto her back again, inched her way up the barrier behind her until she was in a half-sitting position. She closed her eyes and fought to catch her breath, exhausted by her efforts.

She tried desperately to concentrate. It was so

difficult to think straight. *Harder!* her mind screamed, *try harder!* Somewhere close to the surface, black funk snickered.

From somewhere above came a faint distinct squeal. The sound snatched her thoughts. Her heart lunged against her ribs. Her eyes fastened on the stairs, as somewhere above her a disused door opened. A flicker of saffron-white light bobbed up and down, sweeping from side to side, coming slowly down the steps. It was a flashlight beam. A pair of legs moved carefully down the steps, a big hand holding the rickety banister.

Arcie's heart somersaulted. She wasn't sure what to do. Remain quiet or make noise to attract their attention? She had to chance it. She didn't want to die here like that wretched creature next to her.

"H-help! Help me, pleaseee!"

The flashlight beam wavered and the legs halted in their descent. The light swept around, centered in her eyes. Blinded, she raised her arms to block it out. She tried to turn her face away, but it seemed to follow her. She was unable to get away from it. She wiggled frantically, scraping her head, pulling hair from her scalp, not caring if she injured herself, wanting only to be rescued.

"Heeelp meee!"

The light left her eyes, leaving her with glowing sparks and black dots which flashed around. *Help me.*

Please get me out of here! her mind screamed as she bumped against the wall to attract attention.

The legs suddenly centered between her toes. A second later, the flashlight beam spun upward and highlighted a face.

Domeno Abadie stood looking down at her.

"Oh, God—D-Domeno . . ." she gasped, staring into his eyes and knowing as she said his name that he would not be her savior. That wasn't what he was here for, he was here to be bringing death, to be her annihilator. He wanted to humiliate her for what she'd done in the past and what she'd done today. She could see it in his eyes. Eyes like gold ice, pale and menacing—eyes of impending danger and death, graveyard eyes.

And for a moment those eyes contained a flash of color, a brilliant scarlet, before the red disappeared and they became cold and depthless. Her stomach bolted up and smacked against her heart, heat hurling upward until she thought she might vomit.

He was going to kill her.

96

Lips twisted in a cold smirk, Domeno squatted near her knees and put down the flashlight. The beam made a moon-circle on the side of the deer carcass. Flies buzzed and scattered. Never taking his eyes from her face, his hand fumbled in the debris to her left. He produced a fat, partially-burned utility candle, the type used in power outages, old and yellowed and gouged. He worked a plastic cigarette lighter from his breast pocket. A single metallic click; then, a second one. The flint caught, the lighter ignited in a hot flare of flame. More light as the candle wick caught. The flame wavered in some miniscule draft from above as Domeno tilted the candle, working it into wax and dirt, forming an artificial holder.

He finally turned his attention to her again.

One big hand reached out and she shrank away, terrified.

"Hullo, Arcie," he said. His fingers touched her cheek, the tips hard and rough.

Maybe, she thought in desperation, *maybe I'm wrong about him, maybe he doesn't want to kill me, maybe he didn't hit me. Maybe it was my imagination, I only slipped and fell. Maybe he's come to save me.*

His fingers trailed down her neck, his palm settled on one heaving melon breast. She felt as if by his touch she had forged a fragile intimacy with him.

His hand closed around her breast, kneading it slowly, stroking across it with his thumb.

Arcie gasped, stunned, flush with a sudden heat. His touch felt as she had imagined. His grip tightened; she felt steely pain push through her, but she didn't want to move.

"D-Domeno," she croaked.

Domeno's hand slid father down, two big fingers burning a path across her stomach until they stopped and hooked inside the waist of her jeans. He popped the snap, ripped open the zipper, the metal making an electric hiss in the silence, then he pushed the denim aside, and poked at her with a finger as her unsightly belly fat poured out. he wrapped the waistband of her panties around his fist and brutally yanked until they pulled up the crack of her ass and through the slit of her sex and the fabric ripped.

His hand pushed the fabric aside and covered her mound. The heel applied pressure, the fingers spread open through her thick dark thatch of pubic hair.

"O-oh, D-Domeno . . ." she whispered, confused but thrilled, a hot ripple whipping through her, as she sucked in her breath and forgot to be frightened.

She stared at his hand as the heel of it continued to slowly massage her, separating the folds of her genitals. She was so overcome by the intense feelings his touch created, she thought she would faint. His thumb slid farther down, pressing, pushing, as it entered her opening. He forced all his fingers inside her. His fingers became a fist. She groaned as her flesh quickened and she wilted, lifting her butt and thrusting her groin against his hand as her orgasm washed over her. She closed her eyes, opened them again, and stared up at him, gasping, enthralled with him and what he'd done to her, thinking he'd finally realized he wanted her and they would be together. Otherwise, he wouldn't have touched her like that.

A sudden grin erupted on his face, as his hand stopped its movement. In the green-gold patina of his eyes, she saw contemptuous amusement and her breath caught in her throat. It was back, as if it had never left, the same ugliness that had broken her heart, the same disgust she had seen all those years ago when he looked at her.

"Bon, chienne?" he whispered. Good, bitch? His hand had stopped moving, but he didn't remove it. He just held it there, pushed tight inside her.

She didn't understand him, couldn't remember a single word of Cajun, but it was his tone, the look in his eyes. She felt as if he had struck her. Arcie flinched and cringed away. The orgasmic flush evaporated as her blood turned glacial. As he removed his hand, a terrified whimper began a slow crawl up her throat. She pressed her legs together and tried to raise them without success, to block his touch, as his fingers tangled in her pubic hair. They curled into a as if his intent was to strip her bald in one strong pull.

"Graisse chienne!" he said, fixing her with a cold stare. Fat bitch!

More Cajun she didn't understand, but it felt like an insult. Her panicked breath whipped up her throat. Amusing himself, playing some perverted game with her, punishing her for whatever sins he thought she'd committed against him. Arcie attempted to buck away from him, her frantic eyes searching the cellar. He leaned forward and pushed an elbow hard into her stomach to stop her movement, taking her breath away. She sucked in air, terrified, her thoughts a maelstrom, as she tried to twist away again.

"What y'u lookin' fer, bitch?" he hissed. His hand came up, reaching toward her face. He held her chin like a vice as he pressed his face close to hers. Only inches lay between their lips, and his breath was hot, smelling of whiskey and cigarettes, and something sickly sweet, tainted.

"Where's Y-Yancy?" she stammered, disgusted by her smell on his fingers.

He laughed, and it was loud, outrageous laughter; mad laughter. He stopped and grinned at her, a predatory grin.

"Why? Y'u th'nk she'll save y'u? She doesn't give a damn 'bout y'u."

"Please . . ." she whimpered, as tears blurred her

vision.

Domeno released her chin and ran his fingers over her lips. His index finger slipped inside her mouth, stroked her tongue, and she could taste herself. The scent of her arousal, the taste of her orgasm was so strong she gagged. She thought to bite him, was too terrified what he might do if she did, entertaining not a single carnal thought, and horrified he would mistreat and use her in such a way,

"Please what?" Domeno removed his finger from her mouth. His hand slipped down and lifted her right breast; he hefted it in his palm as if weighing it. He cruelly tweaked the nipple. "Y'u want more? Y'u beggin' me fer more?"

Arcie winced, dragging her head hard against the wood and pulling out more hair, feeling splinters break off and slide into her scalp.

"Ain't I give y'u what y'u want? Ain't that what y'u come fer? *Oui?*" His eyes followed the jerky movement of her head. *"Non?* Then what y'u beggin' fer, bitch?"

"P-please . . ." she sobbed. "Please, don't kill me."

97

Kitty was nestled in one of those gray zones between sleep and wakefulness, not quite in dreamland, but sensing herself close, as she drifted slowly back to consciousness.

The full effect of the herb hit her system like a sledgehammer. She had slid down an incline, slipping into a damp, soft paleness. Her mind had settled, snug and content, and rolled gently over.

She thought she had wanted to say something before it happened. Remembered trying to speak, to tell him something, but her mind was empty now. Her lips wouldn't move; her tongue unable to produce words. She slowly lifted her hand and touched her face. The slightest pressure made her wince. Her face felt so huge and tender. Her jaws ached into her ears, far down into her neck. Her eyeballs felt like stones. She was sure she had a lovely pair of shiners.

She held her hand away from her face. It was raw, the skin shredded off palm and knuckles, all her fingernails broken off in the quick. She lifted her other hand. It was the same. Her foot was propped on a pillow, wrapped haphazardly in a cloth and taped with masking tape. She tried to move it, and pain raced up her leg. Her ankle had a fiery drum beat. She wondered if it was broken. She remembered her bare feet striking everything in their path, imagined cuts and gashes, the soles in worse shape than her hands.

"Welc'me back," Domeno said softly.

Kitty jerked up. Pain whipped hard and brutal through her body. Her brain slammed against the back of her skull. He placed his hands on her shoulders and pushed at her and she fought him, but the struggle didn't last long. Her injured body rebelled. The pain was so intense, she felt as if someone had scored her with a blow torch. He won, holding her against the mattress with a firm hand.

And as she stared up at him with terrified eyes, she remembered and wailed, *"Oh, my God—Lacy!* Did you see Lacy?"

"Oui."

Kitty clutched at his arm with both hands. A couple of her abrasions cracked and began to bleed.

Domeno studied her with serious eyes. *"J'ai fait tous ce que je povais."*

"What—what did you say?"

"I said 'I did all I could.' There was nothin' I could do for 'er. She was already dead when I foun' 'er. I needed to he'p y'u. I used *pied de mamou* salve on y'ur wounds and in y'ur tea. Good fer healin', inside and out. The cuts and bruises will mostly heal in a week or so. Nothin' broken, not even y'ur nose or y'ur ankle. No scars, y'u'll be as beautiful as ev'r."

Kitty's thoughts were a locomotive rushing down a track. Lacy was dead, Arcie had gone nuts. Where was Yancy during all this? It didn't matter; she wasn't sure she wanted to see her again. What was important was how she was going to get away from here. She might have Domeno's protection as long as she was here, but she sensed he had no intention of taking her back to New Orleans, not even to the nearest town.

"Lacy . . . Lacy looked—shit, Domeno, she was torn apart! She looked—*eaten!*"

Domeno said nothing, offered the magic cup again. *"Boisson,"* he urged.

"I don't want anymore," she whispered, skepticism in her voice. She pushed his hand away. "What happened to her? Did some kind of animal kill her?"

"Do y'u th'nk I'm tryin' to h'rt y'u?" he asked, avoiding her questions.

She didn't know how to answer him, Part of her thought exactly that, part of her wanted to believe he was trying to help her. Would he understand if she tried to explain it that way? No, not likely. He would be offended, maybe get mad that she didn't trust him and thought so little of his efforts.

"No," she whispered and closed her eyes, filled with inner turmoil, not wanting to look at him, for him to see her lie. She opened her eyes again, looking everywhere except at him.

He'd told her she was in his house. She was in

his bedroom. It was a plain room, sparsely furnished, with a sloping raw-beamed ceiling. There were two large windows with faded flowered curtains, the exterior wooden shutters almost closed, blocking most of the light. The wooden floor had no carpet or rugs. Off to the right was a huge fireplace, the mantel adorned with a pair of brass candlesticks. No candles.

The hearth held the remnants of a fire, one partially burned log jutting like a blackened, naked elbow from the ash. Above the mantel hung a magnificent buck's head, with an impressive rack and dark eyes that glistened in the half-light.

"Drink," he said, the single word almost an order. "It'll he'p the pain."

"It made me sleepy. I don't want to sleep again." She was afraid to sleep again. She suspected he knew but didn't want to tell her what had happened to Lacy. He was staring at her throat maybe watching the steady beat of the pulse in her neck. His tongue crept out, caressed his lower lip, as if he felt the rush of blood there, almost as if he could taste it.

Kitty looked away. He could tell she was afraid of him, but his eyes said he wouldn't hold her fear against her.

"Please," he said softly, holding out the cup. "Trust me. I won't let anyth'ng hap'en to y'u when y'u sleep."

Kitty eyed the cup. His expression said he needed her to trust in him, he wanted her to give him another chance. He wanted her well and would never again let anything happen to her if she trusted him. "Are you leaving me when I fall asleep?"

"No," he lied. "I'm righ' h're, keepin' y'u safe."

"If I drink, will you tell me what's going on, why all this is happening?"

"I promise to try," he said, pressing the cup against her lips. "I promise to try."

98

Arcie found herself drifting after Domeno left, thinking over what he'd said when she asked him not to kill her.

"Don't kill y'u?" he repeated, his voice raised a notch or two. "It's 'kay to kill Kitty . . . it's righ' fer Yancy to kill my wife and *bebe*—for her to kill Lacy . . . but don't kill y'u?" He laughed. "It's 'kay fer ev'ry-one else to die, but not y'u?"

She didn't fully understand what he said, found no humor in his hurtful, angry words. Some of it didn't make sense. *What's he saying? I tried to kill Kitty?* She couldn't remember so well. *Lacy is dead? Yancy killed Lacy? Yancy killed his wife and baby? What baby? She knew nothing about a baby. Yancy never told her about a baby.*

She just didn't understand. *Not possible, not possible, not possible!* she chanted to herself, her mind racing to find words to defend against his accusations.

"You have it wrong. I would never kill Kitty," she stammered. "I only wanted to scare her." Her throat muscles constricted, her vocal cords twisted so tight her voice sounded squeaky and distant. She no longer knew if what she said was a lie or the truth. The black funk had crawled back inside its hole, but she could feel it at the edge, eager, waiting until it was safe to come out. "I was angry with her. I-I only wanted to scare her, make her understand how I felt."

"Why wo'ld y'u want to scare 'er?" he asked, nodding slowly as if he might be trying to understand her side of things.

"She makes fun of me." How to explain to him she had lost control? She had suddenly been so *angry*. Surely he could understand that? All her years and years of anger, it came bubbling out. How to explain about the black funk, how it had taken over? She wouldn't have really hurt Kitty, would she? She just wanted her scared—wasn't that what she wanted? It was the funk that had egged her on and had wanted more. She wasn't a violent person, she wouldn't kill anyone.

And then she remembered the knife . . . .

. . . and Mama coming at her, striking her, knocking her hard into th e old refrigerator, the handle of the refrigerator trying to punch a hole through her back. Mama pulled her up by her hair and she broke away, ran into the bedroom, knife held tight to her chest. Mama was screaming at her, saying she was a burden, telling her she needed to earn her keep, she was old enough for that, that men liked young girls, she could make lots of money, she would learn to like it. She kept shaking her head, it hurt, she wouldn't do it, she wouldn't let those dirty old men touch her like that . . . and Mama came at her again, threw her up against the chiffonier, raising her hand to strike

again, and she raised the butcher knife and stuck out . . . .

... she realized she couldn't let herself think about that now, maybe later, but not now. Yes, she had killed her mother, but that didn't mean she could kill Kitty, and this wasn't the time to think about things that no longer mattered. What mattered was him not killing her. She realized how she must look, a fat quivering blob, begging for her life, stripped of her dignity by this man she had loved for so long.

The words tumbled out of her mouth, "Please—please, let me go. I—I love you, Domeno . . . I've always loved you."

He had stared at her, eyes dark and deprecatory. And she had recognized the spiral of disgust that rose up in those eyes because she had seen it before.

She felt her mouth go completely dry. An intense pain stabbed at her heart. How stupid could she be to blurt out such a thing! It wasn't going to make a difference. It hadn't made any difference when she admitted it the first time.

The buried memory is abruptly back, and formed in her mind as vivid as the one of her mother's death, as if it happened yesterday. She cringed as the remnants sprung to life and she lost herself in the humiliation of it . . . .

. . . *as she waited to catch him alone. She had come by herself to the* fais do-do. *She stood hidden behind some adults so she could watch what was going on, followed him and Lacy outside, saw Lacy leave and Kitty approach him. She listened to his exchange with her, feeling a little smug, thinking he would never speak to* her *like that. She waited until Kitty left, waited until he came back outside for a cigarette. And she couldn't wait any longer. She grasped him around the waist from behind, pressing herself hard against his butt.*

Startled, Domeno had jerked around, a fist raised, ready to strike. "What the hell y'u doin'?" *he demanded, as she threw herself against him and they almost fell to the ground. She pressed into him, wrapping her arms around his neck, trying to cover his mouth with kisses as he struggled to push her away and free himself. She desperately clung to him, needing him to want her, hold her, confess his love for her. They tumbled to the ground, his fingers like steel, digging into her shoulder as he roughly pushed her off and managed to get to his knees. She fell backward, hitting her head on the metal bumper of an old pickup truck.*

"I love you!" *she moaned, clutching at the bloody gash on her head as he only stared at her with disgust. It felt as if he'd taken a knife and sliced out her heart. As he turned away, her bloody hands scrambled frantically for his legs again, her fingers hooking in his trouser cuffs.*

"I love you, Domeno . . . I love you, I love you so much!" *she repeated, over and over, as he dragged her along, scraping her knees and elbows in the shell. Her jaw popped as he shook her loose and her chin struck the ground, her heart fluttering in a strange combination of jerks and rapid bird-wing movements that made her think she was dying.*

He shook her off with a hard kick to the shoulder. She grabbed for him again and as he stepped away, out of nowhere the gob flew into her face.

He spat on her.

Then he turned and walked away without a backward glance. As she wiped the spittle away, her cheek felt as if it had been burned . . . .

. . . and she swore she would stop loving him. But she didn't.

She prayed she would stop loving him. She never had.

She had forced herself to not think about the disgust she had seen in his eyes.

And now he just stared at her. The disgust was back like it had been then. Nothing had changed.

"Y'u love me?" he said, his voice a soft growl. He leaned in close to her, that same venomous look in his eyes before he spat on her.

"Y-yes," she panted. "Oh, God, *yes—I love you!*" She felt her heart leap into her throat. the words burst from her again, explosive with emotion, thinking she had earned a reprieve.

She knew she sounded pathetic. She didn't care.

If only she could make him believe her. She would

forgive him again. She would forgive him a thousand times if that was what it took to make everything right between them. Whatever he wanted, she would be his slave, his servant, he could do anything he wanted to her. He would learn to love her, she knew he would.

"Y'u love me," he repeated, a statement not a question, his tone dull and flat.

"I do, I do! I've always loved you, always. I tried to tell you when we were kids. Don't you remember?"

Domeno nodded slowly. *"Oui*, I 'member."

"I don't know how I got here, but I need you to take me out of here, let me show you how much I love you," she begged. "I'll do anything you want— anything." She ran out of breath as she ran out of words. She stopped, panting, her eyes beseeching.

Suddenly he laughed, such a brittle, impassioned sound it withered her soul. And in its hidey-hole, black funk snickered, peeking out its head. She felt awash with another intense wave of shame. His laughter seemed to reverberate off the walls, bounce around inside her skull, touch someplace deep inside her hungry aching heart. She felt flush with a terrible heat. Her head was throbbing. The black funk was crawling out of its hole.

She struggled against the ropes. She could feel the fiber seesawing into her flesh. The burning raked up her arms and gnawed at her ankles. She'd broken skin and there was blood, but it didn't matter. The longer he laughed, the more she filled with fiery outrage and the closer the black funk came. This time she didn't want to forgive him, she wanted to hurt him. If she had been free, she would have tried. Nothing else mattered. She was empty of everything else, except for the creeping nasty funk, choking on all her righteous anger.

It was her turn. She spat on him.

The back of his hand casually wiped her spit away with a derisive grin.

It infuriated her. She wanted to do it again, but she thought she saw his eyes flash red for an instant, and terror leaped across her chest and seized her heart. Her terror became vocal.

It came so fast, she didn't see it coming. The blow from his fist almost tore her head from her shoulders. It silenced the next scream in her throat.

"*S'arreter!*" he growled. Stop! "It was *Minou*—only *Minou* I loved, y'u cow."

Arcie jammed her spine against the rough cellar wall, slipped sideways, and felt her elbow sink into the stinking rot of the deer. Gnats and flies lifted in an agitated cloud. She heard the wet whisper of maggots near her ear, could feel them wiggle up her arm.

You fucking bastard! Go on, kill me! she screamed, then realized her words had only been thoughts, had never reached her lips. In her outrage, the words formed but froze like ice against her tongue.

"You're going to k-kill me," she managed to say aloud.

He looked at her with a bemused expression, and asked, "Sh'uld I?"

"N-*no!*" she wailed.

"What sh'uld I do w'th y'u?"

"L-let me g-go—"

"No."

The black funk broke free. *He's laughing at you! Making fun of you!* Rage flashed through her like a lightning strike, filling her with a power she would never have imagined. In one swift movement, she lifted her legs and kicked at him, catching him in the groin. He grunted, reached down to cup himself as he stumbled backward.

He held himself, his face gone white with pain, and regained his balance, breathing heavily, lips curled contemptuously upward, revealing the sharp white edges of his teeth. She thought she saw red flash in his eyes again before the pupils blackened with his own rage.

He gave her a final look, hands fisted at his sides, turned and quietly moved away, stumbled up the stairs, and disappeared from view, leaving her with nothing but the flickering candle and the rotting deer.

Now he was back. She watched him step through the pale rays of milky sunlight from above into the dimness of the cellar. He stopped to stare at her again before he leaned down to pick up the candle. The candlelight revealed tremors darting through his cheeks, lifting the shadow of his beard like burrowing insects. His lips pursed, ready to blow out the candle and commit her to darkness.

"I should have killed her!" Arcie kicked out at him again, her feet sliding off his kneecap

"Y'u'll rot here, bitch," Domeno said as he side-stepped. The candle flew from his hand, tumbling over and over in the air.

Her eyes followed its movement. It seemed to be moving in slow motion, flip over flip, over lazy flip, toward her. The flame flickered when it struck, but didn't go out. The candle nestled in the gauzy material of her shirt, the painful lick of hot wax scoring her stomach.

He backed away from her, turned and didn't look at her again as he climbed the steps.

Her eyes followed him and she screamed his name once, but he didn't look back.

And suddenly her mama was there, smiling above the slash across her throat. Arcie wondered why she smiled, there was nothing to smile about when countless slashes crisscrossed her body, the wounds weeping blood that ran thick and wet and warm.

Something was cooking. Steaks? Maybe spare-ribs—she liked ribs with lots of barbecue sauce—or a roast? Definitely meat of some kind was cooking. She could smell it, meat cooking on a grill. It smelled strangely good, made her hungry. Someone had decided to have a barbeque. She liked barbecues. She hoped she was invited.

And there was a bonfire, but she was too close to the center. It was scorching hot, felt like the flames spread up and down her body, and blurred out her thoughts before they fully formed, so she had to do something about that first, before she ate.

She thought: *Maybe this is what death feels like, hot, all hot and sweaty and painful, do you think this is what death feels like, Funky?*

Black funk didn't answer her.

How many times had she wished for death, to end her misery, wished for someone else to do it . . . was it here? If it was, she hadn't expected it to hurt—*sweet Jesus, it hurt!*—it hurt so much she decided she didn't like it, she didn't want death anymore.

Alone—she sensed it, she was completely alone, black funk had deserted her.

She heard the echoes of cries inside her head. She didn't recognize them as her own. She thought for a moment: *So much noise. Terrible screams. Who is making so much terrible noise?* She wished they'd stop.

Pain now, real pain, spreading across the back of her head, gray fog rising out of nowhere, twisting, flipping, circling, morphing into black and losing itself in the cavernous space between her ears. Her skull pulsed with fierce cutting agony, a smell like chitlins cooking. No more steak or ribs.

Such dreadful, awful, hideous blue-white pain filled her up, deflecting off her skull, and twisting in her mind. Growing, widening, all-encompassing, the crunchy sounds of aluminum foil as her skin curled up and her flesh melted away from her bones.

She wanted to scream, couldn't scream—*why can't I scream?* she wondered. *It hurts so bad, I should be able to scream.*

Her last thought, as her consciousness slipped away, she realized why she couldn't scream . . . she had already been screaming.

99

Yancy followed Domeno a short distance after he deposited Arcie in the Blanchard cellar, then turned back and followed the curls of smoke. She stood watching the tinder evaporate in flames. It didn't take long for the house to fall in on itself. What she didn't understand was why he had set the fire, knowing Arcie couldn't get out. Why had he chosen to kill her in such a way?

Two dead now, she thought, *one on me, one on him.*

She had cast a spell that led to this. It had been a terrible mistake.

There had been unknown elements involved in that spell, elements that changed the outcome of it. Elements she should have known about, but hadn't. Her *Grandmere* might have known about the elements, never thought they applied, so hadn't warned her. Or had it been just another withheld secret?

And when Euphrasine's anger had passed, her mother told her those secrets, told her everything.

Kinship—the most powerful element of all, a bond of blood . . . .

The same bloodline . . . sisters.

They were all half-sisters.

Kitty . . . Arcie . . . Lacy . . . *her*. The same father. They all had the *same* father.

Freddie Chauvin, that bandy-legged, perverted, shit-faced little snot, spreading his seed around French Gap. He had wronged Euphrasine, like the other women, her sisters, the ones she thought were friends, had wronged her. But she wanted them to know, felt they should know who they really were. People didn't treat kin that way. Sisters didn't turn on each other.

Anger flared up, sharp and liquid hot, and she felt herself tremble. A growl formed deep in her chest. Anger worked against her, advanced a change, sometimes forced a longer shift.

She fought it, but it was useless. She could feel it sliding to the surface, a rampant surge of estrogen tightening her womb, and taking away her control. Rich and thick, like sticky sweet syrup, racing through her, causing a wasp-nest buzz in her head as the shift ripped through her.

100

Kitty stirred restlessly, coming half-awake. Her head felt fuzzy, her eyelids felt grainy and glued together, and her mouth was uncomfortably dry. She touched her cracked lips with the tip of her tongue. The room was chilly and her bare skin was covered in goose flesh. *Bare?* She no longer wore any clothes.

She tried to turn on her side, but something had her body pinned down. Her heart began a furious pounding. Slowly turning her head, she half-opened her eyes and glanced down the length of her body. For a startled moment, she froze. There was a hairy leg over hers, the weight like a log, a thick, muscular arm flung across her ribs. The arm terminated in the wide, naked shoulder of Domeno Abadie.

Domeno slept, shoulders hunched deep into his pillow, lips twisted, teeth bared. Tousled hair had slid across his forehead, fans of pale lashes underscored with dark smudges of exhaustion, his eyes dancing under his eyelids. Not a restful sleep; bad dreams of some kind.

And *all* of him was naked.

Kitty couldn't help herself, she gravitated toward him with the beginning of sexual flickers, incapable of turning away. She tentatively touched his cheek. He seemed unnaturally warm, hot enough to have a fever.

His facial muscles felt hard and lean, bristly with beard growth. He'd said he wouldn't leave. He hadn't lied; he was here, he'd stayed with her. She felt shame for her doubt and a twinge of sadness that she had thought he would hurt her.

She touched his hair, ran her fingers lightly through the soft thickness. He stirred, mumbled something in his sleep—it sounded like *Minou*. He shifted a little, his groin pressed against her hip, his leg sliding more across her thigh, his knee tight against her mound, the toes curling under the bandages of her injured foot. His arm inched higher, tight under her breasts, fingers splayed against her armpit. Desire shot through her, heat pooled between her thighs, and her nipples beaded into hard knots.

She had imagined what he would taste like a thousand times during those early years. What his skin would feel like under her tongue and hands, between her teeth. Running a hand down his muscled chest, across the flat plane of his belly, her eyes scanned every inch of him, as she moved her hand shamelessly lower, her fingers brushing over his dark-blond mat of pubic hair. His penis was thick and wide, heavily veined, partially erect, the mauve-shaded crown peek- from under the foreskin.

Oh, God, what am I doing? She had taken him into her hand. She couldn't seem to stop herself; decided she didn't want to. Her hormones were making her stupid. She had been terrorized, attacked, found her friend dead and mutilated, ran for her life, maybe come close to being killed, and had no idea what might happen next. Her body was battered and bruised and torn. She could barely move without pain and she was thrusting herself blindly into sex. It was almost lunatic crazy; she didn't understand it, was bewildered by it all, but the urge was there, no denying it. She wanted to feel him buried deep inside her. She couldn't seem to focus on anything else—wanted nothing more—than to take him in her hand, and wrap her fingers around him.

Kitty angled her body into his, watched him grow to not quite a full erection with each slow stroke. He moaned and shifted slightly, his penis suddenly solid against her palm.

She raised her head. He was looking at her with those deeply brooding green-gold eyes. Their glances locked.

"Minou," he breathed.

Her arousal twisted through her as his mouth found hers. Sweet torture as he stretched himself against her; his hand stroked her with a slow motion from her throat to her pelvis. Intense ripples, deep waves, entrenched in her lower regions. His hand settled between her legs, fingers moving with deliberate pressure. The sensation drove her head back with a gasp. He rolled her onto her back, raised himself up and locked his elbows, hanging suspended above her, knees pressed tightly against her hips.

Kitty strained against him, aching for penetration. Lowering his body slowly, eyes transfixed on her face, he slid down between her thighs but didn't enter her. She lifted her legs, wrapped them tightly around him and dug her fingers into his ass, urging him for more, and a second later he penetrated her.

His rhythm was fast and hard, almost brutal. She surrendered to his movement. Each thrust brought a raw sensation deep in her lower belly, took her deeper into need. Kitty felt her body leaking around his hardness, muscle clutching tight, sucking at him until she had all of him, their groins locked in a furious demanding tempo. She screamed, biting into his shoulder as her orgasm seized her. He made huffing sounds, continuing to plunge into her, hard and harder with each stroke. When he came, a shudder ran the length of his body, his ass bunching and knotting under her hands. His release triggered a second orgasm for her.

When she opened her eyes, he was still looking at her. He had never closed his eyes. They swirled with the dark aftermath of his orgasm, and when he spoke, his voice was low and gruff: "Did I h'rt y'u?"

"It was wonderful," she whispered, delighting in him, wanting to live for the moment, forget everything else aside from the enjoyment of their sexual episode without complications. But a niggle of something bothered her about her willingness to enter into the experience so quickly and she knew it wasn't going to be that easy to simplify things.

"It was too fast. It's been such a lon' time fer me." His voice was a little angry, but the anger was directed at him, not her. He was apologizing, disappointed in his performance.

"It was wonderful," she repeated.

He scowled at her. Kitty ran her hands over his face, wiping away sweat, brushing damp hair from his eyes. The sex had been fast and rough, but completely satisfying, and she saw it for what it was—plain old fucking spurred on by a natural instinct, it had nothing to do with tenderness or making love. She imagined he saw that, too, but knew he had wanted more. He had wanted to make slow love to her.

Her glance dropped down, her eyes widened, shocked by the damage to the rough scarred flesh of his shoulder. Why hadn't she felt it, even noticed it before? She had been too filled with hunger, too absorbed in her sexual need.

"Oh my God!" she gasped, reaching up to touch the ugly twisted skin. "What happened to you?"

Domeno grabbed her wrist, twisted it away from his body and held on tight for a second. Then he pulled away from her and threw himself off the bed. He stalked to the windows, stood looking out, and began to pace, all dangerous energy. His eyes burned hot and dark under his eyebrows, like the embers of a dying fire. It happened so fast, Kitty was startled. Her heart began an unsteady palpitation.

Such terrible scars, she thought, *they embarrass him, make him angry I've seen them.* She was unsure what to say to him. She waited for him to speak, but he didn't, and the silence between them became awkward.

Domeno stood in the dappled light of the shuttered windows, a giant in shadow, and eventually turned back toward her. Emotion flickered across his face, multifaceted, calm and benign, cold and angry, in the same racing instant. Eyes that glittered, more gold than green, seemed slashed through with scarlet that vanished as quickly as it appeared. His penis had a heaviness that hadn't disappeared as it rested against his thigh. She stared at his tantalizing nakedness, feeling nervous, and thinking she should feel something besides desire, the need to touch and have him again. She didn't. She shuddered. There was something feral there, raw, primitive steel of every tense inch of him, that filled her with a hungry need. She sat transfixed, staring toward him, pulling tiny sips of air into the tightness of her chest.

"Tell me," she whispered, unable to keep quiet any longer. "What happened? Who did that?"

He took a step toward her. Light slants touched on his shoulders, slicing across him, splitting him in half, one side horribly disfigured, the other sleek and magnificent. The scarring was terrible. It looked as if his shoulder had been ripped apart, and healed without medical treatment. She couldn't imagine how much he must have suffered, how long it must have taken to heal, the amount of pain he had experienced. What had done that, animal or human? Had it been on purpose or been an accident? Had Yancy been involved? Was that another reason why he had brutalized her?

Kitty gathered the sheet around her and swung her feet out of bed. She had a dozen questions, but a subtle warning in her mind told her not to ask, not to pressure him, to let him explain at his own pace. *He can be dangerous*, she thought. And a frightened part of her wanted to run away, while another part felt sadness and wanted to comfort him.

When he spoke, his voice was dangerously low. *"Sa fait pas rien . . ."*

"What?"

"Sorry, I—I forget myself," he apologized. "I said, 'it doesn't matter.'"

"Of course it matters."

Domeno turned away again, fisted knuckles pressed hard against the windowsill, his nose almost touching the glass. "I'm strange now, Minou—"

"Aren't we all, in some way?"

"Non, y'u don't see. I'm dif'erent."

"What do you mean by 'different'? A few scars don't make you different," she said, pointing at his shoulder.

"I'm not who I used to be. I'm not what I seem to be." His voice grave, his breath was a foggy vapor on the windowpane. "I wanted to tell y'u 'bout it . . . for y'u to know 'fore we—" He cut himself short, sighed deeply, and said, "Oh, damnit, *Minou. Je t'aime, Minou.*"

Her heart went bumpty bump. She knew that much French, it was the same in France or in Louisiana.

No, he can't possibly love me. She had wanted him, knew he'd wanted her, but the sex hadn't meant more to her than it actually was. Had it meant more to him than she thought? A long time for him, not so for her, but he didn't know that. It had been terrific, fast and powerful, but it certainly didn't deserve a declaration of love.

When she said nothing, he asked, "Did y'u he'r?"

"Y-yes . . ."

"I h've alw'ys loved y'u." He turned toward her again, offered a tiny shy smile, almost as if embarrassed by his confession, and ran his big hands across his face, wiped the smile away. "I alw'ys loved y'u."

"Domeno—"

He silenced her with an abrupt sideswipe of his hand. *"Toujour."* Always. "I liked to th'nk we'd be to-get'er when the time was right." He reached for the Camels on the nightstand, jabbed one between his lips, flicked flame from a disposable lighter. Smoke curled from his nostrils and the corners of his mouth. "I wanted to die the first couple years w'thout y'u. I wanted to find y'u, didn't know wh're to look fer y'u."

Domeno paced in front of her, running his fingers through his hair, naked without discomfort, baring his soul. "Then Tansie came into my life" He glanced at her with pain-filled eyes. "She didn't deserve what hap'en to 'er. Jest a kid wantin' to get 'way from too many bro'hers and sis'ers, par'nts that mistreated 'er. I took advan'age of that 'cause I needed someone." He sighed, drew deeply on his cigarette. "I loved 'er, y'u know. Not at the start, not like I loved y'u . . . *non,* ne'er like that, but I loved 'er." A wistfulness in his voice, a gentle reflection, before a quick subtle change overtook his tone, deep and passionate, a little sting to it. "Fer a lit'le while I forgot 'bout y'u, pushed y'u to the back of my mind. I didn't h'rt so much. Can y'u underst'nd, Minou?"

"Yes," she whispered. It was easy to understand. She'd been in that desolate place, more than once. The need to replace someone you had lost and loved or cared about, even a little. It seemed to make the loss and transition easier. What she didn't understand was his feelings toward her now, after all these years.

Domeno stiffened, hands bunched into fists. *"Fils de putain!"* Sonofabitch! His outburst startled her.

"That *fou* bitch! She wanted me, one way or 'nother. She thou'ht all she needed was her *gris-gris* and spells and I'd want her and that *bebe.*"

Kitty was stunned. "What baby?" she breathed.

"The *bebe* she made w'th me. The *bebe* she got by usin' one of her spells on me."

Kitty stared at the red that sparked in the depths of his eyes and said, "You made a baby with Yancy?"

"*Non,* she used me to h've a *bebe.* Spells to h've sex w'th me . . . used me like a stud horse, fill up 'er belly w'th a *bebe.* She had it, I knew she had it, but I ne'er seen it. I tried to, but I ne'er did. It might h've died, but maybe she jest killed it. I don't know what hap'ened to it." He shook his head sadly. "She done terrible th'ngs to me w'th spells . . . but she ne'er had me of my own free will. Y'u should know that, *Minou.* Ne'er my own free will."

His hand rested on the ugly scars, fingers curled as if he wanted to dig into his shoulder and tear the flesh away. "What she had of me, she took, but she ne'er had me of my own free will," he repeated, like he couldn't emphasize his point enough. He needed her to know he would have never slept with Yancy, under any circumstances, on his own. She didn't now why, but it seemed urgent that she know.

"Even after she did this to me," he added quietly, touching his shoulder.

101

Creely sighted the spiral of smoke and allowed the Porsche to coast down the street. It was nothing as simple as chimney smoke, something large was burning. He was curious about it and wondered if it was wise to find out what it was. After his last vision, he had been cautioning himself to not allow himself to be distracted. He didn't know enough about what he might be walking into. He was impatient and angry with himself for not being able to piece everything together. Kitty bloody, but not dead. He could sense the warm strength of her pulse with his mind, knew she was close.

He parked in front of Schexnaydre's, the exact spot as previously, and he entered the store. The old woman stood in almost the same spot.

"Foute ton quant d'ici!" Get away from here!

Creely didn't understand her, but he caught the gist of it quickly enough. It made him furious. She might want to use Cajun on him now, but he knew she spoke and understood English. She had spoken it with him the last time he was here.

"Listen to me, you old fool! You have a fire somewhere around here. I saw the smoke. You could be in danger." He was tempted to leave and forget about her, but he decided to stand firm. He sliced at the broom handle with the side of his hand, almost knocking it from her grasp.

"Foute ton quant d'ici!" she repeated.

"A fire! Don't you understand what I'm saying?"

"Fous ton camp!" Leave! *"J'avoir rien a dire!"* I have nothing to say.

It was no longer the two of them. A sinewy old man with a full white beard, wide, fuzzy eyebrows and a straw hat had appeared from the shadows. He held the stock of a shotgun tight against his shoulder, the barrels pointed directly at Creely's chest.

"She tole ya to leave," the old man said. "Ya might be 'bout doin' that."

"You have a fire. You might not be worried, but I need to know about the women who came here a couple of days ago. They could be in danger."

"We got nothin' to say." He gestured toward the door with the gun barrel, his finger firm on the trigger. "Ya best be a listenin' 'fore I fill ya fulla holes."

Creely stepped away, backing out the door. They made no move to follow him. He kicked out angrily at the rocker. It slid a few inches across the porch, and almost toppled over.

"Abadie!" he called a minute later, as he abruptly pushed open the door to the Sheriff's Office. Empty. Sunlight from the window threw off the same small squares of pale light, dust motes swimming near the glass. The ashtray still overflowed, Creely's business card peeking warily out. The holding cell was empty.

Creely went back outside. At a loss, he scanned the area. The old Chevy was still there; the sheriff apparently occupied elsewhere. Creely didn't know know which way to go, but he felt he was being watched. He took a few steps, did a complete circle. A few feet beyond the Chevy lay a well-used walking path. He started toward it, a hard pulse in his throat as if it was trying to jump out of his skin. Six or seven yards down, the path twisted to the right, went past a well-kept little house guarded by a couple of dilapidated ones, and abruptly turned left. The sky above the tree canopy was gray and wanted to rupture with rain again.

He froze in his tracks and listened, feeling superheated inside his clothes, perspiration warm and oily under his arms, around his balls, and in the crack of his ass. His hands trembled a little. He could taste salty air on his tongue and smell dead crustaceans that had washed up against the marshy bank. He briefly wondered if it was his imagination or if he smelled his fear on his own skin.

Silence surrounded him. It was now a race against time. His subconscious felt itchy. Alarm bells rang inside his head. He knew he was a little bit of a mess, nervous and having a hard time dealing with his own fear about what he would find, what might happen when he found it. Nothing seemed so far-fetched anymore. he had to rust his own instincts, no matter how vulnerable he might feel or how fearful he might be. He had a feeling things were about to get intense, and if force became necessary, he was determined to use it.

He stepped carefully along the tract of ground, looking in all directions, trying to focus solely on his task and not his unease. He felt certain the day wasn't going to end well. He had come prepared as he would ever be, the rail spike tucked in his belt, the gun hard against the small of his back. He couldn't gauge the extent of his disadvantage, but he never doubted it.

Breathe! he told himself. *Just breathe!*

Through the trees, he could see a dark gray cloud and smoke heavy in the air. His scalp prickling, his pulse jumping all over, fear spurted through his system. He wondered if he had made a mistake in not contacting Sal to send the state troopers. Enough criminal cases had taught him what anger, money, love, power, or insanity could do. Most of it was ugly, very ugly. Sal had been trying to remind him of that. Did his pride get in the way? He had made an edgy decision, taken a big leap and walked into a huge pile of shit.

Not handled right, this could end up being the last day of his life.

102

Domeno's fingers uncurled and moved in small circles, caressing his scars almost intimately. "She did this to me—w'th her teeth."

Kitty gasped, horrified. "What's that mean—with her *teeth?*" She tried to envision Yancy running toward him with bared teeth, sinking her teeth into his shoulder and ripping away a hunk of flesh. Her imagination couldn't work that out; it didn't seem right.

Domeno realized he wasn't telling it right, he was saying everything wrong. He had left out too much. He should've told her the other things, the most important things about Yancy, about himself . . . how everything had come to this. He should've done that first. He no longer knew how to tell her. He didn't know how to backtrack, and start over. She was afraid, petrified, staring at him in wide-eyed horror.

"I'm scarin' y'u," he said softly.

"Of course you are . . . you're scaring the hell out of me."

"I'm sorry."

Kitty felt a slick of temper rising. "Don't be sorry," she snapped, her voice hard-edged. "Tell me what the hell you're talking about. I'm losing my mind here. Saying you're sorry doesn't get it."

"I wanted to 'plain it bet'er."

"Domeno, damnit, just *tell* me!"

He flinched. She seemed to have lost some of her fear now that she was angry. She didn't love him, he could feel it, but he needed her to understand. She might never love him, once he told her the truth . . . that he was no longer simply a man, that sometimes he became—a *wolf.* An animal that craved raw flesh and the taste of blood on his tongue, but he wasn't like Yancy, no, never like Yancy. There was no easy way to explain that.

Domeno knelt in front of her, buried his face in her lap. Kitty hesitated, and then she ran her fingers slowly through his hair. He lifted his head, moved back and opened his arms. She hesitated again, but went into them, and pressed her face against his terrible scars, feeling his pain. He clung to her and they didn't speak. Kitty's expression revealed her intense sadness for him, her confusion and a wave of fear, but she held onto him, as if sensing his need to touch her, and she didn't pull away.

Domeno shoved his face hard against her shoulder. He should let her go. If he kept her, Yancy would cast one of her spells and harm her, try to kill her, or one day he might turn on her and she would see him lose his last scrap of humanity.

"Yancy is *maudit*—evil," he said. "She's a . . . she can change—into a wolf." He looked up to see her reaction, watched her eyes widen, the pupils dilating with mistrust, lips suddenly askew.

I misunderstood him, she thought, and stammered: "A-a—a *w-wolf?*"

"*Oui,* a werewolf—*loup-garou.* She has a power." He leaned back on his heels, rested his hand against his ruined shoulder. "I tracked her while she was wolf. She did this to me."

"That's *crazy,* Domeno. People can't turn into animals." Bubbles of stuttering, nervous laughter rose from her throat, sounds that seemed to come from someone else, not her. "Why are you trying to scare me like this?" She jerked away from him, lost her grip on the mattress, and slid off the bed, tumbling him back, ass to the floor, and breathed, "Oh, my God, is that what happened to Lacy?"

"*Oui.*"

Kitty's hands flew up to cover her mouth; she gasped through her fingers. Yancy was touched by madness Kitty couldn't imagine, seriously fucked up, killing Domeno's wife and baby, tearing his shoulder apart, now killing Lacy, and others, no telling how many others, before that. "You *are* the one that cut out her tongue, aren't you?"

"*Oui,* after she killed Tansie and the *bebe.* I was so angry—so *angry.* I wanted to kill 'er for every strike she made aga'nst me. I wanted it more than I wanted to breathe, but I couldn't do it—" he touched his his scars again—"even after what this did to me. I didn't have it in me, so I only h'rt her 'fore she could h'rt me ag'in." Bitterness curled the corners of his mouth. "Y'u th'nk me as crazy as 'er."

Do I? Thoughts raced wildly through her mind, reflected in her eyes. *Gris-gris*, monsters, werewolves! Kitty couldn't answer him. He sounded crazy, if she believed him. Yancy was crazy, yes, she didn't doubt that. And Arcie. Only crazy people did those sorts of things. But him—she couldn't be sure.

"I h've somethin' fer y'u." Domeno stood and walked out of the room.

Kitty heard a door open, heard a scraping sound, and stood. She dropped the sheet, and it pooled at her feet as she reached for her bloody robe that lay crumpled beside the bed. She jerked it around her and tied the belt. He might be comfortable with his nudity, but she suddenly found she wasn't so secure with hers. He reappeared, dragging something behind him. It had an irregular shape, stood three feet or so off the floor. He moved from shadow into the meager sunlight. When he stood in the slants of sun again, she saw what he had. She felt a sudden sting behind her eyelids.

An old wooden rocking horse, its colors faded, its coat dulled an unbecoming beige, its lips drawn back in a frightful grin of cracked, yellowed teeth, stared at her with one shattered eye.

Kitty felt struck numb, remembering his hard

sides between her thighs as a child, the smooth movement of his stride as he bolted through green pastures and over flowery fields, and carried her into a fantasy world where there was no pain and nothing bad. A Christmas present from *Grandpere* when she was two—or had it been three? Her most prized possession until she grew too large to ride it and her mama moved it to the shed.

She reached out and touched a broken ear, ran her fingers down his forehead to the flaring chipped nostrils. Set him in motion with a fingertip. He no longer moved smoothly, burdened by age and neglect.

"Where did you find him?" she whispered.

"In the shed 'hind y'ur house," he said, and thought: *just before I burned it to the ground trying to erase your memory.* He took her hand off the rocking horse and pressed it against his chest, just below the jagged scars. "It was the only thin' I had left of y'u. I would h've let my *bebe* ride it."

Kitty reached out, cupped his cheek. He hung his head, leaning into her palm. Tears came, spilling down her face. If he meant her harm, wouldn't he have already done it? He had saved her, treated her injuries, given her satisfying sex that somehow she knew they would never experience again. Now, this special gift. She hoped she could take the rocking horse with her when she left. How could she not believe what he told her?

"More . . . y'u need to know more, *Minou.*"

It showed on her face that she didn't want to know more, because she knew he expected her to stay. She couldn't, she wouldn't. There was nothing here for her, not even him. No love, only sadness, and tenderness, sexual feelings banished. It had been momentarily good and quelled her curiosity, but she sensed there was more to their coming together, a lot more she didn't know, wasn't sure she wanted to know. Had a spell brought them together? *Compelled.* Lacy had used that word. Was it the truth? Had there been a twisted spell that had brought him and her together, like one that had brought them back to French Gap? A *gris-gris* spell much stronger than their natural instincts and desires? She was guessing and would probably never know for certain.

"I'm not sure I want to know more," she said.

"Y'u need to know," he insisted. "Y'u h've to know what I am."

"I believe I know who you are."

"Not who—*what.*"

Domeno studied her with sharp tawny eyes filled with such sadness. No doubt he loved her, at least he thought he did, it was like a vapor drifting off him. She knew, even if she tried, she would never love him, not as he loved her.

"Tell me," she whispered.

"I am wolf," he said softly. "She made me wolf

w'th 'er bite." His features twisted up like someone had shoved their balled-up fist into soft clay. He paused, his eyes glazed and blank for a moment as if the simple act of his confession had required all his willpower and concentration, and he'd forgotten who Kitty was for a second. "I am wolf."

Kitty felt fear spurt through her as he grasped both her hands that had suddenly gone cold. Her fingers screamed. She tried to tug them away, but he held on tighter. "Stop it, you're hurting me," she said.

Domeno jerked away, releasing her hands. "I ne'er want to h'rt y'u."

"I don't understand what you're saying. She bit you and turned *you* into a *werewolf?*" she said in a strangled voice. She tried going over in her mind his words, all the things he'd told her. Most of them were difficult to believe. If what he said was true, that made him dangerous, very dangerous, didn't it? Would he kill her if she rejected him? It didn't feel that way, but she couldn't be sure. Her protector could easily turn into her slayer.

"Non, a wolf—not a werewolf, *not yet,"* he said, a wash of unlimited sadness blanketing his face.

103

Yancy poured a glass of water and drank slowly to wash away the dryness in her mouth. She sighed deeply. If Domeno and Kitty had bonded, if the spell had completed itself as Euphrasine said it would with the bonding, she wouldn't accept it. It would be unfair. She had imagined the bite would work. That turning him wolf would make him more receptive toward her. How many times had she done spells to have him love her, to bind him to her, and they had all failed? Why should the one used to eliminate her rivals be the one to work?

She would have to conjure up another elimination spell and do something about it. Or maybe not. Maybe Domeno would destroy the bond himself. Maybe he would shift. She knew Kitty wouldn't accept that, couldn't live with him knowing he was wolf, so things could still turn out okay.

She didn't know if he was really content with the flesh of rabbit or squirrel or deer or nutria. She had no way of knowing if he experienced the same exhilaration over the scent of human flesh that she did, the satisfaction the taste of their blood gave. Or the burn in her guts, the loss of humanity in her mind that left her with only the hot licking, primal, animal desire for food, hungry for a kill. Not just any kill, a human kill, live flesh—warm, struggling, terrified human flesh to satisfy that hunger and fill her belly.

It was the nature of the beast, so he must feel it, at least a little, but maybe he had something different about him she didn't understand. Maybe he had a stronger will, was determined, no matter how difficult it could be, that he would never make a human kill. Deep down, she felt a human kill, one human kill, would change that for him. Make him like her. Maybe he knew that. She hadn't known at first, but maybe he'd figured out that one taste of human flesh, and there would be no going back.

She wanted it to happen. She felt if he was more like her, maybe, just maybe, he wouldn't hate her so much . . . maybe he'd mate with her as wolf—like normal wolves, a mated pair for life—and they would be bound together . . . maybe, just maybe, he'd have sex with her as a woman—and her next conception would produce the female child she so desperately wanted before it was too late to conceive at all.

104

Creely felt the hair rise up along the edge of his collar. He stopped, staring at the deeply rutted trail almost hidden between pine, oak, and cedar saplings. Palmetto as tall as a man guarded the trail's entrance, barely revealing it to a casual glance. If he hadn't been in search of a hint leading him closer to Kitty, his senses so alive, nerve endings buzzing with fear, he would've walked past and never noticed.

He pushed palmetto fronds aside and stood to stare into the uninviting shadow where the sun offered only dapples of pale light. The hair on his arms stood on end. He could have sworn his pubic hairs were curling also. He knew he was going in the right direction.

Squatting, he studied the ground. The trees and foliage were thick, but the trail had been used, frequently and recently. It had deep old dried mud ruts made by tires, but also patchy new areas of cool, damp earth from the recent storm.

And it had footprints. Human footprints, two pairs, one larger than the other . . . *and* animal prints. Paw prints, huge, much larger than his hand.

A warning signal sounded in his head. Every hair on his body twitched as Creely's pulse kicked up a couple of notches. He removed the gun from the small of his back. *On the side of caution,* he thought, *for safety's sake, maybe just to prop up my faltering courage.*

He groped his way through the sharp palmetto and naked berry bushes rife with piercing thorns that scored his hands and arms. They started to bleed and itch and he cursed softly, pulling out a couple of large thorns and sucking at a bloody scratch on his hand.

He had to keep going. This was where he needed to be. No dream or vision or premonition; just a strong intuitive hunch. He didn't doubt it. It was a positive, a certainty.

He just knew.

This trail, wherever it went, would lead him to Kitty.

105

Kitty had goosebumps the size of marbles on her arms. The bloody robe was too thin to give much warmth. A surge of fear-driven adrenaline made her heart pump faster. He had insisted he show her what he was talking about, that she go with him so he could show her. *Go where, show me what*—she argued. He had caught her hand. *Trust me,* he said and pulled her out the window behind his naked body. *Come,* he urged, tugging her along through weeds and trees when she balked, until the bandage broke away and she could feel the shrieks of her injured feet. *Where are we going? Where are you taking me?* she asked. *'way from my house,* he insisted

They broke through the trees. The foliage and weeds had thinned into a small clearing, space maybe twelve by twelve feet, almost a perfect circle, a stone fire pit in the center. He toed the charred remnants in the pit. *H're,* he said, *h're's wh're she'd bring me, take me against my will.* He swung her around, startling her, almost jerking her off her feet. He pulled her against him; his mouth came down hard on hers, so hard she felt the pressure of his jaw and teeth behind his lips.

His arousal burgeoned against her belly, but she didn't dare to look. Icy dread filled her stomach as his erection grew larger and she wondered if all niceties and promises to keep her safe would be forgotten, and he would rape her. Had he brought her to this place to do to her what Yancy had done to him? She knew he could smell her fear, feel the stiffness in her body as her skin crawled against his palms. She could tell he was fighting against the hot rush of her blood under his lips and hands. He wanted to shove his erection into her, maybe so hard and fast he'd make her scream with pain, but he fought hard against it.

"Y'u're afr'id of me!" he growled. Hurt and disappointment shadowed his face, boiling up inside of him. He could feel his beast tremble, uncoiling muscle, issuing silent howls to claim release.

The growl skittered down her spine. His features twisted, his voice and eyes flaming angry.

"I-I—yes, I am," she admitted, scared shitless, afraid to move.

Domeno felt the blood surge in his manhood and his brain at the exact moment, releasing a stream of fire that rushed from each direction to center explosively in his chest. He loved her so much, wanted her so much. She hadn't understood what he was telling her and he never shifted near his house, so he'd brought her here to show her where it happened, what he would become. He realized now a shift would terrify her more, push her further away, but he didn't know how to do anything differently. He needed her to understand, and maybe she never would.

"Don't hate me," he said.

"I don't hate you." She choked on the shallow, mechanical sound of her words. His voice had filled with sorrow, torment, the anguish in his expression so palpable it tore at her.

"Not want to scare y'u. Don't be afr'id of me."

"I-I don't want to be . . ." Anxiety rose from the back of her throat in a thin wail. Fright slithered along her skin, coiled around itself deep inside her belly, and she knew he could tell when he looked into her eyes.

Domeno released a deep gasping shudder. "I can't tell y'u . . . y'u cain't know how it is to become an animal. It rips me apart—" he said and he stepped away. He couldn't be close to her any longer. The smell of her fear had the density of sun-baked rock, hot and hard, and it clogged his nose, sent his blood into a boiling surge. His wolf touched the surface under his skin, struggling to free itself, driven by the fear and the wild hot pump of a beating heart, the strong scent of rushing blood. He fought against it, but the pungent fear-scent was so delightful, so tempting. His wolf began an anticipatory tremble and Domeno, in turn, felt his body tremble.

Kitty felt the need to scream, struggled with the need to run, but didn't make a sound, didn't move.

"Minou, Minou," he muttered, more to himself than to her, but his voice curled like smoke in her blood, filled with all the salacious scraps of distress,

unhappiness and misery of his life, wringing from him all the hurt and grief and disappointment. He stood staring at her with longing, but he didn't touch her.

"He's comin', *Minou*," he said, barely above a whisper. "I cain't keep him 'way."

"Who's coming?"

"My wolf." He felt the power of the beast, its hunger and excitement as it padded closer to the surface and pushed against his skin. "I'm afr'id—" he began. In the next second, he fell to the ground, limbs jerking, muscles contracting and twisting taut against his frame in some kind of seizure.

Domeno pushed himself up on palms and toes, his body arched, beseeching eyes turned toward her. A terrible sound came from his mouth, nothing remotely human, an animal in deep distress and pain.

"Domeno!" she screamed and took a single step toward him, unable to go farther. Was it a hallucination? No, it was real, just as all the things he'd told her were true, nothing a lie.

Domeno rose unsteadily to his knees with a gut-wrenching snarl, got one foot under him, caught his balance and raised his body from the ground. The transformation moved in high-speed motion, a chaotic smear of animal and human spliced together. A transparency of glistening flesh was outlined by angular, jutting bones. An elongated muzzle and pointy ears rose against the distorted features of his human face, one terrible disfigurement whorled into another.

Golden fur sprouted, bristled around his shoulder and along his spine, long legs and giant paws, fangs, and a long tongue inside huge jaws. He lunged to his feet and shook his body. He lifted his muzzle to snuffle the air before his massive head swiveled toward her and a growl flowed like liquid from between his lips. His immense legs spread wide as he took a deep shuddering breath. He appeared to suck air up from the ground through those giant paws.

Kitty froze. "Oh, Domeno . . ." she breathed.

Her stomach bounced into her throat as she stared at him, this gigantic, magnificent tawny creature that a moment before had been a man, sunlight trapped in its fur, its spine burnished gold. No longer was there anything human about him, but for a stunned moment, she thought him the most beautiful thing she'd ever seen—until she saw the brilliance of his red-gold eyes, dark lips pulled away from the formidable fangs. Her lips moved soundlessly. She no longer had any doubt what a deadly killer he could be.

She now no longer needed to struggle to understand what she'd seen that night in the Arceneaux house long ago. Now she knew what it had been—a specter of Domeno, a vision of what would happen.

Domeno Abadie—a half-man, half-wolf creature.

106

Booming cracks of thunder, jagged lightning, more than a drizzle, less than rain, but brisk, as if the trees were physically leaking instead of just the sky. The storm had brought air with a considerable nip in it.

Creely plodded along, tall grasses making wet *swishing* sounds against his legs and faint squeals under his shoes, tripping on the muddy, rutted path. He stumbled over his own feet as dense vines and plants grabbed at him. Mosquitoes sucked on him, gnats out of nowhere swarmed around his head, darted against his eyelids. He was wet and chilled and impatient, but his senses abruptly alerted him to danger.

The trail ended. He heard the low desolate keening before he located the opening in the thicket. He stared, blinking away rain, disbelieving what he saw, his blood a maddening pulse in his throat. A wave of despondency washed over him—*almost too late!*

The flickering anomalous, one moment man, one moment wolf, took a step toward her. Kitty side-stepped and the ground was unstable under her feet. Her toe found a small sinkhole in the swampy soil; it grabbed at her ankle, threatened to suck her foot under, and she almost lost her balance. She thought, as surely as her pounding heart tried to escape her chest, if she moved again he would attack and kill her.

"No! Abadie!" Creely shouted, lifting his gun.

The sharp desperate command and the silence-shattering crack of the gun were almost simultaneous. The creature spun around, fully wolf, its paws leaving the ground, as a thick jet of blood flew from its side and sprayed the air.

Kitty thought she had dropped into hell. She saw the man running across the clearing out of the corner of her eye—recognized him without comprehension as to what he was doing there—but she couldn't take her eyes from the wolf . . . from *Domeno*.

The giant wolf lifted itself off the ground. There was a hole in its side, where its huge ribs curved into the hollow before its haunches. Blood leaked out, matting thick fur. It stood with legs spread wide, sides heaving, fangs bared, its tongue lolling out in a long, thick curl.

It looked at her with a momentary swirl of passionate emotion in its eyes, a reflection of its pain and humanity in the gleam of those brilliant gold wolf eyes, before it bolted across the clearing. But in that second she had recognized the Domeno that had declared his love for her. *I don't believe he's evil, but if he is, he never wanted to be evil—it's not his fault he's no longer human.*

Creely fired the first shot without thought or aim, feeling lucky when blood spurted and he knew he'd hit the wolf. The second shot was more focused and echoed in the silence. The wolf's huge head whipped around, eyes alive with rage, as its left front leg buckled and it stumbled. Creely fired a third shot. The bullet slid through the thick fur around its neck, near its shoulder, releasing another burst of scarlet. The wolf snarled its pain, its movement so quick it was almost a blur as it vanished into the foliage.

A sob caught in Kitty's throat as her eyes tracked the wolf's movement a moment before her legs melted and the ground came up to meet her face.

107

It happened so fast, it stunned him, halting his thought process, but Creely found himself running, filled with an energy he hadn't known he possessed. As he ran, he could hear his breath coming in a strained whistle. The rail spike jammed against his stomach with each step. He pushed the .357 out in front of his body, his eyes frantic as they searched for Abadie—no, the wolf. Abadie was no longer a man and, although he didn't want to believe it, Creely had seen the transformation. He had seen Abadie's human form twist into a giant wolf. His bullets struck home, taking chunks of flesh and drawing blood from that immense muscled body.

His scalp prickled, his nerves doing a trembling sing-song. A warning flapped around in the back of his mind, flipping and tumbling like a chicken with its neck wrung.

Careful, careful . . . careful—be careful, careful, careful!

His gun hand trembled as he stood above Kitty, breath quickening as he jerked right, then left, made a fast 360-turn, his eyes crazed in their sweep, thinking Abadie might come back. He knelt on one knee, quickly turned Kitty onto her back and cursed over her battered condition. As he gaped at the patchwork of bruises on her face, he tried to imagine what had been done to her, thinking it done by Abadie and hoping he had killed the bastard. If he hadn't, given another chance, he'd make every effort to do so.

"Kitty," he said, shaking her shoulder. "Wake up! You need to wake up . . . *Kitty!*" He stuffed the gun inside his jeans next to the rail spike and lifted her.

Kitty floated back to consciousness with the teasing scent of familiar cologne, big hands scooping her up, strong arms pulling her tight against a broad chest, hot breath against her ear. A voice was calling her name, husky with emotion, urgent with fear. She fought her way through the fog. It took a moment for her thoughts to connect, but she knew that voice, recognized the welcoming heat of that body, the security of those strong hands and arms, the delicious scent of that cologne. How he came to be here, how he had known where to find her, she had no idea. It didn't matter. It wasn't important. He *had* found her. He was holding her, he'd saved her from . . . she squeezed her eyes tight, blinded by tears.

Domeno. No, not Domeno—*the wolf.*

Are they really one and the same? she wondered. *Does killing one mean killing both? Is Domeno dead? All because of Yancy and her spells. He doesn't know what he's doing when that happens to him, he doesn't deserve to die!*

"C-Creely," she whispered.

Creely pulled her up, caught her before she fell to her knees, hugged her close as she sagged against him, and pressed her bleeding face tightly against his chest. He tried to help her walk, but her legs weren't working right. He grabbed her around the waist and lifted her listening to her mumble someone's name.

Her thoughts were a whirlpool of craziness, but Kitty knew everything had been wrong. She felt it, didn't know what it was, only that it wasn't natural, that attraction, the urgency for sex with Domeno that she'd been unable to resist. Had Yancy done that? All of it voodoo, all part of a spell, part of Yancy's madness to hurt them? Had Yancy cast a spell over them all? Why would she do that?

But now it was over; Creely would take her away from here. Kitty had no idea how she would repay him, only that she was thankful he'd come for her. She was sure without him she would be dead. *How does a person go about repaying someone for saving their life?* she wondered.

108

From a distance came a long-drawn howl.

It drifted through the air with an eerie quality, freezing the blood in Creely's veins. A scintillating sensation washed over him; he felt his testicles draw up and the skin of his scrotum tighten against his groin. His heartbeat sped up, racing so fast and thudding so loudly, for a moment he was aware of nothing beyond the lump in his throat making it difficult to breathe. And he had to breathe . . . because he knew he was going to have to make a run for it—*run, you jackass, run as fast as you can!*—to get himself and Kitty to safety . . . because he hadn't killed the wolf.

He hugged her against his chest as if she were a weightless package, his long legs eating up ground. Her teeth clacked together with each pounding step he took. He sprinted the clearing, broke through the barricade of wild growth on the other side, used his body as a wedge and whipped them inside the small opening. Vines entangled them, palmetto points stabbed, berry thorns raked at exposed flesh.

Creely held her tighter against his chest and kept running. His foot hit a pothole and he felt the depth of the hole into his upper molars. He could feel the soft tissue knotting up, threatening to give under his weight. He pushed through the pain, pressed Kitty's face deeper into his shoulder, and she moaned. He stumbled on something, felt pain shoot up his leg as his ankle twisted sideways, and he cursed aloud, but righted himself before he fell or dropped her. Tightening his grip, he kept running, his heart a frenzied drumbeat. His mind and body surged with fear.

The terrible howl came again.

Creely burst through the trees. He paused to drop Kitty onto her feet. She staggered as her feet hit the ground, her eyes flew open, her head jerked back, and he heard her neck pop as she stifled a scream of pain. He held her upright with one hand, fumbling in his shirt pocket. He heard the *beep-beep* of the automatic key fob. He yanked open the door, thrust her roughly and without hesitation inside, a breathless, "Sorry, love," whispered against her ear.

He leaned against the Porsche's fender, struggling for breath. He felt lightheaded; thought he might pass out. His legs screamed from exertion. He was fucking tired and scared shitless. He pulled the gun from his jeans, held it in front of him with a shaky two-handed grip, and edged his way around the car, thighs and butt pressed against metal. His head jerked side to side, eyes searching for an attack. The next moment, a strong physical shift filled the air.

A second later, a different wolf appeared at the end of the street.

109

Yancy sniffed the air. Their scents enraged energy inside her nostrils. Her growl morphed to a full-throated snarl. Fury snapped through her with such force the shift was almost instantaneous.

My territory! her mind raged, burning with mania.

Her large paws barely touched the ground as she leaped through foliage and briars that clawed at her pelt and wound around her thrusting legs. Her heart lunged against her ribs, pounded and jerked, driving blood with throttle force through her body. Her brain was inflamed. Froth slid from her lolling tongue, her eyes flaring a brilliant red.

Leaping from between the trees, sides heaving, fur bristling along her spine, she uttered a single warning growl: *He's mine!* the growl declared.

Adrenaline accelerated through her system. She'd come to protect what was hers.

The breeze lifted the thick lupine collar around her neck, riffled through the raised guard hairs along her shoulders and spine into the aggressive flag of her stiffly erect tail. She stood with shoulders hunched, legs spread wide, muscle coiled, panting and huffing. Her head dropped low, lips curled, fangs bared at the man who crept around the shiny silver car. A whisper hiss of air slipped from her lungs, turned into a heavy chuffing noise, and thundered out her muzzle as a murderous roar of sound.

The assault of thrumming rage, hot killing blood-lust, blinded her to everything except the man center-ed in her vision.

Creely stared at the massive dimensions of the animal. The wolf growled, the ruff around her neck flaring wide with each vibration. He was positive this was a female; something about her stance, her heat, her fierceness told him so.

The wolf launched itself through the air.

Creely pivoted a little, thrusting out his shoulder as the full weight of the creature hit him, and he lost his balance. He forced his left side and knee up be-tween them. Frothy jaws snapped near his face. Toe-nails scrabbled against his chest, and the animal drove him to the ground, knocking the gun from his hand and the breath from his lungs. Its angry eyes made hostile crimson pools against its dark fur. Rancid saliva dripped in his face. He clutched the dense roughness of the animal's fur in his fists, those blaz-ing scarlet-slashed eyes inches from his own.

Catching a handful of flesh and fur between the leaking jaws and the bridge of the animal's broad muzzle, he dug his thumb into its right eye. With a painful grunt, it jerked up and away from him.

That was all the time he needed.

The huge dark body stiffened, its jaws gnashed

together, its hind legs clawed for purchase, and fetid breath bellowed from its throat in a bubbly, bloody snarl.

Creely used all his strength to drive the rail spike in, then deeper, into the wolf's side.

The massive body hung momentarily above him, and he could feel the resistance of muscle and tissue against the metal. Its blood spewed, the powerful surges of the animal's heart opening and closing around the rail spike. The strength ebbed from its legs. The red gleam vanished from its good eye in the same mercurial moment. The body was suspended in the air for a moment. A glaze slid over its undamaged eye. A haunting rattle escaped its lungs.

He felt the wet heat of its blood soaking his clothes as the wolf collapsed on top of him. He hadn't realized he'd closed his eyes when he used all his strength to drive the spike into the wolf's body. When he opened them a second later, he found himself underneath the naked body of a woman.

110

Kitty pulled the tattered satin of her robe tightly against her body and sat huddled into herself. Every couple of minutes her eyes flitted sideways at Creely's bloody hands. He buried his foot against the accelerator, sideswiping weeds and saplings, barely missing a tree. The Porsche fishtailed through oyster shell and dirt, hitting the blacktop with an engine roar and tire shriek at such speed her spine jarred forward into the back of her skull. Her stomach lurched up under her ribs with each pothole strike, her heartbeat a painful thump.

Rain made round droplets on the windshield, a soft ticking sound on the car's roof, then stopped; weak sunlight made intermittent flashes through the glass. The tires hissed, expensive shocks and suspension groaned in protest. Metal occasionally caught a dip and scraped the roadway, discharging a shower of sparks they saw in the wing mirrors.

Kitty hazarded a closer look at Creely. Covered in mud and blood, his lips pulled back in a grimace, features rigid with determination, his eyes were wild with fear. She was unsure how much, if any, of the blood belonged to him. He had shoved Yancy's body off, scrambled to his feet, retrieved the mean-looking gun he'd used on Domeno and threw himself inside the Porsche. He hadn't looked at her, or spoken to her, since slamming the car door and barking at her to fasten her seat belt. As the car circled, he'd taken a final glance at Yancy's body, losing most of his color, before kicking the Porsche in the ass.

She watched Creely look down at the steering wheel, lifting his fingers one at a time from the blood-soaked leather, breaking its hold on his skin. The clotted blood, crinkly, like balled-up cellophane, had dried under his hands. He glanced at Kitty. She stared back at him, knowing she looked battered and exhausted.

"Did you see it?" he breathed. "His eyes. It was in his eyes—he was going to kill you."

Kitty shook her head. Had she? She seemed to have a lapse of memory.

"Did he do this to you?" he growled.

Kitty shook her head again. "No, I did, running away from Arcie."

"Why would you run away from her?"

"I thought she was trying to kill me." Kitty wondered if she would ever forget Yancy's naked body with the metal protruding from her side. Or Lacy—reduced to a mutilated corpse. "Is it . . . is she dead?"

"Yes, she's dead," he said.

Kitty began to sob softly. Lacy had mentioned someone special. When she didn't come back, would he look for her? She should try to contact him, or at least her company, but if she did, she wouldn't know what to say. How did a person tell the bereaved their loved one was dead, a casualty of a werewolf attack? They would think her insane and immediately call the police. She wasn't sure she could give an accurate account of what happened. And Arcie—what had happened to her?

Creely slid his hand gently over hers. "Don't cry. It doesn't seem like it now, but it'll get better," he said. His grip tightened, his eyes met hers briefly, but he looked away. He could imagine what she had been through since leaving New Orleans. Feelings, waiting for recognition for a long time, squeezed tightly around his heart. He loved this hurting, terrified woman, loved her with a raw gut intensity, would do his best to help her repair her torn psyche.

Kitty's sobs eventually hitched into hiccups, and she managed a few shaky breaths. Her thoughts were scrambled, like cracking open and dropping a raw egg. She whispered, "I . . . I don't know what happened here, but Arcie went crazy and tried to kill me. She chased me with a knife. She had a million chances to do that over the last twenty years. Why do it now, like this?"

"There is no logic to madness, sweetheart. No accounting for human behavior. Crazy is crazy." Creely's lips quirked up at the edges. "Sort of like that *thing* back there. What was that? Who was that?"

"Yancy Arceneaux, the reason we came back. Domeno said she was a werewolf."

"Abadie was one, too."

"He said he wasn't—he was just a wolf. I have no idea what it was, but I think there was a difference between them . . . it seemed to be important to him for me to know that. But—yes, he was a wolf."

"A hell of a big one. Both of them. I didn't want to believe something like that was possible." He ran his hand across his forehead, leaving behind a flaking smear of red.

"You knew about the wolves?"

"I had an idea, but I guess I really didn't believe it until I saw him change, saw her coming at me. An old guy in the next town told me about them. *Loups-garous*—werewolves . . . a *human* turned into a *wolf*. It seemed impossible."

"It was true."

"Yes, it was."

"My other friend, Lacy Kennedy, she's dead. Yancy's dead now. Domeno's dead . . . I have no idea about Arcie."

"Probably dead, too. Why would she want to kill you?"

"She gave me a dozen reasons, but none of them were true, at least I don't think they were. I think it was all in her mind." Kitty sucked in air, rubbed her lacerated hands against her bruised legs, wincing.

"We've known each other most of our lives. I thought Arcie was my friend. I should have paid more attention." She rubbed a nervous finger back and forth over her upper lip. "I thought she was my friend," she repeated.

"Time doesn't always allow you to know everything about another person," Creely said. Kitty nodded. "Do you believe that would've stopped her? She was apparently damaged, Kitty. Damaged people can be very dangerous. Not your fault you didn't see it. We all make mistakes. Don't blame yourself for this fucking mess."

"She blamed me for everything wrong in her life. Like I stole all her chances for happiness."

"She had to blame someone, if she couldn't take responsibility for it. You made an easy target."

"She could have left a long time ago. She didn't have to hang around."

"She probably felt she couldn't for some reason. Maybe she felt dependent on you. Looks like she was a late bloomer, an inept one, living behind a dark wall of insanity. That made it easy to blame the wrongs in her life on you. When she saw you succeed, that made it easy to blame all the wrong in her life on you. She finally slipped off the edge."

"Can you imagine how it feels to trust someone, think they're your friend for thirty years, and find out they hate you? Probably hated you the entire time?"

Creely shook his head. "No, I can't."

"It's a horrible feeling. I took her away from *this*—" She waved her hand at nothing in particular. "How could she hate me so much?" She stared at him; she looked wounded but fierce, clasping and unclasping her hands.

"Why did you come back here anyway?"

"Arcie said it was a twenty-year reunion."

"Hell of a reunion."

"I never wanted to come. It got complicated. I ended up doing it just to shut her up."

Creely glanced at her. Kitty sat staring into the distance, maybe trying to empty her head of the horrors she'd witnessed. Feeling the pain of loss, she would grieve for her friends; those she had thought were her friends. She'd need time to stop finding fault with her own self. He wondered how long that would take. Everyone mourned differently. Right now she wasn't as resilent and strong as the Kitty he had always known. Not that it mattered. He would be there for her, no matter how long it took.

He saw the flash of fangs, remembered the feel of thick, gritty fur clutched in his fist, the push of all his strength behind the spike, the gush of hot blood. For a second Creely closed his eyes against it all. How long before the body of a woman with a spike protruding from her side would no longer prey on his mind? How long would those creatures haunt him?

"Yancy was a witch. She used *gris-gris*. She killed people, Creely—she killed Domeno's baby, killed Lacy . . . did terrible things. I'm not sorry about what you did to her," Kitty said. She lifted her injured hands, stared at them, then dropped them back into her lap. "Domeno tried to help me after I ran away from Arcie. He didn't hurt me." She realized she was rambling, and turned big, bewildered eyes up at him. "How—how did you find me?"

"One of my premonitions—the rest isn't important right now. What's important is I found you." He wiped his hands on his jeans, crusty blood flaking off, and frowned at the leather steering wheel and the seat between his legs.

All the detailing in the world wouldn't remove the damage. *Ruined,* he thought, feeling his flesh crawl and a little sick to his stomach, realizing he would have to dump the car. The blood-soaked clothes, his nerves curled like steel bands, his breathing still shallow, he smelled that *thing* on his body. He needed a scalding-hot bath, a bottle of Scotch, and a soft bed, with his arms wrapped around the woman sitting next to him. She needed her wounds treated, to be stroked with love and care like the animal her name represented. They both needed a good meal and rest, and a few hours of solid sleep, hopefully without nightmares.

Reality was a kick in the ass. *Werewolves!* Who would have thought such a thing? He had shot a man

. . . no, a wolf. He had no way to know if Abadie, man or wolf, had more than flesh wounds, was seriously injured or dead. He had killed a wolf turned woman. These were people Kitty knew, had thought her friends. She was traumatized, more lost than he was. In time, when they felt sane again, they would try to figure all of it out together. Not right now. Right now he wanted a lot of distance between them and that nasty little place—not French Gap any longer, now it was No More, Louisiana—an empty space where people no longer wanted to live. He would continue to think of it that way. It didn't belong, and thinking that way would makeforgetting easier. Kitty was safe, and he was safe; they never had to go back there. The experience had left them with a lot to work on.

"Hello, beautiful lady," he said softly, resting his hand against hers. *She's pretty busted up, but she's alive, she'll heal,* he thought.

Kitty offered a miniscule smile. "What made you come?"

"I think you're pretty special."

"So you just came . . . by yourself?"

"Of course."

"Of course," she repeated.

"Did you expect me to bring the entire New Orleans police force?"

"No, but . . . you came with only a gun and whatever that was you used—"

"A rail spike."

"A what?"

"A spike used on old railroad ties. I picked it up along the way."

"Thank you." It sounded lame, but that was all she could think to say. She knew there were other words, better words, to express her gratitude and feelings. At the moment, she couldn't remember any. She hoped he understood how grateful she was, how much it meant to her that he had come for her. It made her sick to think what could have happened to her if he hadn't come. Or what might have happened to him because he did.

"You're more than welcome."

"Are we going to the police?"

"I don't think so." The police would believe they were fucking lunatics. Sal might believe him, but he didn't want to compromise their friendship, raise a problem with Sal's job, or put him in an awkward position holding onto such a secret trying to protect Creely from the casualties of murder, the possibility of losing his reputation, his career or going to prison.

Kitty stared straight ahead lost in thought, face masked by confusion, trying to sort it all out. He thought she was looking far beyond anything he could see, maybe even understand. He wanted to hold her, to give her some small comfort. He felt he could do with a little TLC himself.

Creely pulled the Porsche to the side of the road, reached across the console and tentatively touched her arm. Her head turned, round, bruised eyes dropping to stare at his hand. He leaned across the seat and opened his arms. She pressed herself into them. He placed a finger under her chin, tipped back her head, and brushed his lips against her mouth. The kiss held no passion but was filled with meaning. He drew her to his shoulder, kissed the top of her head, and held her.

"There are three, maybe four, dead," she said. "Yancy killed Lacy, you shot it . . . *him*—stabbed . . . *her*—isn't any of that called murder?"

"More like self-defense. People are always innocent until proven guilty. Someone will have to prove it was something different. We have more important things to worry about right now. We're going to stop in one of these little towns at some cheap no-tell motel. Get hot baths, clean clothes, fresh bandages, food, and a couple of stiff drinks. We can't arrive home looking like this."

"Don't you think we should tell the police?"

"No."

"Why not?"

"They will probably never be missed."

"Lacy and Arcie will be missed."

"If explanations are needed, we'll find them."

"So we're going home—as if nothing happened."

"Yes."

"Are we ever going to tell?" she asked, voice muffled by his dirty shirt.

"Do you think anyone will believe us?"

"I-I don't know." After a moment, she shook her head. "No. No, I don't even believe it. How can I expect someone else to believe?"

"You can't."

"Arcie might be alive."

"She's probably dead."

"That sounds cold. We don't know for sure."

"She threatened to kill you—how much colder can you get?"

"I'm listed as her emergency number. What am I going to tell anyone who asked about her? Her boss will call when she doesn't show up for work, when he can't reach her. She always went to work."

"Would she have told anyone where she was going?"

Kitty thought a minute. "No, I doubt it. I can't think of anyone in particular."

"We'll wait until someone misses her and calls you. You can say you haven't seen her for days."

"People could have seen us leave my condo."

I made inquiries, and you were seen at the airport. "We'll figure something else out."

"And Lacy? Someone will look for her."

"A husband?"

"A boyfriend. Employees. She owns a business. People will miss her."

"Do you think she told any of them where she was going?"

"I can't be sure, but she said she didn't."

"Don't worry about all that right now. We have to work our way through this one step at a time."

"Will we ever be able to forget this?"

"I hope so. We'll work through it together." Creely looked at his bloodied hands. How much scrubbing would ever get them clean? Even once they were clean, he thought he still might feel the blood, knew he definitely would remember it. He could throw away his clothes, get rid of his car, scrub his body, but he was yet unsure what to do about his mind. He needed to work on that.

Kitty was staring at him. He knew he was scaring her. He could see it in the angst deep in her eyes. She wanted him to give her all the right answers. It wasn't that easy. He wasn't sure what the right answers were. Maybe she was thinking he was being too cold-blooded and calculating about everything. He felt he was thinking logically, under the circumstances.

"You're looking for the right answers and I don't have them, sweetheart . . . not right now. What is, just is. We'll find the answers together, I promise," he said, and lightly touched his lips to her forehead, burying his face in her hair.

She started crying again. He let her. She seemed to have lost the aura of her strength. He had to be the strong one; she needed his help to get it back.

"He—he said he loved me, and I believe he honestly thought he did," she murmured after she stopped crying.

"Abadie?" Creely felt a twinge of jealousy. It came out as a rough edge of anger in his voice.

"Yes."

"He turned into an animal, and he looked ready to kill you. That's not love, that's insanity." Creely felt that familiar intense electric spark fluttering between them, cutting through the pain. "I don't care what he told you, I promise to never let anything hurt you again." But he did care.

Kitty lifted her head, her eyes were enormous and dark. "It wasn't his fault. He told me Yancy did terrible things to him. She did spells and forced him to have sex with her. She bit him."

"Bit him?"

Kitty nodded. "When she was a wolf. It turned him into one."

"I don't know much about that type of thing. Some kind of lycanthropy, I guess. It's crazy to think of where it might have come from."

She pushed tight against his chest, a sensation like a bird settling securely into its nest, and he tightened his hold. An intense sweet fire took hold of him, surprising him with its strength. Sal was right, this was a lot more than like, and it made him feel good, complete. "Everything will be okay," he promised. "It'll be difficult, but I'll be there for you."

"I know you will." She pulled back a little, looking down at his strong, familiar hands. A faint smile formed. *Always dependable. No white horse, but maybe one day I'll buy him one.* "How can you be sure?"

"Trust me."

"I do. I know at some point it will probably get better and I might be able to let some of it go," she said softly, "but right now it's hard to think straight and I can't."

"I think you're doing a good job of it." He touched his lips against her temple. "And, yes, you will let go of it, eventually. Maybe not all of it, but most of it. Enough to make it easier to live with."

"I hope I can."

"You will. I'll help you, even if it takes the rest of our lives."

"I hope that's a very long time," she whispered.

"Me, too."

Epilogue

The wolf had run full out, riding an adrenaline wave, until it felt the strength drain from its limbs. It tripped over its own paws, stumbled, and collapsed. It lay at the edge of the coulee, panting as its faltering breath came back. Sprawled in the alligator grass, trembling, it felt the blood seeping through the hole in its side, as a spasm of pain tore through its body and needles of agony pierced its skin.

A moment later the wolf was gone and Domeno lay stretched in the grass. The shot in his side had been the worst. The one in his arm would probably leave a scar; but the one that skimmed his neck had been a clean through-and-through slide, almost like a shallow knife cut, without much damage. Th bleeding had stopped. The wounds began to heal, the one in his belly closing around the bullet still lodged in his side. He couldn't leave it there, couldn't let the flesh heal around it.

Domeno plunged his thumb and index finger into the hole and worked them around until he felt the bullet. It was a big fucker. Crane hadn't brought a peashooter. He had come prepared to kill, or at least inflict serious damage. He hooked it with his fingernails and pulled it out. It bled a little more and the wound burned. He pinched the skin together and held it until the bleeding subsided and the wound begin to close again.

He had lost enough blood to make him weak and lightheaded. He had to rest for a few minutes, but by tomorrow he would be completely healed inside and out. Only scar tissue would remain. It was the only possible advantage he'd found in being a shapeshifter. Once, in wolf form, he had slashed his paw on a broken whiskey bottle chasing a rabbit, and he had noticed it healed almost instantly. It made him wonder why Yancy's tongue had never come back. Only after working on his old car when a wrench slipped, nearly cutting off his little finger, did he realize a wound gotten in wolf form healed and remained healed in human form, but a wound gotten in human form did not. It would have to heal normally, and depending on the wound, sometimes not at all.

Using a young oak for support, Domeno dragged himself to his knees and stood on shaky legs, palm pressed tight against the bullet hole. He worked his way back toward his house. He needed to clean himself up. He needed a bandage and clothes. He needed the tea and rest to get his strength back.

His mind was suddenly chaos, a jumble of thoughts and emotions that seemed to want to eat him alive. He thought of Kitty—and the man who took her away.

A knot tightened in his chest. He had wanted to

kill Crane, but that was foolish, only his jealousy talking. He might not have liked Crane, but he felt the man was honorable, a man of integrity. They just happened to want the same woman, and that made them rivals. Crane could provide for her, something Domeno couldn't do.

No doubt Crane loved her. He wouldn't hurt her or let someone else hurt her. She wouldn't have to fear him. He'd come in blind, believing her in danger, having no idea what kind of danger, but he'd come anyway. Domeno grudgingly admired him for that, but it didn't help soothe the burn of his bittersweet envy of Crane, or the knowledge that Crane was a better choice for Kitty than he was.

He knew his love, his need, wasn't a good thing, like he knew Kitty would never feel for him what he felt for her. She'd never love him in return, and she'd never be completely safe with him. No doubt, Crane could give her a wonderful life, the kind of life she deserved, and she could love Crane, and feel safe with him. Maybe she already loved him. Maybe that was why Crane came, even if he wouldn't admit it.

That wretched emptiness would return soon enough, tormenting his sanity, eating at his guts. Only now he would have new, different memories. He'd held her, kissed her, been inside her. He would never forget, it would stay with him forever.

The solitary frenzied howl cutting through the

swamp jolted him from his reverie.

He knew that howl, knew what it meant, and he had to go, but Domeno felt the weight of his weakness as he stumbled through the foliage in time to see the wolf launch her attack. He'd wanted this, waited for it—for someone to come along and kill her—and he had no doubt Crane was up for doing that, if she didn't kill him first.

Yancy, filled with rage, was intent upon the kill.

Crane was intent upon surviving.

The two bodies fused together for a moment.

Domeno thought she had killed Crane until Yancy collapsed and shifted.

Crane pushed Yancy's human body away, rose shakily to his feet, retrieved his gun, climbed in his fancy car and spun away, taking Domeno's heart with the woman in the passenger seat. He knew he'd never see her again.

Domeno dropped to his knees, threw back his head, and howled.

The sound that rose and cut through the quiet wasn't wolf.

It was mournful, deeply anguished—and very much human.

A minute later he began to cry.

After he had composed himself, Domeno felt the elation. Palpable flutters of joy, heated pleasure running a course through his veins. It was finally over.

His tormentor was dead. He stood motionless, arms hanging limply at his sides, staring down at her without compassion. Today he felt no shame, only the distance of strangers between them.

I'll never mourn you, he thought, eyes touching on the spike, a smile curving his lips. Crane had unintentionally set him free.

Whether he had known it would work or not, that had been really smart of Crane, that big old spike. It was a surprisingly perfect weapon. It had pierced her heart and killed her almost instantly. There would be no shifer healing.

Yancy's eyes were fixed on something only she could see. Her mouth gaped open in a dark hole. She'd always wanted what she couldn't have, a twisted wire that made them different. He would've liked to leave her to rot where she lay, allow the animals to drag her away, but it wasn't in him, even as he wished to avoid and not touch her. She was dead, but death didn't make her any less his albatross. What she'd left him with would be with him always. He would move her, but he didn't owe her a burial.

Domeno stooped, picked up her body, and threw it over his shoulder.

The simplest and easiest thing was to burn down the Arceneaux house, with her inside. Fire was good, it cleansed away bad things.

Domeno felt the drag of his feet, the weight of

the burden on his shoulder, as he paused on the steps
the steps of the Arceneaux house.

There had been a flicker of the curtain at the
kitchen window.

It only took a moment to lose his inner peace
and contentment, to have his skin prickle and his
blood run slushy.

Was there someone *inside* the house?

Impossible! Everyone was gone, except the old
people at the store. The house should be empty. Had
it only been his imagination? Maybe an open window?
Or a breeze blowing through the house?

Except there was no breeze.

Domeno climbed the gallery steps, stopped
outside the door, and listened. A noise inside. Shuffling sounds moving away from the door.

He yanked open the screen door, it thwacked
against the wall. From somewhere close in the
shadow came a thin wail of fright. The old frame
wobbled and bounced back to hit him in the shoulder. He cursed as he stepped inside the dim interior.

He could see it in the shadowy hallway, trying to
run away.

"Arrete!" he shouted. Stop!

It stopped in the middle of its crab-like shuffle
down the hall, the most terrible abomination he had
ever seen.

It had a cobby little body, a short slender muzzle,

deformed black lips lifted permanently back to reveal elongated eye teeth in an overshot jaw. Fat round ears tufted with long wispy hair pressed against the sides of its nearly bald head. One large green eye was human, the gold one was wolf. The pair of mismatched eyes stared out from a face that was otherwise mostly human.

It was naked and stood sideways, the shoulders hunched and sprouting wispy black hair. Short arms ended in thick-toed canine paws. A hairless chest was thin and pale, leading down at an angle into hips that were twisted into bowed lightly furred animal—*wolf*—legs. A strip of gold fur ran along its spine, terminated in a thick stubby dark tail with a fringe of fur curling overs its hairy hindquarters. In front hung shrunken male genitalia.

Mon Dieu! Domeno thought, as the wide black nostrils quivered, scenting him, and the luminous mismatched eyes flickered toward the body thrown over his shoulder. It trembled.

The muzzle opened wide and *"Mommiieee!"* escaped in a husky, blood-chilling wail, the instant it launched its snarling self forward.

Domeno dropped Yancy's body.

The body struck the floor with a wet thud. He caught the wolf-child mid-air and pressed its clawing, snapping, struggling body tightly into his own. It wailed, screeched and snarled. Sinewy hindquarters kicked upward against his chest. Paws with thick black nails slashed the air, soft pads grazed his cheeks—smooth pads that had never touched the outside ground—seeking a grip on the side of his head. Gnashing teeth slid across his arms, ripping away skin, drawing blood.

It fought wildly, grunting and growling, emitting wrathful snarls, but it was not strong. Eventually, its struggles subsided, and it began, like any frightened child, to cry.

Domeno continued to hold the limp, pitiful creature, knowing without a doubt what he held had come from his loins—his sperm, Yancy's womb . . . this little creature was his malformed whelp, a monster caught between human and wolf forever.

It was young, maybe five years old. Not old enough for the pregnancy he'd seen. He had been unaware, but there had been another pregnancy. Why she hadn't flaunted this pregnancy in his face, he had no idea. Maybe because something had happened to the first one and the baby had turned out this way, he considered.

He'd always suspected she killed the first baby. He had never understood why she would do that, but seeing this one, he thought he now knew why. Maybe it had been like this one. If it was, it confused him as to why she hadn't rid herself of this one. It would've been the most humane thing to do.

Holding the weeping creature tightly in his arms, its wet muzzle dampening his shoulder, Domeno carried it from the house. He walked slowly so as not to disturb its misery. It continued to cry softly, but no longer struggled. He stopped under a willow beside the old turtle pond and lowered himself carefully to the ground.

It was shady here, the humidity lower. A small breeze provided a peaceful moment for both of them. He sat a long time under the tree in the quiet afternoon cool, his ears buzzing, his hammering heart echoing inside his head, and watched the sun cast bright, shimmering circles on weak chocolate-colored water flashed through with veins of deep green. Domeno thought the water pretty, thought maybe the little creature might think the water pretty, too.

An egret turned a curious eye in their direction and took flight. Somewhere in the distance, a bullfrog croaked. The creature paid no attention. Domeno continued to hold it, even after it stopped crying, afraid if he released it its first instinct would be to run.

Domeno surprised himself when he impulsively reached up and stroked the almost-hairless head, thinking he shouldn't think in such a damning way. It wasn't an *it*, it was a *him*. A boy; a little boy. He patted the trembling shoulders, set to rocking him until he quieted and Domeno thought he might have fallen asleep. Finally, the child lifted his head, staring sadly at Domeno with his huge glistening eyes.

One *wolf* eye . . . one *human* eye

Domeno stretched out his legs, dropping the boy lower and letting him slide into his lap, but holding tightly to one crooked leg. What had happened to produce this strange hybrid creature with his mismatched eyes? Was it his fault, something in his sperm? Or something in Yancy's body? Maybe the curse they both shared.

The boy sat quietly. Domeno closed his eyes, his stomach queasy, his body slick with sweat and taut with stress. He opened his eyes again when the boy spoke.

"Quoi—quoi arriver du elle?" he asked softly. What happened to her? The Cajun was heavily accented. He had trouble speaking through his animal mouth, twisting his thick tongue around his teeth to form the words.

Domeno stared at him, surprised he spoke so well. Yancy had taught him, spent time with him, maybe even loved him like the mother of a normal human child. Maybe a spark of humanity had still existed inside her.

"Elle aboutir en mal," he explained. She come to a bad end.

"Comment sa ce fait?" How come?

"Je connais pas." I don't know. The lie slid easily off his tongue. No need to hurt him more. A small lie,

for a small, frightened, misshapen boy.

A flash of anger appeared in those huge eyes. *"Tu?"* he demanded. You?

"Non." Domeno could feel the weight of his gaze, assessing him as a friend or a threat. Intelligence was shiny bright in his eyes. *"Etranger."* A stranger.

"Crache dans l'aire et sa tombe sur? A moi?" The boy patted at Domeno's scarred shoulder with his paw, his eyes flickering over the puckered reddish spots of the new wounds. The same thing could happen to you? To me?

"Non." Too smart, Domeno thought. The boy no longer appeared frightened or angry, but resigned, questioning his new position. He wondered about his safety, if he was in danger, what kind of danger it might be, where it might come from. *He's never been outside. His pads are too soft. He has no idea the terrible things that have happened, no idea the terrible things his mother has done. He only knows his mother is dead, there's no one else to care for him.*

Domeno sensed the boy's need to form a new bond. He was willing to trust, to transfer his loyalty if security was involved. He was intelligent, seeking out help and protection until he could care for himself. Domeno wondered if he would ever be able to do that. How would he feed himself? Had Yancy cooked for him or had he eaten raw? Having never been outside, he probably had no idea a rabbit or a squirrel could outrun him.

The boy looked slowly around, suddenly aware of his surroundings, his eyes widening a little, awed. His muzzle hung open, his long tongue curled over the edges of his sharp teeth, and his nose twitched as he sniffed the air.

"*Joli,*" he said softly. Pretty.

"*Oui* . . . yes, it is," Domeno agreed.

Curious eyes turned toward Domeno again. *"Quel est ton nom?"* What's your name?

"Domeno. *Tu?*"

"Emile."

"Y'u speak English."

"*Oui,* Mommy taught me both. I don't use it much. She spoke Cajun with me." The dark lips curled slightly upward, the best semblance of a smile the boy could possibly give. One paw lifted to wipe at his damp face, rubbing the end of his leaking nose. Such familiar, childlike human gestures.

"Hello, Emile."

"*Bonjour,* Domeno." He studied Domeno's face with those serious mismatched eyes. He sniffed Domeno's arm. His paw patted at the slashes his fangs had inflicted, wiping away streaks of drying blood, and he said, very softly, *"Triste."* Sorry.

Domeno felt a sudden tightness in his chest, a constriction in his throat. His heat began a heavy thud. He stared at the child, flush with warmth. His eyes grew damp with unshed tears. He blinked them away. Emile wasn't a monster. He was only a child—a little boy. Hate and anger had produced him, deformed and unfit for the outside world—but they didn't live in the outside world. The outside world didn't need to know about Emile, frozen in a body he couldn't escape, an ugly little creature that was part of Domeno, and belonged to him. Emile might be the only child he would ever have.

Was he an accident or just the horror of mixed genes gone awry? Had he been born that way or the product of an incomplete shift? Domeno had no way of knowing, no idea how the genes had gotten all gobbed up and produced this pitiful abomination of a child, but they had. A creature permanently trapped between two worlds. Domeno could do little to keep him from feeling alienated, but he would do his best to help guide him forward through the unjust unknown they both faced. Sometimes he would wrap his arms around him, absorb his warmth, but mostly he would just love him, he decided.

Swirling emotions filled him. He would attempt to let his past die into a decaying memory, put aside all the pain the mother of this child had caused him. He was going to try to give this half-wolf boy a chance, whatever it might be.

Crane and Kitty might tell what happened here; he couldn't trust that they wouldn't. No one from around here would care, they had learned long ago to stay away, but Crane might come back, bringing outsiders with weapons intent on ridding the world of the horrible creatures that lived here.

French Gap was no longer safe. He and the boy would have to be careful, hide, and stay out of people's way. If they found they couldn't, he would plot an escape, and they would run and keep running. Get as far away as possible until they found a safe place. If people saw them, they would think them a pitiful pair, both of them better off dead, and try to kill them. Or try to put the boy in an institution, take him to a lab where scientists and doctors would study him, do terrible things to him, probe and cut him, experiment on him in painful, inhuman ways. Make a lab animal out of him, slice him into small particles and study him under a microscope as they searched for modern answers to the mystery of his existence.

Or worse, someone might try to put him in one of those sideshows with other freaks, making money while people stared and laughed at him. He wouldn't let that happen; he would do whatever was necessary to protect the boy. No one need ever know about this special wolf-child.

Domeno couldn't have his old life back—he was no longer sure he even wanted it—but he could build a new one with Emile. After all, Emile *was* his son Not the child he'd always wanted—but his son, his

blood, just the same. It no longer mattered who birthed him, they had made him together. Yancy had given
him life, decided to keep him, and had taken care of
him. It was now Domeno's turn. He would try to
make the right choices, right some of her wrongs.

He felt sorry for the boy and started to feel sorry
for himself. Something deep in his mind told him not
to go there. Crane hadn't managed to kill him.
There was a reason for that, a reason his life had been
spared. No doubt that reason was Emile.

He had been given a purpose. His life was going
to be different now. Everything was going to be different. He needed to be strong for the boy.

Most of all, he wouldn't be alone anymore.

Domeno reached out, slowly tracing a gentle
finger along the slender muzzle. Emile was so soft,
his skin like velvet, his fur like silk, a deep, dark gold
with black-tipped guard hairs.

The boy pulled away, stared cross-eyed at his
finger. It amazed Domeno the wisdom and trust he
saw in those huge, so strangely different eyes.

Emile tilted his head, his eyes bright and curious
and without fear. *"Et qui tu?"* he asked. Who are you?

Domeno smiled, a slow tender smile, and
answered, *"J'sus ton Pere, cher 'tit negre."*

I am your father, precious little fellow.

ABOUT THE AUTHOR

Judith D. Howell, a writer since young and
editor of her high school paper, has written
and published short stories in national magazines
and anthologies for years. A longtime resident
of Louisiana, she now lives in Virginia near
family with her rescued Beagle, Abbe.

This is her first published novel.

38187900R00371